# WHAT PEOPLE ARE SAYING about...
## Hood Rich

"Crystal Stell shines in her sophomore project. She paints a clear picture with her words and often makes you feel as though you're a bystander in the story. **Hood Rich will be a National Bestseller.**"
**Monique Bruner**, Author/Co-Editor Strategies that Empower People
**Reviewer**

"**Hood Rich** kept my eyebrows in the raised position. When I read some of the pages, my mouth literally fell open, making me say, "What?" **I simply love and can never get enough of this author's plot twisters.**"
**Looseleaves Book Reviewer**

"Perkins-Stell has crafted a best seller. **HOOD RICH** is a raw, riveting and captivating novel that will surely open your eyes to life in the hood. Those who have a love for Urban Fiction will definitely love this book, and those who don't, may find themselves **jumping on the urban fiction bandwagon.**
**Rawsistaz Book Reviewer**
**Atlanta, GA**

"**Hood Rich is a must read.** All I have to say is Winter was cold as ever, but DeMarques Prince is off the chain. If you put this novel down after reading the synopsis, you're missing out on a powerful read. It's amazing to see how this sista has realistically brought this male character to life. **Hood Rich is Bestseller Bound.**"
**Abu, Ubaida**
**Wichita Falls, Texas**

"Mrs. Stell, I got three words......... **Bestsella' Fa' Sho!!!!!**
**LaToya Martin, College Student**
**Tulsa, Oklahoma**

"**You Go Girl!!!!!** Hood Rich is such a realistic read. Every encounter Prince faced made me think, **"This is the best book I've ever read."** Keep the stories coming 'cause I'm ready to read your next one."
**Cassandra,**
**Detroit, Michigan**

"**I must BOW DOWN to ya' on this novel**. Hood Rich reached out and grabbed me in Chapter 1. I'm hooked and a new fan for life."
**Mark Murrell, Bondsman**

*Silk*

"Young Playa, when you're on top of your grind, money, murder, and hoes rule the block. If you're ***Hood Rich***, you have to be true to the game. You got to be cold as ice and hard as a rock, feared by many and loved by few, always on top of your hustle and ready to square off for your cause. I'm warning you to keep your enemies and your friends close. Oh, and always remember, when you're rich off the hood, trust is always a factor. Most of all, a Baller never confesses to a damn thing. "***Loose lips, sink ships***," and often cost heavy hitters their empires and sometimes their lives."

Re-edited     2/2005

**BOOKSTORE DISTRIBUTION**
**Contact:**

**CRYSTELL PUBLICATIONS**
**P.O. BOX 8044**
**EDMOND, OK. 73083-8044**

**Place orders via our website**
# www.Crystalstell.com

ISBN: 0-9740705-0-5
Library of Congress Control Number:  2004094135

Cover Credits
----
**Model:** Teretta
**Photographer:** Derrick Brown   **dbrownphotos.com**
**Model:** Jermaine Chiles / **Photo taken by:** Kimberly Lewis
**Cover Design:** Doris

This is a work of fiction. Names, characters, places and incidents either are a product of the author's imagination or are used fictitiously and any resemblance to actual persons, living or dead, is coincidental.

Printed in the United States of America

Sex, Status, and a Baller's Confession

# HOOD
## *Rich*

Crystal
Perkins-Stell

HOOD *Rich*

CRYSTELL
PUBLICATIONS

Copyright 2004

A Novel by Crystal Perkins-Stell

*Ant*

"***Hood Rich*** ain't nothing more than a state of mind. Most often, it's about a few Ballas trying to get their shine on before they learn the real lessons of the game. As a hustler, I'm a firm believer of the infamous motto, "Nothing Ventured, Nothing Gained." Therefore, chumps better respect my gangsta and try to vibe on the tales of the Prince Family. We ain't no joke, and we certainly ain't to be flexed with."

# *Acknowledgements*

I asked God to bless me with a gift I could share with the world. He gave me the talent to write, and a spirit to love others. Damon, thanks for all you do to encourage me. Makya, mommy sprouted wings with Soiled Pillowcases, now I'm trying to soar like an eagle, and you inspire my altitude.

Mom, Miles, Marcus, Kimberly, Dawn, and Delmar you all are simply the best. You got your shout out in Soiled Pillowcases, so I'll end here with you. Miles Lewis Sr. I appreciate all you've done for me. Also big thanks to the Perkins, Horton, and Stell family for your support. Tonya Bell, my ghetto lovely home-chick in Detroit, thanks for breaking down the new and old skool street terminology. Lawanda smooches. Hey now Scooter & Moses, I love you guys. Mike May there are simply no words for you. I am speechless. Just thanks for believing in me. You have been such a great friend for the past nineteen years. Victor thanks, for believing pushing my first book as if it were your very own. Marc Flemon & Currie Ballard, thanks for your encouragement and my first plug on the Radio. Mrs. Thelma Wallace thanks for reading all my drafts. You're a sweetheart. Monique, LaDonna, and Tajama my sisters in Delta, y'all are simply the bomb. Iris, and Marilyn thanks for reading when I needed you most. My wonderful students, Mike Cozart, Author O'sha Shamir, and the rest of my wonderful supporters at Langston University, I appreciate each one of you.

I want to extend a super special Thanks to my beautiful cover model Teretta. Girl, you're going places. Not only are you a pretty face, but your spirit is right. You have the gift to soar. I pray that this is the beginning of BIG THANGS for you. Derrick Brown, founder of DBphotos, you are a Bad Brotha.... Any authors, models, common people, companies, entertainers, etc, looking for a quality photo shoot, this is your man. Contact him soon and watch him bring your hidden qualities to life. Jermaine Chiles, thanks for that Big Balla photo with your Benzo....(wink) You added the last bit of flava my cover needed. James Hicks thanks for being my eyes inside the various prisons. Mook, the new and improved Ant, you got the look for real baby. Silk, you know I got mad love for you.

To all of my family, friends and supporters who were not mentioned, know that I didn't leave you out intentionally. There are just simply too many of you to name. No harm intended, so don't take it personal. I'd like to send a shout out to all of the authors who've inspired me along the way ESPECIALLY, Winston Chapman for his help.

To all the book clubs and dedicated readers who have purchased my books and supported me in my efforts to accomplish my dream, thank you. I'll never forget how you embraced me as a new author.

Finally, I'd like to say thank you once again to Tom Joyner for inspiring me to follow my dreams. A person never knows exactly where every seed their planting falls until they witness their harvest blossoming.

"Hey! What's this ***Hood Rich*** stuff all about
anyway?"

# 1

## NGN

"This is Ken Peters, Chief Editor for *Big Successors Magazine*. We're interviewing DeMarques Prince this afternoon as he shares stories about life inside the walls of Michigan's Department of Corrections. Today Mr. Prince will recap tales about his heart-wrenching journey to win an appeal, after falsely being convicted on First Degree Murder charges. Good afternoon, DeMarques."

"Good afternoon."

"DeMarques, many convicted felons often claim they are innocent, when in fact, they are truly guilty. What makes you different?"

"I was falsely convicted on some shadiness."

"Shadiness, Hmm…... Well, many African Americans often slander the judicial system. What are your views about what happened to you and the manner in which you feel you were railroaded?"

"Ken, I'm going to stop you right now. First of all, please call me Prince. Secondly, did you come here to ask me all these bullshit ass questions or do you want to have a real interview?"

"Man, straight up, I want you to tell me your story."

"Straight up! Are you sure you're ready for some *real talk*?"

"Yeah. Why do you think I'm here?"

"I know you're here for a story, but do you want the raw, uncut version of a Prince in chains?"

"Prince, it took you forever to agree to this interview, not to mention that I came a long way to get this story. You know I don't want to waste time BSin'."

"Okay. Turn off your recorder, get out a note pad, and remember regardless of what I share, there's only a small portion of my story you may actually print. I'm trusting you to honor the contract I've signed with your company. If you don't, we gon' have issues."

"P, you're about to put me on the map with this story. You know I'm not going to jeopardize the integrity of my magazine or risk getting sued."

"Cool, turn off your recorder like I said. Oh, and put it over here in front of me. I'd hate for it to accidentally get turned back on in the middle of my story."

"Yeah, right…… Here… It's off. I'm ready whenever you are."

"Man, the city *ain't ready* for these dreadful tales I'm about to share, but I *ain't for no half steppin'*, so brace yourself. With this *confession, I feel like* if I'm gonna tell it, then I'm gonna tell it all. Most often I'm ashamed of my past, but I've accepted that *only God can judge me;* therefore, I'm about to *clean out my mental closet,* trash some of these skeletons, and move the hell on with my life. Ken, at one point in time, *Me against the World* was my theme song. I swear I had the worst run of fuckin' luck during my teenage years."

"Oh yeah?"

"Man, for a youngin, I had far more than *ninety-nine problems,* and I don't know how I let it happen, but I can guarantee you that a bitch was most certainly in the top five. Most often, I thought I hit snake eyes on my way out the womb. The struggles I've endured have been so painful that I've *shed so many tears* when I consider the *hard knock life* I've overcome. Excuse me, I hope my language isn't too offensive, but I don't know any other way than to keep it real."

"Naw, you're straight. Please continue."

"As a shorty, I was so busy trying to *get my hustle on* and blow up like my uncle and brother. My mind stayed focused on big ballin', but it seemed like the *mo money* the *family business* made, the *more problems* we experienced. I can't deny that I've always had to *do things my way*, and though I was frequently warned to stay out them streets, *grindin'* and crime was in my *bloodline*. Man, I had that *bad boy for life* mentality. You know, *can't nobody hold me down.* For a while I got so cocky that *my mind was playing tricks on me,* it had me thinking I was invincible. So I turned out to be a straight bad-ass, just living for the moment, and caught up in this fantasy of being the HNIC like my uncle Silk."

"So actually, you started slangin' dope pretty young?"

"Yeah. Obviously and I was *livin' it up* too much. I say that because while I was trying to be a *playa with game,* the law stepped in and checked me. That's how I fell on my *hard times.* "*Game over,*" is all I thought as Jeffery Lesure, the District Attorney informed me that I wasn't *above the law.* Man, Mr. Lesure was hip to the mischief in the hood. Hell, he was a low-down *grimy* nigga himself. I can't really say how he came up with me as the prime suspect, but *some how* that sneaky bastard managed to accuse me of being under my brother's influence and made an example of me."

"Your brother?"

"Yeah, at the time, Ant was a *menace to society* and most definitely *paid in full.* I tried to *shake* the law *off* of me, but you know *game gon' recognize game.* Mr. Lesure, like most prosecutors, swore I had a *motive 4 murder,* and you'll understand what I mean by that better, once I tell you my story. My juvenile record didn't help much, which is why, when it was all said and done, *Murder One was the case* that he gave me. How he won a guilty verdict, when he knew I was completely innocent, still baffles me to this day. But I'm a *survivor,* and I know in time I will prove my innocence."

"Damn, Prince. The state is *ruthless.* Are you sure you still want to do this interview? Man, I don't want you to have any regrets later."

"Yeah, I'm sure I want to because I'm tired of carrying all this pressure. And Ken, I'm not worried about you crossing me 'cause if you do, you'll be a *dead man walking.*"

"Prince, *you gots to chill* on the threats if we're gonna talk. I'm trustworthy. I promise your story is safe with me. Plus, with all these street titles you just rattled off, you're starting to sound like a Greatest Hits CD."

"Oh, you caught my flow? I threw in a few lyrical hit titles, but they weren't just titles to rap songs to me, they were more of a synopsis to describe my life. Actually, a rapper could never illustrate what I've been through in just one song. But it's good that we're on the same page because you know in the hood, the consequences for *dishonor is death.*"

"Yeah, I know."

"Good, with that in mind, I'll start with this letter I got from my mother back in 1990 and we'll go from there."

### *"Mail Call"*
Is what the Correctional Officers always yelled before dropping mail into my cell.

*September 11, 1990*

> *Prince,*
>
> *I hope when this letter finds you, your health is well. How are you? Sorry I haven't written in a while, but things have been very hectic around the house. Renzo and I are still having our little domestic disputes, and last week they got way out of hand. You'd think after getting enough of your brother and Silk's beat downs, he'd learn not to fool with me. Last weekend that idiot lost his damn mind and tried to break my arm. He came in all hours of the morning ranting and raving about some cigarettes he'd left on the coffee table. I told his drunk ass, I work a 9 to 5, with benefits at the supermarket. Don't nobody need to steal no damn cigarettes. I guess my comment offended him, and the*

fight was on from there. But don't worry about me, I'm doing fine. You know your mom has a survivor's spirit. That means I'll get through this battle as well.

Anyway, I've complained and complained, and two weeks ago Anthony finally got someone to repaint the outside of the house. Boy, paint was chipping off, so our house looked a mess. I don't know what got into him. I'd been asking him to get it done for the last year 'cause my money wasn't right. With as long as he made me wait, I wish I could've afforded to do it myself. I hope I don't sound ungrateful, but lately your brother drives me crazy with his split personalities. I guess that's what the stress of living as a supplier of Street Pharmaceuticals will do to your mind. Nonetheless, it's done, so I'll move on.

Oh, before I forget, I sent money along with this letter to go on your books. It isn't much, but Ant said he's going to take care of you next week.

Prince, you should see KeKe. She's really growing up. She calls herself being into boys. Now that has my nerves bad. I keep telling her don't bring home no babies. With the amount of time I spend bitching, she knows I'm not playing with her grown butt. Shoot, Lord knows I'm not ready to be no grandma again.

Boy, bear with me. I know my letter seems odd today. I'm just jumping around like I've smoked a joint. (Smile) Well, I haven't. In fact, I haven't smoked any weed in almost a month. I'm trying to quit. No I'm not sick. I've just been thinking about my life, and right now my conscience is uneasy. It's been eating me up these past few months. Sometimes, with the way I worry, I wonder if I'm about to die. I've been beating myself up about some of the poor choices I've made in the past, especially how I've cheated my kids. Prince, there are so many things I'm ashamed of pertaining to my parenting skills.

Now that I'm older, I know I should have been a better parent to you and your brother. At times, I beat myself up because of your situation. I feel like I should have shown you far more love. Had I not been so caught up on doing my thing, maybe I wouldn't have neglected you and Ant to the extent I did. I

4

often blame myself for your situation and wonder had I been more focused on motherhood would you be in prison today. If my conscience were at least clear about that, I bet half the skeletons I deal with wouldn't torment me so much. There are days when I struggle to even look at myself. Sometimes, living is extremely hard for me. I know I didn't give you what you needed emotionally, and that rips at my soul.

In the future I hope to sit down and have a heart to heart with you about some things from my past. There are so many family secrets you and KeKe need to know about before I die. Well, I've got to go. I wish I could come see you. I love and miss you very much.

P. S.

GG and Daddy Ruenae will be out to see you next weekend.

Love you,

Bean

September 14, 1990

Bean,

It's always good to hear from you. Seems like Renzo ain't gon' ever get his act together. I'm glad Silk and Ant are there for you. If not, he'd stay in your ass. Why you stay with that chump for so many years anyway? He's been beefing with you over bullshit ever since I was a shorty. I keep wondering when you gon' wise up and drop that bitch? You know you've tolerated that zero far longer than you should have, and I swear you deserve someone way better than his punk ass. Shit, I'm about to change the subject 'cause I can feel myself gettin' mad. I don't even know why you mention him in your letters to me. You know I got issues with him. In the future, don't even bother to tell me about your man. Then I don't have to fantasize on the many ways I could kill him when I see him again.

Hey, how are things going with raising money for my appeal? I'm desperate for y'all to be working on that. It's clearly obvious that me and my jailhouse attorneys ain't gon' win me no new trial. Recently, I submitted my first appeal to the Circuit Courts and lost. That's why I need to make sure a highly skilled professional files the few appeals I got left.

I have to hurry up and get out of this dungeon because my mind's starting to play tricks on me. I've been in solitary confinement since our last visit eight months ago. Bean, the pressure of this hell hole is getting me down. Ms. Anderson, my case manager, informed me that I was up for a transfer. And get this, they're moving me to Ionia, Super Max. Talk about pressure, prison ain't no place for a dapper twenty-year-old like myself, and super max is going to fuck with my head for real. Twenty-three hour lock down, no windows to see the sun, no communication with other inmates, and yard takes place in a two by four, one hour, a few days a week. Damn Bean, the thought of that place makes me feel troubled. I can't take much more of this. Y'all got to beef up the hustle so I can come home soon.

Say, you must've been drinking while writing my letter the other day. It sounds like you were on a pity party. You know alcohol is a depressant. I done told you a million times to leave that Cognac alone. Everybody makes mistakes, Bean. Regardless of what kind of mother you were in the past, you've been here for me since day one of my incarceration. That may not seem like much to you, but I appreciate your support more than you'll ever know. I don't care about your skeletons. We all have them. Huh, I got a few that might blow your mind to this day. So look here li'l lady, you keep your secrets to yourself and I'll hold on to mine. Deal?

Tell GG and Daddy Ruenae not to come see me. I can't have contact visits no way. Seeing you like this is already hard, but I don't want my grandparents to see me under these circumstances. They keep me in belly chains during the entire visit, and GG ain't gon' be with that. Once she sees how the cuffs cut into my wrist and leave deep imprints on them, she'll bawl. I know you can recall how she tripped the first time she saw me shackled. I still remember the way she whimpered when I was sentenced. That memory alone haunts me to this day. Sometimes in the middle of the night, I wake up tearing. I think about the judge saying, 'Life without parole,' and really sob like a baby when I recall GG crying out in despair. She and Daddy Ruenae invested so much in me while I was growing up. Bean, I really feel like I let them down.

Being incarcerated is a heavy pill to swallow. Sometimes I wonder why it required me losing everything that matters to me to finally realize that I had a real purpose in life. Survival in this place is like a nine to five. There are cold-blooded killers, rapist, and niggas that simply don't give a damn in here. Bean, I'm not any of them, but to endure, I have learned to adapt and camouflage who I really am. I will say that I am blending in well with the best of them. Killers, that is, and to defend my manhood or stay alive, I'll do whatever it takes to protect Prince.

Tell Ant to get at me. Kiss KeKe, and you stay up.

Love,

Your Prince

That correspondence took place between my mother and me almost nineteen years ago. When I reflect on my past and think about all my sacrifices, I must admit that my life was very fucked up. At that time, I was twenty-years-old, in solitary confinement, and had already served four years of my *Natural Life* sentence. I was detained at Carson City Correctional Facility, which primarily housed lower level inmates in Michigan's correctional system. It was one of the newer facilities linked to the Department of Corrections, and here I'd sabotaged the lovely time I was doing on a stupid drug trafficking misconduct.

Officials knew narcotics were getting into the prison, so they beefed up security on everybody. Prison officials weren't stupid either. They knew drugs generally came in, one of two ways, visitors or correctional officers. One day during a visit with Bean, we were caught trying to smuggle drugs. We got busted as soon as she attempted to pass them to me. I didn't realize that an observation camera was above us. Actually, the nosey-ass police zoomed in on our visit right after Bean returned from the restroom. That wasn't a mandatory requirement, but one of the guards monitoring visits that day felt a little suspicious about something, so he zoomed in to watch until he got us.

We were big time slipping. When the police rushed me, I tried to swallow the balloons containing the drugs. I knew if I could get them down, I'd go to my cell, drink lots of water, and after my belly got full, I'd throw them back up. The guard grabbed me around my neck, which cut off my oxygen. His grip not only prevented me from getting air, but swallowing as well. Bean got mad about the manner in which they were roughing me up. Not to mention, I was turning red from not being able to breath. Before I knew it, she'd jumped on the back of one of the guards restraining me and punched him.

After minutes of kicking, biting, screaming, and wrestling around on the floor with CO's, I was finally under control, so was Bean. They pulled me off to a secluded room, stripped search me, and sent me straight to the hole, bloody, battle scars and all. Bean went to jail and was banned from visiting me for the next two years. The Department of Corrections also decided that once her privileges were reinstated, we would only be allowed non-contact visits. She'd never be able to hug me again, unless the warden approved a special contact visit, which at the time, I couldn't see happening. For me that meant I'd never be able to feel the empathy in my mother's touch for the rest of our lives.

When I look back on how it all began twenty-seven years ago, there are times when I want to slap myself for not paying attention to the lessons of the hood. In July of 1982, I was twelve and living in the heart of Detroit. Like most shorties in the ghetto, my mother's income was limited, so I was very impressionable. My father was a sorry bastard who'd been missing in action since day one of my arrival. Early on, he had deprived me of the opportunity to know and appreciate a father's love and guidance. After getting my mother pregnant, he decided that plans for his life didn't include a full time woman and most certainly not no kids. His personal failures regarding me made it possible for my brother and the other Ballas in the family business to serve as my role models.

My mother's man, Lorenzo, was supposed to be my father figure, but that tired chump was a taxicab driver and an alcoholic. I had real playas in my family, so I couldn't look up to no knucklehead like him for my hero. Back then, my Uncle Silk and my older brother Anthony were the only ones who really taught me anything about the lessons of survival in the ghetto. My uncle was big time gettin' em. I mean, he wasn't paid like YBI, the Young Boys Incorporated or the McGerck Brothers, who were kingpins of some of the largest drug empires in the city. However, he had the Westside on lock and was paid in full. He owned a few strip clubs, some after hour joints, and a pager store, which served as his cover-up. The kind of money he floated weekly was ridiculous. One day after seeing him count the cash made on a drop and watching him conduct real Dope Man business, I was ready for Ballernomics 101.

"Prince, before I ever let you get on, you gon' have to learn some lessons about the game. First, keep your enemies close and your friends closer. I know most people say it the other way around, but in this line of work, you can't trust anyone, especially not your friends and family. Secondly, I don't care what you get caught up in, a real nigga on the grind never confesses. I don't care what I expose you to, remember, loose lips sink ships and could cost me everything, including my life." As Silk talked, he had a real gangsta stare in his eyes. He wanted me to understand the seriousness of the business, and from watching for so long, I did.

"Uncle Silk, I don't care what you make me do. I just want to be down."

After having that discussion with him and trying to understand how the game worked, I found myself a place in the family hustle, and quickly learned the game of grinding from the best. Initially, my uncle used me as eyes. I'd take note of new faces trying to slang in our hoods, keep a look out for 1-time, and ran off broke junkies before they brought unwanted attention to some of our most lucrative dope houses. After beating down a few crack heads, preventing a bust or two at the family spots, and catching a host of petty charges myself, Silk finally allowed me to get on.

I'll never forget it. In December 1983, one day before my fourteenth birthday, I was walking around one of our fairly profitable dope houses, acting like Baby Scarface. Ant tossed me a stack, which at the time was a lot of money to me. Hell, as a thirteen-year-old, a thousand dollars in my hands made me feel super powerful. From Silk and Ant allowing me to kick it with 'em like they did, I often walked around acting like this fictitious Superhero. To some people on the block, I behaved like I sported the letters KPM on my chest, (**K**ingpin in the **M**aking). Really, I was just on top of my game for a small guy. So niggas simply hated on me because they envied my come up. There were several brothas who wanted to get put on, but so few got the chance to be on Silk's payroll. Trust was always a factor with him, so he kept most niggas at a distance.

Anyway, I was actin' a fool. Finally, after getting on Ant's nerves, he blurted, "Prince, stop acting like you ain't had a G before."

"I haven't had one that belonged to me," I sarcastically replied.

"Chump, come on. We 'bout to go get you fresh for yo' fourteenth. Then, I'm gon' let you holla at a few of my bitches," Ant arrogantly stated.

"Oh, I'm with that. I can tell you right now which one I wanna be on," I said, smiling like I was the man.

"P, you been checking out my females like that?"

"Yeah! Some of 'em are fine as hell."

"Who got you waking up to a hard on?"

"No one," I lied.

"Right! I bet one of 'em got you pounding your li'l dick throughout the night on the down-low."

"Man, I got mad women. I ain't jackin' off over no bitch."

"P, I don't know why you frontin' like you get major ass."

"Frontin," I repeated, smiling. "You're frontin'. Nigga, you're the one that's supposed to be big ballin, and you just as *Hood Rich* as ever."

"Hood Rich? Where did that come from?"

"I don't know, it just seemed like the thing to say."

"How the hell you figure I'm hood rich then?"

"You're the one drivin' around the D in a Benz. You be draped in major gold, sportin' the freshest gear, and here you are livin' in a busted crib. If anybody frontin, Nigga, it's you. Your car cost more than your house."

"That's alright 'cause one day I'm gon' own a spot out in West Bloomfield, and you gon' really be on my dick. That hood rich nonsense you spittin' ain't nothing more than a state of mind. Suckas that try to blow up too fast get caught slippin' in the game when they style for show. I ain't that sucka. And don't be tryin' to change the subject, we talking about you, Li'l Nuts."

"Man, stop tryin' to dis me. You act like I ain't got no women."

"I ain't dissin' you. I'm statin' facts. All I'm saying is if you ain't slangin' major dick, you ain't ready for none of my women. For example, my girl Toni's pussy is so deep that she literally likes a nigga to pound the bottom out of that thang."

"That sounds like the kind of work I'm puttin' in," I suggested with confidence.

"Nigga, please! You ain't old enough to put in work like that. Either you're pumpin' or spankin', but a combination will get you off."

"I can handle Toni and anybody else you send my way."

"Playa, you ain't lookin' well hung to me. I don't know about that comment you just made, so if you ain't jackin' off, you better start." Ant laughed, giving Melvin five.

"Ant, how you figure I need to be jackin' off. Hell, I'm packin' more dick than you, and you got me by ten years?"

"You're playing right? Have you seen all that ass on Renee?" He asked.

"Yeah."

"How you think it got like that?"

"Not you!" I quickly replied to shut him up.

"Boy, I put in work," Ant bragged.

"Whatever, that's not what Peaches said the last time I bust one in her mouth."

"Damn, Ant, he threw Peaches in yo' face like that. Now that was low," Melvin suggested, grabbing me around my neck to keep Ant from hurting me.

"P, you better stop talking about that one there, and come on before I bust your li'l ass," Ant replied, looking serious.

Right then, I flashed all thirty-two of my pearly whites on Ant. I had just done something I was never able to do. Shut him up. Ant didn't know if I was serious about his ex-girl or not. Her reputation had gotten so bad. He didn't know what to think, so he didn't want to play the big dick, little dick game with me anymore. Especially since Melvin was cracking on him along with me.

At one time, Peaches was Ant's main squeeze. She was probably the only girl he ever really loved. However, since their separation, her status had been reduced from classy to Chicken Head. She was a high dollar sack-chaser who wore the latest hoochie mama fashions and oversized jewelry.

From the first time I met Peaches, she was always on a mission to get paid. She was fly, she knew it, and sleeping with Ballas was her full-time J.O.B. Right before Ant blew up and started grinding major weight, Peaches crushed him big time. She kicked him to the curb for a sorry brotha off the Eastside. Ant didn't ever have a chance to appropriately put closure to that relationship because of the way it abruptly ended, but whenever we saw ole girl, it was clear that she had moved on. The sad part about their entire situation was that he was still feeling her long after she moved on, but she clearly wasn't thinking about Ant, which is why he was kind of sensitive to jokes about her.

◆◆◆◆◆◆◆

Later that day, I walked out of Fairlane Mall with three Run DMC Adidas trackies, a few pair of Top-Ten sneakers that matched each suit, some Cazal glasses, two Calvin Klein jean hookups, and the leather Max Jullian jacket. Shortly after leaving the mall, we rolled Ant's turquoise Benz-190 to the Gold Plaza on Greenfield to buy a few cable rope necklaces, and some two finger rings. That's when Ant got his first fat pinky ring with this plushed-out diamond. That stone was so phat that all the haters acting like they didn't know Ant was the man, would be forced to pull out their sunglasses to block the bling. Some still didn't give him his props on that piece of jewelry, but most couldn't help but bow down to acknowledge his come up.

After shopping, I had Ant run me by the house to drop off my things. I figured I'd chill at the spot with Bean for a minute, shower, and get back with him later that evening. When I first walked up in the house, Bean and Renzo were arguing as always. At first, I tried to ignore them, but as soon as I heard some loud slaps, I walked back to Bean's bedroom. I briefly listened, then kicked the door open like I was 5-0.

"Punk Ass Nigga, get your hands off my mama!" I yelled with authority.

"Prince, you better get out of here, close that door behind you, and stay in your place," Renzo replied, staring me down like he wanted to square off on me.

"Fool, this is Bean's spot. She's paying all the bills while you lay around here sleeping and scratchin' your nuts like a damn dog. Cab driving ain't bringing in no major loot to this crib. You better recognize that you're a temporary tenant. If anybody got to step, Nigga, it's gon' be you, not me."

"Boy, you better watch who you trying to run up on. I'm a grown ass man. I'm not one of these kids you be around here regulating."

"You better watch who you disrespecting," I insisted, giving him direct eye contact.

"Prince, I'll snap, go off, and break a foot in yo' young ass with the quickness. You better take your li'l frail behind out of here talking to me."

Bean immediately started looking crazy at Renzo. She wasn't feeling his comment, though generally, she was known for being on his side. She looked him up and down, then quickly intervened on my behalf that day. For a change, I was actually in shock because she'd come to my defense like a parent's supposed to.

"Lorenzo, don't talk to my child like you're crazy. You ain't about to do nothing to him!" she yelled.

At that point, I was impressed. However, like always, she pulled her same ole, I'm gon' cut for my man nonsense.

"Prince, you're out of line. Get the hell out of my room and close my door behind you. I done told you once, I don't need you in my business. I can handle my own affairs!" she screamed, looking at me.

"Yeah, right, I guess that's why Ant and Silk are over here every other month checkin' yo man," I angrily shot back, slamming her bedroom door behind me.

I walked to the bathroom thinking, *Bean's a stupid bitch. I know GG taught her better than this old fer-doop mess she over here on. My little sister is watching the stuff she does. I wonder what kind of example she's trying to set for Ke?*

Kenyatta, also known as KeKe, was my seven-year-old sister. One evening after going to a Christmas party out in Oak Park, Bean and Renzo got mad drunk and came home on one hell of a high. Bean was stunned when she found out she was pregnant with Ke 'cause she had just celebrated her thirty-eighth birthday. Prior to that, she swore she'd gone through menopause two years earlier. Well, that's what she was always telling Ant and me because she was moody as ever and hot flashing like crazy.

Anyway, Ant made it to the house about two hours after my incident with Renzo. The entire time he was there, Ant sat in the living room mean mugging Zo. Renzo didn't say one word to my brother. He feared him 'cause he knew Ant held grudges. He also didn't bother Ant like he bothered me because Ant was mentally on something different and as vicious as Manson. Right before Ant moved out of Bean's house, him and Renzo got into a big fight. Ant had Zo on the bedroom floor begging for his life. He put a gun in Zo's mouth and told him, "The next time you touch Bean, I'm gon' kill you. Then I'm gon' pay one of my boys to have you cremated."

Renzo knew when Ant said something, it was clearly evident that he meant it. Plus, he wasn't going to push my brother's buttons. Ant's temper and his rep on the streets were too ruthless to ignore. Ant had this odd smirk, a violent history, and everyone knew he wasn't to be tried or the consequences could be grim.

Right when Ant was about to go off on Zo for beefing with me, Bean came into the living room popping off at the mouth.

"Anthony Lavell Prince, I don't want any foolishness up in my house tonight. Do I make myself clear?" she asked, reaching for some Coke to mix with her Hennessey.

"Bean, you got to live with that nigga, not me. But I will say this, he better not threaten or put his hands on P or else!" He replied, looking her dead in her face with his cold eyes.

"Well, he is your sister's father, too, so while you're making threats, you need to take that into consideration before you do anything to him."

"KeKe is seven. He ain't ever been a good daddy to her. Hell, I've been helping you take care of that girl since she was born. So to me, he ain't shit more than her sperm donor."

"You need to leave. Leave my house right now. You ain't about to sit up in my place and disrespect my man like he ain't a man himself."

"Bean, he ain't. As soon as you accept that, the better off you'll be."

Right then, she walked to the door, twisted the lock, and ordered Ant out.

"Anthony Prince, get the hell out! Get out of my house right now, and don't come back until you can show some respect for me, my man, and our house."

When Ant stood up to leave, I went walking right behind him. Ant was not only my older brother by ten years, but he was also my idol. I wasn't about to stay. If he had to go, I had to go.

"Prince, where do you think you're going?" Bean asked with clear anger in her voice.

"See there you go. Don't start trippin' out on me because you're mad at your eldest. I ain't got nothing to do with this argument. Here I was defending you, and now you going off on me for your man like you always do. You're never on my side. You let that sorry nigga say whatever he wants to me. I'm getting tired of that. You always show your boyfriend way more love than you show me. That's bold as hell, too, because I'm your child."

"Prince, most of your life I've made sure you had what you needed in spite of your trifling father walking out on me. He denied you as his own, but I've always loved you. You can say what you want, but don't try to send me on no guilt trip. You can save that nonsense you're talking right now for someone who doesn't know any better, because I do."

Bean was right; I knew she'd always treated me the best between my brother and I. However, as a mother, there were several instances in which

14

she fell short. I really wasn't trying to dog her out. Actually, I only wanted to send Bean on a guilt trip long enough for her to let me go with Ant. I figured I better stop while I was ahead, so I didn't reply to her comment. Instead, I explained my plans for the evening, hoping that would calm her down enough to allow me to depart with her blessings.

"Bean, Ant's supposed to let me hang tonight. He and the fellas are sneaking me up in *My Fair Ladies* to kick it. I'm gon' be out all night, so why you don't want me to leave with him?"

"Prince, Anthony is 24, you're 13. What's reasonable for him is much earlier for you. I really don't want you out in them streets with Anthony period. He's involved in too much, and anything could happen to you. I don't need or want any extra-added stress in my life. I'm sick and tired of you trying to be so grown. You need to get some friends your own age, and stop trying to act like you're Anthony's equal."

"I know I'm not his equal, but I will be fourteen in a few hours."

"So what! You said that like it's a major difference. You're still a child. Sometimes you forget that. I'll let you go this time, but you better have your ass in this house by 2 A.M."

"I'll have him in early," Ant stated, aggravated.

"You better or he's not going any place else with you," She responded just as annoyed.

I don't know what got into Bean that day. She was on some real nonsense talking about I wouldn't be hanging with my brother. She really didn't care anyway. All that mess she was talking was a front. I'd been doing what the hell I wanted to do since I was ten. Now all of a sudden she wanted to play the concerned Mom role. We didn't even refer to her as mom. After we were born, GG and Daddy Ruenae raised us for the longest because Bean was too busy trying to kick it. When she first had Ant, she didn't even want him. She refused to let him call her Mom or Bonita, which was her name. So when Ant started talking, he called her Bean. He was trying to call her BB like we called my grandmother GG, but Bean kept coming out. By the time I came along that nickname was a given.

Just as I was making my way down the walkway, Bean came to the screen door yelling, "Prince, you're so busy trying to be grown and run behind Anthony. You gon' keep on and these streets gon' be the death of you." I looked at her with clear disgust on my face. I was extremely uneasy about her comment, but what could I say in my own defense.

"P, Bean gone on one of her Henny Henn adventures. She's been drinking all day like a damn fool. Don't even let her get at you like that. You know how she trips when she's been sipping," Ant suggested.

"Yeah, I know," I replied, feeling a little like Bean had just put a curse on me, talking about some death shit.

Ant wasn't about to let her mess up my first major outing with him and his boys. He fired up a phat joint, took a few hits, and then insisted that I take a few drags as well.

"Prince, we got to get you ready for tonight. You need to relax. Hit that blunt a few more times before you pass it back to me."

"Naw, I'm tight," I struggled to reply 'cause my lungs were full of smoke.

When I extended my arm to pass the J back to Ant, I started gagging and chocking. I was trying to get the full effects of my hit, but the smoke was overpowering my lungs.

"Boy, this stuff is the bomb, you better slow down," Ant insisted, looking at his pager. It was beeping like crazy. "799-9952, that's Melvin. This is his fourth time calling me." Just when he lifted the joint to take another hit, his pager started beeping again. "Damn! It's Melvin again. Why this nigga keep beeping me?" Ant mumbled, exhaling.

"Maybe something's up at one of the spots. You should pull up on this payphone and buzz him back right quick."

"We're almost at his house. He knows I'm on the way. If something's going down, stopping would only take longer."

By the time we rolled up on Melvin, he was standing on the porch bugging out. I could tell he was worried about something, but he was trying to maintain his manhood.

"What's the problem?" Ant yelled with his arms extended.

Melvin broke down, "It's T," he replied, anxiously making his way to us. "We got to hurry up and get to him. While I was on the phone with T, somebody ran up in his spot. I heard someone say something to him about Silk. Then T dropped the phone and started screaming like he was being tortured."

T was short for Terrance. He, Ant, and Melvin had been boys since the second grade. They were thick as thieves, too. He was one of the coolest friends Ant had, not to mention something like a second big brother to me. That evening, while riding to his house, I remember sitting in the back seat speechless. I was thinking, *If something really happened to T, Ant was gon' nut the fuck up, and Silk was gon' trip as well.* T was Silk's stepson. Though his mom, Monique and my uncle weren't still married, Silk was still pushing up in that fatty-girl every now and then, so there was still a family connection between him and T.

When we rolled up on my boy's crib, the door was pulled up, but it wasn't locked. Ant told me to stay in the car, but *fuck that*, I thought, after sitting there for a second. I grabbed his extra heat from under the dashboard and ran in behind them. Before taking the steps two at a time, I remember slowly pushing some chick walking on the sidewalk out of my way, "Is T alright?" I asked, breathing hard as my heart raced from the excitement of everything. Neither Ant nor Melvin said a word. They didn't have to either. I could see for myself. T was sitting tied to a chair with his pants pulled down to his knees. His nut sac had been slit open, NGN was carved in his chest, blood was all over everywhere, and I was in shock. I guess that's why I didn't realize that his brains had also been blown out the back of his head. When I finally noticed brain tissue splattered all over the wall behind him, I became sick to my stomach. I locked in on this thick brown stuff oozing from his mouth. The look of terror I saw in his half-open eyes horrified me.

"Call the police!" Ant screamed, crying like I'd never seen before. But I didn't move. "Prince!" I jumped. "Call the police, I said!" Ant yelled a second time before I picked up the phone to dial 911. I'd never seen death first-hand before, and I never wanted to see it again. I was so nervous that I was literally shaking. Most of all, I was scared, but I didn't want Ant or Melvin to know. I tried to remain as calm as I could while the line for the operator rung, but no matter what I did, a queasiness continued to fill my stomach.

"911. What is your emergency?"

"Yes, we need you to send the police to 04441 Rutherford."

"04441 Rutherford, what's the emergency?"

"There's been a shooting. I just arrived at my cousin's house, and he's been shot."

"Sir, can I get you to hold while I dispatch an officer to your address?"

"Okay."

While waiting for her to return, Ant was making me nervous. He kept asking T, "Who did this to you?" I wanted to tell him stop asking that man questions. All I know is had T attempted to answer with him being in the condition he was in, I was bouncing out of that house with the quickness. As I cased the house from the spot I was standing in, my eyes started to wander. There was so much blood in the room that I was becoming nauseous again. Especially, after I looked at the large puddle of blood resting beneath T's chair. I'm glad the operator came back when she did because I was becoming ill, and she distracted me.

"Sir."

"Yes, I'm still here."

"An officer and ambulance is on the way."

"Okay, but I don't think we need an ambulance."

"May I please have your name?" the operator asked.

"Yeah, Prince."

"Prince, I'm going to have you stay on the line until an officer arrives."

"Alright."

Finally, after holding for about two minutes, I told the operator a few officers were walking in, so she allowed me to hang up.

After half-butt casing the crime scene, those assholes started asking tons of questions. At first, they were trying to insinuate that we had done that horrific killing. When we told them about T talking to Melvin right before he was killed, they eventually excluded us, but wrote down our information for future contacts. Mrs. Hicks, T's nosey neighbor, said she observed us running into the house, which confirmed our story and saved our asses. She said the only reason she knew what time we pulled up in front of the house was because Ant skidded rubber when we arrived. Lucky for us he was driving like a maniac, but most of all, lucky for us Mrs. Hick's snooping old butt loved peeping out of her blinds.

That old lady was not only able to spare us, but she also gave a great description of the assailant's automobile. She described their vehicle as a black Laredo Jeep. Based on her description, the jeep was on rims and had a special paint job. The only problem with that was the fact that there were a bunch of brothas in the city rolling jeeps on rims. And, in the city of Doe, most of them had custom paint jobs. That meant once an investigation started, finding T's killer would basically come down to a process of elimination.

I stood looking around in complete shock. At first, seconds, minutes, then hours passed. When the coroner finally arrived to get his body, the reality of T's death hit home for me. I stared at him while he remained tied to that chair for the longest. To me, T appeared to be on display for the various people coming to investigate the crime scene. One photo after another was taken. Then the lead investigator pissed me off when he informed us that we'd probably contaminated the crime scene by coming into the house. At that point, who gave a damn about a crime scene? We were more concerned about our boy's well being, not preserving any evidence.

After several questions and telling our story a thousand times, it was extremely late when we finally finished. I was crushed about not getting to enjoy my big birthday celebration. On top of that, I didn't even get to rock my new Calvin Klein jean hookup or my fresh new Top-Ten sneakers. Most of all, I almost died myself at the thought of missing out on my chance to lie up in some warm mature pussy.

Considering the circumstances, I didn't even care that I'd missed my curfew. Bean was gon' swear that Ant deliberately had me out 'til all hours of the morning anyway. I knew she'd vow that we were involved in some kind of drama. Most of all, she was gon' nut up when she found out she was half right. I didn't stress it though. Bean was a natural born nag who loved to hear herself talk shit. There was no reason for me to trip about what she was gon say, 'cause a cussing out was guaranteed.

I finally made it to the house about 5A.M. When I got to my room, I slowly undressed. I threw my clothes on the floor next to the foot of my bed and kicked my sneakers in the closet. While crawling up onto the mattress, I thought *December 5, 1983. What a way to bring in my birthday.* As I pulled my blanket a little above my waist, all I kept seeing was T tied to that chair. The slash in his nut sack stood out most. When I envisioned the look in his eyes, I considered the kind of pain he must have endured, and then I grabbed myself a time or two out of sheer compassion for his suffering. *NGN, what the hell did that mean, and why would someone carve those letters into T's chest?* I thought, looking through my blinds at the sunrise.

I noticed my clock as 6:58 flashed on the monitor. I was fighting to keep myself awake. Finally, I turned over to get comfortable, but I couldn't. I thought about T one additional time, again grabbing myself for reassurance. I was tripping so much about the manner in which my boy had been mutilated that I must have held my nuts for what felt like a lifetime. For some reason they seemed to feel much safer in my hands, so I kept holding them without shame, until I finally fell asleep.

## 2

## *Triggerman*

"DeMarques Brandon Prince, what time did you get in here this morning? And don't lie either!" Bean yelled, standing in my bedroom door.

"It was late." I moaned.

"I know it was. I stayed up until after three o'clock waiting on you to come in."

"I know!" I grumbled a second time, looking at the clock, which had just changed to 8:20AM. "I know I missed my curfew, but don't start fussin'. I just got in about an hour ago. T got killed last night. I rode with Ant and Melvin to his house, and I was late because the police kept us there forever."

"My God! T got killed? What! How?"

"Shot and cut up."

"Has anyone called Silk or Monique?" she frantically asked, covering her mouth.

"Umm hum, Ant called Silk while we were still at the house with the body."

"What did he say?"

"Nothing nice, I know niggas better watch they back 'cause it's about to go down. Silk gon' have a few suspect niggas hit, so I hope they got an alibi or else."

"My God, the last thing we need is more people dying! Well, are you okay?"

"I'm fine, just tired," I responded, rubbing my eyes with my fist. "I don't know all the details of what happened. When we got there, he was already dead."

"Prince, I can't believe that. Is Anthony okay?"

"He's as well as can be expected, but Bean I'm tired. Can we talk later?" I asked, cutting her off because she was popping off a million questions.

"Talk later, what kind of question is that? I want to talk now."

I looked at Bean, and then covered my head with the sheet. I was so tired I couldn't force myself to talk another minute. "Can we please talk later?" I asked, sucking my tongue.

"I guess. Go back to sleep. I'm about to run to the Eastern Market. We'll talk when I get back."

"Okay," I replied, turning over to hug my pillow.

Bean walked out of my room sniffling. It seemed like after I gave her the news about T, she didn't even feel much like fussing any longer. For the first time in a long time, Bean was able to show that she still had a human side to her. I could tell she sincerely felt some genuine compassion for my brother, which also made me feel better.

♦♦♦♦♦♦♦

T's funeral marked the first Home Going service I'd ever attended. Silk was a stylish kind of guy, so I already knew he was gon' put T away real nice. He special ordered a tailor made, lavender suit, which he set off with a killin' it shirt and some lavender gators. When I questioned him about the color, Silk said lavender represented status. That means we were gon' put T away like he was a king. I didn't even know that you could be buried in shoes, but at a very early age, I learned that money rules when you got loot like that.

As arrangements were being made, Monique didn't want to ride in the normal family cars. To honor her wishes, Uncle Silk rented six stretched limos for the family and a few of T's closest friends. The morning of the funeral, limos pulled up in front of the church one behind the other. I swear you would have thought we were the first family with the way heads turned to check us out. Our chauffeurs opened the rear passenger doors one right after the other like a domino effect. Everyone that stepped out was wearing lavender, even me. From the time I stepped out of our car, all I kept thinking was, *Damn, T should see this.*

I looked over at Monique, immediately noticing her pain. She was crying so hard that it broke my heart. When I saw that she had to literally be supported while walking towards the church, I felt bad for her. My uncle stood to her left side. Her brother Larry stood on her right. Bean and I walked in with Ant. Melvin's sister Porsche escorted him. As we assembled, we were instructed to form two lines before entering the sanctuary. I zoned out for a moment. I wanted to be strong for my brother, but I'd been having nightmares since I'd seen T dead. I understood death very well. I knew after that service, I wasn't going to ever see him anymore. Though I wasn't ready to say goodbye to my boy for good, I had no choice, his life was over.

As we passed the first pew in the back of the church, Ant clutched my hand. I could hear Monique crying louder and louder the closer we got to the casket. The scent of the many floral arrangements posted around T's body filled the air, and sniffling could be heard all over the church. Ant started to break down right as we made it to the front, which was a good thing because that's where we ended up sitting. I immediately noticed T's casket was closed. To distract my fears, I focused on the sound of an organ playing soft music while it echoed a soothing sound throughout the room. Obituaries were already going back and forth. I know I counted about fifty people using them for fans. Finally, the preacher stood to speak. Shortly after, he opened the floor for two-minute remarks. People started making their way to the front in packs. I swear there were so many homies trying to give farewell remarks that we almost ran out of time. Wouldn't you know it, everyone had great things to say about T. He was just that kind of guy, friends with the world and loved by many.

The breaking point for me was when the mother of T's son went up holding their three-year-old to give her final remarks. When she started to cry, Li'l Terrance asked, "Mommy, why are you crying? You know my daddy told you he don't like for us to cry." Then he reached up to wipe her tears with his tiny bare hands. After repeatedly wiping her face, he hugged her. "There, don't you feel better now, Mommy?" Almost everyone in the church was crying after that.

Once they returned to their seats, I couldn't help but observe that li'l boy for a while. He was trying to be a man for his mother and Monique. It was so obvious that he didn't even realize the magnitude of what was going on. That's what broke my heart the most. For me, it was amazing to see T's son exhibit such strength on the day his father was laid to rest.

After the Eulogy was given, the funeral directors prepared the body for the final viewing. Porsche gave the musical selection. To hear that girl sing *Precious Lord* instantly put me in the mind of Patty LaBelle. She gracefully hit each high and low note like a true professional. The way she delivered that hymnal made everyone cry. During the entire selection, ushers passed boxes of tissue throughout the church. Bean, Ant, and I had already used up an entire box ourselves. By the time Porsche finished singing, she had me wishing I'd owned stock in Kleenex. There were so many boxes going around that day, I could've easily been a millionaire.

When people started walking up for the final viewing, I sat watching many of T's women break down. They sobbed their hearts out over their loss. Some of his girls dropped mementoes into his casket, others simply stretched out all over his body, begging him not to leave them. "Damn, this is hard," I whispered to myself as my eyes watered repeatedly. I didn't know the effects a funeral could have on a person, but seeing people weep to no end, brought it all home for me. *T is really gone, we'd never see him again nor have a chance to share anymore memories,* I thought, wiping my eyes.

The funeral directors finally made it to our row. When it was Ant's turn to view the body, I remember tears streaming down his face. He and Uncle Silk always told me 'Real niggas don't cry, they deal with the pressure, and then move on.' I guess he made an exception for T's funeral. It was obvious that Ant was hurting because he cried like a bitch. It killed me to see my brother go through that kind of pain. I knew there was nothing I could do to console him either. Nonetheless, had I been able to remove his heartache that day, it would have been done in an instant. As we approached the casket, all he kept asking was, "Damn T, why they do this to you?" His inability to rationalize that a dead man couldn't speak helped me understand what Ant truly lost in his friendship with T.

Though he was an emotional wreck, I thought it was real gangsta of him to lean over and slide a fresh one hundred dollar bill in the pocket of T's suit jacket. I heard him say, "Man, you ain't ever been without, and you ain't going out without." Right then things went from bad to worse. Melvin walked up, and he and Ant had to be physically removed from the sanctuary. My cousin Delmar finally had to escort them out to the limo because they were an emotional mess.

Bean grabbed my hand to pull me away from the casket. I was stuck in my tracks, crying like a girl, and in denial. I thank God they got me out of that place before Monique and Silk did their final viewing. As I exited the sanctuary, I could hear Mo cutting up. All that screaming and loud moaning she did that afternoon made me real nervous in my stomach. When she fell out on the floor, I knew she wouldn't be able to handle much more. As for a matter of fact, it was a definite given that once we made it to the cemetery, Mo would have to remain in the car.

When we arrived at Rose Hill, it was so cold outside that the last portion of T's service was held in the mausoleum. I didn't even bother to go in, Mo didn't either. Silk brought her a few carnations and some other flowers to press in her bible. After noticing fresh tears in her eyes, I thought that was even going to be a little much for her to handle.

Everything regarding the service had gone pretty well. But as always, someone's gon' show their ass during a nigga's funeral. Once we made it to the fellowship hall to eat, people started cutting up. When funeral arrangements were initially being made, Monique wanted everyone riding in the limos to also sit together at the family tables. Though T and his son's mother were no longer together, she was still allowed to sit with the family. Denise, T's main girl, got so upset about that decision that while the family was eating, she decided to confront Mo.

"Mo, I want to know why I wasn't allowed to ride in one of the limos or sit at the family table. T and I have been together for over a year. I know I wasn't your pick for him, but he was my man. Shit, whether you like it or not, I did deserve some kind of acknowledgement."

"Denise, this isn't the time or place for you to start questioning somebody. My auntie's mourning the death of her son. You know you need to show some respect for this occasion, so please move away from the table. It's a shame we can't put my cousin to rest without some bullshit jumping off," T's older cousin Stacey interrupted.

"Stacey, you know how it was between T and me. You know I should've been at this table or at least in a family car. When T was killed, we were living together. What, y'all don't think I'm mourning, too?"

"Denise, I know you are, but we don't have to do this here. The limos are gone. It's not an issue that matters right now. It was a small oversight. I know you're upset, but you can take this up with my auntie at another time. I'm gon' ask you to move away from this table one last time or you gon' piss me off. I'd hate to get up and show my butt in this church, but I will."

"Oversight my ass," she replied, exiting the fellowship hall in tears. Denise was one of T's many women, but he really did love her, and though she was highly upset about the way things had been done, out of respect for T, she left the issue alone.

◆◆◆◆◆◆◆

Ant and Melvin laid low for the first few months that followed, which shocked me. Ant wasn't the kind of guy that was easily spooked, but he appeared to be real uptight for weeks. Ant immediately limited my hanging out with him to a minimum. When I questioned him as to why my time had to be reduced to after school hours only, he explained that he didn't know why T had been murdered. "P, I don't know who might be looking for me, Melvin or Silk, what to expect from these Simps trying to come up in the hood or what kind of danger I might unexpectedly run into. I'm not gon' put your life in jeopardy, so you can't hang with me or at any of the houses until further notice."

Since I loved hanging with Ant so much, I tried to convince him that I could handle mine. "Ant all you got to do is let me get out on the hustle with you again and I'd show you I'm a real gansta." Regardless of what I said or felt, Ant was firm about his no. He even insisted that I stay off the streets trying to grind by myself for a while or at least until some questions about T's death came to light. I didn't want to honor his request because it was going to tap into my finances. I hated being broke with a passion, so I wasn't trying to hear him. Actually, for Ant to be the G he was in my eyes, I was disappointed in what he was asking me to do. To me, he was asking me, a Prince, to walk in fear. Our family never walked around on eggshells. A Prince just didn't step lightly for anyone. "Ant, you're representing like a wimp, and I ain't gon' lie, that's pissing me off. We should be out looking for the chumps that killed T, not hiding out."

"We are looking for them, you're not. You're going back to school to get your education and that's final."

Once he put the clamp down on me, all the excitement that once went on around the house had changed. I was still trying to do my thing on the sly, but after my uncle found out, he insisted that I chill. That's when I accepted the fact that they were serious about me laying low. If Silk was worried, something grim was goin' down in the city that was way out of my league.

Since there was really nothing for me to do, and it had pretty much become mandatory that I attend school on a full-time basis, I started hanging with a few of my old friends from middle school again. By the time March rolled around, I was back to big kickin' it with two of the coolest cats in the ninth grade, besides me of course, my boy Julius O'Neal and the homie Duran Jones, who we all called Chew-Chew. Those cats had been my dawgs for what seemed like forever.

Everyday after school, we'd all go over on Evergreen to the projects and hang at Chew's place. He had all the latest Atari games, and the luxury to do whatever he wanted in his mother's house. Weekly, about six of us would meet up for this Space Invader's Tournament. That nigga's crib wasn't the best, but his mom, Faye, she was the home girl. Occasionally, she would even blow a few J's with us before leaving for work. She ran the local neighborhood Laundromat, so when she showed up at work high, no one cared.

Though Bean was out there sometimes, she certainly wasn't getting high with me and my friends. I knew she'd have a fit if she found out, so I kept the extra curriculas we did at Chew's house on the down low. GG and Bean would have both kicked Faye's ass had they known she was smoking weed with minors, especially considering that I was one of them.

All Chew's homies loved his mom. She was the only parent that allowed us to come over and be ourselves. She didn't care about us talking loud, smoking urb, cursing or nothing. Everyone else's mother, including mine, only let us hang for a few hours. Aw, and Julius's mom, Man, she got on my nerves. She was always correcting our grammar and butting in our business. At the age of thirteen or fourteen, who cares about using correct English? As soon as we set foot in her door, she started questioning us about homework. After she started buggin', it was usually time to bounce. Shortly after arriving at his crib, I was always like, "J, I'm out." Shoot, I wasn't feelin' what his mom was talking about nor was I trying to do any damn homework right after school.

Everyday Julius, his little brother Carlos, Chew, Damon, Big Mike, who was actually 5foot even, weighing in at 100 pounds, and me, all crammed into Chew's bedroom for hours. We'd all be up in there talking noise and tossing joysticks. After every game, losers always had to give up their game control to the next victim. Of course, I had major skills, so I barely loss or tossed. I often talked trash about my repeated wins, which made all my boys spit more than a little bit of shit to me.

It was rare for me to lose, but when I did, I usually blamed it on my not being able to concentrate. Chew had the biggest, blackest roaches in his house I had ever seen in my life. I'd never seen roaches that came out during a bunch of confusion, carried on like they were a part of the party, and sat around like they were next on the game. Whenever I first walked into his house, I'd always be like, "Chew, get your damn houseguests." My boys thought I was trying to be funny, but I was serious. I wanted that fool to get a can of bug spray and clear they li'l nasty assess out. Sometimes he did, sometimes he didn't, either way our competitive spirit was high.

Once the competition got heated, I became so caught up on making my paper that I didn't even care about the roaches. There were some days when I felt like they gave me luck. Every now and then, one would crawl on one of the homies or fall off the ceiling in someone's lap, and that was it. By the end of my visit on a day like that, the roaches were my peeps. I'd make about fifty dollars thanks to them cutting up.

◆◆◆◆◆◆◆

Two months before school let out for the summer, I started diggin' on this cutie in my Home Economics class. Naw, I didn't care about sewing, cooking or nothing like that. The class was full of females, it required little brainwork, and that's where I wanted to be. That's also where I met Carrington Horton.

Carrington was a tenth grader. She was bowlegged, fine as hell, and had a body like an hourglass. I think the reason she first caught my attention is because she had the biggest titties out of all the girls in the class. She was a year older than me, had a phat rump, and her jeans hugged that beaver just right. Whenever she walked around the class, my attention stayed focused on that gap between her legs.

Beaver was the nickname my boys and I used when we didn't want females to know we were talking about their poodie-cats. Once they got hip to the terminology, they tried to trip. Shit, we didn't care. We were just like any other mannish ninth graders, horny and lying on our dicks to make ourselves look good.

Whenever I was around Carrington, I wasn't myself. As cool as I thought I was, most often, I found myself carrying on like a Wankster. That wasn't even a word back then, but had it been, that would have certainly been me. Carrington knew I was feeling her, but she wasn't one to be on no thug like me. Plus, she was from a far different kind of background than I was. First of all, she lived with both her parents. They were established professionals in Detroit, and lived in the "Boochies" (**B**allin **O**ut **O**f Control, **H**appy, **I**ndependent, & **E**conomically Secure,) neighborhood.

Had Carrington even tried to get involved with me, she would have certainly been on the verge of jeopardizing her family inheritance. In spite of her snootiness, I still wanted to get to know her better. I tried inviting her to meet me a few times at the Norwest Theater, but she was so stuck on this Simp named Derrick that she repeatedly let it be known. "I got a man." She tried to convince me that she was in love. I wasn't buying it though. She stared at me too much in class to be all into her man like she claimed. "Prince, I'm not interested in no wanna be thug," she always expressed with attitude. But I wasn't nobody's thug. To this day, I don't know why I ever told her I wasn't a thug 'cause a few weeks following her comment, I proved her right.

One Sunday afternoon, GG loaded Chew, Julius, my cousin Juan, and me up in her Suburban. She dropped us off at the Norwest to meet up with some of my other cousins. When she left, all hell broke loose. While we were waiting to get into the theater, Juan started beefin' with some dudes over a female. This nut named Antonio started talking crazy to Juan and then our crew. He walked up, trying to call us out just as Ant's boy Raynard and his date walked by, so I nodded to acknowledge his presence. When I turned around, I was unaware that Juan and Antonio were about to throw down until he got in my face talking ignorant.

"What ch'all li'l Niggas wanna do?" Antonio asked, acting like he wanted some of me.

"Nigga, what you wanna do?" I snapped back with much bass in my voice.

I wasn't one that got into lip serving brothas. That made a person vulnerable. When he tried to reply, I socked him square in his grill so hard that spit squirted out of his mouth on contact. There we were locked up. We were rolling around on the ground. I was punching him, and he was socking me back. As the fight escalated, people immediately started closing in on us to watch. I won't lie, he did get a few good licks off on me, but I was taggin' his ass. Of course, his boys couldn't take the pressure of that beat down I was putting on him, so they jumped in. Once my boys got involved, we had a small riot going on. When Antonio's brother Charles pulled out a gun, then fired it into the crowd, all the spectators surrounding us scattered like a pack of wild dogs.

"Don't nobody fuck with a Nutty Gangsta Nigga and live to tell about it!" he yelled, firing his gun a second and then third time. After his gun went silent, I got up off the ground with blood on me. Immediately, I noticed my cousin Juan rolling around over in a corner. I knew he'd been shot. Before I could reach him to provide help, I wondered how critical he was. After I ran over to check him out, my side started burning. I looked down at my waist and there was blood everywhere. That's when I realized a bullet had grazed my side. Antonio was lying on the ground gasping for air. He'd been shot in the chest. When I glanced at him, he appeared to be fighting for his life, but I wasn't about to help his ass. He wasn't one of my guys. I didn't give a damn about him dying. His death wouldn't have bothered me one way or the other, which is exactly why I kicked him one last time while he was on the ground in distress.

Suddenly, I could hear sirens. Before I had a chance to run or do anything, the police rushed in with their firearms drawn. They started cuffin' brothas, throwin'em up in squad cars, and askin' questions later. I sat in the back of the officer's car casing the crowd. My eyes locked in on Charles. I wanted to remember his face for three reasons. One, he'd just shot me. Two, he said something about them NGN chumps, which I wasn't real hip to, but most certainly had beef with. And three, in time he was gon' have to deal with the consequences of bringin' it to a Prince.

To this very day, I could still tell you every visible scar and tattoo on Charles Casey's upper body. That's how focused I was on burning images of him on my brain. I caught a glimpse of a tat he had on his left arm, with every intention of not ever forgetting what it looked like. His tat was of a scroll with these distinctive letters that spelled out D.R.E.A. Shortly after noticing his tat, the officer got in the front seat to question me.

"What's your name?" he asked.

"Prince."

"Prince, what?"

"DeMarques Prince."

"DeMarques Prince? The Prince that played little league football with P.A.L.S (**P**olice **A**thletics & **L**ost **S**ons)"

"Yeah, that's me. Who are you?"

"Your old coach, Officer Williams."

"Coach Jeff?" I said with some excitement in my voice.

"Yeah."

"Man, you're on swoll."

"I've been hitting those weights."

"I can tell. What's been up?" I asked, acting like I was cool.

"Not much. What are you doing out here fighting? Prince, when I think about all that talent you had while you were playing Pee-Wee ball with the Broncos, I know you're on something more positive than what I'm seeing right now. Right?"

"Not really."

"Boy, your grandparents would die if something happened to you," he stated, pushing buttons on his computer.

"I know." As he punched in the letters of my name, I focused on the screen. I knew I had priors, but I didn't want him to see all my charges or be all up in my business. Before anything came up, I confessed. "Man, to save us both some time, I guess I should tell you I have a criminal history."

"Yeah, quite an extensive one," he mumbled, scrolling through my information. "It looks like you're on the verge of becoming a real menace to the department. I can tell you right now you don't want that for yourself," he advised with sincere concern. I didn't want to hear no good guy stories or be lectured by "Detroit's Finest," so before he could even get started, I cut him off.

"Man, I've been shot. Is there any way you could get me some medical assistance?"

"Yeah, I'll get you a medic in a minute."

As he walked over to the ambulance, I sat watching the two of them talk until I became distracted. I noticed Carrington walking up to the ticket booth with her boyfriend, Derrick Mason.

Derrick went to Cass Tech, which was one of the academically accelerated high schools in Detroit. Not only was Derrick a lame bookworm, but he was a car owner as well. He was a junior, almost dressed as fresh as me, and was on a mission to steal my girl. Well, Carrington wasn't really mine, though my infatuation for her was strong enough that I believed she was sometimes. Had Derrick not been running major interference and getting on my nerves, she could have been mine.

There I was sitting in the back of the police car, shot, and about to catch a few new charges. As Carrington turned to look in my direction, I tried to duck down. I didn't want her to notice me, but our eyes met at the exact same time. She looked, did a double take, and rolled her eyes. I tried to extend her a partial smile, suggesting that I was still "the man," but she looked away, clutched Derrick's arm, and walked into the theater completely ignoring me. *That punk's about to come up with my woman fa'sho now,* I thought as they made their way through the door.

Officer Jeff transported me to the hospital for a medical exam. Somehow, everyone shot during that altercation obviously had somebody praying for them that day. After I was cleared to leave the hospital, I was transported straight to the police station for questioning. I thought I was gon' just make a statement and leave, but I was charged, and then booked on some bullshit. For the record, I'll go to my grave believing that there was no way I should've been charged with anything, especially when you consider I was defending myself. Due to my juvenile record, no one cared that I was a victim. Hell, I'd been shot over some nonsense, so where was the justice for me?

That night, I was released to Bean's custody. Shoot, with the way her and Ant fussed, I would have preferred Juvie Hall.

"Prince, what the hell were you thinking about? Why would you be at the movies fighting?"

"I was mindin' my own bi'ness. Those chumps ran up on me."

"Can you go anywhere lately without getting into some foolishness?"

"Like I said, they ran up on me, Juan, and my guys. We were chillin'. They brought the drama to us. What was I s'posed to do? You expect me to just let 'em kick my ass?"

"Boy, I can't take no more of this stress. I'm starting to really worry about you. You're so busy tryin' to be like your brother. You're going to learn the hard way that these streets and this fast living ain't all it's cracked up to be."

"Bean, I done told you once, I wasn't doing nothin' this time. They called me out. The punk that shot me started popping them gums about some NGN niggas, who are obviously down with them same guys that killed T."

"All the more reason you should've avoided them. Boy, you're not bulletproof. You ain't gon' be satisfied until I'm burying your grown ass or visiting you in prison. I don't care about no ABC's, no NGN's, no

XYZ's…none of that shit. Keep your ass at home on the weekends, come straight to the house after school, and don't ask to go anywhere. Do you understand me? "

"What! Bean, I…"

"Damn it, Prince! That's the end of this discussion. Stop talking to me. I don't want you to say anything else to me about nothing, especially not that foolishness."

It was rare that Bean tried to play mom. I couldn't believe she was trying to crack down on me and enforce some rules. I wanted to keep defending myself, but I was waiting on Ant to say something on my behalf. He usually came to my defense when she got on me, but not then. For once, he was in agreement with her. He didn't say one word to help me out. I think in his heart, he knew she was right, and so did I. That still didn't change the fact that I was disappointed in him for not trying to help me plead my case. We always double-teamed Bean. Even when we both knew I was wrong, Ant still had my back. When Ant pulled up in front of the house, he told Bean he needed to holla at me for a second. She got out, slamming the door with a major attitude.

"Anthony, I know you're about to smooth this over with Prince, but I'ma tell you right now, if something happens to my baby, I'm holding you accountable."

"Bean, that's crazy. I stay on Prince. You can't make me feel guilty about anything. I've always looked out for this boy. Hell, I was watching his back when you didn't care one way or the other about either one of us. Right now, I'm not trying to hear that noise you're talking. I already got a lot on me, so you can take that mess to the house."

"Ant, you heard what I said, and that's what I mean. If something happens to Prince, I'm holding you accountable."

Ant sat in the driver's seat with an empty expression on his face. He was totally silent for about two minutes. I think he was trying to shake off the vicious words Bean had cut him with. Usually, when it came to me, Ant was selective with his words. He always picked them wisely. I guess that was based on the respect he had for me and the bond we'd established.

"Prince, you know you're my boy. I mean, Man, we're brothers, but I love you like you were my son. I've always tried to be that person you come to for anything because like me, you didn't have a father either. It makes me proud to know that you look up to me like you do, but things in our lives are about to change. Before T got killed, being the dope man was the thing to strive for. But seeing T dead haunts the hell out of me. The scandals associated with these Detroit streets ain't no place for a fourteen-year-old gangsta wanna be. You aren't ready for the game. Man, you can't survive the daily hustle that goes along with grinding. P, I don't want this kind of life for you. Boy, if something happened to you behind me, Bean would see me in Hell. You know you're her favorite. Man, to this day, she already blames me for the petty charges you have. After I served three years in the joint, and didn't get to finish high school, you were supposed to be the son that made Bean proud. When you think about it, I was her first born, but out of the pride she felt for you, she coined you as the one to carry the family's last name as your nickname. Prince, I want you to focus on things like girls, school, video games, and stuff the average fourteen-year-old focuses on. Don't be like me. Graduate from high school and make Bean, GG, and Daddy Ruenae proud. Better yet, be a better example for KeKe than I was for you. Shit's getting hectic in these streets. I don't wanna have to blow a nigga's mouth out for fucking with anybody in my family. To be honest, I think because I'm gettin'em so tough right now, you'd be the perfect target for a bunch of brothas trying to get at me. If something shady jumps off with you, I swear I'd do life or lose my own in seek of revenge."

"But, Ant," I stated wanting to plead my case; however, Ant cut me off.

"Prince, I can't and don't trust anybody, not even my closest friends and family some days. Something faulty happened with T. His death just doesn't make any sense to me. For that reason alone, everybody is suspect. Since I haven't heard or don't understand why he died, I can't take any chances with your life. I don't know who killed him; therefore, I got to even step lightly because I ain't ready to die."

As I listened to my brother, I could see that he had a real fear for my life. I'd never seen fear like that in him before, but I understood it. I could see that he was seriously worried about me.

"Ant, I promise I'll do better about trying to stay out of trouble. But what we gon' do about those punks from the movie?"

"Man, go in the house before I have to hurt your mother. Don't worry about them. They already hit."

After mentioning what Charles said about his connection to NGN, I didn't stress it anymore. I believed in my brother's wrath, and I knew if anything else went down, Ant was gon' most certainly be present to put straight fear in the triggerman's heart.

# 3

## Summer Parties

My doctor had me stay home for a week to recover from my injuries, so my first day back in school, I felt like a star. I walked through the double doors of Redford High with my hands full. As I stopped in front of security to be scanned, I tossed my backpack on the conveyer belt, got searched for weapons, and observed my classmates on the other side of the window, worshiping me like I was Big Shaq himself. Carrington still wasn't feeling me. I'd finally started to accept the fact that if she didn't get wit me, it was just gon' be her loss. Chew and Julius kept sweating me about being so weak behind her, but I couldn't help myself or the fact that at times she had me acting stuck on stupid. Hardheads don't always like for other brothas to know a female has him weak, but there is no denying it in my older age. Carrington had me gone.

That Friday, our Home Economics class baked cookies. Well actually, Carrington and some of the other females baked cookies. I sampled.

"Prince, how are you feeling today? Did you like the chocolate chip cookies we baked for you?" Carrington asked.

"They were straight. I'm not really a cookie fan, but since they were baked with some TLC, they were sweet like the person that prepared them."

"TLC! Sweet! Boy, you're so corny," she replied, staring at me with her deep dimples and the biggest smile.

"Why are you looking at me like that?" I asked, thinking, *Yeah, she's feeling me.*

"You're always so nice to me. I was just reflecting on how I sometimes trip for no reason, and how glad I am that you weren't seriously hurt on Sunday. Prince, I was angry when I saw you in the back seat of that squad car. I just knew you had done something stupid. That's why I rolled my eyes at you."

"Carrington, you don't give a damn about me, my criminal encounters or my well-being. You're always acting so stuck up or like nobody's good enough for you. That's why I'm wondering why anything pertaining to me matters to you anyway?"

"Prince, I like you as a person. You get on my nerves sometimes, trying to always be so hard. You act like a thug, which I find very unattractive. But, overall, you have some real good qualities. I just don't think you see them."

"Girl, I ain't trying to be no thug, and you don't know me like that to know about any of my personal qualities."

"Why are you getting so defensive?"

"Because the only person I try to be is me. If you want to be friends, I'm cool with that, but I'm gon' still be me."

"I'd like for us to be friends. But what does "being you" consist of?"

"Being real."

"What's real?"

"Not trying to be something I'm not."

"So how do I play into that?"

"I'm not from Rosedale Park, West Bloomfield, Dearborn or any of those other uppity ass, Boochie areas like that. You have to accept me for who I am. Most of all, you need to realize that what you see, is what you get."

"Prince, I can live with you being real. I can even live with you being who you are, but you're not a thug. You just think you are."

"I'm glad you feel like you can accept me the way I am 'cause if we're gonna be cool, you gon' have to. Now what's up on lettin' me get those digits?" I teased to change the subject.

"Don't push it. I said friends."

"I heard what you said. Friends can and do exchange numbers, don't they?"

"Sometimes, but we're not going to today."

"That's fine, one day you gon' want me to have your number. I ain't gon' take it though."

"I highly doubt that," she sarcastically stated, laughing in my face.

I didn't come up with a number that day, but I stayed on Carrington for the days that followed. By the last day of school, I had worn her down. She still wasn't on me like I wanted her to be, but we had become better friends, though at times, she sent mixed messages. I know she did that because I was so irresistible in my own way. I found it to be real funny how she'd rush home to call me, but always made it clear that we were only going to be friends. *Ain't that just like a damn woman,* I frequently thought as we talked many days into the wee hours of the night. There were times when

Carrington would get off the phone with her man to talk with me. Then turned around and rushed me off the line after her conscience started kicking that butt. I think because she claimed to be so much in love with Derrick, she wanted to honor him as much as she could. At that age everybody thought they were in love, but in my eyes, Carrington's thing with Derrick was nothing more than a "Puppy Love" I planned to sever.

Sometimes it appeared as though Carrington was on a mission to break my heart. The more I felt like I was wearing her down the more she talked about her man. *Here I am feaning over this woman like a dope-addict. How the hell she gon' tell me she's in love with another nigga?* I thought, listening to her stories like a trick.

◆◆◆◆◆◆◆

Julius threw the biggest summer house party of the year. His mother had a huge crib in Rosedale Park on Glastonbury, so J's party was a big deal. Everybody that was somebody in high school was making an appearance. I had to make a grand entrance, so I needed to get a new jean hookup and some fresh sneakers. After Bean got off work, I had her run me to Northland Mall. She fussed the entire time about me dressing like a thug. "Bean, just because I bought some fat shoestrings for my Pumas doesn't mean that I'm a thug." She rolled her eyes at me a few times, irritating me so much that I was almost tempted to put them back. Nonetheless, I was a fashion king. Whatever was hot, I was rockin' regardless of the price or what she had to say. All the way home, she fussed and got on my nerves. Finally, I jokingly told her, "Bean, you better be glad the stuff I like ain't as pricey as some of the gear the Ballas around here sportin'. Stop sweatin' me and just deal with my need to be trendy."

"When you live by yourself and pay all your own damn bills, then I won't worry. As long as you live in my house, what you're spending on any and everything will always be my business."

*That was a typical reply for her.* I thought, walking into the house. I could tell my comment pissed her off, so I didn't bother to say anything else. When we made it into the living room, I could hear the phone ringing off the hook.

"Prince, get that phone. I know it ain't for nobody but you. We haven't been in this house a good five minutes. Tell your friends don't start blowing up my phone. And make sure you let them know you'll be out, so don't be calling my damn house all night. I got to go to work in the morning, and I don't want to be bothered."

"Okay," I grumbled before answering. "Hello."

"Hello, is Prince there?"

"Speakin'. Who 'dis?"

"Hey, it's me, Zena. What 'cha doing?"

"Zena? What's up, Baby? I ain't heard from you in a minute. Where you been?" I asked, sitting on my bed.

"You haven't heard from me because you ain't returned any of my calls. What are you doing tonight?"

"I'm going to J's party."

"Can I see you?"

"Right now? You want me to come by tonight?"

"Yeah, I want to see you or I wouldn't have called."

"You're not going to J's party?"

"Yeah, I'm going, but I want to see you first. Can you arrange that or what?" she asked in this mouthwatering tone.

"What you got for me if I can?"

"You gon' have to come find out."

"I'll cum alright."

"Stop playing. Are you coming or not?"

"I told you I'll cum, but not quickly."

"Are you going to make it by my house this evening?"

"Fa'sho. I'll be over in a minute. I'm not staying long, so don't even ask."

"Ain't nobody asked you to be here all night. Just hurry up. I'll be waiting."

I was geeked. I knew Zena was making a *"Booty Call."* I hung up the phone, jumped on my Mo-Ped, which was a gift from Ant, and bounced that mug all the way to her house.

Zena was my ex-girlfriend. She was the first female I'd ever allowed to sucker me into having a serious relationship. It was cool while it lasted. When I started trying to be a playa, she decided to give me my space. Seconds before dumping me, she said she wasn't with me cheating on her. I was okay with her decision. I'd only hooked up with her because she was one of the few girls giving it up in middle school. I was lucky enough to be the first guy she'd ever slept with, so she was no longer a challenge for me anyway. During that time, neither one of us really knew what we were doing. After we moved on, one thing she always told me was that she hadn't had any dick better than mine since we broke up. That's probably why she couldn't move on.

We'd been separated for over two years. But shoot, by the time we'd made it to high school, Zena had developed, and her body was on point.

Hell, the thought of possibly getting some before J's party inspired me to push my scooter to the max. When I arrived at Zena's house, I was all ready to lay up in some warm gushy stuff. I pulled up by the front door, and like a damn fool, I just laid on the horn, honking it. She was looking good when she came outside. She had on this fitted "Baby girl" T-shirt, and that rump was looking right in her tight Sergio Jeans. Her hair was in two long French braids to the back, which she always wore. There was something sexy about the entire look she had that turned me on. "Prince, park your Mo-ped on the porch. Once you finish, come on in." I wrestled my ride up the steps, excited about the thought of getting busy. After my scooter was secured, I rushed into the house like I was being stalked. Before I could even get in the door good, Zena was all over me, kissing and sucking on my neck.

"Prince, I've missed you so much. When I see you at school, I get so jealous about other girls being all over you. You know you're supposed to be my man. We had a good thing a few years ago. I think we need to try getting back together," she stated, pulling me into her bedroom.

"I've missed you just as much," I replied, lying *Well, I don't actually miss you as much as I've missed the pussy.* I thought, taking off my draws. I wasn't stupid enough to verbalize my true feelings and take a chance on striking out. I could tell Zena was hot. She started rubbing my chest and licking my navel, which was the sign for me to do what I do, *Pop that coochie 'til it talked ta' me.*

I pulled her shirt over her head, unfastened her bra, and started sucking her fresh plump titties like I was her child. I rubbed, fingered, and pumped that coochie 'til she started screaming. Zena was begging me to stop, but ut'un, I flipped her over and got me some doggie style 'cause in my mind I owned her shit. I wasn't just the Prince of my family, but also the Ruler of Zena's little pink erotic kingdom. I put in firm long strokes, trying my best to touch every section of her guts. "Whose is it?" I asked, pumping, grinding, and pumping some more.

"Yours," she'd whimper, trying to take all of me.

"Tell me again how good it is," I insisted.

"Shut up," she ordered, covering my mouth. "Just hit this," she demanded, working her ass and hips like a hula dancer.

Zena continuously moaned as she tried to receive all twelve inches of me. Okay.......... I'm getting a little carried away with my story. Let me stop lying on my dick; it wasn't quite twelve inches back then. It was actually more like eight. What ever it was, it was more than she could handle, and her whining confirmed that I had the magic stick.

When I came, I was so far up inside of her, I know she was full of nut. Like a damn fool, I didn't even wear a condom nor did I try to pull out. I was sure she was on the pill 'cause when I told her I was about to bust, she didn't push me out or pull away. As a matter of fact, I actually remember her grabbing my butt cheeks and pulling me further in. That was all I needed to mentally confirm that she wanted to feel every bit of what I was giving.

After we finished, I was worn out. Zena wanted to lie in bed talking, but the last thing I remember was falling asleep inside of her, still somewhat firm. When I woke up thirty minutes or so later, I was in the same spot. The only difference was that my dick had gone retarded and looked like someone had forced it to drink a glass of soft-peter.

I glanced at the clock, noticing that it was almost eight thirty. J's party started at nine. I still needed to go home, get cleaned up and dressed. Zena was trying to give me a little more sex, which I truly didn't want. At the time, one nut was good enough for me. Plus, I knew I wasn't gon' miss my boy's party for nobody. She started talking about some she'd see me there, but I wasn't with that either. She wasn't about to have me on lock down. Carrington was gon' be there, too. Ut'un.........If anyone was going to be on my arm or have me on lock down, I wanted it to be her.

"I'll call you when I'm headed to the party," I stated, rolling my scooter off Zena's porch.

"Okay," she replied, puckering her lips for a kiss.

◆◆◆◆◆◆◆

When I made it to the house, Bean and Renzo were sitting in the living room, acting half civil. "Sup." I stated, walking to my room. My clothes had already been ironed. They were lying out on my bed, so all I had to do was shower and make sure I looked good. After getting ready, I stood in the bathroom mirror flexing my muscles and smoothing down the peach fuzz over my lip. While putting on my shirt, I noticed about five hickeys on my neck. There was one right below my ear, on my lower jaw also. *That damn girl done branded my ass. Carrington's gon' see this and I'm done.* I was about to put a cold spoon or some toothpaste on my face, but Bean called me from the back to get the phone.

"Hello." I answered.

"What time you rolling out tonight?" Carrington asked.

"I'm leaving here in about fifteen minutes. Why?"

"I was trying to make sure you were coming to the party."

"Why you so concerned about me and where I'm gon' be? Ain't that busta Derrick coming out tonight? Oh, let me guess, that nerd has to study?"

"Get off my man. This conversation isn't about Derrick. I was calling to see what time you were showing your face, not to get a lecture about my boyfriend. What you need to do is get off his jock."

"His jock? You know that punk wear panties. Chew and J told me they boy Kish got PE with Derrick and that nigga had on a purple thong the other day."

"Oh you wish."

"Oh I knooooooow," I repeated, talking proper like her.

"Bye, Chump. I'll see you later. Save me a dance."

"A'ight, I will. Holla back."

"There you go with your ghetto terminology."

"Oh, here we go. Don't try to dictate the way I'm s'posed to talk now. And before you show up tonight, you better think twice about dancing with me. After I put these moves on you, I might not be able to keep you from wanting me."

"Yuck," she laughed, before hanging up in my face.

I walked back to my room, sprayed on some Polo cologne, and grabbed my wallet.

"Bean, I'm about to be out."

"Wait," she replied. "How are you getting to the party tonight?"

"I'm riding the Scooter."

"Oh no you're not! With everything that's been going on over the past few months, I think you better come again. Go get my keys. I'll take you. When you're ready to come home, call Anthony or me and one of us will pick you up."

We pulled up in front of J's house, and everybody's hormones were raging out of control. The lawn was full of my high school homies, so I anxiously jumped out of the car, almost completely forgetting to say goodbye to Bean. "Prince, remember to call when you're ready to leave. I expect to hear from you by 1:15."

*No Bean ain't giving me a damn curfew on one of the biggest nights of the year. She couldn't possibly be serious,* I thought, smacking my tongue. I walked up to the side door with definite intentions of ignoring her.

As soon as the door opened, I could hear my jam coming on. "Party People, Party People,"... *Planet Rock* was humping out of the speakers.

"Aw, that's my jam," I yelled as everybody inside the party went buck wild. I walked downstairs to the basement with my hands in the air. All eyes immediately shifted my way as Zena ran up grinding all on me.

Zena wanted to make sure she put claims on me before anyone else had a chance to. She pulled me onto the dance floor and worked it out. Planet Rock was one of the biggest hits of the summer. It had the kind of groove that made you want to bust a sweat. I stood on the dance floor with my hands up in the air. I wasn't about to get sweaty. I stood there with Zena doing what I call my "Cool P" dance, and the ladies loved it. I was way too cool to boogie, but my dance served its purpose. It was different, it was mine, and it allowed me to get much action on the dance floor.

Zena had that young firm butt of hers planted right on my jewels. The way she was pumping her mid-section made a bunch of the girls mad. I have to give it to her, that girl could "Jungle walk." Dancing just came natural for Zena. She was really limber and could flex her body like Patra. When I compare her moves back then to those of the new millennium, they often put me in the mind of some of them fly sista's on rap videos. Don't act like you don't know which ones I'm talking about. I'm referring to the *Freak-a-leaks* that *stop then jiggle wit it* like they were born to do nothing other than *drop it like it's hot*. Man, all I can say is, *I like it like that*, too, but Dawg, let me get back to my story.

Hell, I can't lie, I enjoyed every bit of her being all over me for a moment. That's before I caught a glimpse of Carrington with that look of disgust she was so infamous for giving a brotha. Her top lip was turned so far up her face that it could have easily been stuffed in her eye. I watched her lean forward a few times whispering something to her best friend Mecca, but I really didn't know what that was about. She wasn't trying to be my woman, so I was free to do what ever I wanted to.

When the song, *My First Love*, came on, the mood instantly changed. Carrington walked over to the area I was dancing in with Zena. She stood right behind us looking at me all crazy. I casually gripped Zena's butt, rotating our position. I wanted to look Carrington in her face and question her behavior.

"What are you doing?" I tried to inconspicuously whisper.

"This is my favorite song. Let's dance," she suggested without considering Zena's feelings.

"What?" I motioned totally confused. "Where's your man?"

If I stopped dancing with Zena to accommodate Carrington, all hell was gon' break loose.

When I didn't rush off the floor to dance, Carrington became irritated. I think she was more so embarrassed. She was probably over there talking noise about me to Mecca seconds before coming to stand in my face. Her expression changed after I didn't move, so she pointed her finger, motioning the word, "Now." *Who the hell does she think she is?* I thought. Because of the effect she had on me, I only made her wait a few minutes longer. That's when.........I made the second biggest mistake of my life with Zena.

Z was snuggled all cozy in my chest. She was holding me around my neck and singing her li'l heart out. From my past experiences with her, I honestly believed I was her real first love. Like the young fool I was, I didn't care about her feelings. All I could think about was caressing Carrington. I pulled Zena off my chest, looked her in her eyes, and coldly moved her to the side.

"Prince, what are you doing?"

"I'm about to dance with Carrington."

"You're about to do what?" she asked, pulling my arm.

"You heard me, I'm about to dance with Carrington."

"You're about to dance with her right in the middle of dancing with me. Boy, if you dis me like that for her in front of all these damn people, I'm done with you fa' real."

"Okay," I rudely replied, like we hadn't just had some bomb, unprotected sex a few hours earlier.

I stepped away from Zena, pulled Carrington towards me, and slow danced with her through two more songs. She tenderly stroked my back, and when Earth, Wind and Fire's song *Reasons* came on, that woman had me fantasizing about doing some freak nasty stuff to her.

"*Reasons* is my favorite song," Carrington whispered in my ear, giving me an erection. Due to us being so close, my partner in crime would give me away. "Boy, something has you distracted."

"Huh," I laughed.

"Prince, this is my favorite song." At the time that wasn't something I wanted to hear. Her comment made me feel a little guilty about dissing Zena. *My First Love* was her favorite song, but that didn't stop me from dogging her out, though she didn't deserve to be treated that way.

Zena stood about five feet away from us in disbelief. I looked at her expression, immediately able to detect that she was going to give me a piece of her mind as soon as she could.

As I held onto Carrington, I couldn't help but wonder what her motivation was behind wanting to dance with me so badly. Her jocking me like she did that night came as a real surprise. I didn't know why she was suddenly giving me so much attention, but I know I liked it. She and I ended up partying together for the rest of that night. I totally ignored Zena along with a few other bucket heads trying to holla at me. When I looked at my watch, it was 1:25AM. *When I finally make it home, I already know what to expect. Dang, I can't believe this girl done made me miss my curfew again.* When the party was over, I walked Carrington to her mother's car, trying to set a good first impression, you know, just in case she gave me some play.

"Carrington, call me when you get a chance," I stated, waving.

"Okay, I will."

Once I found my way home, everyone was asleep. I tiptoed through the living room to my bedroom, dragging the phone cord behind me. I thought Carrington or Zena might call, but neither one of them did. *Damn Prince, you know Carrington was probably geeking you up at the party, and Zena is definitely pissed about the way she was treated,* I concluded, lying my head on my pillow. I couldn't beat myself up about anything that happened that night. *If Carrington played me, her bad, and if Zena wanted to stay mad about my ignorance, her bad, too,* I told myself before falling asleep.

Saturday morning, the telephone rung, which disturbed my rest, "Now why isn't Bean answering that phone?" I mumbled, rolling over to reach for the receiver.

"Hello." I answered.

"Prince, you sorry punk. Why did you do me like that last night?" Zena asked.

"Girl, what the hell are you talking about?" I yelled.

"Why did you embarrass me and leave me standing on the dance floor in front of all my friends to go dance with Carrington?"

"You ain't my woman. I can dance with whoever I want to dance with. I'd already danced about five songs with you, so why are you trippin'? You ain't got papers on me. We ain't committed, and I don't have to explain myself to you." I defensively yelled.

"Well, we were fucking before the party earlier that day like I was your woman."

"That's 'cause you gave it to me like you were my woman. I didn't call you asking for no pussy, you called me."

"You didn't have to come."

"Yeah, right! And since when have you heard of any real niggas turning down some ass?"

"Prince, I can't believe you did me like that."

"Look, I'm sleep. Get at me later," I rudely ordered before hanging up in her face. To make sure she didn't call right back, I took the receiver off the hook. Afterwards, I rolled over on my stomach and went back to sleep.

◆◆◆◆◆◆◆

During the summer of 1984 there were five different murders involving teenage males in one week's time. Actually, that entire year a few teens a month had been murdered, but never five tight. GG, Bean and Ant were on me like never before. I knew Ant was going through some things, but he was tripping me out. He still wasn't letting me hang with him that much, which bothered me. I know he was trying to keep me away from all the nonsense, but his approach was getting on my nerves. Any summer event I was trying to be at, Ant provided a reason I shouldn't get to go. For a minute, I thought he had a personal vendetta out for me or something. He was blocking all my summer entertainment, which made me question his behavior.

All he'd ever say is, "Prince, I am my brother's keeper."

"At the rate you're going, I don't want a keeper," I'd reply.

♦♦♦♦♦♦♦

During the school year everybody did the movies on Friday and skating at Detroit Roller Wheels on Saturday. Since that had been our weekend routine for so long, we decided to continue those same activities during the summer months. Seven weeks into our summer vacation, Chew and Julius three-way called me. It was the weekend, and they were trying to make plans.

"What up, Playa, Playa?" Chew yelled when I answered the phone.

"What up doe?"

"You know it's going down tonight."

"What is?" I asked.

"Beat Street's at the Norwest. You hangin' wit'cha' boys or what?" Julius asked.

"Fa'sho. I'll be there. Y'all need to fall through later on. Pick me up about 7:45, so we can all walk or catch a cab together."

"Man, I ain't with walkin' nowhere, but we'll be over to your crib about 8:15 tonight," Chew stated.

"That's cool. I'll be ready. How y'all gettin' here?"

"Chump, how else? We're walkin.' Are you tryin' to be funny?"

"Punk, you just said you wasn't with that, so I thought you had some wheels."

"Naaa Playa, but you gon' provide some when we get there."

"Whatever. I ain't got no car, so we must be rollin' out on my back."

"You don't have wheels, but you've got money."

"And?"

"That means you can pay for a cab."

"You always moochin'. Holla back."

When we hung up the phone, I arranged my gear for the evening. I wasn't even about to beep Bean at work to ask if I could go out. I didn't want to hear her mouth. I decided I was just gon' hang and deal with the consequences later, if there were any.

Chew and Julius arrived a little early. We all sat around in the den jammin' Run DMC's *It's Like That* on the radio. When that song went off and *Flashlight* by the Parliaments came on, Julius jumped up and started jittin' around the room like an electrocuted chicken. Chew was generally mellow with his moves, like me. For some reason the Funkadelics had him so hype that he, too, started pop locking like a maniac. I threw my hands in the air doing my "Cool P, Thug Life" dance that a lot of perpetrators were starting to bite. That dance was so gangsta. I owned it though, and there were very few people that could duplicate my style. You had to have real G tendencies to perfect such a dance. Since I created it, no one looked quite as good rocking it as I did.

After clowning with them for about half an hour, I called us a cab. We waited about twenty minutes, still bumping WGPR or JLB on the radio. Deejay Mojo was off the hook. He played Whodini right before we left, so we rallied together like real boys and flowed *Friends* like we were in concert. "Aw this is our theme song," I stated before my boys and I started wildin' out. We all sung the lyrics to *Friends* like we had written them ourselves. *Friends is a word we use everyday.......* Shoot, we were jamming something serious, when out of the blue our moment was interrupted by a horn.

"Damn, my man got bad timing," I stated, turning off the radio.

"No lie." J replied.

"Come on bustas let's be out," I suggested, as Chew and J looked at me like I was stupid.

"Busta, P, you the busta with yo whipped ass." J replied.

"Whipped, whipped on who or what?"

"Boy, you foolin' now. P, if somebody said Carrington's name, you'd about break your neck trying to see where she was or what she was doing. Punk, if you could get up in Judge Horton's house, I bet you'd hide in Carrington's panty drawer just to get a wiff of the pussy."

"Chump, I hope you would, too. If you say something different, I'm gon' be concerned about your manhood."

"I bet you'd be sniffing her dirty thongs," J argued.

"I bet he would, too" Chew agreed.

"So would you," I responded.

"No I don't think so. I can't stand Carrington. If I were in her house, I'd be hiding in her closet."

"Chew, what you gon' be hiding in there for?" J asked.

"So when she gets undressed, I can pop out that mug, surprise her prissy ass, and take pictures of her saggy titties to post them all over the boys' locker room. That way every nigga at Redford's gon' know Carrington has to put them big tits of hers in a miracle bra to make them bad boys stand at attention the way they do."

"She told me they naturally stand like that," I said, getting him going even more.

"Man, her stuff is too big to naturally stand. She's just like a grandma watching television."

"Grandma?" J repeated.

"Yeah, you can best believe when Carrington takes off her bra, them tits go from young and perky, to resting on her knees like my grandma's when she's watching her soaps."

"Fool, you're stupid. I ain't even fin'na fuss with you about Carrington. I know she ain't got me gone like y'all think."

"Oh…Okay," he replied, sounding like Baby Huey.

After arriving at the theater, our cab fare came to six dollars. While getting our tickets, I noticed a few females walking up behind us. One was pretty and smelled hella good. Another one kept laughing like she was in middle school, which got on my nerves. Chew introduced himself, then started talking that suave BS he'd be shooting on females to break the ice.

"Hello, Beautiful." Chew stated, and they all started laughing. "Y'all meeting somebody tonight?" he quickly asked.

"Naa, we're here alone. Are you and your friends meeting some chicks up here?" Tasha, the cutest one asked.

"Do you see anyone with us?" I asked, inviting myself into their conversation.

"Nope. That don't mean y'all aren't meeting some chicks inside."

"Well, we're not. You and your friends are welcomed to sit with some real playas if you like," I informed her, grinning.

"If you show us some real playas, we might consider sitting with 'em."

"Oh, you got a smart mouth. I like that. What's your name?" I asked because I was feeling her snappy convo.

"Tasha. What's yours?"

"Prince."

"Prince! Prince, like *Do Me Baby*, Prince?" she asked as Chew and Julius burst out laughing.

I looked at her like she was crazy. I didn't appreciate her fronting me in front of my guys. To be honest, I was digging her sharp tongue only because she was cute. Had she been a butt ugly chick, there's no way she would have gotten away with dissin' me in public.

"Yeah Right! Do I look like a rich nigga that wears fitted pants, frilly shirts, and bitch ass boots?"

"No, I was only playing, sorry. Dang! Calm down."

"Prince got some jams, but don't play me like that again, you don't know me like that."

"Okay, I said I was sorry."

Once inside, I stopped by the concession stand to buy a drink. I was trying to come off like somewhat of a gentleman, so I asked the girls if they wanted some popcorn or something. None of them did, which pleased me because I really didn't want to spend no extra money anyway.

As cute as Tasha and her girls were, they got on my nerves talking through the entire movie. There were so many times I wanted to tell them to shut up. A few times, I gave them ignorant looks, thinking, *That's why I can't stand sitting around girls. They talk too damn much.* They ignored me and kept talking, so I looked over at them one last time before straight telling them to, "Shut the hell up."

When the movie ended, everybody exiting the theater was all pumped up. As we saw the girls to their cab, I exchanged numbers with Tasha. "Call me sometime soon. Maybe we could hook-up on the solo tip and have a little you and me time," I suggested, closing the door.

Once they were gone, Chew and Julius ragged on me about talking to the finest girl as always. Those wimps didn't have any game. They always got mad at me because I had conversation and a way with the ladies. I repeatedly told them just because I seemed thugged-out didn't mean I wasn't able to have a quality conversation with a classy honey.

"Don't trip on me because chicks feel me the most. I can't help it that I've got mad character. Chew, you can't stand seeing ladies jock my unusual hazel eyes, my good hair, smooth skin, and these pretty white teeth," I said, smiling. "I dress fresh as hell, always smell good, and they can't help themselves. What you gone offer the women, J, with yo whopped Gumby hair cut that needs to be tightened up. And Chew, while you're over there smiling so big with that chipped tooth of yours. What you got to offer a lady that I don't have?"

"Man, please get off your own nuts," J insisted, walking away.

"Whatever, y'all the ones that's perped out! Don't get mad at me because I'm that guy folks love to hate."

"Shut up, P," Chew replied.

"Okay, I can see I'm being hated on, let me change the subject. It's real obvious that y'all niggas mad about my come up tonight."

"Yeah, right!" J replied with much sarcasm.

"So, what are we about to do now?" I asked, running to catch up with them.

"We don't know what you're doing. We're going to Zena's house party," Julius answered.

"What! Zena's having a house party? She didn't invite me? I guess she's still mad about the little ordeal at your party."

"Yep."

"I thought she'd be over that li'l Carrington incident by now."

"Fool, are you crazy? The way you dogged her out in front of everybody for that trick Carrington was out cold. She might not ever holla at you again. I know if you did me that way, I wouldn't," J suggested, looking all crazy at me.

"Man, it was only a dance."

"Yeah, right in the middle of one you were having with Zena. Anyway she told us don't bring you."

"What the hell does she mean don't bring me?" I defensively asked. "It ain't like y'all can tell me where I can go."

"Man, we're not about to argue with you. Come on, J. Let's be out. We'll tell you about the party tomorrow," Chew cynically informed me.

I was heated about not getting an invite to Zena's party. She knew I loved to party, so for her to invite my friends, and not invite me, hurt my feelings. Zena was gone for me, like I was for Carrington. I couldn't understand her obsession with me though. *She's just being vindictive,* I thought, playing it off for a minute. *I wonder if she's testing me,* I considered, attempting to ignore my friends' taunting.

To maintain some degree of self-respect, I went anyway. "Man, I'm going to the party wit ch'all."

"Okay, you gon' get fronted on."

"Whatever."

As soon as we hit Zena's street, DJ Ekin was bumping *La-Di-Da-Di*, by Doug E Fresh. The block was packed, and the music was humping. Everybody on the street was smoking bud and drinking forties. My crew showed up like we were all that. I walked up Zena's long driveway to the wooden privacy fence, grabbing the gate latch. Ekin started spinning *Hard*

*Times,* by Run DMC. Like always, my hands went straight into the air. I started pumping my arms up and down as I walked through the gate to get lost in the crowd. I was bobbing my head, trying to slide past the entrance 'cause I thought I could sneak past Zena without being noticed. I was wrong, Zena stopped me in my tracks.

"Prince, where do you think your black butt's going?"

"Aw, what's up with that Z, I can't come in?"

"Oh hell no! After the way you dissed me last month, you ain't welcomed here at all."

"Why it got to be all like that?" I asked, easing up on her to rub her back.

"Prince, just leave. I'm not falling for your BS. You're sorry, and that mess you pulled at J's party was bold."

"You're right, and I apologize. I didn't think you were going to get as mad as you did. Dang, it was only a dance. Why don't you stop trippin'? I'll make it up to you. We can dance all night tonight with no interruptions." I suggested because I knew Carrington wasn't gon' be there. After that, I flashed my pearly whites on her. As usual, wouldn't it be my charm and warm smile that was my ticket into the party? She bit bait and by the time *Hard Times* was going off, my time had improved, and I was up in the party mingling.

While I was standing along the fence drinking a beer with some of the fellas, *The Message* by Grand Master Flash came on. Zena walked over, wanting to dance. She pulled me out to the center of the yard, and then worked it out from there. Though that song was a hit, it wasn't one I'd pick to dance to. That was one of the few songs me and my boys frequently smoked to. It was so mellow, and you could chill to it after getting ripped. Zena wasn't feeling that song either. With the way she liked to shake her ass, I knew it was way too slow for her. She didn't really care about doing her thing; her focus was more on paying me back.

I stood there doing my dance, when out of nowhere, Zena started pumping her fist in my face singing, "Don't push me 'cause... I'm ......trying not to lose ...." I backed up, thinking, *Naw you wanna lose your head or something. If you didn't, you wouldn't be pumping your fist in my face.* I tried to laugh at her ignorance because I didn't want to snap and go off on her. After all, she had allowed me to stay.

"You didn't have to front me like that," I stated walking away.

"Neither did you, but you did. I recovered from it, so you do the same. And enjoy the rest of my party."

No matter what jam DJ Ekin bumped that night, every song sent the crowd ballistic. To be honest, Zena's party was just as off the chain as J's.

As a matter of fact, it was so phat, I didn't even allow her tripping to affect my mood for long. She said what she had to say, and I acknowledged her bitterness.

As the party continued, my boys and I downed a few more forties. We chilled up in Zena's gig that night like we were Big Ballas. By the time the party ended, we had a few brews, a nice buzz, and the girlies were on our jocks like crazy. Out of respect for Zena, I had to mack on the sneak tip. But shoot, I didn't care 'cause by the time we left, we were "Crunk" like Li'l John and ass was leaving with us. The only thing we lacked was a decent place to get laid, but Hoodrats don't rate quality shit anyway, so Chew's basement came in handy for the red light specials that went down after Zena's big event.

# 4

## *Greektown*

Seems like time stood still for no one, and my summer break from school played out just as fast as the fashions did that year in Detroit. The last week in September, Henry Ford High School was playing football against Cooley High. All my boys wanted to go to that game. For some reason, I wasn't feeling them twisted nuts over on Eight Mile. They got real stupid in that hood for no reason at all. Plus, I didn't want to bring no unnecessary beef on myself.

"I ain't feeling that move to the game tonight. It's all kind of stuff we could be on besides a football game. It's movie Friday anyway. What's up with that? Why y'all want to break up the weekend routine without a vote?" I asked.

"Man, it's gon' be mad freaks at Ford tonight. We need to be representin' up in that mug. Don't nobody want to always go to the movies. Plus, it's good to play your hand a little different every now and then," Chew responded.

"I'm not with that, I ain't gon' even lie. Bean and Ant got me spooked about going to certain hoods. Besides, I can't afford to get into any trouble period. I got court next week on that stuff that happened at the movies back in May. Judge Cheatham is just looking for any reason to lock my black ass up in Juvie Hall. That's cool, if y'all going, but I'm sittin' this one out."

"I guess you're sittin' this one out then. Julius, everybody else, and me gon' be up in that game tonight. It's Ford's Homecoming, too. Aw homie, you know all kind of ho's gon' be there."

"P, you stupid if you don't go. What you gon' do while we at the game?" Julius asked.

"Damn J, you act like I'm a sucka. I got something I can get into without y'all. You act like I can't function since something different goin' down."

"Why you getting mad? I just asked a question."

"Because, you acting like you hold my dick when I piss. Newsflash, Nigga, if you ain't present, I can drain the weasel by my damn self."

"Man, you on some BS. Your mom's got you acting like a pussy." Julius replied, giving Chew five.

"Man, I'm hip. That's exactly why he ain't going," Chew cosigned.

"Keep my mama out of this conversation."

"Damn Dawg, calm down," Julius quickly replied. "We're just playing."

"I'm not. Don't talk about my mama."

"I'm out. Chew, you coming? Your boy's trippin'. I ain't got time to be fooling with nobody's kids."

"Kids, Boy, I'm a grown ass man," I yelled, as J walked away.

Julius looked like he had lost mad respect for me. I know he was heated after I bugged out on him. My temperament wasn't intentional. I was just dealing with a lot of stress. As boys, every now and then our raw-dawg side came out on each other, but our anger never lingered like females. We'd have our little dispute and move on.

While they went to the game, I caught a cab to Zena's house. We'd hooked up a few times after her party. Long before I decided I wasn't hanging with my guys, she'd already called me over to watch movies with her. The only reason I spent my Friday evening with her is because my evening ended up being free.

When I got to her house, her brother Ray was chilling in their basement with some of his boys. Ray was grinding, too, but compared to Ant, he was a featherweight in the game. Ant didn't have any respect for Ray either. Whenever he said anything about him, he frequently referred to him as 'Shady Ray the Big Balla Wanna Be.'

A few times Ray tried to get Silk to put him on. But Silk, huh, he didn't trust anybody. He most certainly didn't trust Ray 'cause he'd done some down low deceptive deals that pissed Silk off. Silk told Ray if he messed over him again, one of his boys was gon' find him dead with toes in his mouth. That was gon' let his crew know that he brought it to the wrong one, and he should have watched his step.

After I discovered Ray was shooting craps in the basement, that's where I wanted to be. Hell, I didn't want to be watching no house movies.

"Prince, we need to talk," Zena informed me as I headed to the basement.

Right then, I figured she was trying to lure me into the room to get busy. For us to be youngains, Zena loved to have sex like a nympho.

"Can't it wait?" I asked, walking back to her room.

"No."

I started unfastening my pants to get undressed. I figured I'd hit, shoot some dice, then take it to the house. Once, I made it into her room, she really wanted to talk. I immediately relaxed on her bed, while Zena sat on the dresser with the blankest expression on her face. From her look, I knew something was wrong. I just didn't know what she was about to say.

"Prince, I'm scared," she stated with tears rolling down her cheeks.

"Scared! Scared about what?"

"I haven't had a period in a few months, and I think I'm pregnant."

"What the fuck? How the hell did that happen? What, you ain't on the pill?"

"No."

"Damn! Why you let me nut all up in you then? How stupid is that when you knew you weren't on any birth control?"

"You should have asked, not assumed."

"Have you told your mother or Ray?"

"Prince, I haven't told anyone. I'm scared to death, and all you can do is bitch. You know, you could've used a condom, too."

"Yeah, okay! You're right," I replied, trying to calm myself down.

"You mad?"

"Hell yeah I'm mad. You should've told me you weren't on the pill, then I would have at least pulled out."

"Well, it's too late for what we should've done. I might be pregnant, so what are we going to do now?" she asked, wiping away tears.

"Let me think for a minute."

"Let you think," she repeated. "Think about what? Prince, I know I'm not getting an abortion, so you don't need to think about that. That's not even an option right now."

"Zena, I'm not ready to be no daddy! I can't even take care of my damn self. How the hell am I gon' take care of a baby? Maaannn, Bean about to trip out for sure. I can hear her talking shit now."

"Prince, you need to relax. I don't know the first thing about being a mother, but I don't want to get an abortion. If that's what you're thinking about doing, then don't."

"Why not? You got the rest of your life to have kids. Why you want to start having babies so early? We'll only be fifteen-years-old when our child is born. We're just starting to live ourselves. I don't want any kids. I don't want to grow old having to deal with no baby's mama; I want a wife and a family. Zena, after we've both had some time to think, we need to talk about this again. Right now, I need to get home. I'm about to miss my curfew again."

"You don't care about a curfew. You violate your mother's rules more than anyone I know. Now all of a sudden, her rules are the law. Give me a break."

"Shut up talking to me. I already got enough stress and now you just added more."

"Well, let me relieve you of a little stress. Go ask Ray to give your black ass a ride home, so you can talk with him about why you want his little sister to get an abortion."

"He gon' tell yo stupid ass to get one, too. He knows we're to young to be parents."

"Prince, get out my room."

After her bad news, I didn't want to walk home. When I went to the top of the steps to call Ray, right as I was about to go down a few stairs, I noticed a muscular arm with this familiar tat. *D.R.E.A. in a scroll. Damn, Ray down with them cats*, I thought, quickly backing up the steps like I had seen a ghost. I walked back to Zena's room, insisting that she get me their phone.

"What did he say? Is he going to give you a ride?"

"I didn't even ask. I forgot Ant told me to beep him when I was ready. We're supposed to go to Coney Island for breakfast."

"Oh, beep him then," she replied, handing me the phone.

I dialed Ant's number, pushing in my emergency code 4357. That spelled out HELP. When Ant called back, he was frantic on the other line. I told him I couldn't talk, but I needed him to come scoop me up as soon as he could. "I'm on the other side of town, I'll be there in about fifteen minutes," he stated.

I chilled in Zena's room with the door pushed up, until Ant arrived. Fifteen minutes later, he was in the driveway. I hugged Zena before leaving to let her know that I didn't want bad blood between us. "Sorry, I yelled at you. I'm sure we'll come up with something we can both be happy with." As I exited, she kissed me on the cheek, looking real sad. I waved bye to her, but I'm sure that didn't provide much comfort.

"What's the problem? Why you push the help code in my beeper? You know you ain't supposed to use 4357 unless it's a dire emergency."

"Man, it really was. Those chumps claiming NGN were in Zena's house with Ray."

"How you know it was them?"

"Ray was in the basement gambling with 'em. When I was on my way down to ask him for a ride to the house, the chump that shot me was standing on the steps."

"Did he see you?"

"Nope, but I saw him."

"P, how you know it was him if you were looking down into the basement?"

"Man, I know who I saw. Plus, I saw his D.R.E.A. tat. I'll remember that 'til the day I die."

""Think, are you sure it was him?"

"Ant, if Silk ain't taught me nothing, he taught me to pay close attention to details. The day my man shot me, I looked him over. I paid very close attention to every visible scar and flaw on his body. I'm telling you, I know for a fact it was him."

At that point Ant didn't say anything else to me. He made a few calls, took me to Coney Island for breakfast, then drove me home.

"Ant, don't say anything to Bean about this incident tonight. If you do, she'll have me on house arrest. I won't be able to go anywhere." He laughed. "Man, I'm serious, she'll start naggin' me to death about my every move."

"She needs to."

"Dawg, I can't be locked up in that house with Bean and Renzo all day, everyday. I'm serious; I'll go nuts or catch a Murder One charge for killing his crazy ass," I stated.

"P, you know I got yo' back. Go on in and relax."

"Thanks," I hesitantly replied, looking pitiful from my news.

"You look a little stressed. Man, you straight?"

"Not really. I got a few things on my mind, but I'll be cool."

"You sure you don't need to talk about anything?"

"I'm sure."

"If you do, I have time to listen."

"Ant, I'm straight. Thanks though."

"P, I hope you don't feel like a simp because you're trying to avoid an early encounter with death. It's cool to occasionally be scared. However, a man can't walk in fear everyday and survive these wicked Motor City streets. Eventually, you got to square up. Let a nigga know that you ain't no trick and demand your respect. When you're in the game, sometimes life comes down to survival of the fittest. Trust me when I tell you that only the strong will survive."

I heard what Ant was saying, but his words were like rubber bullets to me. Since T's death, Ant had been on some scary shit himself. I didn't want to crush his ego, so I just pounded him down before going in the house.

♦♦♦♦♦♦♦

That Monday at school, Chew and Julius talked about all the numbers they'd gotten the night of the game. I told them about Zena's news, and they both swore I'd better have a blood test done as soon as the baby was born. Shortly after ragging on me about not wearing a condom, they started tripping because I didn't go with them to the game. "Man, get off my dick and chill with the jokes," I stated, clearly frustrated. Neither of them were fazed by my outburst and continued to piss me off. I was already feeling beat down from my weekend news. The last thing I needed was for them to make matters worse.

Without taking my issues into consideration, the two of them went on with their story, insisting that I should've gone with them. "P, you probably would have had a better weekend had you gotten Zena's depressing news at school today," Julius joked. I didn't even get into it with them; Zena's news would have been depressing no matter when or where I got it. Seeing how they carried on after getting my first bit of news, I opted not to say anything about seeing the guy that shot me at her house. They would have sworn Zena set me up, but I knew that wasn't the case.

Another reason I didn't mention anything to them is because I knew loose lips sank ships, and both of them talked way too much, so I wasn't taking any chances.

♦♦♦♦♦♦♦

One afternoon, I was sitting in Mrs. Young's Algebra class, thinking about my life. My court date was quickly approaching, I was about to be a daddy, and I had beef with some lunatics. I still hadn't shared my news with Bean or Ant. I knew I needed to eventually say something because Zena was almost five months pregnant.

As I looked out into the hall, I noticed Carrington walking by. She obviously saw me as well 'cause she backed up, motioning for me to come out of class. "Excuse me, Mrs. Young, I need to use the restroom." Once that hall pass was secure in my hands, I walked out smiling.

"Hey, Sexy. Where you been?" I asked.

"Derrick's a senior this year. He's been doing a few college tours, so I went with him and his family the past two weekends to do campus visits."

"How wack! And I guess you enjoyed doing that?" I asked.

"Yeah, actually I did."

"That's 'cause you're wack, too," I replied, rubbing her hair.

"Boy, don't touch my hair. That's my man's job," she said, punching me.

"That's why I'm rubbing it. You know I'm the closest thing you got to a man. Soft ass Derrick would prefer to rub my hair over yours."

"Derrick is a man. He's just doesn't behave like you think a man should. He isn't a thug like you. He's good people, and he's going places in life. You wouldn't notice qualities like that since all your role models are street people."

"Derrick's a lame, and so are you. I'm out! I have to get back to class," I replied, turning with my face all frowned up. As usual, she'd gotten under my skin talking about her boyfriend. Her comment pissed me off, too. It sounded as though she was insinuating that all I'd be in life was a zero. Huh, little did she know that once I became focused on my purpose, there were great things in store for my life.

When the date for my court proceedings rolled around, almost my entire family was present. Bean, GG, and Ant, sat right behind me for support. My grandfather didn't come; he'd been having chest pains. GG said court might be too stressful for him, so she insisted that he stay home. All during the trial, Charles Casey kept mean mugging me. He called himself intimidating me, but I wasn't moved. I wasn't worried one bit. As far as I was concerned, I knew he wasn't going to be an issue much longer. I was banking on DOC dealing with him, so I let his looks ride.

After the prosecution rested their case, I could tell from the way things were going, Charles feared he would be found guilty. Turns out I was right. The last day of court, Casey didn't even show up. Once my family realized he wasn't coming, we all became noticeably worried. What pissed me off the most is that he was so hard when he shot me. But the fear of going to prison caused him to avoid facing his sentencing like a man.

When the decision was given, the juror's walked into the courtroom and read the "Guilty" verdict without any regret. I was thrilled to hear that he was found guilty on four felony counts. Two charges of Attempted Murder, one count of Felony Firearm, and the other was Possession of a firearm as a previously convicted felon. Although Charles didn't show up, I was certain that whenever the law finally caught up with him, he'd be forced to face his punishment of forty years to life.

Though Casey didn't get sentenced that day, I wasn't walking around in fear until he was caught. Had GG and Bean had it their way, I would've. That Friday night I tried to relax. I called my boys to see what was up. They wanted to hang, and so we did. Ant was on this cautious mission. He dropped us off at the movies, then forced me to see what time it ended. Before leaving, he assured me he'd be back to get us.

When we entered the theater, we sat in our usual seats in the middle row. By the time we walked out, Breakin' had us all trying to do the Electric Boogaloo. Chew and Julius were the real dancers among our clique, so they argued about whose moves were the freshest. After they exchanged a few words, Julius grabbed Chew around the neck. I watched them for a moment. Before I realized what I was doing, I jumped in to horseplay also. Ant pulled up right after I did and snapped.

"Cut out all that playing!" he yelled, pissed off. "Now you punks come on and get in the car. All y'all slipping big time. P, you know we got you laced up better than that. Did you forget that a man was found guilty for shooting you today? When y'all standing around, y'all better be doing way more watching each other's back and less playing or else you might end up dead."

While Ant was raising hell, none of us said anything in response to his comment. From his tone, we could tell that he was angry. At first, I thought he was being a little over protective, but shoot, at the time, I dare not tell him that. Though, I didn't verbalize my thoughts. I didn't believe for a minute that anybody wanted to kill us over some BS. Yet to appease him, I tried to divert his anger.

"Ant, can we hang with you tonight?" I asked

"Nope, I'm taking your girls home first, then you next. I got to take care of some business."

"My girls?"

"That's right. Y'all behaving like bitches, so I'm treating y'all like some. Only females get comfortable and let they guard down like y'all did tonight."

"So now we some bitches?"

"I guess so. You're acting like it."

"Man, I'm hungry. Could we at least get some Coney Island before you drop me off?" I asked as Chew and J got out the back seat.

"Naw you gon' have to eat when you get to the house. I just told you I got business," he rudely replied before driving the rest of the way in complete silence.

Ant had the most serious look in his eyes. I could see that something heavy was on his mind. I figured one of his runners was short on their dope tab. Whatever the case may have been, something was about to go down. *What if Ant's being short with me because he found out I was about to be a daddy?* I thought *Naaa, I'm trippin,* after pulling up in front of the house.

"Holla at you later," Ant stated.

"Yeah, Man, thanks for everything."

I went inside straight to the kitchen to find me something to eat. I was starving, so I ate the other half of Bean's corn beef sandwich from Lou's before settling in with thoughts of Charles Casey invading my mind. Him being on the loose suddenly made me uneasy. The more I thought about him, the more unsettled I felt. *Damn, I can't stress this*, I thought pulling back my sheets to get into bed.

Around two o'clock that morning, Carrington called. She said she was up and just wanted to talk. I think that was BS. That girl knew she secretly loved me. I don't know why she tried to front like she didn't. After being on the phone for about ten minutes, she started talking about her man.

"Prince, Howard University sent Derrick an admissions letter for this upcoming fall."

"Sooooooooooooooooo! And what is your point?"

"Aren't you excited for him?"

"Wayne State, Howard, you're talking to me like I'm supposed to know something about colleges. I've already made it quite clear to you that I don't care about that nigga."

"Boy, everyone knows about Howard University."

"No, not everyone. I'm somebody, and I don't. But before you get all off into explaining, let me tell you now, I don't want to know either."

"Howard is one of the most established HBCU's there is. Derrick wants to be a neurologist and they have a great Medical School program."

"First of all, Carrington, I don't even know what an HBCU is. It sounds like some kind of girly device y'all use for birth control. Secondly, why are you always talking about your man when you know I do not care about yo nigga?"

"Prince, stop tripping and let me enlighten you."

"Ut'un, I'm out."

"An HBCU is a Historical Black College or University," she responded, ignoring me.

"Well, let me enlighten you. I don't care what those letters stand for. The only way they would matter to me is if they represented a **H**orny, **B**eautiful **C**arrington, **U**ndressed in my bedroom ready to get dicked down," I ignorantly replied, laughing.

"You make me sick sometimes. There are moments like now when I wish I could take some of Derrick's qualities and put them in you. You have so much potential, but it's rather unfortunate that you don't realize your own talent. Sometimes you act so damn immature. It drives me crazy."

"Carrington, I don't give a…" Right when I was about to curse her out, my other line beeped. "Hold on while I answer my line," I said, pushing the flash button to click over.

"Hello," I answered. Afterwards, all I heard was a female's voice. She was frantically screaming on the other line. I couldn't make out anything she was saying, but I knew she was saying, 'My brother's dead.' I was trying to confirm if she was telling me that my brother was dead.

"What did you say, and who is this?"

"It's me, Zena. Somebody just killed Ray in our front yard," she clarified in distress.

"What? When did this happen?"

"About ten minutes ago. Ray was standing outside in the driveway with some of his boys. Suddenly, I heard gunshots. When I ran to the door, I saw some guys driving away, talking bout NGN."

"Damn, those chumps done did a drive-by on Ray and his crew now?"

"Yeah," she cried.

"Are you alright? Did anyone inside the house get hurt?"

"No, everyone inside the house is fine. I can't believe Ray is dead."

"Want me to come over there?" I asked out of concern.

"No."

"Which of his homies was he with?" I asked, hoping it was Casey.

"Two of his boys got shot. Joe is in critical condition and Big Man was transported to the hospital to be treated for minor injuries."

"Did anybody see or hear anything?"

"Nope! Nobody saw the guys' faces. All of the shooters were wearing dark, hooded sweatshirts. Those punks road down on them in an old Cutlass that didn't have any tags on it."

"Damn, Baby, I'm sorry. Are you okay?"

"No! How could I be? My brother just got killed," she replied, crying. "Prince, I know it's late. I probably shouldn't have called. I'm sorry; I just needed someone to talk to." Suddenly, there was an abrupt pause. "Sorry for crying on you like this, I'll let you go."

"Wait! I'll talk if you want to," I responded out of compassion.

As much as I was digging Carrington, seems like Zena needed me more. Though we primarily just held the phone saying absolutely nothing at all, I ended up staying on the line with Zena. Considering that Carrington had already pissed me off, I never bothered to click over to tell her I'd call her back. I knew whenever we spoke again, she'd swear I left her holding on because she was talking about Derrick. However, that truly wasn't the case. For once, I was sincerely concerned about Zena. While listening to her cry, I considered why someone would want to kill Ray. He was a family man, and he and Zena were close like my brother and me. Though I hadn't lost a sibling, I could relate to what she was going through from losing T. I realized she was going to have a hard time recovering from Ray's death. Out of sympathy for her situation, I decided I would be as supportive of her as I possibly could for the weeks that followed.

After Ray's funeral, I spent a lot of quality time with Zena. I tried to keep her occupied to help her cope with the death of her only sibling. I believed my being there for her was only right, considering she was the mother of my child to be. My acts of kindness ended up working against me though. Zena started falling in love with me again, which was not a good thing. I didn't think I was doing anything special by giving her so much of my undivided attention, but she did. I wasn't trying to establish any kind of romantic ties between us either. But because of her crisis and the pregnancy, I didn't know how to tell her. Hell, I was still feeling Carrington. Plus, she and I had worked through the disagreement we had before Zena called that night. We were still communicating as friends on a regular basis, but for Zena's sake, I decided I'd keep the extent of my friendship with Carrington concealed as much as possible or at least until after the baby was born. As far as Carrington was concerned, she didn't sweat me about the time I spent with Zena. She already knew there was nothing she could say. Even if she wanted to express her thoughts, she knew it was best to keep it to herself. Derrick was her man, not me.

◆◆◆◆◆◆◆

A month later Zena wanted to get out, so she and her cousin's invited me to go downtown to Greektown with them. I considered going at first, but Carrington called at the last minute inviting me to go out with her for a post Sweet Sixteen birthday celebration. Her parents had bought her a brand new 1984 red Camero for her birthday. Since Zena had been occupying all my free time, I'd been missing her. After she extended the invite, I immediately called Zena with this sorry excuse as to why I couldn't go out with them. She accepted my story without question, which was cool with me. That way I had to tell less lies, and less to remember later, if it ever came up again. "Zena, with all that has been going on you probably need to stay home and rest as well," I recommended, trying to prevent her from becoming suspicious of me.

I also stayed on the phone with Zena an additional thirty minutes to throw her off. I continuously watched the clock, and the closer it got to the time for Carrington to pick me up, the more I played sleepy. I let out a series of superficial yawns, convincing Zena that I was exhausted.

"I guess I'm going to go to bed early," I suggested, trying to rush her off the phone.

"Okay, talk to you tomorrow. If you wake up late and want to talk, call me."

"Call you? You're not going out with Wanda and `em?"

"Naaa, I think I'm going to take a long bath and turn in early myself."

"Alright, hollar," I replied, excited that she was staying home.

Shortly after hanging up, Carrington arrived about forty minutes later. When I made it to the car, she looked so beautiful. She was grinning from ear to ear, her dimples were driving me nuts, and she was giving me this look only she could explain. I thought it was one to confirm that she was glad to see me or that she possibly missed me, too. To break the ice, we had our casual conversation about our friendship while we headed to a shrimp shack on 6 Mile. After I ran in and got us a pound and a half to share for the ride, we were on our way.

"Prince, you're dropping crumbs in my new car. Stop talking with food in your mouth `cause you're making a mess."

"I got this. When I get out, I'll dust off my seat," I replied, gulping down my drink.

"You better."

"I better or what you gon' do?"

"You better or you'll be walking."

"Shit, you'll try to put me out. Carrington, you'll get your li'l hundred pound self snatched up for even thinking some craziness like that. Then I'll put you out of your car."

"If you say so. You might not want to try me. The last time I checked, I was in control of this."

"You sure are," I sarcastically replied, "but mess with me if you want to. You won't be in control for long."

We cruised East Jefferson and Belle Isle for the longest, talking about life, relationships, and some of our classmates. I noticed once Carrington became more relaxed, we ended up having a really nice time together. At about 12:45 that morning, we found our way to Greektown. Since Zena decided to stay home, I thought it would be cool. Like always, there was bumper-to-bumper traffic. Everybody was hanging all up and down the strip and niggas were deep. While rolling, we came up on Julius and Chew. Those two were trying to get their mack on with some dog ugly chicks. "What's up, chumps? I see y'all Bustas." I yelled to let them know I saw them at their worst. Right before we turned onto Monroe, they ran over to the car talking noise.

"What's up with that? Y'all on a rescue mission or are you just rounding up all the stray dogs in the city tonight?" I asked, grinning big.

"Aw Punk, ugly girls need love, too," J stated.

"Yeah, but you and Chew looked like y'all were trying a little too hard to get some conversation for them to look like that."

"P, who are you trying to rescue or should I ask are you trying to be saved?" Chew asked, looking at Carrington before she turned her nose up at him. "Oh, what's up, Carrington? I almost didn't see you," he stated.

"Hi, Duran."

"Daran! Bitch, you ain't in my family. I don't like you. Don't be calling me by my real name in public like we're cool," Chew rudely insisted.

"I got your Bitch!" Carrington yelled.

"P, your baby's mama is hanging out tonight. Man, you better get out of Greektown." J whispered in my ear.

"My baby's mama is where?" I asked out loud not feeling as though I needed to be secretive.

"Her and her girls are right up the street."

"Good looking out," I replied, before Carrington pulled off on them.

We turned the corner, drove about a half a mile, and were caught in traffic at another light. All I remember was bobbing my head to some LL while listening to Carrington fuss. Out of the blue, somebody walked up and smacked the hell out of me. When I came to my senses and was able to regain my focus, I noticed Zena standing in my face, plump bellied and all, and talking major shit. *Oh hell naw! This ho done slapped me in Greektown in front of every damn body*, I thought, regaining my composure.

"What the hell are you doing down here? I thought you said Bean was trippin' about you being away from the house so much."

"Who you trying to question? Bitch, we ain't married? I'm not your man, and what the hell did you slap me for? If you weren't pregnant I'd get out this car and beat yo ass."

"You told me you were staying home. Why are you here with that slut? I'm carrying around your baby, and you're hanging out with another tramp."

"Honey, I'm no tramp," Carrington replied with her well-spoken self.

"Bitch, shut up! You're about to make me hurt you. You're starting to get on my nerves. I don't appreciate you disrespecting my pregnancy or me. Prince and I are about to have a baby. Besides, you got your own damn man, so why are you always with mine?" Zena asked, walking around the back of the car to get to the other side.

"Pull off, Carrington," I suggested because Zena and her cousin Wanda were about to snatch her up and give her the beat down of her life. Carrington quickly pulled off, barely making it through the red light. I mean we just missed a car going in the opposite direction, which scared the hell out of me.

Chew calling her a bitch and Zena's outburst didn't help our evening one bit. As she talked about what she was going to do, I tried to calm her down because she was driving fast and selling major wolf tickets. Carrington couldn't fight worth a lick and she knew it.

"Carrington, let it go and I'll resolve things in the morning." Initially, she continued to play hard, but as I kept talking with her, she finally chilled out.

"Prince, you've spoiled my birthday weekend."

There was nothing I could say. I already felt bad about what had jumped off, so I listened to her fuss all the way back to the Westside. Zena was my baby's mama, but Carrington was my baby. The last thing I wanted to do was bring some unnecessary drama her way. I apologized for the incident, yet that didn't seem to change her mood. She pulled up in front of my house, finished cursing me out, and pulled away without bothering to see me in. That's when I knew exactly how mad she was.

I was furious with Zena about her outburst, especially her slapping me. I thought about calling to snap off on her, but I figured she was probably still out. After I'd been home for a good twenty minutes, my beeper started blowing up. It was Zena. I didn't call her right back 'cause I needed time to cool my head. However, I didn't get a chance to do that either because she called me.

"Hello."

"Prince, you sorry bastard. I'm getting rid of this damn baby. I'm getting' an abortion 'cause I'm not about to be trippin' over no sorry nigga that keeps me stressed out on some kind of bullshit every other day. I am not about to deal with you for the next nineteen years. Nigga, you ain't worth the stress you be trying to put me through behind a bitch who has her own damn man."

"I don't care what you do with that baby. I didn't want it to begin with. Go do what you got to do, and don't call me no damn more with no nonsense," I angrily yelled, before hanging up in her face.

I rolled over to close my eyes and the phone started ringing again. Zena wasn't going to let our conversation end like it had. She was notorious for having the last word, which is why she really called right back. Had it not been all hours in the morning I would have just let it ring. The thought of being nagged by another woman made me hurry up and answer. If I had not picked up the phone on the first ring, Bean would have been all on me.

"What?" I yelled.

"Don't hang up on me again."

"You said what you had to say. I told you my outlook on the situation. There's nothing else we need to talk about. Zena, I don't give a damn what you do. If you want to get an abortion, get one. Like I said before, I don't want no kids, so do what you gotta do."

"Prince, you know I'm speaking out of anger. I'm not about to get no abortion this far into my pregnancy. I'm pissed off because you continuously disrespect me for Carrington. Why? I'm always good to you, but you don't appreciate me. So tell me, what is it about that girl that makes you so weak?"

"Zena, I'm not weak behind Carrington. We're just friends. She doesn't want me and has made that quite clear. You don't have to worry about her because we're nothing more than friends. Like I told you tonight, I'm not your man. We're not married, so I can see and hangout with whomever I want."

"If you're not my man, then what are we? One minute you act like you want to be with me. Then the next minute you don't. I'm getting tired of you sending mixed messages. Until this baby comes, I wish you could at least be a little more respectful of my feelings. I don't need any extra unnecessary worries. I'm already stressed out enough."

With Zena being as far along in her pregnancy as she was, if all she actually wanted was for me to be more considerate of how me being out with other females looked to her family and friends, I could respect that. I heard what she was saying, and I understood her request. Maybe she was telling her family and friends that there was more to us than there really was. I didn't know if that was the case and couldn't worry about it. What I had to take into consideration is that we were about to be parents. I also knew if I kept stressing her out there was a great chance that she'd go into early labor and our baby might experience complications. I didn't know much about parenting, but I didn't want my child to live with physical or mental impairments behind me tripping.

I promised Zena I would do better to make her pregnancy as stress free as possible. In doing so, I didn't see or pursue Carrington as much as I had. Plus, she was mad at me for the longest, so that was a good reason to stay away.

# 5

## *1985*

On March 28, 1985, at 4:15 in the morning, the phone started ringing off the hook. As always, I slept with it by my head, so I quickly grabbed the receiver. Usually, when someone called that early in the morning something was wrong. With the way my brother was living, I didn't want Bean to get any bad news before me, which is why I always kept the phone in my room. If it wasn't bad news, I didn't want to hear her fussing about the phone ringing all hours in the morning, which is why I always rushed to answer it.

"Hello."

"Prince, I'm in labor. I'm on my way to the hospital," Zena moaned in pain.

"You're in Labor? Damn, already! Are you okay?"

"Hell naw, I'm in labor. Meet me at the hospital!" Zena yelled.

"Alright, I'll be there as soon as I can."

I hung up the phone, and my heart started pounding like a drum. For a minute, I thought it was going to burst out of my chest. Here I was about to be a father three months after my fifteenth birthday. I hadn't done anything to prepare for a baby. I hadn't told anyone in my family, and I wasn't ready for the responsibility. I stretched out in my bed staring into space. I didn't move for a few hours because I knew I couldn't leave the house that early in the morning without a good explanation. When it was time for me to leave for school, instead of catching the bus to Redford, I caught it to the hospital.

I arrived about ten minutes before my daughter was born. Wow, to actually witness the birthing process nearly killed me. I almost threw up a few times because I never imagined that a pussy could open like it did. For me to see Asia's head come squeezing out to the extent of making Zena's skin stretch to its max, made me vow that I'd never tell another lie about putting in work. If a vagina could deliver a head like that, I knew if we ever had sex again, my dick would be like a red toothpick in a bowl of red Jell-O. Lost!

At 9:15 AM, I became the father of Miss Asia Dominique Prince. A daughter was the last thing I needed. I took one look at my baby girl and knew that she was mine. Asia looked a lot like her mama, but she had my nose and eyes. In spite of my past feelings for Zena, I instantly fell in love with my little girl. At first I kind of wished that my first-born had been a boy because at the time I would have raised him to be a G like me. With a daughter, well, she was gon' have major troubles with her ole dude. When she finally started dating, I wasn't even trying to have no knuckleheads like me running behind her. Anyone that even considered trying to holla at my Butterfly was destined to catch hell from me, especially if they were on some thugism. Oh, and any little chump that even tried to treat Asia as out cold as I'd treated her mother was certain to get his cranium split.

While I sat around enjoying the birth of my daughter with Zena's family, I became jittery when I considered that I still needed to tell Bean, Ant, and the rest of my family the news. They were all going to lose it. For some reason, I feared what my brother would say the most, but the day Asia came home, I discovered it should have been Bean.

Zena brought Asia by the house on her way home because I told her I wanted my family to see her. When they got there, Bean, Ant, and GG were all at the house, so I was able to kill three birds with one stone. I felt queasy and kind of light-headed when I walked into the den with a baby carrier. Actually, I realized how scared I really was when I felt my throat trembling before I spoke.

"Excuse me, everyone, I'd like to introduce you to the newest member of the Prince family."

"The newest what you say?" Bean asked as GG sat on the couch with her mouth wide open. I instantly looked over at Ant who didn't seem to have an expression at all before repeating myself. "The newest Prince."

"How long have you known about this?" GG asked, looking directly at me.

It was rare for her to ask me questions, so before responding, I cleared my throat. Though no one could say anything about my situation at that point, I didn't want to sound rude when I replied. I had mad respect for my grandmother, so my words had to flow correctly.

"I've known for the past five months."

"Prince, why would you spring something like this on us after the baby is here? You should have told us long ago."

"Yes Ma'am, I know. I was scared and not thinking clearly."

"You sure in the hell weren't." Bean angrily replied, pouring herself a drink. Zena was in shock. She didn't know I hadn't told my family, so she was as surprised as they were.

Everyone started fussing at me at one time, and my little doll must have known her daddy needed some help. Asia let out this little whimper, followed by a full fledge cry, which rescued me.

"Prince, hand me the baby." GG stated with authority in her voice. As I put Asia in G's arms, she looked at my baby and cried. "Prince, she's a very beautiful baby. I never wanted this for you. I wish you had informed us sooner. That way we could've been supportive. I'm sure this young lady's family wondered where we were while everything was going on."

"Maybe, but they never asked."

"I'm sure they wanted to. Well, it's done now. The two of you need to work out something. Bean and her parents need to meet since they now have a common interest."

"G, that's exactly what I was thinking," I assured her.

"Well, he's not getting off that easy with me," Bean slurred.

"Bean, we're not about to go into it right now," G callously replied.

It seems like G's approval of my situation was the icebreaker that eventually set the mood for everyone else. I was relieved to get the kind of support she provided. Yet, I was still very nervous about being a daddy.

For the weeks that followed, fatherhood became an extra task, but not a priority in my life. Early on, I reminded Zena that I wasn't ready for a kid. I told her when she decided to keep the baby and forced fatherhood upon me that Asia was gon' be her responsibility. Since she decided to make us teenage parents, she kept Asia most of the time. I refused to give up my lifestyle and friends to stay home and change diapers. After about two weeks of playing daddy, I was back to big kickin' it with my boys and my weekend activities.

For Zena, motherhood turned out to be more of a challenge than she expected. She was missing out on a lot of activities with her friends, so she frequently complained about needing more help from me. I tried to do better, so there were times when I'd keep Asia, but never on the weekends. That was my time, and even though she fussed about having to stay in every Friday and Saturday, I wasn't giving in.

Neither Zena's mom nor Bean did much babysitting either. They both claimed they'd raised their kids. Since Ke was only nine, Bean didn't allow her to baby-sit for us period. Bean always made it clear that Ke couldn't baby-sit because she didn't want her to associate having a baby with being fun, then turn up pregnant herself. After experiencing a few weeks of motherhood and seeing that her role was a fulltime commitment, had Zena been able to do things over, Asia might not exist today.

That year my boys and I highly anticipated the release of Krush Groove. We were Run DMC fans and mad crazy about hip-hop music. When it hit the big screen, day one, we were there. The weekend that movie released, Zena already knew she could count me out for daddy-sitting period. I had plans to hang with my guys, and that's exactly what I did.

About twenty of us went to see that movie. We sat in the theater talking loud, being obnoxious, and partying through the entire show. On our way out, everyone was talking about the sexy, female drummer that left us all in aw. Ms. E was packing a real phat rump and her body was on point.

"Sheila E is fine," I stated, knowing an argument would start over her.

"Man, she gon' be my baby's mama." Chew replied, smiling so hard his chipped tooth was showing.

"Punk, you so broke, you know you can't even afford a fine woman like that. Now me on the other hand, I could keep her pleased," Julius stated.

"Broke? How you gon' call somebody broke? Dawg, your pockets ain't stacked either. Your mom's got money, Fool, not you. Man, I'm sure a classy woman like Shelia E don't want to be rolling nowhere with you in your ole G's ride. She's used to being chauffered, but your mom's driving y'all around would be a major turnoff," Chew responded.

"I don't think she would care."

"Fool, your old G ain't no chauffer," Chew yelled before I cut him off.

"Sheila don't want neither one of y'all lames. Did you see how she was filling out those heart jeans? Now think about it. What y'all wimps gon' do with a woman like that? What she needs is a man like me."

"P, SHUT UP! *You talk too much.*"

"J, you shut the hell up. Nigga you're not DMC. And, P why you always talking about somebody a wimp? Is that what you act like when you're around that bitch, Carrington?" Chew asked.

"Man, you do be simpin' out over her high-si talking ass," Julius confirmed.

"Both of y'all need to get off my jock," I replied, stepping into the cab.

"Man, you're mad because we're spittin' facts. But that's okay. At least Chew and I are in love with a woman that's loved by many. We realize we can't ever have her. Now you on the other hand, do you seriously think you gon' ever get with Carrington?"

"I might."

"Dawg, let me answer that for you. Ut un, no way.... Daddy Horton, ain't havin' his little Sunflower with a thug like you. She ain't all that to me any damn way. I just don't know why you can't see that she's not feelin' you," Chew replied, cutting my pride.

"Chew, I'm not about to argue with you about no bitches all the way home. Let it rest. You win tonight. I'm done with that discussion."

"What y'all think about LL bustin' up in the office like that?" J asked to change the subject.

"Aw that was on point." Chew and I agreed, getting back on track. That's just the way we were. Something as simple as LL coming hard about his radio had us back to being boys in no time.

The following Saturday, Detroit Roller Wheels was having their big annual after hour skating party. Joe Skee Love was gon' be up in the house, and they were hosting the Pee-Wee Herman dance contest. I knew I was going, so to be nice, I agreed to watch the baby that morning while Zena went to the beauty shop. Asia gave me hell that day. She shit all over herself, and I'd only perfected changing pissy diapers. I looked inside the padding, only to discover that it was full of a yellowish mushy substance I'd never been required to clean. I blanked out for a second. Then I looked a second time, realizing that mess was all over everywhere. Stuff was oozing out the side of her diaper, up her back, down her legs, and had gotten all over her Onesie. When I tried to take off the diaper, she started moving her legs, and then her socks were destroyed.

"Bean, Asia needs her butt cleaned. She has mess all over everywhere. Could you please come help me?" I screamed, feeling very overwhelmed.

"That's your baby, you handle it," she yelled back, without budging.

"Bean for real. I need some help."

"Bean said that's your baby, so you clean her nasty ass," Ke informed me.

Ke could see that I was irritated by Bean's unnecessary comment. *Like I don't know Asia's mine,* I thought before trying to clean her up myself. Ke could tell I didn't know what I was doing 'cause I was struggling big time. After looking on for a minute, she helped me out. Good thing she felt sorry for me.

Twenty wipes later, a wash up, and some clean clothes my baby was back to herself. She was looking good and smelling powder fresh. For a nine-year-old, Ke had done an outstanding job. I thanked her, hit her off with ten dollars, then asked her to watch Asia while I jumped in the shower. I needed to get ready for my outing to the mall with my guys. Zena was supposed to be back by three. After that, the fellas and I were hitting up the mall to get a new hookup for the skating party.

At about two, I dressed Asia and fed her a bottle while we waited. From the first time I'd ever kept the baby, I was instructed to always burp her after she drank an ounce of milk. After two ounces, I put her up on my shoulder and rubbed her back. She let out the loudest burp. "Dang, Li'l Greedy Butt," I stated, lowering her to my knee. As soon as I saw her face, I noticed spit up around her mouth. I wondered if I'd fed her too much, and shortly after, my thoughts were confirmed. Suddenly, I felt something wet all over my shoulder. Asia had thrown up all down my back.

"Aw man, this girl done spit up all over my silk shirt!" I yelled, lifting her as I got up. Once I was standing, she spit again. That time this foul-smelling vomit got all over my jeans.

"Huuuuuuuuuuu!" I exhaled, smacking my lips. "Where's your mama?" I asked in frustration.

Three, four, and then five o'clock passed. No Zena, and no call. I was mad and cursing her out at that point. *She knows it's the annual Easter skating party today. She better hurry up and come get this baby,"* I thought before looking down at Asia who was knocked out. She was lying on her blanket in a little ball with her butt sticking up in the air. I smiled at her, then kissed the back of her neck. "Where's your mommy little girl?" I whispered to avoid disturbing her rest.

The more I looked at the clock, the angrier I became. Finally, the phone rung. I ran to the dining room to answer it, thinking it was Zena. It wasn't. It was Chew and Julius again. They were calling to say that they were on their way to my house. "Man, I still can't go to the Mall. Zena hasn't come for the baby." With the way they carried on, I almost thought Asia was theirs. Both of them were madder than I was. Zena was interfering with our Saturday night mission, which they didn't appreciate. They were so pissed off, but there was nothing I could do about her not showing up. One thing I knew for sure was that Bean wasn't babysitting. "Call me before y'all leave for the skating party and I'll let you know what's up."

I looked through my closet for something to wear. I hated the thought of rockin' an old outfit to one of the biggest events of the year for teenagers. The thought of being out in something I wore to school or the last big event made me even angrier with Zena.

I kept calling Zena's pager, but she never responded. By the time my boys were ready to leave, they ended up going without me. I was crushed. I sat around the house looking pitiful. I must have truly looked terrible because Bean finally felt sorry for me. "Boy, go get ready, I'll keep the baby this time, but you and Zena need to get it together," she impatiently suggested.

I got dressed as fast as I could to avoid giving her a chance to change her mind. When she drove me to the skating rink, she left KeKe watching the baby because she didn't want to bring Asia out in the cold. *I must have really looked pitiful if Bean felt sorry for me,* I thought because she had broken all her babysitting rules.

"Prince, how are you getting home?" she asked.

"J's mom will bring me." I stated, quickly shutting the car door because I wasn't telling the truth. "But if she doesn't have enough room, I'll call you or Ant."

I walked up to the entrance like I'd hit the Pick Four Lottery. After paying five bucks to get in, I fell up in the building like I was big time. I found my boys at the concession stand and had them walk with me over to the lockers. When I sat down to put on my skates, I noticed Carrington skating backwards all wrapped up in Derrick's arms.

"There goes your girl," Chew stated.

"Man, I see her. What you think I'm blind?"

"Oh, I know you're not blind. But you look like you got a frog in your damn throat from the misery of seeing yo trophy in another man's hands. Plus, I know you weren't 'bout to say you saw your Boo all wrapped up in her man's arms. So, I was just letting you know that I saw what you saw. That way you wouldn't be over there wondering if I did."

"Nigga, it don't matter who you saw or what you think. Besides, I'm not sweating her like that. We're homies and that's all."

"Right!" J sarcastically replied, laughing.

I stood up to put my stuff in the locker, and Chew started pointing again, "Aw Dawg, this must be your lucky night. There go your other woman, too."

"My other woman who?"

"Zena." My eyes followed in the direction in which he was pointing, leading me straight to her.

Zena was all up in some fake playa's face, grinning from ear to ear, and looking her best. She wasn't wearing those two long French braids she always wore either. She had gotten the top of her hair cut short and the back was still stretching more than halfway down her back. I won't lie; I had to do a double take because she was looking sexy, but we had so much bad blood between us that I didn't feel her like that. "Umm!" I replied, going on about my business.

Just as I was about to skate over and holla at a few females from school, I noticed Tasha. She was the girl that I'd met at the movies. I hadn't spoken with her since that night, but she was looking too sexy for me to pass her by. I remember her being kind of cool, so I approached her.

"What's up, Beautiful?"

"Heeeey. Long time no see. How are you doing?

"I'm straight."

After my greeting, she was on me from there. We talked for a minute, and I guess I was more excited about being at the party than I realized. I rarely ever skated, but when Prince's *Do Me Baby* came on, I allowed her to talk me into couple skating. We laughed when she reminded me of the joke she made the night we met at Norwest about Prince. Chew thought we were laughing at him because he had fallen right in front of us. "Get up, chump," I yelled before he turned around to flip me off. Right when he was getting off the floor, Zena skated by with some nigga, looking shocked to see me out. I noticed her saying something to him before making her way back to us. As mad as I was, I was hoping she kept it simple.

"Prince, where's my baby, and what are you doing here? I left you babysitting, not whoever you left my baby with." *This bitch done lost her mind,* I thought before replying.

"Zena, you better get the hell out of my face. You were supposed to be back by three, and you didn't even bother to call to say you weren't coming. The baby's with my mother, her grandmother! Now beat it, Trick."

As I tried to skate pass her, she pushed me in the back of my head. I stumbled into the rail, trying very hard to keep my balance, but didn't. I got up off the floor, skated over to Zena, and before I even realized what I was doing, I had grabbed her around her throat. Due to my embarrassment, I choked the hell out of her. She started hitting me, then spit at Tasha. Tasha was from the hood though. She wasn't soft like Carrington, so things got out of hand from there. I recognized that she had a little gangsta in her by the way she whipped Zena's ass.

About ten security guards ran over to break up our fight. They put every last one of us out and demanded that we get off their property or go to jail. Once again, Zena and her cousin Wanda got into it with Tasha and her girls outside the skating rink. At first, Zena didn't realize it, but her and her clique definitely called out the wrong group of chicks. Tasha removed her skates from around her neck, and without thinking twice swung them at Wanda. She hit that girl so hard in her face, I could hear her grunt when the skates made contact. As the skates came down, Wanda's forehead revealed a knot that was large enough to be seen from the other side of the street. We tried to break them up a few times. Security had already warned us that they were going to call the police. So I felt it necessary to get us moving. "If we don't get off Schoolcraft before the Po-Pos arrive, we're all going to jail for violating curfew," I stated.

On weekends, anyone under eighteen had to be in by midnight. None of us were eighteen, so if we got picked up, all of us were jail bound.

Schoolcraft was a major street, so it was jumping off the hook. Once we heard sirens coming in our direction, most of us started running towards the street Asbury Park. Zena and her people jumped in a cab. When I finally arrived home, they were all waiting on me.

"What the hell are y'all doing on my porch?" I asked, walking up the steps to enter the front door.

"I came to get my baby."

"She ain't going out at this time of night. You should have come by in the morning when all these people weren't with you. How you gon' disrespect my mother and her house like that?"

"Prince, get my baby now!" she yelled, following me in.

"Bitch, be quiet. You need to respect my house. My family is trying to sleep. Like I said, Asia ain't going anywhere. Now you and all your people can get the hell out my house," I replied, grabbing her arm to escort her to the door.

"Prince, you ain't about to do nothing," Wanda replied.

"I know you're not talking to me with that knot on your forehead. You must still be coming to your senses after getting clocked upside your head with 'dem skates. You know better than talking shit to me, so I advise you to mind your own business."

"Boy, you need to grow up," she replied, rolling her eyes.

"You need to get out before I get ole girl on you again. Better yet, all y'all get the fuck out before I go off."

Suddenly, Zena got mad and started hitting me. I grabbed a hand full of her hair, then flipped her on the floor. "I haven't touched you, so don't put your hands on me," I stated, putting my hands around her neck to hold her down. "I still owe you from Greek town. Don't make me hurt you tonight, Zena. Just leave. I'll get Bean to bring Asia home in the morning."

As I removed my hands from around her neck, Zena got up still trying to fight me. We ended up back on the floor fighting again. By the time they got me off of her, I'd choked her so hard she had handprints all over her neck. All the confusion caused Bean to come into the living room fussing.

"What the hell is going on with you two?" Bean inquired, looking at me, then Zena, who was still breathing hard. I didn't say a word. I let Zena do all the talking.

"DeMarques you ain't shit. Excuse me, Ms. Prince, but I'm tired of your son disrespecting me. He don't have to ever worry about seeing his baby anymore. I don't have to take this from him. Your son is sorry and a sorry excuse of a daddy. He has put me through so much unnecessary nonsense. And, I refuse to tolerate it any longer."

"Zena, I know my son. He can test a person at times, but Honey, it's really late to be transporting that baby out of here. Can I bring her in the morning?"

"NO! I want her now," Zena snapped. She was too angry to be reasoned with.

"Prince, go get the baby, get her things, and give them to her mother," Bean insisted. "Zena, I hope that you reconsider your decision about not letting Prince see her. Asia will be the one you'll be cheating in the end. When you calm down, you and Prince need to talk. Be careful and call me to let me know you made it home safely."

When Zena left the house, she vowed I'd never see Asia again. For the first time since my daughter was conceived, I felt like Zena had the upper hand. I didn't like that either. And for once her threats bothered me.

# 6

## Palmer Park

When July rolled around, it had been three months since I'd heard from Zena or seen my daughter. I tried not to let her foolish decision affect me, but it was hard not to some days. Carrington was out of town for the summer touring various colleges for consideration and Tasha had become my new main squeeze. Ant had finally come around again, so he was back to himself. He appeared to be over whatever he was tripping about, which excited me 'cause he and I were back to hanging like old times. I was glad to see that my brother had returned to himself because to me we were starting to grow apart.

Ant, Melvin, and some of the other old playas were hanging at Palmer Park on Sundays. Everybody looking for a hot spot to mingle was gon' be there, and I wanted to be down, too. I wanted my boys and I to be included, so I made sure we got to kick it with Ant before the Sabbath even rolled around. Ant bought in to my request and let us roll out with him and Melvin. The fact that we were bouncing a Benz gave us status with the women from jump. We pulled up in the parking lot making a major statement. In Detroit, when you were riding lovely, stacking major loot, blinged out, and had some style about you, females were on you. Gold Diggers were always trying to pull brothas that looked like money. That particular day, all kinds of older women were jocking me. The funny part about that is that I was a passenger in the back seat. Knowing that, it's easy to imagine the kind of digits and conversation Ant got, considering he was the driver. I hadn't pushed up on an older woman before, but with me being the playa I thought I was, I believed I could put it down.

We were all standing around Ant's car talking to some chicks when this beautiful twenty-six-year-old honey walked over to the car. Felicia was her name. She had all my crew going nuts because she was fine, fine, fine.

"Hey, Anthony, I haven't heard from you in a while. Whose been keeping you so occupied that you couldn't call?" she asked.

"Not you."

"What's up with the smart mouth today? Where have you been?"

"I've been busy making my paper."

"And that prevented you from calling me?"

"Obviously so, you haven't talked to me, have you? Fe, I told you I'm not interested in you anymore!" he coldly replied.

"Why are you always acting so hard?"

"Beat it, Fe. You know I ain't feelin' you like that. You got nothing coming from me. I told you I'm not dealing with you period. So move around."

"Anthony, we all make mistakes. When are you going to let bygones be bygones, and forgive me? Baby, you know how I feel about you. Let's start over."

"Never that! I said I'm not fooling with you. I mean just that. Bitches like you put Niggas like me in harm's way. You've spent your last night with me. This dick don't play in dangerous waters like most of these chumps out here. Fe, you ain't to be trusted. Now beat it, I'm trying to chill with my guys," Ant insisted, without giving her any kind of eye contact.

I looked at Ant like he was smoking some serious crack that day. Felicia was beyond sexy. I was trying to understand how and why Ant was dogging that fine woman in the manner in which he did. She didn't look like the kind of woman a man treated like Ant was treating her. She was finer than most of the bought faces in Hollywood, so she already had status in my mind for simply looking like a doll baby. Not to mention that my boys and I argued over women who looked like her everyday. Either one of us would have died for five minutes with a woman like that.

"Ant, what's up with the fox? Why you treating her like that?" I asked.

"Man, she just another pretty face with no substance. Felicia's a Professional Sack Chaser. I thought she was top of the line, but she got with one of my enemies on the down low, and Silk saw them out. I can't take any chances on her; she's scandalous, and risky."

Since Ant said he wasn't feeling her, I wanted him to prove it at my expense. I begged him to give her five more minutes of conversation in order to talk her into giving me some ass or some head. I'd never had my dick sucked before, but I fantasized about it. And if anyone could make my fantasy a reality, besides Tattoo off Fantasy Island, Ant could.

"Man, come on," I begged. "Please, talk Felicia into giving your li'l brother the hook up of her choice."

"Boy, once she lock them jaws on you, you're gon' be stuck on stupid. And if she pops that coochie just right, she'll have yo li'l ass stealing money from me like a crack head to get the pussy."

"Duuuuh, Man, I don't care. Hook a brother up."

"Felicia," Ant called. As I watched her walk back over to the car, my mouth watered once my eyes locked in on that gap between her legs that was being hugged just right by her tight outfit.

"What's up, Baby? I see you're coming to your senses."

"If you say so. You say you want to be with me, but if you want me to forgive you, you've got to prove your loyalty to me."

"How am I supposed to do that?"

"Give my li'l brother some head to show me that you're really down for me like you say you are."

"Is that all you want me to do?"

"Yeah, for now."

"Done deal."

My mouth fell open in disbelief. I couldn't believe she said that. I was shocked by her reply. *It's about to be on,* I thought, opening the door of Ant's car to push his front seats up as far as they would go. Felicia walked around to the other side of the Benz in her jean cat suit and got in the back. I quickly climbed in behind her, unzipping my pants. I tried to keep my thoughts right. Huh, as a fifteen-year-old about to get my first blowjob from a beautiful older woman, who was almost twice my age, made me act stupid. At that point, my mind and my dick did their own thing.

Felicia was obviously a pro at what she did. She got in, immediately insisting that I relax.

"What's your name, Baby?" she whispered, nibbling on my ear in this sexy tone that made me more erect.

"P."

"P, tell me the truth, have you ever had this done before?" *This chick about to give me a damn aneurism, and have my black ass in here scratching up the back seat of Ant's Benz like an electrocuted cat,* I thought as she lowered her head to insert my Johnson into her mouth. "Relax," she insisted because she could tell I was inexperienced.

I relaxed, and then fine Felicia went to work. I couldn't hold my nut for nothing. The stuff she did to me made my toes curl and my feet tingle. Prior to dealing with her, I thought I had the magic stick, but the only illusion jumping off after our encounter was in my mind. I came faster than I ever had before, which embarrassed me. I skeeted all in Felicia's face without warning. I mean, I really felt bad about making such a mess all over her pretty lips.

"Ohhhhhhhhhhh!" I grunted as my orgasm came to an end. "Sorry, Felicia," I stated, regaining my composure.

"No problem, Handsome. That comes with the territory when you're getting off a good one," she replied, like it was no big deal. I frowned as she wiped her face. I was really done when she got out of the car like all in a day's work and went about her business.

"I'll call you later, Ant." I was floored behind her nonchalant attitude because though it wasn't a big deal to her, it was to me. Fine Felicia had turned me out.

"Damn Ant, I can't believe pretty bitches get down like that? She's a straight freak."

"Fa' sho."

"Man, if you don't want her, I'll take her," I jokingly affirmed.

Chew and J anxiously walked over to me to get all the details. I wasn't telling them anything, though. I didn't want them to know that their boy came in less than three minutes. Those chumps would have never let me live that one down. All the way to the house, they kept asking me for details.

"Come on, P, how was it?" they asked.

"Man, y'all ain't supposed to ask a man about his freaky tales. Dang, wait 'til I'm ready to tell y'all."

"Chew, that means ole girl rocked P's world."

"Why you say that?" I asked, wondering if they heard me grunting seconds after we got in the car.

"Because you love to tell on your dick. Had you put in work, you'd be telling. You know that grown ass woman turned you out. But it's cool, she would have turned me and Chew out, too." Julius responded, laughing.

I argued back and forth with them about having skills until we pulled up in front of the house. Ant couldn't take anymore of our pettiness. Finally, he ordered us out. "You sissies get out. I got to go get ready for Silk's party tonight!"

Silk was throwing a Summer Playas Ball at the Palace. I begged him and Ant to let me hang even though I was under age. I wanted to bat for my boys to go, too. But it was all I could do to get myself in.

After getting my little brain gummed by an older woman, my head was on swoll. I asked Ant to let me rock one of his nice linen suits 'cause I was gon' try to look the part. At the time, I didn't want to spend any of my own money on the kind of gear people in the twenty-five and older club rocked. Had I worn one of my jean hook-ups to an event like the ball, my age would've been a dead give away 'cause nigga's in the D will pull out their finest for any event with an extravagant title. Finally, after begging for a minute, Ant agreed to suit me up.

At fifteen, my conversation wasn't remotely close to most of the women in the club. So standing around the bar, kicking it with real women was the highlight of that night for me. Most of them knew I was underage, but kept telling me how cute I was. The fact that I was Silk's nephew helped me out quite a bit. Actually, he was the real reason most of them paid me any kind of attention to begin with.

Shoot, all the ladies wanted a piece of my uncle. Just about every female in the club tried to make sure he had fun. They kept so many drinks in his hand that every time he went out on the dance floor, I finished up most of his drinks. I know I had at least seven of his drinks. I got so lit, I just sat back and observed my uncle in action. *What a life,* I thought.

"That's how I'm gon' be when it's my turn to shine," I stated to Melvin and Ant.

"Right! In your dreams, Lightweight. Come on, we're about to bounce," Ant stated.

When we left the club, I had a nice buzz. All those glasses of Crown and Coke I drank had taken a toll on me. Afterwards, my speech was slurred, and I was hungry. I didn't want to go home on an empty stomach, so I asked Ant to run me by the Coney Island on Seven Mile in route to the house. I made it in about three that morning and was still hyped up about the mouth work Felicia put on me. Thinking about it made me horny, so I called Tasha to say Hi.

I hadn't spoken with her all that day. I actually wasn't missing her until she answered the phone with that sexy 900 voice of hers. She was trying to sound all sexy 'til she discovered it was me. Then out of nowhere, she got mad.

"Why haven't I heard from you all day? Have you been out with another bitch? I beeped you a few times, but you didn't return my calls."

"I was taking care of business with my brother."

Immediately, the questions ceased. She knew the rules, and she knew I didn't talk about my family's business with anyone.

The Crown and Coke I had on top of my breakfast finally kicked in. Suddenly, after about an hour, I could feel myself getting tired.

"Tasha, I'm falling asleep on you, I'll call you later."

Monday morning, I woke up to Bean and Renzo arguing. Renzo was pissed about Bean withdrawing more money from their joint account than she'd deposited that month. She told him since she'd been paying the majority of the bills longer than he had been paying on them period, her funds were low, she needed some extra money, and so she used some of his. As young and inexperienced as I was with women, even I'd learned over the years that a man couldn't win an argument with one. Why Renzo kept trying to with Bean baffled me.

"What did you use the money for?" Renzo asked.

"I'm not explaining anything. Had you asked me right the first time, I might have felt persuaded to explain. Since you came at me sideways, you figure it out." He was about to go on a cursing frenzy, when I walked into the living room. He stared me down like he was daring me to say anything. He knew better than to call me out, though. Renzo gave me a few additional dirty looks, then did what was best for us all. Without saying another word, he left for work.

*That chump gon' make me hurt him*, I thought to myself before asking Bean. "What's your man tripping about?"

"None of your business."

I held up my hands and went back to my room. I really didn't care what they were arguing about to begin with. I already knew. It was just my intent to stop them from arguing, which I did.

Carrington was returning to Detroit that Monday afternoon. I wondered if she would call that same day to say she'd made it back safely. Derrick had already left for college, which I was excited about. He was participating in a summer biology research program at Howard, so I figured with him finally being gone, I'd have a better opportunity to work on Carrington.

Carrington was a senior, so the upcoming school year was going to be her last. I was going to the eleventh grade, which meant I only had one year left to wear her down. If I didn't get on her during the approaching school term, my chances of ever making her mine would never happen.

As much as I was looking forward to hearing from Carrington, she didn't call the first week she was home at all. That sort of bothered me. Here I'd been anxiously anticipating her return, and she didn't even think enough of me to say she'd made it home okay. I'd been counting down the days 'til her arrival, too. I thought we were better friends than that, but she definitely gave me a reality check.

One evening Tasha and I were watching Sanford and Son when my pager went off.

"235-5555.... Who is this?" I mumbled, looking at the numbers to dial them into the phone.

"Hello."

"Yeah, did someone beep Prince?" I asked.

"Oh, so now you don't know my voice?"

"Who dis?" I asked.

"Prince, stop playing. You know who this is."

"Oh, I do?"

"Yeah, Silly. It's me, Carrington."

"Oh! What up doe?"

"What up doe! Is that the best you can do?"

"Naa not really, but I'm occupied. How are you doing?"

"Good. You want to call me back when you can talk?"

"Ummm, nope you're cool." I responded, looking at Tasha who had gotten a serious attitude. "Well, then again, yeah. I'll hit you back later."

"Okay, I'll be here."

"Who's number is this you're paging me from?"

"My granny's. Call me back when you can talk."

"A'ight."

I hung up the phone smiling, but not too much. I didn't want to piss Tasha off any more than she already was. Damn! Carrington did something to me. I would have been all in had Tasha not been there. Carrington was the only woman I'd ever dealt with that had me like putty in the palms of her hands. I knew I had it bad for her when I discovered that she kept me tripping up on my words. She had my thoughts all confused, and I was a straight sucka for her like Zena was for me. With the kind of influence she had on me, you'd think she had given me some. But the only thing she gave me was smiles, good conversation, hard times, and a challenge, which is why I jocked her so hard.

Tasha became a little quiet after I hung up the phone. I started playing around with her and within a matter of time she was back to herself. After hanging up with Carrington, it was hard for me to pretend like I was still focused on Tasha's visit. I watched the clock for about an hour because I was ready for her to go home.

"I don't want you to be out alone real late," I mentioned when it started getting dark. Finally, after I couldn't maintain any longer, I told her that I was going to call her a cab. She seemed to be cool with that, considering she'd spent most of the day with me.

When the cab arrived, I helped her collect her things, walked her out, and quickly kissed her goodbye. I stood on the sidewalk with my hands in my pocket, looking innocent until her cab was out of sight. I briefly talked with my neighbor Mr. May about his lawn before running back into the house to call Carrington.

That girl was long-winded like most women. We talked for hours about her break, college, and getting together that following day. Carrington suggested that we have lunch downtown or ride out to Belle Isle. But I didn't know if Belle Isle was necessarily a good idea. During the summer, it was always packed with a bunch of niggas 'til all hours of the night. My phone clicked a thousand times during our conversation. I figured it was probably Tasha calling to say that she'd made it home. I didn't want to be disturbed, so I didn't bother to click over. After Carrington and I hung up, I returned Tasha's call. To play if off, I fussed her out about not calling.

"I did call, but no one answered," she replied.

"Oh, you might be right. Bean was on a long distance call with my grandaunt and probably didn't want to be disturbed."

"Right."

"Right? You said that like you think I'm lying."

"I do."

"I ain't got to lie, but bye then, since you don't believe me," I replied, hanging up to make her feel guilty.

◆◆◆◆◆◆◆

Carrington came to get me that following afternoon. When she pulled up, I went to the door after she honked, motioning for her to wait. Actually, I was all ready to go. I just didn't want to run out like I'd been anxiously waiting. As soon as I opened her car door, she smiled.

"Hey, Handsome, I've missed you."

"Yeah right, sure you did. That's why you called me as soon as you got back to Detroit. Right?"

"Don't start. And put your seat belt on."

I refused like always, then leaned over to affectionately peck Carrington on her cheek. She tried to act shy at first, but I quickly put an end to all that.

I'll never forget the way she looked at me that day. It was a given that my consistency to pursue her was working. During lunch, sexy Ms. Horton finally had to let the cat out of the bag.

That evening Carrington revealed that she had been attracted to me since our Home Economics class.

"Home Economics? That was two years ago," I stated.

"I know when it was. I've always liked you, I just know you're not the kind of young man I could take home to my family. That's why I never allowed my interest in you to go any further than it has. As much as I wish we could have more than what we do some days, I have to insist that we maintain nothing more than our friendship."

"I knew you were feelin' me. I told Chew and 'em that I wasn't crazy."

"Prince, Derrick is the kind of guy my parents want me to be with. He's perfect in their eyes. I mean, he can do no wrong."

"They better come again. Every person can and will make mistakes, but he's going to show them his deviant side one day. Then what?"

"I'd never be comfortable with you around my parents. Besides, you're too much of a womanizer for me."

"That's not completely true. Give me a chance. I'll prove to you that I can be all about one woman." Realistically, I knew I could never only be involved with one female. In my mind it sounded real good at the time, which is why I said it. Though, I knew as a Prince, it simply wasn't in my genes to do such a foolish thing.

After our discussion, I concluded that Carrington was absolutely right about me. I was a womanizer and probably wouldn't have done her right. When I thought about it, she would have been like every other female I dated back then. Once she became my woman, I would have won her over, hit it a few times, ran a little game, became bored, and moved on to the next victim. After thinking about our discussion, her decision to leave me alone was wise on her behalf.

◆◆◆◆◆◆◆

When September rolled around, I still hadn't received a call from Zena. For some reason, I found myself thinking about my daughter, so I thought I'd call to see how Asia was doing. She was about to turn six months old, and I hadn't seen her in a little over four months. When Zena answered the phone, I wanted to call her all kinds of bitches, but to prevent making a bad situation worse, I politely said hello.

"Who is this?" she asked.

"Zena, how's the baby?" Once she realized I was on the line, she cursed me out.

"Sorry loser, what do you want? I haven't heard from you in months. If you really wanted to know how the baby was doing, you would have called sooner."

"Look, I didn't call to argue."

"I don't know what you called to do, but lose my number and don't ever call my house again."

I tried to talk some sense into that girl. If I was Asia's father, I wanted to see her. But Zena wasn't trying to hear me.

After she hung up in my face, I was so angry about her behavior that I considered kicking her ass. I called Ant to see if he could get a few of his street chicks to beat her down, but he wasn't with that.

"P, lay low, calm down, and later on in the week, we'll go over to her house."

We never made it to Zena's house for some reason. Two weeks later I was in the hallway at school being silly with a few of my friends. Neither my boys nor I were dancers, but we found ourselves trying to do the Pee-Wee Herman. When the bell rang for fifth period to begin, Zena walked up talking about Asia wasn't mine.

"Bitch, what you say?" I asked with clear anger in my eyes.

"You heard what I said. Asia.. Is.. Not.. Yours," she repeated, talking to me like I had a learning disability. "So now that you know the truth, don't bother us anymore."

"Tramp, I called you over two weeks ago. You should've told me that then. Don't walk up on me out of no where with some stupid shit like that and think I'm gon' be cool with it."

"You been cool with not seeing her for the past four and a half months, so why worry about it now. Obviously you didn't feel any kind of connection to her anyway."

"You don't know what the hell I feel. What I don't feel is your ignorant ass."

"Good, because I don't want you to feel me, you sorry ass bitch. My current man, who happens to be Asia's real daddy, does an excellent job at keeping my attention."

"That baby has my last name and everything. If I wasn't her father, why did you have me tell my family she was mine? And, if I'm not her daddy, why did you let us buy all that shit for her?"

"Because at the time I thought you were."

"Well tell me this, who the hell is the father?"

"None of your business. All you need to know is that it's not you."

"You're a damn lie. That baby looks so much like me, I couldn't deny her if I wanted to. I'm not about to argue with you, we'll just do a blood test. That is, if your ignorant ass wants to take one."

"You take a damn test. I'm not doing anything." She firmly screamed, walking away.

I could have killed Zena. She'd caught me off guard and hit me way below the belt with her remark. She'd embarrassed me in front of all my friends, some of my enemies, and made me think about doing some stuff to her that I knew would get me some major time in lock up. I was done with her tripping on me in public. That little stunt she pulled was gon' be our final encounter. I kept thinking about her showing her ass in Greektown, then the skating rink and became angrier. *If she knew Asia wasn't mine when she was born, why would she allow my family to get attached to that baby?* I couldn't even believe that she allowed me to fall in love with that little girl, only to rip my heart out six months later. *How is she gon' turn around and tell me that another nigga is Asia's father like I don't mean shit.* I thought. Before I realized what I was doing, I ran up behind Zena and socked her in the mouth.

"Now go suck a dick with them lips. Tell yo man if he got a problem with it, see me," I replied, walking off.

By 2:20 that afternoon Zena had about six niggas waiting up at the school for me. I beeped Ant to tell him what was going down because I wanted him and Melvin to be there in case something jumped off. When they arrived, I walked out the front door straight to my brother. Zena's man and a few of his boys eased their jeep right up behind Ant's Benz. They were in a Laredo on some phat rims. It had this rare paint job that was off the hook, so if anything went down, people were gon' be able to ID them. I looked at Melvin and Ant, and it seemed like we all automatically knew who we were dealing with.

"I bet they are the same guys that killed T."

"Prince, I think so, too. Get in the car and pull off if something goes down," Ant stated, stepping out with his piece exposed. "What's up, Man, is there a problem?" Ant asked.

"What you say?"

"Nigga, you heard me. I said is there a problem?" Ant repeated, drawing his Nine-millimeter.

"Naw Dawg, everything's cool."

"I didn't think so," he stated, exchanging a few more words before returning to the car.

I sat in the back seat looking out the rear window at the guy that Ant confronted. T*hat's Antonio Casey, the punk I'd fought at the movies*, I thought before catching a view of his brother Charles who was sitting in the back seat. Charles was real humble. He knew he couldn't say anything due to being a fugitive. Redford was right across the street from the police station. I imagine he was a little leery about getting out 'cause he didn't want to take any chances on being caught. The whole time Ant was talking to Antonio, Charles looked like he wanted to do something. He was smart to stay in that jeep, though. I bet the threat of going on one of DOC's all expense paid vacations restrained him. When Ant closed the door, I told him who I thought we were dealing with. Melvin immediately suggested that he didn't think those cats had enough juice to kill T. Ant and I agreed that in the D, all things were possible. Everyday life on the block revealed how scurvy suckas could be, so I don't know why he thought a Youngian couldn't pull off a hit like the one T experienced. Hell, they were and still are the ones you really need to watch.

"Those are the same guys I was beefin' with at the movies," I mentioned to Ant.

"P, this is some bullshit. Zena is probably trying to set you up. You better watch your back and stay away from that Ho. Give me some time to see what's up with these chumps. They may be working for somebody. Just chill out for a while and for the rest of the year, I'm gon' make sure you get picked up by somebody until we see what's really going on."

"Okay," I responded just to appease him.

At fifteen, I thought I knew everything, so most often I did what I wanted to do. My brother was very knowledgeable about living in them streets, which is why I should've listened. That same Friday Zena had a hundred niggas at my school to beat me down. I had the nerve to still go to the movies that night. I wasn't about to let the Casey boys keep me in the house.

While Ant was in the den counting money, I went out to his car to get his extra gun from under the dashboard. When I was getting out of the car, I noticed him and Melvin standing on the porch. When I shut the door, I quickly tucked the gun in my pants. I didn't think Ant was gon' question me about being in his car, but he did.

"Prince, what are you doing in my car?"

"Lookin' for my keys," I replied, holding them in the air.

"Did you lock my doors back?"

"Yeah," I stated, tossing him his remote.

My boys were uneasy about walking to the movies. I asked Ant to take us, but he refused to give us a ride. I called a cab 'cause I knew Chew and J didn't pay close attention to their surroundings. With all that was going on, I had to be the eyes for all three of us. That night, I was far more cautious of my surroundings. When we got to the movies, I kept my guard up at all times. Before claiming a seat, I looked around the theater four or five times to scope out the area. Though things appeared to be okay, I decided we needed to sit in a different location. I wanted to deviate from our normal routine just in case someone came looking for me. We picked seats way in the back by the exit just in case we had to make a quick get away.

With one chair between us each, and our feet braced on the backs of the seats in front of us, the lights dimmed. While the previews were playing, I noticed Zena with a different dude. They were locked arm in arm as they walked towards the front. Shortly behind them, Tasha and her girls walked in. She knew we were gon' be there and was headed to our usual area. I whistled to get her attention, and they came and sat with us.

With as much time as we'd spent at the Norwest over the years, something didn't seem right about the environment to me at all. In the middle of the movie, I asked everyone if they were ready to leave. None of them wanted to go. J asked, "What for?" Chew chimed in to explain that the guy with Zena wasn't the one from school that I'd been beefing with. He also reminded me that Ant had already checked Antonio and his crew earlier, so I probably wasn't going to have any more problems with them.

"Man, Zena knows your Uncle Silk got status. If anything goes down with you, Zena and her people will have to either relocate or go into a witness protection program. Silk or Ant would nut up and definitely put a hit out on the Johnson family. Hell P, babies and all would have to die if something happened to you," Chew stated.

"Nigga, my family ain't that ruthless. My brother wouldn't kill my daughter to pay Zena back."

"Zena said Asia wasn't yours, so yeah she might get put on the hit list. And Ant might let her live, but if Silk got something to do with it, her toe is tagged, too."

To some extent, Chew was somewhat right. With his pertinent points made, I allowed him to talk me into staying longer. I tried to enjoy the movie, but I kept feeling too unsure of my surroundings. Finally, I decided that it was best for us to leave. About thirty minutes before the movie ended, I told Julius to call us a cab. I went to use the restroom. Chew, J, and the girls went outside. On my way out, I walked right into Zena and her date. I was still heated from earlier that day, so I tried to ignore them. I didn't want to start any unnecessary confusion. Plus, I knew I was packing a gun in a crowd of innocent people. If I had to shoot somebody that night, I didn't want it to be someone that had nothing to do with my situation. If I had to bust a cap, innocent bystanders were certain to fall victim to my wrath.

Tasha came back inside to see what was taking me so long. She didn't see Zena or me when I motioned for her to turn around to walk in the opposite direction. Before it even registered, Zena ran up on Tasha talking noise. She was trying to get revenge from the incident at the skating rink, but I didn't want to get caught up fighting at the movies again.

"I know you're no punk, but I can't afford this. Keep walking because Chew and J are waiting on us in the cab. The meter's running, and she's not worth going to jail over tonight," I stated, grabbing Tasha's arm.

By the time we got to the door, Chew came back to make sure everything was cool. I saw him making his way through the crowd of an opposite door, so I yelled for him to turn around. I walked Tasha to her mom's car, and then I walked to my cab. Out of nowhere Charles Casey came running across Grand River, yelling and pointing a gun at me.

"Pull off, pull off," I yelled to the driver, jumping into the cab. He floored it. We went zipping through red lights, speeding down side streets, and he safely delivered us to J's house without any additional problems. I beeped Ant 4357 to let him know what went down.

"Prince, did you just beep me?" he calmly asked when he returned the call.

"Man, did you get the code?" I asked like he was crazy 'cause he was too calm for me. "Charles Casey was at the theater. He drew a firearm on me. I need to be picked up from J's house ASAP."

"He did what? I told yo li'l hardheaded ass to stay out of them streets. Man, I'm on my way."

Within ten minutes he was there, pissed off, and ready to kill somebody.

Ant dropped Chew off at home. He thought Zena might show her boys where I lived, so he kept me with him. I hoped that wasn't the case because if they brought it to my mother's house, all hell was gon' break loose for sure. Bean and Ant didn't see eye to eye, but he wasn't gon' let no one harm her or my sister. We headed towards Zena's house because Ant wanted to talk to her before things got out of hand. When we got on Zena's block, her, the Casey's, and some of their boys were standing on her porch. Ant pulled out his gun, turned off his lights, and rode down on them blasting.

"Man! Damn it! Have you lost your mind?" I asked as it registered that we had just done a drive-by on Zena in his car.

My adrenalin was going. Ant was so hyped afterwards that he continued to speed long after we were out of Zena's neighborhood.

"Man, slow down, Melvin finally insisted. Unfortunately, his request came a little late. A police car going in the opposite direction hit a u-turn and flashed his lights on us.

"Aw Dawg, we're about to go to jail," Melvin stated.

"Just relax. I got this," Ant insisted.

The officer positioned this bright light on the car, then sat for a minute. After he got out, he walked up, and tapped on the window with his flashlight.

"What's the rush?" he asked.

"There's no rush Officer. I just didn't realize I was driving that fast."

"I need to see your driver's license and insurance."

Ant got his insurance out of the glove compartment. He handed his verification card and all his information to the officer. My heart started pounding. I was nervous, and I knew we were on our way to lock down.

"I'll be right back," the officer expressed, walking towards his squad car to run Ant's information. We sat for about ten minutes then he returned. "Who's Renee Pittman?"

"Oh, that's my girlfriend. This is her car."

"Alright, Mr. Shaw, you're free to go. I'm going to only issue you a warning this time. Slow this Benz down before you hurt somebody. Okay?"

"Sure. Thanks Officer."

I figured the drive-by we'd just done and a description of our car was already in the system. It wasn't. When the officer handed Ant back his ID and walked away, I was in disbelief. The only conclusion I came up with was that the specifics of our crime had not yet been reported to the dispatcher. Lucky for us, if that was the case.

I was hype about us getting away with our crime. Like always, Ant had a backup plan ready to work in his favor. My boy had given the officer a fake ID, so when the police report finally went out they were going to be looking for a guy with the last name Shaw, not Prince.

## 7

## *In the lake!*

As I laid in Ant's living room thinking, I could barely sleep. Ant's couch was hella uncomfortable, and the complete silence was driving me crazy. I finally turned on the television about seven that Saturday morning, hoping to find something to occupy my mind. There was nothing worth watching on that early, so I found myself looking at the news. When I set the remote back on the table, Deborah Binkley, the morning anchor, was reporting the breaking news.

"A drive by shooting on Detroit's Westside has left one twenty-year-old, black male dead and a fifteen-year-old female fighting for her life. Zena Johnson is in critical condition after being shot in the face and chest earlier this morning on her front lawn. The gunman is unknown at this time, but the police are searching for a Mercedes Benz. Anyone with information regarding this incident is asked to call the Detroit police homicide unit at (313) 555-2260 or Crime stoppers at (800) TALK-2ME."

Damn, I felt terrible after hearing news like that. I didn't always see eye to eye with Zena nor did I respect her much, but I certainly didn't want anything like her being shot to go down as a result of our differences. After hearing that report, the reality of what Ant had done settled in. *Everyone knows my brother has a Benz,* I thought before worrying about Zena's condition. *Surely they're going to associate this incident with me and swear I had something to do with this.*

Right after Zena's story aired, I said a quick prayer for her. It was out of character for me to pray, but Zena was the mother of my child. As I sat there in a daze, my beeper started blowing up. *This is Saturday, why is everyone up so early calling me?* I thought.

Finally, the call I'd been dreading came in. Bean beeped me four times. At first, I considered not returning any of her calls period, but after two more back-to-back pages from her, I went on and responded to her last page. Just as I expected, she answered the phone yelling, cursing, and raising hell. I knew it was in my best interest to stay quiet, so I did just that as she vented. After minutes of going off, she paused as if she were waiting for a reply. I still didn't say a word. She exhaled, fussed a little more, and then hung up in my face.

After she abruptly ended our conversation, I walked back to Ant's room to tell him that Bean was on the rampage. I thought he might want to know about our crime being featured on the news, too. When I knocked on his bedroom door, there was no reply. I slightly pushed it, discovering that his bed was empty, and he was gone. *I wonder how he'd slipped by without me noticing. I don't sleep that hard, do I? Maybe he left shortly after I initially fell asleep because he needed to take care of some business, which was too risky for me,* I thought. *But damn, he could have said something, that way I wouldn't be worried.* "Man, Ant's out driving that car around and doesn't even know Deborah Binkley has all his information out there like that," I mumbled, walking back to the living room.

I sat questioning his moves for over two hours. After hearing nothing from him, I wondered if the police had already arrested him. Because he never returned home, I ended up calling a cab. About fifteen minutes later, the cab driver was honking out front. I quickly opened the door, motioning for him to hold. While I took a moment to grab my coat, I noticed the gun I'd taken from Ant's car. It was still in my inner pocket. *I guess I should leave this gun here. Then again, with the way fools nuttin' up, I probably need to keep it with me for protection.* I thought. After a discussion with myself, I decided I'd keep the gun a little longer. For the record, that's when I made another very bad decision, which would demolish my life in time.

I remember arriving home a little after noon that day. On the way to my room, I heard Bean crying. Immediately, I thought Renzo had done something to her, so I angrily pushed open the door.

"What's wrong?" I yelled.

"What! How could you burst in here asking me something like that? You know very well what's going on."

"I know what's going on with me, but I heard you crying. Like usual, I assumed Renzo had done something to hurt you."

"Prince, nobody's hurting me more than you and your brother lately. Between the two of you, I don't know who I worry about more, you or Anthony. Y'all stay in so much nonsense now that I don't know what to do. Everyday I'm worried about the police bringing me some kind of bad news. I can't even envision them telling me that one of my children is dead. And though I haven't always been the best mother, one thing for certain is that I genuinely love all of my kids, and I don't want to bury either one of you."

I felt sincere compassion for Bean's pain, but we were so distant that I didn't even know how to comfort her. I sat on the bed next to my mother, allowing her to have her cry. For the longest, I just looked on without touching Bean at all. She cried nonstop for over ten minutes and longed to be embraced. Though we didn't do stuff like hugging in our home, something finally forced me to hold her. My compassion for my mother might have been a result of the fact that I sincerely sympathized with her pain. It bothered me to see her going through so much agony.

I can't explain it, but I felt extremely awkward hugging and consoling Bean. She always said boys didn't get hugged or kissed on because they'd grow up to be soft, so every since I could remember, Bean had never been the affectionate type. She had her own little hang-ups with my Uncle Brian's sexuality, so she rarely showed us any kind of affection. As a child it bothered me that everyone else had to pick up her slack. What I found most heartbreaking about her behavior is that she truly believed she was doing the right thing by neglecting us. Sometimes when she'd start in on that foolishness, I'd instantly think, *Damn Bean, all kids need affection and want to feel loved, I don't care what gender they are.*

◆◆◆◆◆◆◆

With all the stuff going on in my life, I wished I could turn back the hands of time, but in reality, there was no turning back. With the way brothas were getting shot up and murdered in Detroit on a daily basis, I was afraid for my life.

"Bean, everything will be fine. I'm straight, and you know Ant's a survivor," I mentioned to comfort her.

"Prince, I sure hope that's true. If something happens to any of my children, they'll have to admit me on one of Northville's psychiatric units," Bean replied, getting off her bed.

After we finished talking, I left her room to give her some privacy. While walking to my room, I thought about my brother. *Where is Ant,* I wondered, flopping on my bed? It was so unlike him to disappear and not call. I couldn't help but think about him being gunned down due to retaliation. Huh, when I envisioned that being a reality, I almost cried.

About three o'clock that afternoon, our doorbell rang. When Bean answered the door, there were two police officers wanting to speak to me.

"Prince, could you come to the front please." Bean yelled.

"Okay."

Once I made it to the living room, my eyes went from the officers' shoes, up their uniforms, to their faces. One of them I knew, the other I had seen around, but didn't know by name.

"DeMarques, how are you doing this afternoon?" Officer Williams asked.

"Pretty good, I guess."

"Great. This is my partner, Officer Gordon. I'm sure you're wondering why we're here this afternoon?"

"Yeah, kinda."

"We're here because we wanted to ask you a few questions about last night. Is that okay?"

"Yeah, it's cool."

"DeMarques, what did you do last night?"

"I went to the movies with some friends and then we went to my boy J's house."

"What time did you leave his house?"

"I don't remember the exact time, but it was late."

"Were you driving?"

"No."

"When you left his house, how did you get home?" *Damn where's he going with all of these questions,* I thought before hesitantly replying.

"My brother picked me up."

"Where did you go from there? Did you come home?"

"No, we went to Coney Island and then to his house."

"Prince, do you know Zena Johnson?"

"Yes. She's my daughter's mother."

"Did you know she and another young man were shot last night in front of her house?"

"I heard that on the news earlier today. Do you guys have any leads?"

"Ummm, maybe. Have you called to see how she's doing or if your daughter's okay?" Officer Williams asked.

"I tried to call her mother, but no one answered," I replied, lying to him with a straight face.

"So you haven't spoken with anyone about your daughter or her mother's well being yet?" he asked with raised eyebrows. "There was a drive-by shooting at your child's house, half the day has gone by, and you haven't spoken with anyone to see if she's okay?"

"No."

"Were you planning to call again?"

"Yeah, I…" Bean immediately cut me off.

"Officer, if my son is not under arrest, you need to leave my house. I'm not comfortable with these questions. They are getting a little out of hand for me. Prince may not have spoken with anyone, but I've been calling the hospital talking with Zena's mother all morning. I've kept him informed on her status; therefore, he's aware of what's going on with his daughter and Zena."

"Prince, do you and Zena get along pretty well?" he asked, ignoring Bean's comment.

"Sometimes," I replied, wondering if he was insinuating that I had something to do with the shooting.

"Someone informed me that you and Zena recently had an altercation at school, is that true?"

"Yeah, but that doesn't mean anything, lots of separated couples with kids have arguments."

"Do you know someone that drives a Mercedes?" Officer Williams asked, still ignoring Bean.

"Officer, this interview is over. Get the hell out of my house unless you have a warrant," Bean rudely interrupted.

"Sorry to upset you, Ms. Prince. Thank you for your time. DeMarques, you take care. If you remember anything else about last night that you'd like to share, here's my card." Bean snatched it out of his hand, then forced the two of them out the door.

"Prince, what the hell happened last night?" Bean asked after they pulled away from the house.

"Bean, everything happened so fast, I don't really know what happened myself. One minute Ant was going to talk with Zena, the next thing I noticed is him shutting off his lights to blast on her."

"You better try to remember something."

"Bean, I got into it with them same guys that shot me. They showed up at my school yesterday and then again at the movies last night. Afterwards, Ant picked me up from J's house, and it was on from there. He said he was gone drive by Zena's house to tell her to squash the nonsense. However, when we got on her street, those same niggas were at her house."

"They were at her house! What the hell? Is she friends with them or something?" Bean asked.

"I don't know, but when we were in school Friday, she claimed someone else was Asia's daddy. I got so mad at her that I snapped and punched her in the mouth."

"What! You punched her? When did all that happen?"

"Yesterday, I was fooling around in the hall with some of my friends. Zena walked up trying to embarrass me. She started talking noise about Asia not being mine. Before I knew it, I got mad, so I punched her."

"Prince, who do you think you are? You know you don't hit women. You were totally out of line when you put your hands on that girl."

"Well, try telling that to Renzo 'cause he happens to be my role model lately," I sarcastically countered, clearly irked by her comment.

"Finish your story and don't be a smart ass. I'm still your mother, and you will respect me. I don't know who you think you are, but you're not grown and you won't disrespect me in my house! That's half your damn problem. You're so busy trying to be grown that you don't know half of the responsibilities that come along with the territory. Now watch your mouth and tell me the story like I asked."

I looked at Bean like she was crazy. She'd gone off, ignored my comment, cussed me out, and was ready for me to get back to my story like nothing ever happened. Since she knew men weren't supposed to hit women, I wanted her to address why she allowed Renzo to hit on her.

"Prince, I said finish!" she yelled a second time.

"Oh, so you're not going to address my comment then?"

"No," she said, rolling her eyes.

"I didn't think so."

"It's not your business why I do what I do. And I don't have to explain shit to you."

"Anyway, moving on 'cause I can see I hit a nerve."

"You sure did," she briefly interrupted.

"Bean, after they started trippin' with us last night, we jumped in cab. Ant picked me up from J's. Then we drove to Zena's. When we turned on her street, she was in the yard with her boys, Ant nutted up and started capping on 'em. I don't think Zena was supposed to get shot. I believe she was accidentally hit." *Well I at least think he did it by mistake,* I thought without saying.

"Prince, bullets don't have eyes and names assigned to them before their discharged from a gun. What the hell do you mean she wasn't supposed to get shot? If Anthony shot into a crowd of people, and she was present, he knew there was a chance she could catch one of those stray bullets. Hell, if you were in the midst of that group of people, I bet he wouldn't have fired on them, would he?"

I didn't reply because I could tell Bean was furious. I hated that I even ratted on Ant, but Bean already knew we were guilty. As she continued to fuss, I sat on the couch looking out the window. That's when I noticed Ant getting out of a brown Jeep. In the middle of our conversation, I got up like she wasn't even talking and ran out the door.

"Man, where the hell have you been? Why you leave me at your crib without bothering to tell me you were leaving?" I asked.

"I had to take care of some business. I knew you were gon' want to go, and I didn't want you riding in that car."

"Where did you go?"

"I got my stuff off the Benz and got rid of it."

"Got rid of it?" I repeated.

"Umm, hum. I took my system out, put it back on factory rims, and sent it for a ride."

"A ride."

"Yeah, the Benz is history."

"What, you burned it or something?"

"Nope, I sunk it. My li'l homie DC drove it out of the city to one of his spots. Melvin and I followed him. We rolled out to some secluded lake he uses as a junk yard and dumped it there."

"Y'all rolled it in the lake!"

"Yeah, it was easier than burning it up."

"What lake?" I asked.

"Now you're asking too many questions. All you need to know is that it's underwater. No one will find it where it's dumped."

" Damn! You sunk the Benz?"

"Yeah, and I left my gun in it, too."

"What?"

"I forgot to get my spare gun from under the dashboard. We were rushing, and it just slipped my mind. No big deal though. I have more and the serial numbers been scratched off."

"So if it's found, can they trace it back to you?" I asked.

"The car's not in my name, and I had the chick report it stolen right after DC left city limits. If someone finds it, there's no way anything could be traced back to me."

I was cool with that. *As always, a young Prince was caught thinking at crunch time.* I concluded that Ant's adventure for the day was another lesson passed down from my uncle. Silk was sharp when it came to getting out of things. It was obvious that he had taught Ant well.

Since Ant thought he'd left his gun in the car, there was no need for me to tell him I had it. I figured I'd just have a gun for myself. That way I wouldn't have to worry about anybody running up on me.

As we walked to the porch, I told Ant about the police coming to the house. I assured him that we didn't tell anything that might lead to us. I also mentioned how Bean stood up for me while being questioned. Ant wasn't surprised by her actions, though. He swore I was her favorite, before vowing that had I not been involved, Bean would have easily turned him in. When we walked through the door, Bean rolled her eyes at both of us before cursing Ant out.

"I saw the two of you standing out there in front of my house trying to have one of y'all's "Down-low" conversations. Anthony, what kind of mess do you have Prince involved in now? The damn police have been here questioning him, and I don't like it one bit."

"You didn't tell them anything did you?"

"No, but I want to know what the hell you were thinking. Did you ever take into consideration that you could've killed that girl?"

"She's lucky to be alive. Generally, I wouldn't go off like that on no bitch, but I wasn't myself for a moment. That girl has Prince involved in some serious drama. I just snapped, Bean, that's all I can say."

"Just snapped? Prince's beef with those boys isn't that serious."

"Do you realize what they did to T? They brutally tortured and murdered him. Bean, you didn't see their work. I did and so did Prince. I know what those fools are capable of. If Zena doesn't die, it wasn't her time, but if something happens to Prince, she'll wish she was dead."

"Anthony, what has happened to you lately? I can't believe you're saying these things. You have lost touch with the beauty of life, and I think you're going crazy."

"You're not one to confront me on shit about life. With all your secrets, maybe I should ask you what you were thinking about at times when you did some of the out-cold shit of your past. Maybe if we share some of your skeletons verses mine, we can see who's the craziest. I'm not crazy, Bean. I'm simply doing what you should have done. I'm being my brother's keeper, regardless of the outcome."

"Whatever, Anthony! Price is not about to be mixed up in this nonsense."

"Bean, you can't just snap your fingers and stuff go away like that. Them punks are ruthless. They won't be satisfied until they hurt or kill Prince. Unfortunately, you can't protect him, so you don't have any other choice but to let me handle things."

"I'm going to talk with Silk tomorrow about this."

"Silk's gon' tell you to do the exact same thing or he'll handle it himself. You know if he gets involved, body bags gon' be on back order, and Zena's gon' occupy one of them for sure."

# 8

## *A Family Affair*

Bean knew Zena had gotten me caught up, so for her sake, I wanted things to come to a peaceful resolution. Bean also knew Ant was right about Silk. If your name went on his hit list, within a few hours, you were good as hit, if he wanted it like that. He had homies on his team that cut hard for him. If necessary, they'd take a bullet, deliver one, and serve time on his behalf. Ant was determined to resolve my problem, so if he and Silk had to devise a plan, it was gon' be one only funerals would resolve.

Ant frequently hurt Bean with some of his out-cold comments. For some reason, he was so bitter towards her and sometimes the two of them carried on like they hated each other's guts. I wondered what kind of dark secrets Bean actually had that she was trying to keep quiet. Some days the slightest remark about her past in front of Ke or me quickly sent her humble.

Bean and GG thought they'd do something special for the holidays and my sixteenth birthday. They planned a nice party for me, naming it, "A Celebration for a Prince." GG sent invitations to our relatives, insisting that they RSVP. My family hadn't gotten together in years, so this gathering was going to be a big occasion. Everyone started RSVPing shortly after invites went out.

The week of the dinner, GG was over at Bean's spot everyday cooking. She had a serious combination of scents going on, and the house smelled delicious all week. Well, that is until her, Bean, Ke, and Renzo started cleaning over 130 pounds of chitterlings. I hated chitterlings, which is why my granddad always said I wasn't a real Prince. I was the only member in my entire family that despised the thought of sucking down a long strip of pork intestines. And the fact that they were connected to an asshole didn't help with winning me over. While I stood around watching them clean off little hints of grain, Bean and Ke teased me about being adopted. I didn't care what they said or thought about me with their soiled hands. I wasn't touching or tasting no shit-lings.

The day of the dinner, Bean made sure little to no sampling took place. I was starving, so by the time we ate, I was ready to grub. I knew from the first day they started cooking, I was gon' fix me a plate for a king, and then eat myself to death. Our family started arriving in packs because they were certainly not going to miss out on one of my grandmother's dinners. I knew everyone that called to RSVP was showing up because no one was asked to bring anything, and the menu was off the hook. GG could cook her butt off, too. Intentionally missing out on one of her meals was like the first step to committing a major sin.

Everyone was instructed to arrive by five that evening, but at five-thirty, we were still waiting on a few guests.

"Mama, you know your kids gon' be on BPT." Bean stated, clearly irritated because GG refused to let us eat until a few more guests arrived.

Most of Bean's aggravation came from knowing that we were still waiting on all three of her siblings. I know she didn't mind so much that we were waiting on Silk because he was her favorite out of the three. But she was furious at the thought of waiting on her distant twin Ka'Nita, whom we called Kay-Kay and her brother Brian.

Bean and Kay had fallen out in the early 80's over an insurance policy. My great-grandmother died and left a nice portion of her inheritance to Kay-Kay, which made Bean angry as hell. When my aunt finally arrived, I was shocked to see her behave so cordial towards Bean. The two of them had been feuding for years. Out of respect for my grandparents, Kay-Kay always tried to be supportive of family events. GG was happy to see Ka'Nita try to get along with Bean, so she and I tried to make Kay feel as welcomed as possible, especially since the dinner was in Bean's house. To see me go above and beyond for my aunt pleased Daddy Ruenae because Kay-Kay was his favorite.

Like always, Silk arrived with one of his many women. Then Brian arrived about thirty minutes later with some dude Bean called his boyfriend.

"Brian, where the hell have you been? We've been waiting over an hour on you." You know dinner was supposed to start at five-thirty. I get so tired of you being inconsiderate." Bean expressed out of frustration. "And not only are you late, but you done brought your damn boyfriend, which is going to make the whole family uncomfortable."

"Sorry, Ma," he said, ignoring Bean. "I was taking care of some business that ran a little long. One of my friends came with me. Is it ok if he comes in?" *Brian's about to show his ass,* I thought, anxiously awaiting GG's reply.

"That's fine, Brian, but please don't start any nonsense."

"Ma, what nonsense are you talking about?"

"She's talking about that 'Ms. Brina shit,' Bean rudely answered.

"Look Fish, ain't nobody talking to you. Besides, I ain't bringing Brina to dinner tonight. I got more respect for Ma's gathering than that."

"Yeah, whatever! That's why you brought a punk to our family dinner, right?" Bean replied, rolling her eyes.

"Ok, that's enough! That's the nonsense I'm talking about. We're here to celebrate Christmas and Prince's birthday. Bean, can you please try to get along with your siblings for once? Stop all that foolish arguing, and let's enjoy dinner as a family!" GG angrily yelled.

Brian went out to get his guest, and then the family crowded around the table. We grabbed one another's hands, with bowed heads, as Daddy Ruenae gave the prayer. While he prayed, I stood there fascinated with the menu. GG had the table decked out with everything. Honey Glazed ham, Cornish hens, smoked roast, fried chicken, chitterlings, macaroni and cheese, candy yams, dressing, greens with hocks, fresh green beans, cabbage, corn on the cob, rice, Giblet gravy, mashed potatoes, potato casseroles, sweet potato pies, Italian cream cheese cake, German chocolate cake, peach cobbler from scratch, banana pudding, beverages, and at Bean's bar there was every kind of liquor one could possibly name.

My granddad loved the Lord. I don't care what kind of occasion our family gathered for, he was gon' give the Father and His Son their props. I envisioned piling loads of food on my plate and because I was so anxious to eat, I don't specifically remember anything he said outside of, 'Let the family say AMEN!' When I opened my eyes, there were about eight people in front of me. I wasn't having that. I was the guest of honor, too. Man, I found my way to the front of the line with the quickness.

"Excuse me, my GG planned this dinner for two Kings, and since one of them is turning sixteen tomorrow, I should get to fix my plate first," I stated, looking at Daddy Ruenae who was first in line.

"Well, if your GG fixed this dinner for two Kings, I know my Savior is one of them, and I'm sure I have to be the other because you're a Prince. Therefore, I think it's ok if I eat before you," he said, flashing his perfectly sculpted teeth on me. "Get in line right behind me. If anyone has anything to say about you taking cuts, tell them to take it up with me. Alright?" he manipulatively whispered.

*If I take those dentures, your butt won't get to eat at all,* I thought being silly, before simply replying "Alright!" because I knew I couldn't win with him.

We ate, we laughed, and we had a good time. Dinner with the Prince family went extremely well that evening. After eating, we all sat around like we sincerely loved one another. GG was notorious for pulling out the flicks that caused major embarrassment. Wouldn't you know it, since it was my celebration, she had a few pictures of me. The two photos that sent me over the edge was one of me with about three of my teeth missing. The other was of me when I was seven with some red plaid floods on and a Don King Afro. I had to laugh at myself on that one because with me becoming the natural fashion guru I am, I couldn't believe I had no fashion sense. Back then, I wore some of the ugliest gear and had absolutely no style at all.

Finally, GG pulled out one of my first baby pictures. That made me a little sad. "Awwwwww!" Everyone chimed in sync, as GG showed a photo of me when I was ten months old. Asia was almost ten months old, too. I hadn't seen her in about six or seven months and suddenly seeing that picture caused me to feel a void.

"Well, everyone, I guess we're going to be the first to leave," Brian stated. "Ma, everything was delicious. Bean, thanks for having us. I had a great time." Before Bean could reply, I quickly butted in. With her, there was just no telling what she might say.

"See you, Man. Thanks for coming," I stated, giving him a firm manly handshake.

After Brian and his guest left, Daddy Ruenae and Silk got on Bean about always embarrassing Brian about his homosexuality. She stood her ground with them as well. "I will never accept him being gay. As long as he's my brother, I'm going to voice my opinion about how disgusting his behavior is to me. If y'all want to accept it, fine, but I never will."

"Bean, it's disgusting to the entire family, but Brian's our blood and instead of isolating him like you've isolated Ka'Nita, you need to pray for him," Daddy Ruenae insisted.

"Bean, it's his choice. Like it or not, deal with it," Ka'Nita agreed.

"You sorry Gold Digger, nobody asked you to comment on anything. I was having a discussion with my father and my brother."

"Bean, you are and have been so selfish and ignorant for so long, I don't think you even realize how insulting you are at times."

"Bitch, yes I do. Unlike so many, I'm glad I'm not afraid to speak my mind," Bean snapped back.

"Look at you now, you're disgusting. I don't even know how or why the family tolerates you and your drunken foolishness."

"They don't tolerate me; I'm a major player in this family. They'd be lost without me. I didn't forget about my parents and run off to start me a new life out in Dearborn frontin' like I've always had money to flaunt."

"But if you could have, you would've," Ka'Nita fired back at Bean, making her livid.

"If it weren't for Grandmother's money, you wouldn't be there either."

"Bean, you sound jealous with your trifling ass. And while you're talking about the family would be lost without you, let it be known that you'd be lost without the family. We don't benefit from you being a part of us in any manner. And why you're so busy passing judgment on Brian and me, you need to examine yourself. You have several of your own issues that cause you to fall short as well, Honey. You may not have run out on your parents, Mia, but you ran out on your sons."

"Mia? Who or what the hell is a Mia?" Bean asked.

"You! You're a MIA, and you've been one for years."

"And just what do you mean by that. Don't talk in codes. Tell me what the hell I've been for years."

"Bean, you've been "**M**issing **in** **A**ction" as a parent long before any one of your children was ever born. You hid your pregnancy for the first five months while trying to decide if you wanted to abort or put Anthony up for adoption. Then after deciding to keep him, you didn't get prenatal care until you were in your last month. That should have been a clear indication as to what kind of parent you were going to be. That's why your kids have and will always refer to you as something other than Mom."

"Ka'Nita, you don't know what the hell you're talking about," Bean replied in defense of herself.

"When has Anthony or Prince ever called you Mom?" she screamed to the top of her lungs. "Why do you think they respect Mama and Daddy more than they respect you? Sweetie, maybe you didn't know it, but being called Mom is a privilege that most Mia's know nothing about. Therefore, I know you can relate to what I'm talking about, since you're president of that club. "

"You're not about to talk crazy to me in my damn place. I don't care if this is a family gathering or not. Bitch, you got to get your narrow, black ass out my house. Prince, get Ka'Nita and her family's shit right now, so they can get the hell up out of here."

"Bonita Prince, this is your sister you're talking to that way," GG reminded Bean.

"Sister or not, she was rude to me, too. Do you plan to say anything to her about the way she just spoke to me in front of my kids?"

"Ma, we're about to go. This is Bonita's house, and if she wants me to leave, I'll be happy to," Kay stated, putting on her fur coat.

In a matter of no time, I watched my mother take a perfectly great gathering, and severely mess it up. Daddy Ruenae didn't say one word while all the nonsense between the women went on. He knew not to get involved in the female family disputes.

Kay-Kay said her goodbyes to everyone, and then I walked her and her family to their car. After shutting her door, I kissed her goodbye.

"I'm glad you all came out for dinner," I mentioned, backing away from her car. She smiled, and from her expression, I knew she wouldn't be visiting the family any time soon. Shortly after they pulled away, Ant came outside with his date.

"Man, I don't care what anyone says, your mother is a trip when she gets a little liquor in her system."

"Yeah, Bean knows how to kill the moment. Doesn't she?"

"When you go back in that house, you're going to catch hell about walking Kay and them out."

"Ant, I don't even care. Bean was wrong for that nonsense she pulled tonight. I ain't even up for her fussing this evening. I might go home with GG and Daddy Ruenae to avoid the bullshit. Hey, who is the new li'l cutie you're with?" I asked cause I'd never seen her before that day.

"Her name's April. I met her at Burger King."

"Burger King? You eat at Burger King?"

"Yeah, Man. I like it my way every now and then."

"Oh, okay. Well, holla at me tomorrow."

"Okay! Say, if you're leaving with GG you better go get your bag because her and Daddy Ruenae are walking out the front door right now," Ant stated, pointing towards the porch.

I could see GG was fussing about something. As my grandfather helped her down the stairs, he tried to listen without irritating her. However, she was giving him hell about not intervening when the girls were arguing. To help him out, I interrupted her.

"GG, that dinner was delicious. You put your foot in everything. Do you think your people left me enough food for some leftovers tomorrow?" I asked, forcing out a fake smile.

"Prince, there is plenty of food in there. I'll be over in the morning to fix me a few to go plates. I would have fixed me one tonight, but your ignorant mother has my blood pressure up. I'm going home to relax and calm my nerves."

"Is there something I can do for you before you go? You want me to go fix you a plate?" I asked.

"No, Baby. Happy Birthday," she stated, getting in the car.

Once I went back into the house, Bean started fussing about me catering to my Aunt. At first I didn't even entertain her drunken comments. However, she kept on, so I lashed out at her. "Bean, this was supposed to be a pleasant family affair. As usual, you've messed it up. You get a little liquor in your system, get juiced, and turn into a damn fool. Brian left embarrassed, Kay-Kay left angry, GG went home with her blood pressure acting up, and Daddy Ruenae got fussed out because he didn't stop you from acting like an ignorant ass idiot. Every time GG makes an effort to move us two steps forward as a family, you drink, get pissy drunk, and sabotage her efforts in a matter of seconds."

"Prince, no I don't. And stop talking to me like that. Kay-Kay was rude to me first," Bean slurred in defense of her actions.

"Yes, you do. It seems like you hate to see our people come together and try to be a real family. I don't even know why I'm standing here trying to talk to an un-sober mind. Goodnight, Bean!" I yelled, walking away.

# 9

## Keeper To Keeper

The last day of school for the fall session was Monday, December 23, 1985. During lunch, some of my boys and I were clowning in the hall. We were having big fun when one of the hall guards came over to our area.

"Cut out that foolishness and get to class."

I was kind of laxed about following her directions, but my boys immediately stopped.

"Okay, Mr. Prince, close that locker and make it to the principal's office right now," she ordered.

"The principal's office? Come on, Ms. Bell, give a man a break. You know I was about to go to class."

"You should've moved faster. Maybe this will serve as a warning that I'm here to do a job. When I tell you to move in the future, next time you'll do it. I'll be down to the office shortly to recommend OCS."

"OCS! I know you're not serious. You want me to do On Campus Suspension for horse playing?"

"I told you to stop. That's what I meant. DeMarques, you have a problem with female authority. I'm not here to play with people's kids, and I don't. If I ask you to do something, I expect you to do it when asked, and not when you get ready."

Mean ass Ms. Bell had her way that day. Here it was the last day of school and Dr. Moulder, our school principal, had given me OCS for that evening. At first, I wasn't going to do the three hours, but I didn't want any problems after the Christmas break. Dr Moulder, wasn't no joke either. She would have found me my first day back, so I stayed to make things easier on myself. I called Ant to let him know I was staying after. He told me him or Bean would pick me up and not to catch the bus home by myself no matter what.

OCS was like jail in our school. They had Mrs. Storr, who was one of the strictest teachers in the school, overseeing that class. Man, she would get in your stuff with that Bahamian accent of hers and put some real fear in you.

OCS didn't have any windows, so the environment was gloomy due to being located in the basement of a five-story building. As I headed to the room, I thought about my daughter. Asia's first Christmas was coming up, and I wasn't even going to get the opportunity to see her or take her a gift. When I considered the way Zena treated me, I didn't feel as remorseful towards her as I did when she first got shot. Actually, I felt kind of spiteful. Though she'd successfully pulled through her injuries, and I hadn't been accused of anything, no one in her family allowed my family or me to visit Asia.

*If Asia's mine, I hope when she gets older I'll have a chance to explain why I was forced out of her life,* I thought, considering the comment Kay-Kay made to Bean about a title like "Mom" being a privilege one had to earn. I couldn't help but think that the same rule applied for fathers, also. I guess I simply had a run of bold luck because as far as I was concerned, my father was a MIA, too. After not knowing him and calling my mother Bean all my life, I always vowed that my child would have a dad who was active in their life. By keeping Asia away from me, Zena was putting me in a bad position with my daughter. She was forcing me to be like my father, whom I despised. That's exactly why I was initially so against having a baby's mama.

As I walked to OCS, I thought about how Zena was depriving my child and me from getting to know each other. For a second, I almost believed that once I had a chance to tell Asia how her mother kept her away from me, we would be able to work through lost time. But when I considered my life and the way I hated my father, I knew trying to fix things after my baby was grown wasn't a realistic option. Thinking about all the years my father missed of my life, I knew there was no way he could've told me a damn thing to change the way I felt about him, and the same rule would have applied for my daughter about me.

When I finally arrived, no one was in the room. I waited for the first fifteen minutes. Once I discovered that no one was coming, I wrote my name on the board and left. I was about to call Ant, but I noticed Chew and Julius standing at the bus stop. I walked over to the bushes where I hid my gun and dug out the brown paper bag I kept it in. Immediately, I slid it in my pants to keep it concealed, and then I ran to catch the bus that suddenly pulled up out of nowhere.

We claimed seats in the back, and then got to clowning and talking loud as usual. Chew ragged on me about Carrington, while Julius and I ragged on him about not having a woman at all. Neither was ready to go home, so they suggested that we go to Northland to do some Christmas shopping. I knew there was no way I was going to the mall. Northland was gon' be packed, and all the fools were gon' be out.

"Y'all I'm passing on the mall. I know what kind of traffic's gon' be out there today. With all I got goin' on, there's no way. That's a certain invitation for trouble. Actually, the kind of trouble I prefer to dodge."

When Chew pushed the button to get off the bus at Grand River and Greenfield, J asked me one last time to go.

"Come on, P, go with us," J suggested, walking down the steps.

"Naw man, I'm straight. Get at me later. I ain't about to stress my family out two days before Christmas."

As I watched the two of them run across Grand River, I noticed a Jeep making a U turn. *Oh my God,* I thought as it registered that it was the Casey's. I knew Chew and Julius didn't see them turn around because they never paid attention to anything, which was one of the issues we always argued about.

"Stop the bus!" I screamed.

"Man, what did you say?" the driver asked.

"Stop the bus, please!" I repeated, as he continued to pull off.

"Man, you'll have to get off at the next exit now."

Immediately, I got up with my piece exposed, and started walking towards the front of the bus, raising hell. "Man, stop this fucking bus, right now!" I frantically screamed to the top of my voice.

At once, the bus came to a squealing halt. I anxiously leaped the stairs and took off running. By the time I got to the corner of Greenfield, I noticed the jeep parked in front of the bus stop. Some guy was hanging out of the window talking to Julius, and Chew was somewhat behind him. Instantly, I panicked, quickly pulling my gun completely out of my pants. Without thinking twice or checking traffic, I ran out into the middle of the street trying to dodge cars. Out of nowhere, I heard two gunshots followed by the sound of screeching tires. Before I could do anything, I was hit and flew about fifteen feet in the air. Once I came down, I landed on the hood of the car that hit me and was out cold.

♥♥♥♥♥♥

My heart thumped.....and thumped...and thumped... In my mind, I could see blurred visions of my family and slightly hear what sounded like mumbling. For some reason, I could never reply. Everything that happened in between the gunshots and being hit by that car was unclear for me. I couldn't understand why either. It wasn't until I finally came to, five days later that I realized I'd been in a coma. Cards and Christmas decorations were everywhere. My left leg was elevated in a harness, and I was in a cast from my thigh all the way to my ankle. I had a few broken ribs, some scars on my hands and face, and IV's were everywhere. Though I was big on being a man, I was in a lot of pain, which is why I cried for the first few hours after waking up.

"Prince, you had us worried, Baby," GG stated with tears of joy in her eyes.

"Where am I?" I whispered.

"You're in the hospital."

"Why am I here?"

"Baby, you were hit by a car."

"How did I get hit by a car? What was I doing in the street?"

My entire family ignored my question. Not one of them gave me an explanation or any details as to what really happened before I got hit that day. I didn't even think to ask about my friends, and no one said anything about them either.

GG stayed at the hospital with me everyday until I was released. The day I went home, I almost broke down when I discovered that Christmas had come and gone, and my family decided that they wouldn't open one gift without me. Everyone knew that Christmas was my most favorite holiday, so that afternoon we opened gifts together. I had so many gifts under the tree that year that I felt overwhelmed with love.

Daddy Ruenae gave this long prayer before my family sat down to eat dinner that evening. After we'd finished our meal, I felt so grateful for my family. I mean, I actually realized what kind of blessing they truly were in my life.

"Thanks so much for everything," I said, tearing. "It's cool to realize how valuable I am to each of you. Though I take you for granted sometimes, I love y'all, and appreciate the support you've shown me."

That moment was one I'll always remember. Everyone was tearful. It was difficult for me to decipher if their tears were out of joy or pain. Whatever the case may have been, I know they were plentiful. So it really didn't matter. Later that evening things started slowly coming back to me; I asked Ant about Chew and Julius. I hadn't seen them in some time and didn't realize that they hadn't been out to see me until then.

"Ant, where my boys at? Why those chumps ain't been out to see me? As long as I was in the hospital, I should have seen them by now?" GG looked away. No one else ever said one word, which made me think. I really didn't remember anything about the day I got hit, and up until then, no one talked about it either. Bean walked over and sat next to me. She grabbed my hands and compassionately massaged my fingers with hers. I looked over at

Silk, who was leaving the room. Ant knew how Bean was, so he sat on the arm of the couch next to her.

Bean could not bring herself to words. She cried as she tenderly brushed her hands across my face, giving me direct eye contact.

"Prince, God spared your life," she whispered. I knew something was wrong, but just not to what extent. Ant grew impatient with Bean beating around the bush, so he intervened.

"Bean, let me do this," he insisted, moving a little closer to me. With tears in his eyes, he began to tell me about my friends' misfortune.

"P, Julius and Chew didn't make it, Dawg. And even though you were in the hospital for three weeks, it was a real blessing that you didn't make it over to the bus stop that day or we would've buried all three of y'all." I couldn't believe what I was hearing.

"Ant, you said both of my boys didn't make it. Does that mean that they're dead?" I asked.

"Yeah, Man.....They died that same day."

"Ant, tell me I'm hearing you wrong. How did all this happen? How did this madness get so complicated? Chew and Julius didn't have anything to do with this from day one. Now both of them are dead." Ant nodded yes and his confirmation broke me down. "Man, fuck them NGN niggas!" I screamed out in anger, throwing my crutches across the room. "I can't believe they killed my best friends."

"P' we gon' take care of this," Ant responded.

"Man, we got to. They were innocent. They probably didn't even see them coming," I said, sniffling.

GG told my granddad she was ready to go. "Ain't no way I'm about to be a part of planning someone's murder. Anthony, you all can't be serious," she said, walking out of the room. I listened to her fuss, but wasn't moved after considering how scantless and ruthless those NGN Gangsta Wanna Be Niggas really were. I shouldn't have asked for details, but I had to know if my boys suffered or died instantly.

"How did they die?" I asked, drying my tears.

"Julius was right up on the car, so he got shot in the face and died instantly. The bullet went into his right eye and out the back of his head. When his body slumped over inside the jeep, Chew tried to run, but they shot him in the neck. Once they pulled off, Julius was still hanging inside the window. They drug him about two blocks before finally pushing him off the jeep. Chew died about an hour later in the emergency room. He was fighting to hang in there, but by the time they got him to the hospital, he'd lost too much blood."

"Damn, I always told those cats they needed to be more careful. I tried to warn them about those NGN assholes 'cause I knew they were wilding out. Seems like the Casey boys would have sensed that my boys were on some other stuff. Ant, they weren't like me. Julius was probably in the window trying to peacefully resolve things. I'm sure he must have come off like a lame to them. I bet they took his level headedness for weakness, and then blew his brains out like he wasn't shit. To add insult to injury, they drug him down the fucking street. Come on, Ant. Man! Why these fools ain't already dead? If something doesn't happen soon, I promise, I'm gon' get them myself. I'll spend the rest of my life in prison to defend my boys. If it has to come to that, I'm serious that's what I'm gon' do."

"P, just chill. You don't even have to get involved," Silk suggested, walking into the room. "I've handled this situation. I can assure you that your boys' deaths will be avenged."

Seems like once Silk gave the confirmation, I knew that death for Charles and Antonio was a guarantee. There was some apprehension on my behalf because they'd been coming up like cats with nine lives. Nonetheless, I trusted Silk 'cause his word was his bond. I knew he was gon' put some scantless killers on the hunt, and some toes were definitely about to be tagged. "Those lightweight niggas picked the wrong family. Now they 'bout to get dealt with, for testing a Prince's manhood," Silk replied.

♦♦♦♦♦♦♦

I had been out of the hospital for a good two weeks, when I had a visit from Detroit's finest. Bean opened the door, and there stood two officers with the blankest expressions. They were there on a mission and exemplified little to no compassion for my condition, which pissed Bean off. She hated the police anyway. Them coming by our house to question me once again without a warrant, made her hate them even more.

"Ms. Prince, we're here to see your son, DeMarques," the officer stated, standing on the porch.

"You're here to see him for what?"

"We'd like to question him regarding a shooting that occurred back in 1984 with Raymond Johnson."

"Zena's brother? Ray?" I asked.

"Yes, that's correct. We need you to come down to the police station for questioning."

"I was at home the night Ray was killed. What do you want to talk to me about?"

"DeMarques, can you come with us to the station? We'd like to talk there."

"No!............ My son won't be talking to anyone without a lawyer present," Bean replied.

"That's fine. We need Prince to come by the station tomorrow between the hours of nine and noon. If he doesn't show up, we'll be back with a warrant to get him."

I was bugging out. I didn't know anything about Raymond's murder. Ant hadn't said anything to me about his death either. Plus Zena said when he got, shot the people carrying out the hit said something about NGN, so I thought somebody in Ray's clique killed him. I knew I was innocent. I was home on the phone with Carrington when Zena called me with the news of his death. I didn't worry myself with it though 'cause if push came to shove, either one of them could vouch for me. The question was, would they?

The next morning Silk's attorney Germany Kennedy showed up to represent me. As I was being interrogated, one of the officer's working the case informed me that the Ballistic Examiner Steve Francis had examined bullets taken from Raymond's body, compared them to some fired from the gun I had on me the day I got hit, and discovered that the same gun was used to kill Ray. In his report, I listened to my attorney read a paragraph revealing the results from the research Mr. Francis prepared for the persecutor. Mr. Kennedy started reading out loud to give me some insight on what the state was working with. I didn't really understand all of what he was reading until he read a paragraph that read, "Firearms have ridges inside the barrel that leave a unique firing pattern of marks and grooves on a bullet upon discharge. The marks found on the bullet in Raymond Johnson's body precisely matched the marks left on the bullets fired in the Ballistic Testing Center from DeMarques Prince's handgun." My attorney said these marks were as accurate as fingerprints. If the examiner said the bullets matched, it was a very high probability that he was right. "Well, the person the state is trying to prosecute for this crime is the wrong man," I insisted.

Though I wasn't the killer, it looked like the state had a strong case against me. The gun that I'd taken from Ant's Benz had a body on it. Unfortunately, I didn't know that until it was too late. Had I known Ant was seriously committing murders himself, I certainly wouldn't have been walking around with his dirty gun on me. If convicted, I was facing some heavy charges and looking at life without parole. After being charged with First Degree Murder, I understood why Ant wasn't too upset about his gun being left in the car once they dumped it into the lake. I tried not to worry about the charges that much. I mean, I was a minor with a solid alibi. *What could those bastards possibly get me on since one of my alibis was the victim's sister?* I thought, knowing I was sure to walk.

I was charged, booked, and sent to Juvie Hall. Bean knew Silk and Ant would pay my attorney fees, so she tried to come up with my bail money without their assistance. Once Ant found out I was locked up, he did early rounds on some of his most lucrative houses. Within two days, I made bond. When I walked out of Juvie Hall, Ant was waiting in the lobby for me. The look on his face was intense, which made me think he was angry with me for getting caught up with his gun. "Man, what the hell were you doing with my gun? I told you not to bother any of my shit, and especially not my guns. All my pieces are dirty and got a little history with the exception of one. That's why I always keep more than one at a time."

"I know you told me don't touch your guns, but I needed some protection. When you think about what happened to J and Chew, you see I was right."

"Where did you get that gun from?"

"Out of your Benz the day before you sunk it. Remember the night all that craziness with Zena jumped off?" I asked.

"Yeah, what about it?'

"You remember when you caught me in your car?"

"Ummmm, kind of."

"You don't remember what I'm talking about?" I repeated, observing the most puzzled look on his face.

"Um, somewhat. I mean, I do…..P, just go on with the story," he insisted, still a little unsure.

"Ant, the same day I took that gun is the same day Zena got shot. You should have told me you killed Ray. Had I known, I wouldn't have touched any of your guns."

"P, I was gon' tell you, but I know I've always been your role model. I didn't want you to know that I had your daughter's other uncle killed."

"What did he do to make you kill him anyway?"

"He was trying to grind with us before T got killed. The two of them got into it about Ray grinding in a few of our neighborhoods, not to mention Ray gave 1-time leads on three of our booming spots. After I picked you up from Zena's house the night they were shooting dice, I figured Ray was probably the one that had T set up, once you told me those NGN niggas were in their house with him. He was into some grimy shit, which is why Melvin and I rode down on his crew. You were not supposed to come up with the gun we used to kill him, though. At first we thought it was Melvin's gun that delivered the fatal bullet until you were charged with his murder. Prince, I used the gun you got caught with, so now I know for sure I'm the one that delivered the fatal shot."

"Ant, I'm not turning you in."

"Well, I'll turn myself in."

"Hell no! I'm not snitching you out, we're brothers. With you already having a record, you'll never see home again. Man, you ain't even got no kids to continue your legacy. If they try me, I don't think they'll have enough to convict me on. Silk's attorney is good, so I should walk. I'm going to just let the state try to build their case against me. I got Carrington and Zena as solid alibis. With me being a juvenile, and them working on my side, there's no way I should do any adult time. If convicted, I'll probably have to do a year in W.J. Maxie Juvenile Center or something like that. For now, we'll just play it by ear and see what happens."

"Prince, I'm not letting you go down for something you didn't do. I'm turning myself in. The state's gon' have to drop their charges against you. If I let you go to prison for me, Bean would talk more than a little bit of shit."

"Ant, you just handle my other business. It's time for me to be a man. I refuse to let you say anything. If you do, I'll just plead guilty. Man, you're my brother. We're in this together. Ant, you've been my keeper for so long. Man, I feel obligated to pay you back for something. It's the least I can do for the most dedicated keeper of the Prince," I boldly stated with my arms extended to show him love. "Ant, as long as you live, I won't ever tell anyone you killed Ray."

# 10

## *Life Without My Boys & Carrington*

Here it was mid-February and Valentine's Day had come and gone without me having a sweetheart to share it with. That was the worse Valentine's Day of my life. Though I still found Carrington hella special, after losing my two best friends, I knew the Casey's were crazy. Spending time with her for a few laughs wasn't worth putting her life in jeopardy. I'd stopped seeing Tasha, too. After experiencing so much drama, I didn't want either of them to accidentally be pulled into any of the foolishness going on with me. Just from knowing what they'd done to my boys, I would've been crushed had either of my girls fallen victim to the Casey's wrath.

My initial court date started on Asia's first birthday. I was extremely nervous, and the thought of spending the rest of my life in prison scared me to death. As I stood before the judge with my small frame and boyish face, I remember him asking, "How do you plead, Mr. Prince?" I cleared my throat because it was scratchy, and replied, "Not Guilty, Your Honor." When he looked at me with this grimace smirk on his face, I thought, *Damn Judge Randall isn't playing. If they find me guilty, he's going to send me up the river for a very long time.*

After my plea was entered, my trial was set to start in late August. I left the courtroom with my attorney feeling as though we had made some kind of positive ground. Hell, I was going back home with my family and not to the detention center, so that was a good sign to me.

I had so many fractures in my leg that my cast didn't come off 'til the second week in April. After going to court, I didn't know what the future had in store for me. One thing I did understand from the incident that occurred in December and my first court appearance was the value of family. I spent the months that followed sitting around the house bonding with everyone and trying to get additional evidence to work in my favor. I'd learned to cherish my family. The little time we might have left together was very important. I realized that all things were possible, and I might have to serve some time. Because everything was so uncertain, I tried to stay around the house gathering as many memories as I possibly could, considering I didn't know how things would turn out.

I got spooked about going to prison. Every time I went outside, I stared up in the sky and admired the sun like it was the last time I might see it. I even went to my grandparents' house a few times excited about helping them with gardening, until Daddy Ruenae insisted that my first experience consist of pulling the weeds out of his collard greens, and watering the grass. Though I hated getting my hands dirty, Daddy Ruenae was firm about me doing something in his garden. I ended up not having to pull weeds, but I did get stuck repotting a few of his houseplants, which I had never done before. I made the biggest mess, which caused GG to fuss for hours about me getting her carpet dirty.

Seems like when my freedom was guaranteed, I sometimes took things for granted. The thought of serving time and missing out on special family events taught me some valuable lessons. And even though repotting plants was no big deal, I still cherish that day because I was able to do something special for my grandparents.

I dedicated my Saturdays to Bean and my sister. I spent the mornings lying around the house watching cartoons and eating cereal with KeKe. When the late afternoon rolled around, I'd sit on the porch with Bean laughing about some of my funniest childhood memories. We'd talk about my goals for the future, which was something we'd never done in my entire life. Suddenly, I had all these plans. I don't know where they came from, but once I thought of losing my freedom, somehow having a future started to matter. The death of my friends and the charges I was facing, humbled me. It's funny how when you're going through something you can go from thinking you're a grown man, to hanging onto your mama for comfort in a matter of minutes. It baffled me how all of a sudden even Bean's advice mattered. I talked with her about my desire to see Asia, which led to me asking Bean for the first time for some motherly advice.

"Baby, I think you and Zena have cheated your child long enough. Asia is the innocent one here, and like you, she deserves to know her father. Now the question is are you willing to swallow your pride? What kind of effort are you willing to make to spend some quality time with your daughter? Your father wasn't willing to make any. To me, you suffered behind his stupidity. Prince, Asia doesn't have to know that same kind of pain you've endured."

I thought about the points Bean presented and the situation I was facing. The idea of never being able to hold my daughter again or kiss her made me swallow my pride. I called Zena after almost six months to inquire about the baby. As the phone initially rung, I got butterflies. Hearing her voice didn't seem to calm me one bit either.

"Hello, Zena, how are you?" I cautiously asked.

"Prince!"

"Yeah, it's me. Before you hang up, could you at least let me explain why I'm calling?"

"I'm not going to hang up. I've thought about calling you a few times to see how you were doing, especially after Chew and J's funeral. I'm sorry about what happened to your friends. I know how close you guys were."

"I don't really want to talk about that. I have no memories of my friends being cold, stiff or in a casket. I was still in the hospital when they were buried. To me, they're still kind of alive. How's Asia?" I asked, changing the subject.

"She's good. She's just as fat as ever and walking. Prince, I'm really sorry about the way things have turned out between us."

"Me, too. I know you heard they are trying to convict me for Ray's murder?"

"Yeah, and I also know you didn't do it. But for you to come up with the gun that killed him is odd. That's why I think you have an idea of who did." I was shocked to hear her say that she didn't think I'd killed her brother. I was also relieved because she had some real hatred towards me and that could have affected my case big time.

"Zena, I don't know who killed Ray. He was my boy. I bought that gun off the streets after I started beefin' with your boys. If I could put his murder on someone, I promise you I would. Hell, I'm looking at serving the rest of my life in prison for something I didn't do. There's not one person that would make me sacrifice my freedom like that. I can't believe all this bad luck I'm having," I sadly stated, looking for some sympathy. "Of all the guns to go out and purchase, I can't believe I bought the one that killed my daughter's uncle."

"Yeah, that is odd, which again is why I think you know who killed him."

"Zena, I don't want to argue. The reason I'm calling is to ask if Asia's mine?"

"Why do you care after so many months have passed? You should have called long ago to question me about that, Prince?"

"I tried to, but you told me not to call your house. Even though you said she wasn't mine, I haven't stopped thinking about her since our fight at school. If she is mine, I want to try to have some kind of relationship with her. If she's not, I'll never bother you or your family again."

"Yes," she said pausing. "Prince, she is your daughter."

"Why did you tell me she wasn't then?"

"I got sick and tired of you treating me the way you did for Carrington."

"You stopped me from seeing my baby because of Carrington?"

"I was being immature. I'm sorry. I never imagined that this situation would get so out of hand. I didn't expect your friends to die behind this, but for whatever it's worth, I'm truly sorry. If you'd like to see the baby, you can."

I was numb. I knew Zena told me Asia wasn't mine to be spiteful. But what made me feel physically ill was the fact that we'd been harassed behind some bullshit, which cost my friends their lives. I started to become irritated, but wanted to keep a level head in order to make sure that I got a visit with my daughter.

"Zena, I want to see the baby. If it's okay, I'll have my mother or grandmother pick her up tomorrow."

"Sure that's fine. Are you going to come as well?"

"No, I think it's best for me to stay away for right now, but if it's possible, I'd like for her to spend a few days with me."

"Prince, we'll see. Let's take it one day at a time. Thanks for calling and I'll have the baby ready."

I hung up feeling as though we made some positive progress in regards to our daughter. When I thought about my friends and their families, I hated Zena and the drama she brought to my life. As I walked to the living room to tell Bean that the baby was mine, I wished I could turn back the hands of time for my friends' sake, but I knew that would never be the case.

"Zena said I can get the baby tomorrow."

"Good. I'm glad you were the mature one. I know you're excited, but you need to be leery of that snake bitch. Baby, she ain't to be trusted."

"I know."

"Mama or I will meet her somewhere tomorrow to pick Asia up. Just let me know where we're supposed to meet," Bean stated, draping her arms around my neck and then kissing me on my forehead. *Damn, Bean is getting soft on me. What's all that about?* I thought, smiling.

The following afternoon, I called Zena to confirm our plans. She said it was still a go, so Bean met her at a gas station on Seven Mile. When Asia walked into the house in her cute li'l Calvin Klein jean hookup, I was proud. She was so beautiful and came in looking just like me. I wondered at what period in her life had she gone through such a major transition. The last time I saw her, she looked more like Zena. When I picked her up, I cried. I quickly got myself together, though. Shoot, we only had a few hours, and I didn't want to waste time torturing myself with thoughts of what I'd missed over the months. I held Asia and blew on her fat cheeks. She laughed like a little lady. Suddenly, she smiled real big, and I focused in on the eight teeth that brought her smile to life. When she told me to "Sop `dat" and swatted at my face, I was hooked.

My loud laughing frightened her a bit. That's when she poked out her bottom lip to cry. I found myself talking to her in a tone that only older people and grandparents could appreciate. *Dang, has it really come to this for me? Have I accepted the fact that I'm a father and there's nothing uncool about acting like a lame for my child? Or am I on a mission to break the cycle of MIA's that both of my parents forced me to know so well?* I didn't have any answers for what I was thinking. I was just extremely pleased that I had a second chance to spend some quality time with my daughter. Our visit went well. For me, it was the beginning of the rest of our lives. After that day, every time Zena allowed us to have a visit, I made sure I arranged for someone to pick my baby up.

School was not the same without my boys. Fortunately, I managed to make it to the end of the year with no problems. Carrington graduated and had been granted a full Scholarship to Spelman. That came as no surprise to me because she was always so sharp. I knew she was destined to be successful in life long before she was awarded a full ride to college.

There were a few parties going on, but I knew I wouldn't be attending any of them. I didn't even do the weekly movie and skating thing any longer. Life for me had tremendously changed. The only thing that mattered was Asia and my family. The closer I got to my scheduled court date the more I questioned what life had in store for me.

In late May, Ant called the house at about three in the morning, excited.

"Prince, come outside in ten minutes," he stated.

"Where are you?"

"About five minutes from Bean's spot. Just come outside. I got something to tell you." I paced the house, awaiting his arrival. Once he finally made it, Ant parked two houses away from ours. I went out to talk with him in his car just like he instructed.

"What's so exciting that your news couldn't wait until the morning?"

"P the Casey boys got hit tonight. I know Antonio is dead. Charles is critically wounded. Silk's boys caught them Simps slipping big time at a club in Highland Park and pumped them and their women full of lead."

"Hell Yeah!" I screamed in excitement, giving Ant high five.

"See P, that's why I never doubt Silk, he always does what he says he's gon' do."

"You know it." I declared with pride.

After the news came out about the Casey boys, it turns out that Antonio was most certainly dead. His brother Charles remained in critical condition. If he lived it was certain that he'd be paralyzed due to taking a few bullets to his spine. Both of the young ladies with them died that night. What was scary is that I felt no remorse about two innocent women dying because of my hatred towards the Casey's. At first I thought, *Shit, it's not my fault they were in the wrong place at the wrong time.* But that's because I was so bitter that I didn't care about them being someone's daughter, sister, grandchild, anything. I wanted those boys dead so bad that I had become cold and vindictive. I wanted Chew and J's death to be avenged at the cost of anyone's bloodshed. I honestly didn't give a damn about anyone or anything that got damaged in the process of making that happen. After Chew and Julius died, I was angry with the world. That's what life had come to for me regarding them. I was tired of losing loved ones to senseless crimes.

Months later, when I thought about the innocent girls, I honestly had a change of heart. I considered that I was a son, grandson, brother, nephew, and a father to innocent women that could have easily been in their shoes. "God, forgive my vindictive heart. Please don't let the innocent women in my life fall victim to my actions." I frequently prayed, searching for some redemption.

◆◆◆◆◆◆◆

The first week of August, Carrington called to tell me that she was leaving for Atlanta for school that Thursday. I was excited for her. My girl was going away to college to be groomed into a professional woman. I was a little sad because though we hadn't really seen a lot of each other, I still had my little crush on her. I hated the fact that she was going off to college to be sweated by a whole different kind of playa. In the D, she was dodging Ballas. In college, she'd be dodging Jocks, smooth talking City Slickers from all over the world, and them Geeks in those Greek fraternities that believed they were the cream of the crop in their tight nerdy Alpha, Kappa, Omega, Phi Beta sweaters.

"Prince, I want to see you before I leave. We need to hook up tomorrow and go to Bobolo for the day."

"Bobolo? I can't go that far away from the house. Besides, I ain't about to catch no boat an hour away to go to an amusement park without no homies or protection."

"What about the zoo?"

"The Zoo?"

"Yeah. The zoo," she repeated. "I think it'll be a safe location for us to go without worrying about running into anyone."

Of course the zoo was not my first choice for a date, but to spend some time with my girl, I was willing. Tuesday afternoon Carrington arrived about 1:45. When I got in her car, she looked at me with the blankest expression on her face. She was silent as she pulled away from the house. For the first time in the history of our friendship, she had successfully made me feel very uncomfortable.

"Prince, put your seatbelt on," she insisted.

"I hate seatbelts."

"We're not going any further until you buckle up," she informed me, bringing her car to a complete stop. I looked over into her sad eyes, discovering a very troubled stare.

"Carrington, what's up with you? Why are you lookin' at me like that?"

"Prince, I really feel bad for you. I hate what happened to your friends. I'm most regretful because I haven't been the friend to you I should have been either."

"What are you talkin' about?"

"I feel bad about not coming to see you while you were in the hospital."

"It's cool, I'm not trippin'."

"I also feel bad because I haven't really bothered to stay in touch with you. I know me acting like I was better than you got on your nerves. I should have humbled myself, but I was so afraid of what I felt for you that I forgot about the value of our true friendship."

"I said it's cool."

"No it's not, and I'm very sorry."

"Carrington, why are you beating yourself up? Shit, you were afraid, and understandably so. I was afraid to be around you. I mean, I didn't want any unnecessary drama for you like Chew and Julius went through. I haven't and don't even trip about you puttin' space in our friendship. Hell, if my daughter is ever dating or has a friend that's a knucklehead, I hope she'll have enough sense to do the same thing."

"I want you to know I'm going to do better. When I leave for school, I'm going to stay in touch. When I get to Atlanta, I'll send you my address, and you better write."

"You think Derrick's gonna allow you to correspond with me? Never that!"

"Never that! What do you mean by that comment?"

"Just what I said. Derrick ain't havin' that. You gon' go to Atlanta, meet you some stuck up college niggas, and forget all about the low life's you once knew in Detroit."

"Prince, that's real bold to say. Yeah, I may act uppity sometimes, but I will never forget where I've come from. My parents didn't. They've instilled values in me to make sure I don't forget either."

"Carrington, that's cool. Let's just change the subject before one of us gets upset."

Moving on to a new topic felt like the best thing for me to do. Half of my disrespectfulness stemmed from dealing with separation issues. I didn't want to hurt Carrington by making rude comments, which is why I apologized like a real man's supposed to, and then tried to enjoy the rest of our afternoon. Shortly after working through our disagreement, she apologized to me as well and moved on with our date. I didn't think a cool guy like me could enjoy the zoo, but we had a blast. Afterwards, we had lunch. We sat around in the restaurant laughing like we were little kids.

I guess the time we spent together made Carrington think. I say that because when she dropped me off that evening, she passionately kissed me on my lips like I was her man. I remember her starting with a peck, but hell we weren't going to see each other for at least four months, so I leaned back in and gave her a big, wet juicy kiss. When she stuck her tongue back into my mouth, I knew she was wishing she'd given me some on the down low to see what my good lovin' was all about.

When I got out of the car, I kissed the back of her hand, "You take care, Beautiful." As I stood on the sidewalk, I watched Carrington pull off. *Damn, what made her allow me to kiss her like that?* I thought, walking towards the porch. Just as I was about to hit the steps, Carrington came back around the corner.

"Prince! Come here!" she screamed.

"What's up?" I asked, looking in her passenger window.

"Get in. I have something to show you."

"Girl, what you got to show me? You just want to be around me."

"Being around you ain't no big deal. Just get your black tail in this car and you'll see my surprise," she joked. Carrington drove us to an exclusive neighborhood I'd never even seen.

"Get out," she ordered as I looked at her like she was crazy.

"Who lives here?" I asked.

"Me, Silly. Don't act like you didn't know where I lived?"

"I didn't. What are we doing here?"

"Just get out."

"I wish you would have told me that you were about to introduce me to your parents. I would have dressed better."

"You think I'm about to introduce you to my parents?"

"You are, aren't you?"

"Hell naw! My daddy would have a fit. My parents are out of town for the weekend. If he knew I had you at the house, he'd die," she replied, locking the front door behind us.

"What the hell you mean he'd die? You said that like I'm scum of the earth."

"That didn't come out right. I meant he'd die if he knew I was here with someone outside of Derrick. I told you my daddy loves that boy to death."

"Oh, so you're about to give me some of that ass?" I asked, being my sarcastic self.

"Prince, stop asking so many questions and go with the flow."

Before I could respond Carrington put her hands over my mouth. She pushed me back on her bed and started kissing my neck, then my lips. I'd wanted her for so long that my dick immediately came to life. Obviously she wanted me to put it down, too, 'cause after minutes of foreplay, she started undressing herself. Once she was totally naked, I realized what kind of stunning body she was actually working with. Carrington's body was beautiful. Her stomach was ripped, flat and firm, her butt cheeks stood at attention, and her breast were on point, Chew was wrong about her, too. When Carrington took off her bra, her breast did not sit on her lap like his grandma's did.

I sat up to undress myself, but Carrington pushed me back down. She pulled off all my clothes, then ordered me under the covers. *I love an aggressive woman,* I thought, watching her straddle me. She put so much work into being sexy that I had to feel what it was like to be up inside of her.

"Prince, I've wanted you for so long," she stated, handing me a condom.

"Me, too," I moaned.

*Enough of this small talk,* I thought rolling her over. After my two minutes of foreplay, she was hot and gushy. As a matter of fact, she was so hot that the bed was wet before I even had a chance to hit. I rose to my knees to put on my condom and the damn phone rung. Carrington allowed it to ring for a second, then she considered that it might be her parents, so she answered. Wouldn't that nigga Derrick be the one to call and blow my action out of the water? After all that passion I had put down, his call caused Carrington to suddenly remember that she had a man and was in love.

"Prince, I can't do this. I thought I was ready, but I'm not," she stated getting out of the bed to get her robe.

"What the hell you mean, you thought you were ready? You don't lead a nigga on, get his dick all hard, let him suit up, and then seconds away from him tappin' dat ass, say you thought you were ready. I was content and on my way in my house with the kiss you'd given me. You were the one that came back leading me on. If you would've brought your ass on home, I would be at my house right now chillin', instead of here with blue balls, a hard dick, and mad as hell."

"Calm down. I wanted this at first, but I don't now. Get dressed, and I'll take you home."

"Calm down? Get Dressed? You ain't about to treat me like no bitch. I'll get dressed, and I'm gon' leave with some damn dignity."

"Stop trippin', I'll take you home since I picked you up."

"Carrington, call me a cab. I swear, you ain't about to take me nowhere."

She called me a cab, and I left her house heated. I vowed that I'd never speak to Carrington again, but after she got settled in at school, she called to apologize about the incident. She said that after speaking with Derrick, she realized that she was wrong about being with me.

"Prince, I didn't want to sacrifice my relationship with Derrick or our friendship. Had we been intimate, later I would have been highly confused. We also might have destroyed our bond. Plus, our sexual encounter would have been nothing more than us fucking, and I've always wanted more from you."

"There wouldn't have been any confusion on my behalf," I replied.

"Well, there would've been some for me, which is why I stopped us both from making a big mistake."

I could have easily handled the one night of passion with her because I was a true P by nature. Man, I would've **pushed** up inside of her, **put** in some real work, brought her some **painful pleasure,** and **pressed** on to the next **potential piece** of **pussy** without any regrets.

# 11

## Life without Parole

A week before I returned to school for my senior year, my trial started. My attorney convinced me to go with a Bench trial, suggesting that he was sure that the judge would rule in my favor. After the prosecutor presented his evidence, I started to think Mr. Kennedy's advice was incorrect. My gut was uneasy from the evidence presented, so I was thinking maybe I should've gone with a Jury trial. It didn't seem like the Bench was going to rule in my favor at all. Judge Randall appeared to be in a foul mood from the beginning of my hearing until the end. I could tell he was fed up with the increase in juvenile criminals. If he found me guilty, he was not going easy on me. I don't know what I was thinking when I allowed my future to be decided by one instead of twelve. But I guess I was too trusting of my counsel. Like a sucka, that joker licked me, and then threw me to the dogs.

The prosecutor and the Detroit Police Department were trying to hang me by my nut sac. They brought in all kinds of youthful offenders as witnesses. Two ended up testifying against me. Joey North and Delvon Stevenson testified that while I was in Juvie Hall with them, I confessed to killing Raymond Johnson. They sat up on the witness stand building a hell of a story against me. But I didn't even know them cats. Though I'd seen them on my floor in the detention center a few times, I never said anything to them about my charges. I don't know what kind of BS they were on, but for them to be working for the prosecutor, someone had to have offered them one hell of a plea bargain or something. I knew I hadn't confessed to anything that was gon' get me life. But those dirty bastards pulled all kinds of false testimonies out of their hats. The prosecutor won a guilty verdict even with Zena's testimony in my defense.

"Mr. Prince, please stand for the reading of the verdict." Judge Randall stated. When I stood, my knees felt weak as butterflies accumulated in my stomach. I looked back at my family, and everyone's expression was etched in my mind. Bean was sitting with her hands in front of her face, GG was tearing, Daddy Ruenae was consoling her, Silk was calm, but biting his nails, and Ant walked out of the courtroom. I turned to face the judge, then carefully listened as he read the verdict.

"Mr. Prince, you have been found guilty on the charge of First Degree Murder. I hereby sentence you to the Michigan Department of Corrections for the duration of your natural life without the possibility of parole."
As his words flowed from his mouth, I listened in shock.

Bean started crying out loud. As I stood to be shackled, tears fell from my eyes when I heard GG scream out in pain, *"A Prince in chains! My Prince in Chains! Lord, I ain't never wanted to see none of my children like this, especially not my baby. Protect my boy, Lord. He doesn't deserve this. He's a child, Mr. Randall. You have convicted the wrong man. I hope you can live with yourself."* Daddy Ruenae had to escort her out of the courtroom. He was crying himself, which I'd never seen. Before going out into the lobby, GG turned and said, "Pray, Prince. Be strong. Only God can undo this mess. We'll get you out of this, Baby. Just keep praying." The pain in her words made me cry even harder.

"Mr. Prince, is there anything you want to say," Judge Randall asked.

"Yes." I replied. I looked at Ray's family to express my sympathy. "I'm sorry for your loss, but I'm not guilty. Mrs. Johnson, I didn't kill Ray. I never would have done anything like that to him. He was my daughter's uncle and a friend to me. I'm not that cold-hearted."

I sat back down and afterwards the judge allowed my mother to say goodbye. When she walked over to hug me, she sobbed her heart out. I had never seen her in that kind of pain, but it was clearly evident that she really loved me. Finally, Silk had to pry her away from me when the guards told her our time was up. Without a second look, I turned to be escorted out of the courtroom. I didn't get to see Ant before I walked out, but once I got into the police car to be transported to the county, I noticed him wiping his eyes on the courthouse steps.

I spent twelve days at the county before I rode out. On Monday, September 9, 1986, I was put in leg irons, and my wrists were shackled to belly chains. "Move out! This female officer shouted as this big black male officer escorted me to a Wayne County Sheriff's transportation van. As I focused on pacing myself to keep from falling on my face, he silenced me along with a few other guys riding out that day. I was headed to Ionia, Michigan, to begin serving my time at Riverside Correctional Facility. That was the facility that housed all male offenders ages 16 and up for quarantine.

Before I left the county, I was informed by some of the habitual offenders that I would probably go right up the street to the Michigan

Reformatory after quarantine. That place had been named Gladiator School for new arrivals, and until you go through the Michigan penal system, you can't really understand the hype of Gladiator School.

As I climbed aboard the van, I asked one of the officers to loosen my handcuff. They felt as though they were completely cutting off my circulation. He looked at me and laughed as though I had just performed some stand up comedy, but refused to accommodate my request. "Move to the back of the van and sit down," he rudely shouted. *Damn, a nigga got to be tortured on this long ass van ride. I know I got some kind of rights in this system,* I thought before going off.

"Man, these damn cuffs are tight." I yelled.

"Let me see your wrist." The officer asked. "I don't see any bite marks yet, so they look fine to me. Now move to the back of the van."

Once I was seated, and the van pulled away from the facility, some of the older offenders riding in with me started telling horror stories about being locked down. Each of them had several war stories that seemed embellished to the max. They also felt it necessary to insist that I be careful once I made it to the other side of the prison walls. I don't know if they were trying to frighten me, but I was scared to death. I tried to be hard to avoid appearing like a punk. I talked major noise to them all, vowing that I would defend my manhood at all cost. Due to my size, a few of them laughed at me. They thought I was playing, referring to me as a Small Fry, but I was serious.

"Li'l nigga who you gon' do?" One of them asked.

"Anybody that fucks with me, including you. I ain't taking no shit from nobody just because I'm small. I swear, I'll die to maintain my dignity if it comes to that." I ignorantly replied.

After a while, I tried to tune out the four professional convicts that accompanied me on the ride that afternoon. I began to focus on another young fellow just like myself. His name was Louis Curtis. He was seventeen-years-old and had been convicted for Distribution of a Controlled Substance. He was apprehensive about talking to anyone, and didn't have a lot of conversation during our ride to Riverside. I focused on a few dark, gloomy clouds that lined the sky, questioning myself. I wondered if I should've told on my brother. *Naa, Ant would have done the same for Silk or me,* I thought before altering my thoughts all together.

While daydreaming, the bite from the steel handcuffs ripped into my wrist with each bump in the road and hurt like hell. Once I considered that I better take in as much scenery as I possibly could, the pain didn't seem to matter as much. I knew it would be an extremely long time before I ventured anywhere in the free world again. As I thought about all I had sacrificed, my heart felt most regretful when I thought about my daughter being raised without her father. Sure I planned to one day win an appeal or even a new trial, but the reality of my situation made me feel sorry for myself. In the meantime, Asia would lack experiencing the real beauty of enjoying her daddy's love.

I looked over at Louis once again, noticing sweat beading down his face like rain on a chemically treated windshield. I could tell that terror was getting the best of him. His constant fidgeting was a clear indication that his fear of the unknown was tormenting him like crazy. I wanted to tell him to get his shit in check before we arrived because prison was no place for the weak or the weak-minded. Instead, I stayed to myself because that was best for me. As the van pulled into the Inmate Assessment and Reception parking lot, I noticed the perimeter security system the state had in place. It consisted of two 12-foot fences with razor-ribbon wire, an electronic perimeter detection system, gun towers, and a patrol vehicle with armed personnel. *All of this to detain an inmate,* I thought. "What a hell of a way to live for the rest of your life," I said to Louis. That's when an older inmate named Freddy B started laughing.

"Welcome to quarantine. This is the first stop before you get to tour Gladiator School," he yelled to bring a new degree of fear to all first-timers.

"Man, what the hell does that mean? All I've been hearing about is this Gladiator School, what's that?" I asked.

"Li'l partner, you're about to do one of three things in convict terms once you get in there. You'll Buck, Fuck, or Lock Up," he laughed.

"What?"

"In English that means you're either going to fight to keep your dignity, get that young ass of yours taken or go on protective custody to survive the rut of the dungeons." Louis was frantic, but I knew older convicts inflated the content of their stories to seem wise or gain respect from younger inmates. Freddy was no different.

I watched the electronic gates slowly close after the van was already parked by the entrance. The next thing I noticed was this large steel door opening like the mouth on a garbage truck would to receive trash. Louis and I eased to the front of the van to have our leg irons unchained. Once we stepped out, they removed our belly harnesses, leaving us in nothing but handcuffs. Finally, we were shuffled to the door and delivered like human cargo to two awaiting prison guards. I massaged the imprints on my wrist that ached from the cuffs digging into my flesh. I pushed my cuffs forward to provide a little slack while entering the facility. As I made it inside the prison, I remember passing the first Guard Control Center. It was a highly secure room with all kinds of colorful switches and buttons that caught my attention. We were escorted to a small holding cell and crammed in with twenty other new arrivals. I sat on one of the steel benches that contained a few rust stains and chipped gray paint. It was the last seat in the holding tank, and a tiny space at that. Louis found himself standing for over two hours. After his legs became tired, he eventually sat on the hard cement floor.

Some of the men that came in after us were standing around for hours. Ultimately, most of the guys in the tank found themselves sleeping to pass time. I stared at this one guy in amazement for a minute. I considered how skilled he had to have been to be standing and in a deep sleep at the same time. *Hum, my man got skills, and if he falls, I'm gon' laugh at his retarded ass,* I thought, continuing to look at him.

At some point, the stench of musty bodies became top dog in the holding tank. For some reason, there was this particular smell that most inmates shared. Everyone that rode in that day carried the scent of their past institution in their jumpsuit. When I scanned the room to observe my surroundings, I noticed Louis anxiously tapping on the floor. By this time, he was sitting sandwiched between two older, hard looking convicts.

Finally, a red neck guard wobbled to the door, looking like Miss Piggy's brother. He started screaming out instructions for us to follow, and the inhumane treatment inmates endured was about to reveal itself to me.

"Okay, Girl Scouts, you're about to become a number. In about twenty minutes your name won't mean shit to me. Whoever you were, whatever you did in the world, no longer matters to DOC. You're in prison now. You will be treated according to your actions, and you can do your time or let your time do you. Once your name is called, follow me, and don't say anything unless you're asked a direct question. Do I make myself clear?" I wasn't about to say anything because at that time, I thought a guard's orders was the law. In a matter of seconds, some of the older inmates quickly taught me something totally different. A few of them rattled off obscenities to the guard, but he was used to the convicts being disrespectful, so he ignored their comments and called two names. "Curtis and Prince," he screamed. After we made our way to the door, he led the two of us to an adjoining processing area. Two different guards took over from there. "Strip down to your birthday suits." They ordered, after uncuffing us. *Butt ass naked,* I thought before unzipping my county jumpsuit to remove it.

As our jumpsuits rested on the only table in the room, orders started flowing like crazy.

"Okay boys, I need for you to bend and spread your butt cheeks for a cavity search. Now, squat, cough, and lift your nut sacs. Raise your arms, open your mouths, lift your tongues, and now finally your feet." I was floored. I felt highly degraded, humiliated, and very overwhelmed with the intake process. Though it was not uncommon for inmates to hide contraband in their rectum, I wasn't one to be sticking anything in my ass. That little process sucked. I wished there had been a different way to do that particular part of assessment. To me, there was a hidden agenda with the ass searches. Its real purpose was to make convicts aware of the fact early on that they had little to no rights. It also made me aware of the fact that the affiliates of the Michigan penal system would become the primary decision makers of my future until further advised. Since they wanted to assess somebody, I felt like telling all those damn guards to huff my sweaty balls, and lick my black ass. Those legal, overpaid violators knew the perfect way to strip a real man of his self-respect was to belittle him by looking up in his ass while he held it open like a bitch.

After being on display for about twelve long minutes, we were then allowed to shower, issued some underwear, a set of "State Blues," and some cheap, black tuxedo shoes. From there we went to the photo room to have our prison ID taken. I couldn't believe they wrapped a chain around my neck that obtained my DOC number like I was a dog. Later, I was fingerprinted and finally sent to medical for a check up.

"Mr. Prince, this is your prison identification card. It is to be carried on you at all times. If you are ever asked to produce your ID and you are unable to, please note that it is a major infraction of the rules developed by the prison administration. You can and will be disciplined for that violation." *Disciplined for not having my ID? Damn! How dumb,* I thought, moving to stand by a wall.

Having completed the initial intake process, me and some of the other guys were escorted to our new living facilities in the Reception Guidance Center. This area is where quarantine took place. While I was held there, it was the officers' mission to mold me into an ideal prisoner. That's where they taught me about the rules of the environment I'd be calling home.

Once I was inside the prison block, I noticed officers enclosed in various stations throughout the prison. The first station issued me my cell number. As I walked through the Guidance Center, I was breathless. That area was a large cellblock that housed several inmates. It kind of reminded me of something I'd observed when Carrington and I went to the zoo, "Caged Animals." I was shocked at the manner in which the facility was set up. As I passed through the block, suddenly a burst of noise hovered over my head like a swarm of bees about to execute a vicious attack on the intruder of their precious honeycomb. Instantly, I started to feel extremely ill at the stomach from the comments being shouted at me. However, I tried to choke back my worries to prevent them from sensing my fear. I knew I couldn't come off as scared. There were too many convicts in the house who preyed on the weakness of others for me to be bitching out.

"Hey li'l Pretty Nigga, if you need some protection holla at me. I'll take care of you," this one six-foot, three-hundred-pound, mean looking black nigga hollered at me.

"Ooooo Weeeee! What's up, Handsome? Billie Jean's the name. If you're looking to rough ride or pound into something tight, look me up. It's gon' be a minute before you get to pound up in some real fish again, so you got to get it off somehow." I looked and kept walking. "For real, Sexy, if your Willie needs to spillie, you better come on and holla at Billie. I got this deep throat fo' ya', and I promise you won't be disappointed." *Is his Bitch Ass crazy? I ain't with that sissy shit period,* I thought, mugging him until he was out of my view.

Finally, right before I reached my cell on the opposite end of the guard station, I saw Raynard Hicks. He was one of Ant's associates from the hood, and a veteran inmate himself.

"P, what's up my guy? Welcome to hell. You better get ready for Gladiator School li'l Mellow. By the time you make it to MR you got to be ready to buck, fuck, or lock up. I'm square business. You're a little small for this block. Brothas gon' test you, try to make you they bitch or send you to protective custody. I hope you got the nuts to endure the initiation process of prison 'cause only the strong-minded and the fit gon' survive in this system."

Though Raynard was older than me, I was a little relieved to see him. As I made it to my cell, the doors slowly closed behind me. I sat on my hard bunk thinking about what I had really done to myself. All the tales about the "Belly of the Beast" had not prepared me one bit for prison. At the age of sixteen, I had become a man. No more depending on Bean, GG, Silk, Ant, and Daddy Ruenae. *Damn Prince, what have you gotten yourself into now?* I thought as I sat looking around my mysterious cold cell. Here I was sitting in my new home. It was a small space, with a hard, narrow bunk and a 3 by 6 footlocker. I hated my living conditions. DOC didn't do much to make a brotha comfortable either. I had a steel desk, toilet, and sink in my cell that helped me understand they didn't plan for me to be comfortable either. "There's no turning back at this point, Prince," I whispered. I was too young to even realize what my foolish loyalty had done to my life. In time, I understood why it wasn't always beneficial for a man to go down or out for his homie, and after losing everything, I discovered that the same rule sometimes applies to a sibling as well. Prison forced me to reflect and realize that my life had real purpose. It's a damn shame my self-value didn't matter to me long before I was forced to spend the rest of my life doing time.

*If these walls could talk, I wonder what they would tell me about those who came before me. Did they survive this shit? Did they get tormented or raped by other inmates? Were they sentenced to serve the rest of their natural lives in prison, like I had been? And for those that had the opportunity to parole, did they make it to the parole board with their mental capacity in check?* These were all questions I asked myself 'cause my mind was going a million miles a minute. As night fell, I tried to think about everything but my family. Thoughts of them made my eyes water like crazy. At times, I cried hard, but silently. I didn't want the other men to hear me. Good thing I locked alone 'cause I know I soiled my pillowcases that night with many tears. Had the other inmates been able to see the way I carried on, they would have concluded that I was a trick for sure. One thing I learned about prison is that some of the toughest killers and the hardest brothas cry at night in the dark.

Louis was locking right next to me. That first night, I occasionally considered hollering over at him to ask if he was tight. Since we were both new to the block, I didn't want to jeopardize our safety by exposing our fears to the untamed wolves that might've been listening. I was afraid to say anything that evening. Finally, I laid on my bunk. All of a sudden, I started tossing and turning. I couldn't get comfortable for the longest. Again, thoughts of Asia came to mind, which caused me to cry all over. That night, I cried 'til my eyes were swollen, which eventually made me fall asleep.

The next morning, I was awaken by the sound of bunks sliding across the floor. I could hear the clicking of the officers' keys as they made their rounds for the first count of the day. While they ensured that every inmate was accounted for and all cells were cleaned, I swiftly made up my bed. I was clueless as to what my first day of prison would be like. I knew I was on spook after fearing that the guards would give me a ticket 'cause my bed wasn't done by the time they made it to my cell. Before anything else could happen, I kneeled down on the side of my bed to pray. My grandfather had always instilled Christian principles in me. I just rarely used them. It amazed me that the only time I could spend some quality time with G...O...D is when I found myself in trouble. One thing for certain, prison was going to teach me to depend on a higher being more often. It was also going to teach me to call on Him at all times, not just when I needed Him due to everything being so uncertain in the joint.

September 10 was going to be my first full day in prison. I didn't want to cause any problems nor did I want to encounter any. When the officer reached my door, I asked what time it was. I wasn't used to being unaware of the time. Huh, how we take things for granted until they're taken away. Since I didn't have an alarm clock or a watch, I quickly discovered that little shit like something as simple as keeping up with the time was a big deal to the average inmate.

"It's 5:50 in the morning. The doors will open at 6AM. Be standing in front of your door as soon as it opens and ready to step out," he stated.

While waiting, I peered into the unknown world right outside my entranceway. I could see the movement of an inmate that was housed about fifty feet across from me. I found myself staring at him, which later, I felt a little guilty about invading his privacy. Yet, in time I would learn that "Intrusiveness" was the nickname for the Department of Corrections and inmates alike. The lack of privacy was something that I had to quickly adjust to. With prison, there would always be someone invading my space, be it other inmates or officers.

When the doors slid back, I apprehensively stepped out. I looked to my left and then to my right, noticing other men forming a line. Louis fell in line about ten feet behind me. Though I was clueless as to where the line was going, I ended up following the others to the chow hall for breakfast. Once we had our trays, we located a table and sat down.

"Louis, tell me a little bit about yourself." He hesitantly looked, which helped me realize that questioning him wasn't a good thing. He stopped all casual communication, and then refused to share any of his business. About fifteen minutes into our meal, Raynard walked over to our table to sit with us.

"What's up, Li'l Playa? What the hell are you doing in the joint?"

"Man, I caught a Murder One charge. My judge was on some bullshit. The prosecution came in with some lames that claimed I confessed to killing Raymond Johnson to them. That's a lie though. I was cheaply framed like one of those dollar store pictures. The judge sent me to this place on some BS."

"Man, I 'mon tell you right now. Don't tell anyone else your story. Talk as little about your conviction as possible, it'll be helpful in the end." Raynard warned me. "If the con's think you're a killer, let 'em. It sometimes works in your favor."

"Okay." I replied without further questioning him.

"Do you know who the guys were that testified against you?" he asked.

"They're two cats I sat in Juvie Hall with. Joey North and Delvon Stevenson."

"Why they testify against you?"

"Man, you got me. I have no idea as to why they'd set me up like that, but they did."

Right as Raynard was about to ask additional questions, the feeling of someone taxing our conversation interrupted us. He couldn't help his paranoia, I believed because he had already been in once, watching his back was simply in his nature. We both cautiously started scanning the chow hall. Immediately, the two of us were on the lookout for adversaries. Raynard had so many enemies from the streets that he had to literally watch his back at all times. I turned to look as well, considering that I might want to start watching my back again, too. My eyes instantly locked in on this thinning brother with a familiar face. This Cat was in a wheel chair and was viciously staring me down.

"What the hell?" I stated as my mind concluded that the person I was looking at was Charles Casey. "Damn, I thought that nigga died." I said out loud to no one in particular.

"What did you say, Man?" Raynard asked.

"Man, the guy about four tables behind us. We were beefin' on the outside. Him, his brother, and a few of their boys killed some of my crew. He's in that wheel chair as a result of one of my connections."

"Well P, I know you ain't worrying about no nigga that's paralyzed. If he tries anything, just from the love I got for Silk, Man, I got your back."

"You know my Uncle?" I asked with a look of shock completely covering my face.

"Hell, Yeah. Silk put me on when all those other lames were shooting me to the left. None of them wanna be ballas gave me a chance. Silk showed me love, got me fresh, and made sure I had a place to live after my mother and father went to the joint together. They were sentenced to serve 35 years of fed time. After they got caught up, I didn't have nobody."

"What spot were you working?"

"As far as the house I held down, I can't tell you all that. Silk got a few underground joints that very few people know about. He had me working one of his most elite spots. I served his more upscale clients out of my spot."

"Why he have you working his best spot and not my brother?"

"Because when my parents went down for Silk, he told them he was gon' look out for me, and that's how he did it. He didn't want to put me in no spot that required I stay mad strapped. Now as far as the president of Ida goes over there in that wheelchair, don't sweat him."

"Ida?"

"Yeah, the Impotent Dick Association."

"Boy, you're a fool." I said laughing. "Now, tell me about these upscale clients you served?"

"You know, doctors, lawyers, city officials, and anyone else of status that was smoking on the down low." *Damn, Silk got some underground spots. I wonder why he didn't have Ant, T or Melvin working any of those spots.* I thought before responding.

"I never knew my uncle was ballin' like that." I expressed with a curious look on my face.

"Yeah, it's a lot of stuff you and your family probably don't know about Silk. Out of my loyalty for him, I won't divulge his business either."

I was cool with that because I knew my uncle didn't tell all his business to anyone. I wasn't that trusting of most people either. However, I really felt a little better about locking on the same unit with Raynard. After ending our conversation, I could once again feel some discomfort from stares. I looked back one last time to check my back, and Charles was talking with a few of his guys at the table. They all suddenly looked up at me almost in unison. I knew from the looks on their faces that within a matter of time a riot between them and me was certain.

"What's up, Playa? Why you looking so uneasy? I told you not to worry. I got your back and I mean that. I'll go check all them chumps right now if you want me to." Raynard informed me, standing to go over to their table.

"Man, just chill for the moment. Allow me to get a few days of prison under my belt before I start trying to make a name for myself."

"Prince, I don't like that clique already. I guarantee you if anything jumps off, we're gon' kick ass together," he stated, hesitantly sitting back down.

I knew right then that I had to formulate a plan of action. Silk always told me, 'Never let them see you sweat, and always leave the round table with something accomplished.' I was pissed off about that nigga bringing unnecessary drama into my life at such an early stage of my incarceration. Despite the fact that I tried to dodge Charles as much as possible in the free world, he was going to force me to show him that I wasn't the lame he assumed I was. Psychologically, I knew I had to be a beast in the new world forced upon me in order to survive, so that's what I groomed myself for.

As we got up to put our trays in the window, Louis finally spoke up.

"I got your back, too."

"What you say, Doc?"

"I said I'm rolling with you, if it's necessary."

*Maybe Louis really got a little heart after all,* I thought, heading back to the block. Where his sudden loyalty for me came from was unknown. If he really had my back, time was gon' tell in the end.

After weeks of adjusting to prison life, Louis, Raynard, and I were getting pretty cool. We often sat around on the block swapping stories about our day in the world. Most of all we talked about how we missed the fresh scent of a woman.

One evening after count, I was heading to chow when some simp down with Charles yelled threats out to me. "Man's going down on the block today," he said, pointing at me. I don't know if he was trying to send a warning or intimidate me. Either one, I heard him and took heed to what he was saying. Raynard got heated and replied before I could. "Nigga, if anyone's going down, it's gon' be you."

When we got to chow, we stood in line to get our food like normal. I made sure I never sat with my back to Charles, which was the only thing I had done differently after learning he was at the same prison. While walking to the table, Charles watched me the entire time, occasionally making gestures as if he was stabbing someone. I nodded at him a few times, giving him this look to insinuate, "Try me and try to survive my wrath." I know he thought I had Kool-Aid flowing through my veins 'cause I appeared to always be running from him in the world. What he obviously forgot is that we were no longer in the world. If he fucked with me, I was determined that he was gon' regret his decision to bring our beef to the joint.

Raynard was so ready to get at him. I can't count the number of times I had to talk him down. "Ray, I'm mentally ready to do what I got to do." I said, meaning I'd prepared my mind for murder if it had to be that way. "But for now, I'm gon' play it cool until I have no other choice but to do something different." He was cool with that, so we let it go for the time being.

Charles and his crew finished eating before we did. I couldn't believe after all my talk to Ray about chilling out that punk tried to check me. After he put up his tray, he had the nerve to roll his wheelchair over to my table.

"What up, Pussy? I see we finally meet again. I knew I was gon' have a chance to see you once more. I just didn't know it would be this soon," he stated.

"What you want with me, Handy Man?" I tauntingly asked, laughing at him. "Why are you over here in my face talking shit to me? You couldn't possibly think that you're about to kick my ass. That is if you can kick at all." I smiled, looking at his legs. "Man, can you even lift up them twisted, lifeless looking motherfucka's period?"

"Nigga, even in this wheelchair I'm still D.R.E.A. Detroit's Rawest Exterminator Alive. Bitch, I'm like a real plague. I will haunt you down, get all over you like a germ, and kill you just like I did your boys. Seconds after they stood in my window begging for their lives, I put an affliction on those weak niggas they'll never forget. You either. Those punks stood in my face trying to compromise with me. When they saw I wasn't budging, they tried to get hard, and go out like men. Once they found themselves looking down the barrel of my piece, they humbled up a bit. But shit, I ain't got no patience or no mercy for no bitch ass niggas. That's why I shot your one homie dead in his eye, then drug him halfway down the street like garbage."

*No this Wimp ain't sitting in my face telling me in detail how he murdered my boys,* I thought, before picking up my tray to repeatedly smack him in the face with it. On contact, his nose bled heavier than a slaughtered pig. Instantly, blood ran down his lips, eventually getting all over his shirt and pants. He started trying to swing on me, but there wasn't much he could do confined to his wheelchair. Finally, he ended up falling out of his chair. That's when Raynard and Louis started kicking him in the face. Some of Casey's boys intervened after the fact. His boy Big Man, punched me so hard in my jaw, I swear I saw every shape in a box of Lucky Charms cereal before finally regaining my composure.

I don't know where the officers were that day because I should have been placed on lock down, but I wasn't. I was told that CO's sometimes turned their heads, and let inmates rumble until death. Since we were all still fairly new to the system, I think someone should have intervened. Somebody paid somebody off 'cause I later heard that I was supposed to go out in a body bag that day. Even if I would have turned up dead, I'm glad no guards intervened. That gave me a chance to beat the hell out of Charles, and let him know I meant business, so he better step, oops, roll to me with caution.

After that fight, I often saw Charles and his boys in chow, but he stayed away from me. I thank God he didn't die that day or I'd be serving a legitimate life sentence. He and his boys probably didn't think much of me prior to our altercation, but I know one thing they concluded after I waxed Casey with that tray is that I wasn't the pussy they thought I'd be. That was also the day they learned to respect what the fear of prison and going to "Gladiator School" could bring out of a new inmate.

I was released from quarantine into general population at Riverside in mid October 1986. I was housed on J-Block and stunned at the manner in which the state saved money on everything, including electricity. The long halls were dimly lit or I guess I should say the light bulbs were spaced so far apart that the unit appeared to be dimly lit either way, lighting was a problem. I noticed several men looking out at me as I walked by. Some of them used their "Hawks" to get a better view of the new man on the block.

A Hawk was nothing more than a mirror an inmate used to see down the walk outside of their cells. Unlike quarantine, this floor was extremely quiet. *Where's all the taunting chatter that went on in the back,* I thought, carrying my bedding to my cell. I later learned that officers discouraged talking amongst the inmates on the block. To maintain order, they frequently threatened to write misconducts or tickets for disobeying the rules. After the officers left the noise resumed. I heard one inmate scream out, "Yo, who's the new fish on the block?"

*I ain't no damn fish,* I thought, standing in my doorway to check out my new surroundings. Suddenly, I noticed this slightly older guy named Everett Storey. I'd served some county time with him. Everett, was from Atlanta Georgia, so he was a long way from home to be serving time. He came to Detroit to visit his extended family and got nabbed. He had a girlfriend in the city who convinced him to stay longer than he anticipated. Initially, he lived with his auntie; however after a few months, she told him that she and her husband were not about to have no grown man living on them. Two months later they put him out. He worked a few low paying jobs to survive the financial demands of a big city. But, he was barely making ends meet. After always being broke and observing the flashy living of the trendsetters in the D, Everett was forced to consider making some fast money. He hooked up with some of his girl's knucklehead cousins, only to become the fall guy for a few of their charges. E later caught some distribution charges while on probation, which landed him in the Michigan penal system. Before leaving the county, I never found out what kind of time he received. I rode out for Riverside the same day his trial ended. Though I rarely concerned myself with another man's business, E was pretty cool.

"Yo, E. What kind of time you looking at or did them sorry bastards railroad you like they did me?"

"Man, they hit me with five to fifteen. I hope to be paroled after three, but that might be wishful thinking."

"Don't hold your breath," I suggested, before providing an example of my brother's first experience with DOC.

# 12

## *Gladiator School*

In May 1987, Riverside had problems with overcrowding, so I didn't stay in general population very long. After a few months, a group of us were shipped up the street to the Michigan Reformatory. Now that damn place was one of the ugliest facilities I'd ever seen in my life. It sat high on a hill, and the closer you got to it, the more it favored a haunted castle featured in a scary movie. I was praying that Gladiator School would be a short tour for me. It was a horrid site for the eyes, let alone a place I wanted to call home for any amount of time.

Gladiator School was worse than I expected. From day one, niggas tested me. Short and tall niggas, skinny and fat niggas, young and old niggas, and hardcore and soft niggas, all tried to call me out. Everybody wanted to try the new man on the block, and that's where they fucked up. Though I was small in size, I wasn't nobody's punk. That first week was like a living hell. I fought and fought and fought and fought. My knuckles were sore, my body was bruised, and my tooth even got slightly chipped from getting hit in the mouth with some rocks in a sock. On the sixth day of my first week, I wasn't taking on any more challenges, so I did the damn fool. This chump name Relo tried to call me out in the weight pit, and I took to that sucka like I was his pimp. I grabbed my towel, wrapped a weight in it, and beat that nigga almost to death. When the guards came in, everybody acted as though they didn't know anything and Relo knew better than to tell. All I can say is that I'm glad I handled things the way I did because after that, I was one of the top Gladiators on my block and got mad respect because I would Buck with the best of them to keep from getting fucked or locked up.

Bean and Ant came out to see me the same weekend I moved to general population. I walked into the visitation room, bearing phat hugs for my family. Bean started her body searches, which had become one of her routine missions during every visit. It was so common for her to hug me and then immediately start searching me for scars. Once she found anything resembling bruises or cuts, she instantly questioned me about how I obtained them. After giving her explanations on each, she always cried due to the harm she feared I was facing. Her tears that day caused me to be hesitant about telling the truth on future visits. For a while, she thought the officers were beating me up. There were times when she would literally ask them if that was the case.

"Come on, Bean, I'm fine. You don't need to worry about me. I learned to survive long before I came here," I remarked, trying to reassure her.

"Prince, sometimes you appear to be too tranquil about your situation."

"Bean, I'm trying to prevent time from doing me while I fight to survive the rigorous trials of prison. If I want to ever make it home alive, I've got to have that mentality. Hell, it's real killers in here with nothing else to lose. They're serving life sentences, so what do they care about doin' a li'l nigga like me. Nothing! I can't even show a human side in this place 'cause that's a sign of weakness."

I looked over at Ant who was quiet. He didn't interject much of anything during that visit. I could tell my bruises bothered him after Bean exposed them all. I'm sure he was probably wondering what in the hell he'd allowed me to do? In spite of their stress, I tried to keep the visit going. Once they were ready to leave, I hugged Ant.

"Man, don't worry about me. I'm maintaining."

"Don't worry! P, that's virtually impossible."

"Man, I'm serious, don't worry about me. I'm the keeper of the Prince now," I insisted as he shot a half ass smile at me.

"I can't help but worry, this isn't your crime. You're not supposed to be here, I am. Plus, I've always looked out for you. The fact that I can't right now, kills me. You hang in there and we gon' get you out of here."

There was so much on my mind that I didn't look back after exiting the visiting room that afternoon. Whenever I returned to my cell, I took a little time to reflect on what my life had once been. The bars that secured me in my cell quickly reminded me that my life no longer went beyond the prison walls or the razor wire. Sometimes after seeing my family, I would feel sorry for myself. I was so emotionally worn down that afternoon that all I wanted to do was relax on my bunk and think about my misfortune.

♦♦♦♦♦♦♦

Over the years, looking at calendars became harder for me. Most brothas were marking off days to count down their time, which was a reality check for me because that often reminded me that I was serving a life sentence without parole. As the years passed, and I matured, I spent my birthday and most holidays deprogramming myself. Actually, I really didn't have much of a choice. I knew if I didn't, it was going to be extremely hard for me to stomach being away from everyone during those festive times.

Raynard, Everett, and I were still locking at the same prison and had become like brothers over the years. Louis was still there too, but he was different. I can't explain it, but he wasn't a part of the brotherhood, though he was a part of our clique. As time went on, we encountered a few more fights, some enemies, and an occasional ticket or two. For some reason, we were still able to avoid solitary confinement or what we called, "the hole." I didn't know why, but something was working in my favor. Maybe my boys were looking out for me with the Big Man from Heaven.

In 1988, a few days before my eighteenth birthday, we were chilling on the yard, talking much noise. Like always, the four of us frequently positioned ourselves where we could watch the others' back. I was sitting on a bench with my back towards the main entrance, telling one of my worldly stories. Big Man walked up on me tripping like I was his trick.

"What up, Pussy? You look like you recovered nicely from that last beat down I put on you."

"Yeah, and you look like you recovered from that split eye I gave you. When did you get your stitches out?" I asked without smiling. "Oh, and the knot you got from that chair I took upside yo' head seems to have gone down nicely, too."

"You caught me slipping, but that won't ever happen again. The next time you get that close to me, Bitch, you'll be giving me head?"

"I ain't the Bitch up in this joint. You may want to go holla at one of these real sissies with that nonsense 'cause I ain't no punk, and you ain't about to make me one."

"We'll see."

"We'll see my ass. And while you still have a pulse, you better move around or at least get the hell out my face. Oh, and by the way, don't you ever disrespect me like this again or it's gon' be some consequences." I said, giving him direct eye contact.

"Consequences?" He repeated, before one of the officers motioned for him to move to another area. "We gon' continue this later. You better watch your ass 'cause I am," he replied, pointing at me.

"Man, I'm gon' defend my manhood to whatever extent I have to. You better recognize that I ain't to be fucked with. Bring it if you want to, but be prepared to leave here in a body bag."

"Ain't no li'l fifty pound nigga sending me home in a body bag," he laughed.

I listened to his threats, thinking *When I came to prison, I knew I was gon' have to be on top of my survival tactics.* I'd mentally prepared myself to do whatever I needed to do to maintain, therefore he was good as dead.

I looked at my boys with the most serious look I'd ever had in my life, "Big Man's getting done on the way to chow tonight." I didn't even bother to ask if they had my back. Actually, I didn't want them involved. If I got caught assaulting him, I was ready to go down alone.

After yard, I went to my cell. I meditated while waiting for count to end. I tried to get my mind prepared for committing a murder because I knew if I didn't kill dude, he was going to rape or kill me. I'd never killed anyone before, so I was somewhat apprehensive about taking a life. I knew if I didn't handle the bullshit, Big Man was gon' continue to torment me. I felt like my hands were tied, it was either him or me. Since I was the keeper of the Prince, I was sure it was gon' have to be him.

Once count ended, I walked out of my cell with my shank tucked in my sleeve. When I headed for the chow hall, there were several other inmates walking right along side me. I maneuvered my way right up behind Big Man, slowly easing my shank out of my sleeve to position it just right in my hand. When the line into the dining hall curved, it temporarily put us out of the officer's sight. I bumped into Big Man, shoving a sharpened spoon I'd made for protection into the side of his neck. I shoved it deep to make sure he died. I was spooked behind what I'd done. I didn't want to be fingered by anyone, so I kept moving with the crowd without ever looking back to avoid giving myself away.

My heart was racing extremely fast. I tried to remain as calm as possible to avoid looking guilty. Once I made it to the window, I noticed my hands shaking. I quickly grabbed a tray of food, trying to conceal what I'd done. I nervously walked to a table, took a seat, and prayed.

Louis and Raynard weren't far behind me. They'd both seen Big Man's body lying on the ground prior to entering the chow hall. Both of them had to literally step over or go around him to enter the room. When they caught up with me at the table, they didn't say anything about the incident, I didn't either. Suddenly, CO's entered the dining facility, informing all inmates that the entrance was being shut down where Big Man's body was lying. Everyone that was in the dining hall was shook down in an attempt to find weapons and his attacker. As a result of their hard work, the officers' efforts were to no avail. Big Man's death never produced an assailant.

No one wanted to get involved or name the attacker. Most inmates respected the Convict Code of Honor, which was "Mind your own business and keep your mouth shut." If the officers didn't see who committed the offense, shame on them. Getting killed in return for telling wasn't a fair trade for any prisoner. Before anybody was gon' say anything, the governor would have to guarantee brotha's their freedom. Big Man's life didn't mean that much to officials, and telling was a hell of a sacrifice for an inmate who had to remain locked up.

I had taken another man's life who was five times my size. Because it was so early in my stay, my victory was like a badge of honor. I was able to make a real name for myself as a little guy. Inmates didn't bother me much after that, which was fine with me. I was tired of fighting anyway. From that day forward, guys really respected me, and I gave respect in return.

In January 1989, after twenty months of what I considered hard time, my stay at M.R. and Gladiator School had finally come to an end. I packed up all my belongings, and once again left my prison comrades who had become like family to me. It was hard to up and leave the friends I'd grown to trust, but that was just one more thing about being incarcerated that a man had to adjust to. Carson City Correctional Facility became my new place of residence. Life there brought about entirely new trials, new tribulations, and was an adventurous journey in itself.

### *"Mail Call!"*

*January 28, 1989*

*Prince,*

*I got your letter last week and as always it's good to hear from you. Zena brought Asia over the other day. That girl is looking more and more like you. Boy, she's sharp as a whip. So why did they transfer you to Carson City? Were you getting into trouble at the Michigan Reformatory or was this move kind of like a reward for good behavior? Huh, I guess that sounds crazy to refer to a prison change as a reward. I probably should've asked if it's a better facility.*

*You're not going to believe this, but you're an Uncle. No, Hell Naw! KeKe hasn't had a baby. I'd kill her! Your brother's finally a daddy. And the real shocker is that he's excited about this baby. His son Anthony Lavell Prince II was born December 31, 1988. I know you're wondering why we didn't tell you before now. I guess it's a new family tradition to keep the pregnant girlfriend a secret until after the baby is born. He claims that he didn't say anything because he wanted to make sure Renee was on the up and up when she got pregnant.*

*By the way, Zena said I could bring Asia out to see you the next time I come. I thought I'd mention that to you in advance to allow you some time to think about that. I wanted to make sure it was okay with you first, since the last time you saw her was almost three years ago. KeKe sends her love. You take care, and call home when you get a chance.*

*Love you,*

*Bean*

February 14, 1989

Bean,

What's up, Baby? Damn, I can't believe I'm an uncle. Man, Ant has a son? Wow, I'm so surprised. Tell him I said what's up, and give him my blessings. So you saw my little angel and she's looking more like me? When I read that news in your letter, you don't know how much that made me smile. I'm really glad that you're able to see her. I know that's probably tough for Zena, but I admire her courage and willingness to stand up to her family so Asia can develop a relationship with us. Bean, I would love to see my beautiful daughter. Please make sure you bring her the next time you come to visit.

For the record, Carson City is much nicer than Riverside or MR, but no matter how nice the facility is, prison is prison. There are other stressors that constantly remind me of that fact regardless of how new or bug free a facility is.

How are you coming along with raising my appeal money? Ask Silk if he could make another donation. Shit, that's the least he could do, especially since he referred that bunk ass attorney who bogusly represented me to begin with. Hell, he should feel obligated to do something else to help me for that reason alone. With the representation I got from that simp, I almost think I was set up. Tell Ke I said hello and kiss Daddy Ruenae and GG for me. And I look forward to seeing you all real soon.

Lots of Love

Prince

Mail for me was very important. It was the one source of communication that kept me connected to my family. It also helped me remember that they knew I still existed. To receive good news from them was like a blessing. There were times between **visits** and **letters** when I felt a little forgotten, but whenever I had an opportunity to experience one or the other, it relieved my stress, and confirmed that my people still loved me.

In March 1989, Bean, Asia, Ant, and his son came out for a visit. I will never forget that visit because it was one of my most special ones. It was a few days before my daughter's fourth birthday. When I walked into the visiting room, my family was already seated. Bean started blowing me kisses as I made my way towards them. I started tearing as soon as I laid eyes on Asia, who was wearing a leopard print fur coat, and her hair was in twisties and a big afro-puff. She was so pretty and had blossomed even more since the last time I'd seen her. She had a head full of hair like her mama, and what touched me most was the fact that she knew exactly who I was as soon as I made it to my seat.

"Hi, Beautiful." I stated, lifting her into my arms for a kiss. "Do you know who I am?" I asked, hoping she would.

"Umm hum" She replied, smiling with a mouth full of little teeth.

"Who am I?" I asked.

"Daddy!"

My tears overwhelmed me when I looked into my Butterfly's smiling face and considered what I had actually deprived us of by doing time in Ant's place. Here I wanted to be loyal to my brother and not tell on him, but had overlooked the one person my loyalty really should have been focused on. Several times throughout our visit, I couldn't believe that I had sacrificed developing a meaningful relationship and bond with my very own offspring for the sake of my sibling.

As I sat looking on at Ant and my nephew, I wondered, once she got older, how I would ever explain my incarceration to her. How would or could I make her understand my thinking at the time I allowed myself to go on trial for Ant's charges. There was no way I could ever tell Asia that her uncle Anthony killed her uncle Ray over drugs. I figured if I ever told her about that, once she developed an understanding of life, she'd never accept me for my brother's actions. Therefore, I vowed I wouldn't ever tell her anything about that dark family secret.

While visiting, I could tell Asia was dying to be close to me. As we spent our first visit bonding, she just kept hugging on me. She was so articulate for her age, clearly expressed each of her points, and the girl carried on a full-fledged conversation like a little woman. *Zena exposes her to quite a bit,* I thought, watching her sit in my lap. Eventually, she stood behind my chair. With her head resting against mine, she hugged my neck. I felt pride and pain all in the same moment. Though, I recognized how blessed I was to have the opportunity to see my daughter. I didn't know how much I could do for her from prison, if anything. Considering the circumstances, I just knew I was going to do whatever I could from that point on to build the best relationship I possibly could with her.

I saw Asia five additional times throughout the year of 1989; my last visit with her that year was right after Christmas. It was the best visit I'd had since the beginning of my incarceration because my entire immediate family and a special guest also came out to celebrate the holiday with me that year. I was ecstatic about seeing my family, but Carrington was the one person that made that visit forever special in my mind. Oh yeah! Carrington came out to see me, stole my heart, and made me remember what I missed most about a black woman. "Hips and Ass!"

I rarely made it to the visiting room before my family because I always wanted to clean up, put on my clothing from the world, and look as good as I possibly could. However, for some reason, I didn't dress up for that visit. I just wore my state blues out to the visiting room. After the officer directed me to the area my family and I would occupy, I sat impatiently tapping my knee. While waiting, I looked out the glass window facing the visitors' entrance for Asia. Finally, Bean appeared, then I saw Asia, Ke, Ant, GG, Daddy Ruenae, and out of nowhere this image of beauty appeared, which I knew so well. I was certain that my eyes were deceiving me. *"Carrington,"* I thought before smiling real big. She gave me this soft wave from a distance that instantly sent me fantasizing. I couldn't believe what I was seeing, but what a wonderful Christmas present. I picked Asia up in my arms, kissing her on her forehead. While I expressed how glad I was to see her, I put everyone else on the back burner to ensure that my baby girl got her one-on-one time in first. Once I had a chance to touch the vision of beauty that stood before me, my dick stood at attention. Hell, it had been years since him or me felt a natural woman, so I wasn't surprised.

"Hey Baaaabeee!" Carrington echoed, hugging me.

"Hey, Sexy," I responded once we embraced. "Damn you're so beautiful! You smell good, too. I see college has really done something extraordinary for you, hasn't it?"

"I've always been fine. College has just shown me how to enhance what I was already working with. Now I'm the refined, superfine version of Carrington Horton."

"Superfine is right. I can see college was what you needed to blossom. You've gained a little weight, those breasts are still big as ever, and you got it goin' on. Beans and Cornbread must be the real deal down there in the south."

"Okay, Prince, cut it out!" she blushed.

"It's true, I can't help what I see. You know it's rare that we see beautiful, black women in here. All these chumps from my block gon' be asking about you later on today."

"Asking what?" she questioned.

"Shit like, who you are, and how you're related to me. So how did I rate this visit?" I asked, cheezing.

"I called your mother yesterday to find out how you were doing. Ant answered the phone. He told me that your family was coming to see you today for Christmas, so I asked if I could come along, and here I am."

"Prince, do you have any hugs for anyone else?" GG asked, looking at me like I was crazy because I'd forgotten about all of them.

"Oh, fa'sho! Sorry G, you know you're my baby. I wouldn't ignore you intentionally, Sweet Thang. This fine woman over here just had me distracted for a moment."

"Yeah, yeah, yeah! Whatever," she mumbled, kissing me on the cheek.

After my grandmother burst me out like she did, I knew I couldn't be all into Carrington and ignore my daughter and the rest of the family. I tried to equally distribute my attention to everyone, but my real interest was more on my sexy home girl. Carrington had my attention on lock.

"Prince, you want some snacks from one of the vending machines?" Ant asked, trying to get me a quick one-on-one with Carrington.

"Yeah, a burrito and a strawberry pop," I replied, without realizing what he was trying to do.

"Here you go, Carrington." Ant stated, handing her six dollars in quarters. "You and P go get him some snacks.

She walked over to the vending machines without me because I was talking with my grandfather. While she walked away, I focused on those hips and all that ass she had stuffed in her designer Guess jeans. I completely ignored Daddy Ruenae for a moment. Again, I hadn't seen a sexy black woman up close in years, so I was salivating like a wild dog.

"Ahhhh, what you say, Granddad?" I asked, realizing he was talking.

"Nothing Son, you better go get on that fine girl before one of these other deprived citizens up in here try to claim your prize," he suggested, bumping my arm for his approval to discontinue our conversation.

"Thanks!" I eagerly responded.

When I got up to make my way over to the vending machine, this little lady locked onto my side. Asia slid her small hand inside of mine as if she was trying to be territorial with her daddy.

"Daddy, can I go with you?" she asked, looking into my eyes.

"Sure, Baby Girl. When we're visiting, you can go anywhere you want to go with your daddy." I responded, feeling kind of sentimental because she wanted to be close to me.

Hand-in-hand, we approached Carrington at the microwave. While gawking at her, once again, I complimented her on her sex appeal.

"Sorry to stare, I'm just so amazed with how you've grown up." I felt like I had to apologize with the way I was behaving. It was all I could do to prevent myself from making her uncomfortable with my staring. "How long are you going to be home?" I asked.

"I'll be here until mid January. Then I have to go back to school. Classes will resume the third Monday of the month. Why do you ask?"

"I was hoping I would get to see you again before you left, but on a solo visit. Do you think you could work that out?"

"Sure I do," she replied.

"You do! So are you saying you'll come back?"

"Umm hum, I will."

Before my visit ended, I felt like I had been rejuvenated. I sat thinking about how 1989 was a year of personal growth for me. For the first time in a long time, I felt some inner peace and joy. I'd come to know what unconditional love from my daughter was like, which was priceless. I'd had an opportunity to rekindle a friendship with a woman I adored, and my family showed me as much support as they could.

Right before leaving, Carrington developed this genuinely sad smirk on her face. Suddenly, her eye contact with me became poor. When I told her to lift her face, she had tears in her eyes.

"Why are you crying?" I asked.

"It's so hard to see you this way. I've been fighting back my tears this entire visit. Let me add that it's been real hard to keep myself together, and it's even harder to fathom the thought of leaving you here."

"Don't feel sorry for me. It makes it harder to say goodbye. I hate to be left here, too. But since I've got no other choice, promise me you'll come back to see me soon."

"I promise I will. That still doesn't change the fact that I wish we could take you home with us." After she promised she would be back, I didn't say much more. I could feel myself getting emotional.

"See you all next time," I stated, hugging everyone goodbye.

"Bye, Daddy. I love you. As soon as I get home, I'm gonna write you." Asia expressed, hugging me tightly.

"Bye, Baby. Give me some more of those Prince kisses," which was this little nose and cheek rub she and I developed as our very own special kiss.

"Goodbye, Prince." Carrington whispered, waving.

"Not goodbye, but I'd prefer for you to say, see you later."

"Oh, see you later," she repeated as her deep dimples defined her smile.

"Thanks for coming. You don't know what your visit meant to me. You stay beautiful, and I hope to see you soon."

I leaned forward to kiss her cheek, but much to my surprise, she wasn't restricting my kisses. Before I knew it, she'd puckered up and pecked me on the lips. Once again, my dick stood firm and ready to beat up something. Too bad it wasn't going to be Carrington. She looked down at my erection and laughed.

"Oh, you want some of me?" she asked in a seductive 900 voice.

I wasn't any good after that question. "Bye," I smiled. "I see you're still a tease."

When I returned to my cell, I couldn't get Carrington off of my mind. All that body she was working with took my imagination to a whole different level. Though I had been pretty much in control of my hormones since day one of my incarceration, I wasn't that day. Hell, her visit had me under a lot of pressure, my sperm count was above average, and there was more room out than in. I hadn't chocked up my boy since Riverside, but I couldn't keep it together. I dug through my footlocker, looking for my petroleum jelly. I needed it to aid in the process of relieving myself. I pulled out one of my *Carmel Pussy* magazines, greased up my hands, then stroked, and stroked, and stroked until I skeeted perfectly good protein all over the damn place. "Ahhhhhhhhhhhhhhhhh! That was a good one right there," I confirmed after I burst one.

## 13

## *Ionia Super Max*

**"Mail Call."**

Januray 3, 1990

Deer Dady,

I luv u. Doo u luv me? _Yes or _No.
Cee u sune
Luv ☺ Asia

January 6, 1990

Asia,

How's Daddy's Baby? I hope you're listening to your mom and being a good girl. I have really missed you. I can't wait until our next visit. After your mom reads you this letter, give her a big hug for me. Tell her I said thanks for letting you be a part of my life. I love you more than words can ever express. You stay beautiful. See you soon Butterfly.

Love Daddy

**"Mail Call."**

January 8, 1990

Prince I hope when this letter reaches you all is well. As for me, I'm doing great. Even if I weren't, I wouldn't complain. I've been thinking about you since we last saw one another. For some reason, I can't get you off of my mind. Hum! Is that a good thing? I know you with your curious self are probably trying to figure out what I was thinking about. Well, I'm not telling you. I thought I'd add a little adventure to your life and make you wait until our visit.

Asia is something else. That little girl carries on like a grown woman. She talked me to death when we were driving back to Detroit. She must have asked me fifty times "What's your name again?" I was a little hesitant about telling her because I didn't want you to have issues with her mom behind my visiting you. Zena has done a really good job with raising her. I'd say from what I've seen thus far, your little princess is going to really make you proud one day.

Well I've got to go, Derrick and I are about to go out for dinner. Oops, sorry, I didn't mean to mention him. And yes, he's still a lame, (Big smile) but he's my lame. Chat with you soon, and I'll see you in ten days. Here's my address in Atlanta so you can stay in touch. After the 20th of the month, you can write me at the address below.

1236 River Oak Rd.  Apt 10
Decatur, Ga 31034

Much Love
C

January 12, 1990

Carrington,

It is so nice to hear from you. I'm glad you haven't forgotten me. I was wondering if it's safe to assume from looking at the date on your letter that ten days is the eighteenth of January. If my hopes hold any weight in your world, I'd like for you to know that I'm hoping to see you on that day.

So Asia was giving you the third degree. Man that's my baby. You should see this letter she sent me last week. It was so beautiful and full of love. My baby is growing up on me. It amazes me how she is aging right before my very eyes. When I think about the fact that I wasn't ready to be a father when she was conceived, I can't tell you how lucky I feel to have been selected by God himself to be her daddy. You know what Carrington? I wouldn't trade her for anything in the world. There are so many days when simple thoughts of her keep me going in this place. She's a remarkable little girl, just like her mother. I know that compliment comes as a surprise to you considering that Zena and I haven't gotten along since Asia was born. But with age, I have grown wiser, and I have mad respect for Zena. She was woman enough to allow me to establish a relationship with my daughter in spite of our situation.

Well, moving on. I see that you still think you know me. You were absolutely correct. I am wondering what you were thinking about, and I can't wait for you to tell me either.

By the way how you gon' go spoil my perfectly wonderful letter with news of you going out to dinner with Derrick. Do you know how jealous that made me? I have told you so many times not to talk to me about your man. But, I see you still like to push my buttons and punish my heart. One of these days you're gonna realize how crazy I really am about you. And when you do, then what?

Well gotta go, lights out. See you soon.

Much love,

Prince

Though I rarely looked at my calendar, it got much play all that week. I counted down the days until our visit like I was a six-year-old getting a new bike. Finally, when the morning of the eighteenth arrived, I sprung up out of bed like an addict. I cleaned my house, which is what inmates called their cells to add a little ownership to the space they occupied, shaved, and then ironed me an outfit from the world. I had purchased a few tickets for us to take pictures, so I didn't want to visit in my prison blues again.

When Carrington arrived, I didn't want to keep her waiting, so around 1:30 that afternoon, I started getting dressed. Visitation started at 2:00. By 3:30, I had butterflies. *Maybe she's not going to show up,* I thought over and over, as time kept slowly creeping by and punishing my mind. I relaxed on my bunk, staring into space. I tried to soothe this ill feeling that was forming in my stomach from disappointment. Nothing I did or thought about worked. Not even thoughts of my little princesses cured the feelings of uneasiness that had overtaken my mood. When 6:45 arrived, and Carrington still wasn't there, I started to undress, accepting the fact that she wasn't going to make it to the prison. *Something had to come up. I know Carrington wouldn't have me sitting around waiting on a visit. She knows how much this visit meant to me,* I thought, pulling up my state issued pants.

That night, I went to bed disappointed, but hopeful that she would come the following day. However, she didn't come nor write to explain why she never made it. By the twenty-fifth, I figured she had made it back to school in Atlanta. I considered if I should write her at all to express my sadness. I was almost sold on throwing her address away, but Papi, an older Arabic inmate, encouraged me to send her a letter.

"Prince, only you can ease your broken heart or put closure to the feelings you have for this woman. Something may have come up, give her the benefit of the doubt. See what she has to say," he suggested.

"Oooooh, I get so mad at myself." I said, kicking a pen across the dayroom. "Papi, sometimes I'm so weak when it comes to her. No matter how hard I try to come off, she always manages to keep my heart captive. What's crazy is that no other woman makes me feel this way. My baby's mama hasn't ever had this kind of effect on me. I've got to shake this hold Carrington has on my life or it's gon' kill me."

"Prince, you're in love. Write the woman a letter expressing your disappointment. What is it going to hurt, besides your pride?"

Papi was right. The only thing I was going to compromise by writing Carrington after she stood me up was my pride. My heart was already broken, so the only thing left for me to do was start trying to bring some form of closure to what I felt for Carrington. So as suggested, I wrote the letter.

January 24, 1990

Carrington,

My heart tells me that you wouldn't intentionally leave me anxiously awaiting a visit like you did without a good explanation. I am sure something came up last week, which is why you didn't show up. I hope nothing tragic has occurred and everyone in your family is well. I'm not going to fuss about no visit, but I do want you to know that I was very disappointed. When someone tells me they are going to do something and they don't, it breaks my heart. I was all prepared for our visit. Dang, you had me ready to share some of my most intimate secrets, and Bamm, you leave me hanging. I even purchased picture tickets. I wanted you to take a photo of us back to Atlanta for memories.

I normally wouldn't feel so let down, but it's something about you that keeps my heart wide open and vulnerable as hell. I know that you're involved with Derrick. I understand that there's not much I can do for you in prison. That doesn't change the fact that I am crazy about you. I have always valued our friendship, and I hope you value it, too. However if that is not the case, please don't reply to this letter. I'll move on with my life and accept that fact that we've grown apart.

I hope your trip home was safe. Write me when you get some time. If time somehow never presents itself, then I'll assume that you see me as more of a headache, and I promise, I won't ever bother you again.

Best Wishes,

Prince

I mailed my letter and waited on a reply. To be perfectly honest, it took me weeks to recover from her disappointing me. The survivor in me couldn't allow that pain to linger long because it would've had me out there bogus. I would have been so caught up on her that my guard would've been down. Had that been the case, someone could have easily caught me slipping, and the consequences could have been tragic.

In early February, Bean came out to visit. She was making her solo ride. This was the trip she took every few months or whenever I asked her to smuggle drugs in for me. She clearly knew what kind of risk she was taking, so she never let anyone come with her. She always told me, if something went wrong, she didn't want anyone else to get caught up with us. We had done this kind of exchange so many times in the past that we had actually perfected it. The first few times she was nervous, but after a while, she became a pro at crab stuffing.

Because the phones were tapped, and various prison officials listened to inmates conversations, "Stuffed Crabs," became a part of the underground terminology she and I used to talk in codes.

"I sure wish I could get my hands on some stuffed crabs," I stated whenever I wanted her to make a delivery for me. Actually, it was a nickname I used to describe a woman smuggling drugs into a correctional facility via her vagina. I know I shouldn't have asked my mother to compromise her freedom or her dignity like I did. But we both knew I needed to survive. We also knew I needed to make money for my appeal, which is why she ultimately decided to help out by bringing in my drug supply.

I think someone tipped off the correctional officers because they sat me under a secret camera for my visit that day, which is how we got caught. I tried to defend myself, but one inmate can't beat a team of CO's. Those officers beat my ass real bad. I felt terrible because I'd also put Bean in a bad position. I knew she wasn't going to watch them restrain me in the manner in which they did, so I should've simply surrendered.

When all was said and done, the officers had their way with me. I sat butt, ass naked in solitary confinement for three days before they gave me some clothes. I had battle scars all over my knuckles, some cuts on the side of my face, a slightly blackened eye, a few bruises on my back, and my body ached for weeks. I felt awful when I considered my mother being in the Carson City county jail for smuggling drugs into a prison. I sat in the hole for days wondering how I would face my grandparents and siblings after our incident with the Department of Corrections. GG was going to be pissed off with us both. Thank God my family was a close family with forgiving hearts. Ke stayed mad at me for the longest, but in time everyone forgave me for my foolish act.

In all those years, I had never been to the hole. I'd heard all kinds of scary tales about it, but the hole was never a place I wanted to end up. A few inmates told me stories about men who had gone to solitary with all their wits. However, they returned to general population as "Bugs" due to years of isolation or mental abuse. "Bugs," were inmates who exhibited abnormal psychotic behaviors. Not all of them were on psychotropic medication nor housed on the psycho ward, but their behavior was unstable enough that most cons didn't trust them.

Though I was an inmate, I wasn't in agreement with the way I was treated. I didn't have to take it either. I filed a few grievances on the officers that restrained me. The excessive amount of force they used to control me was unnecessary. The fact that they'd left me naked in a cold cell for three days was inhumane, considering I wasn't a threat to myself. The administrative officials ignored my complaint and never bothered to respond. Some inmates didn't have family to assist them with fighting the system, but I did. I got my family to start making calls to prison officials in hopes of seeing some results, but nothing happened.

I don't care how old I got, I was always gon' be my grandmother's baby. She wasn't accepting no for an answer from anyone, not even the Mayor. GG became livid when her calls weren't being returned. Her neighbor's son was one of the top board members with DOC. He worked at the State Headquarters and could make something happened if he wanted to. After GG spoke with him about my treatment, she asked him to have me moved to a different facility. He promised her he'd see what he could do.

"GG, he ain't to be trusted either. He works for the system as well," I remember writing in one of my letters.

After my altercation with the guards, the many grievances I filed, and the contacts GG made weekly, forced me not to trust any of the staff at that facility. I feared for my life. The officers were so mad at me for getting board members involved that they tried to break me during my stay in solitary confinement. My persistence for some kind of justice regarding their actions was frowned upon. Placement was slow about riding me out to another facility, which put me in a position to experience some of the most inhumane treatment a man could ever endure for the nine months they left me rotting in that place. Once I felt myself starting to give up, I wrote letters to my family again for help. GG started calling state gurus and they assured her that I would be transferred. Due to security purposes, they never told her when or where. As long as I was leaving Carson City, I was fine with their confidentiality policy.

The pressure I was under from total isolation caused me to start hallucinating. At times, I was in my cell talking to myself. I was losing my grip on reality. That scared me. Everyone knows that inmates and free people alike are social creatures by nature. In order to maintain some form of sanity, we all require interaction between others to maintain our mental stimulation. There was no reason in the world I should have been in the hole that long. At first, I think I was dealing with the pressure too well for them. In their attempt to control me like an animal, I was left caged and barely fed, which took a toll on me.

Finally, in October, I rode out to Ionia Super Max. That was a facility that housed level 6 inmates. Level 6 was the highest level of security one could encounter in Michigan's correctional system. My security points weren't nearly that high, I was a level four. As soon as I arrived, I immediately knew what was going down. I was being railroaded for speaking up for myself. That was DOC's way of humbling me. I couldn't believe what I was seeing or how I was living when I arrived. I was escorted in shackles and belly chains everywhere I went throughout the prison. There was always a correctional officer walking on my left, my right, and sometimes one walked directly behind me. We were allowed to take showers three days a week, which lasted for ten minutes each. To top that off, they had to be taken in handcuffs.

"How the hell is a man supposed to wash his ass good in some damn handcuffs?" I asked the guard.

"I don't know. You got seven minutes left to figure it out," he responded.

What ticked me off most were the times when I was in the middle of lathering, and the water was turned off. So be it, a dry towel or the sink is how I finished rinsing off the remaining soap on my body. I was supposed to be given an hour of yard in a two by two everyday, but if we got three days recreation a week, we were doing something. My cell wasn't as spacious as the one at Carson City either. It was real tight. It had this thick steel door with a feeding slot and a small peephole for the officers to look in on me. My cell had this paper-thin mattress that rested on a slab of concrete, which served as my bed frame. Everyday of my life, one thing that was certain while at Ionia was the fact that my back was gon' hurt from a bad night's rest.

*My stomach is going to kill me from eating this nasty food. I don't know if my mind can endure the isolation of this facility either. Too many years of this kind of confinement is certain to make me go fucking crazy from no communication with other inmates.*

Ionia had given us televisions in our cells for entertainment, but mine turned out to be a pain in the ass as time progressed. I enrolled in school to get my GED, thinking I was doing myself a favor. I thought it would aid in helping me get reclassified with lower points, which would eventually result in a transfer.

There were days when even getting my GED felt like a punishment. I thought being in the program would allow me some out of cell time. I was certain that we'd have to leave our cells to attend class in a different area. Huh! That was not the case. We didn't have to be escorted anywhere. Anyone enrolled in school got their lessons and assignments via the television in our cell. When I didn't feel like doing any schoolwork, DOC didn't care because the TV automatically turned on and the channels couldn't be changed or turned off until class ended. If yard was called while I was in class, then I was going to miss out per the CO's judgment. Ionia Super Max was no joke. It had me wanting to go back to Carson City everyday I was there.

Since I had been incarcerated, I rarely thought about Chew or Julius. The pain and guilt that came along with memories of them, was often too much to endure. Due to complete isolation, that was another uncomfortable issue I found myself dealing with at Ionia. I had lots of idle time to think about nothing, but everything I'd lost.

The only kind of excitement on the block that offered my worried mind a sense of peace came from a brother named Perk. That brother could sing his butt off. There were times when hours of silence would take a toll on all the inmates. Perk would stand in the window of his cell, taking request from anyone who wanted to hear something. Though I tried not to think about Carrington that much, every now and then there was one song in particular I'd occasionally request. It reminded me so much of her, and some days I couldn't help myself.

"Yo Perk, kick that *My First Love*, by Renee and Angela," I would shout. And like a radio station, no matter what he was singing he'd stop and begin singing your request from the heart.

"Silhouette….. of a perfect frame…." From the first verse to the ending, once he started singing I'd envision Carrington standing in J's basement whispering how that was her favorite song. *Damn! After all these years, Carrington still has my mind gone.*

I was convinced that my family wasn't going to come up with any appeal money for an attorney. Twice a week, I was allowed to receive material from the Law Library. Over a few months, I had written and submitted my first appeal to the Circuit Court. Within a matter of weeks my appeal was denied. Though I was very discouraged, I learned more about my case, which I initially missed during the actual court proceedings, so that was a good thing.

I had clearly been set up. When I assessed the court recorder's draft from my trial, I discovered that there were so many important facts my attorney neglected to address. He didn't raise any kind of objection to several points that required one. Any judge in the United States that read the draft from my trial could clearly see that my ineffective counsel aided in me being railroaded. As I read the court documents, I understood the errors Mr. Kennedy made while representing me, and I cried. I started to seriously wonder if he had taken a pay off for my fall as well. The thought of being set up by my attorney was painful, considering the fact that it had cost me my life. I vowed that whenever I could afford another attorney to represent me for my appeal process, I was going to be more involved in my defense. There were some valid issues I wanted to bring to my next attorney's attention 'cause my first one completely missed many valid points that could have put major holes in the prosecution's case and probably prevented my conviction.

In August 1991, Zena brought Asia out to see me. It had almost been two years since I saw my daughter. I hadn't seen Zena in almost five. She was still very beautiful, but had gained a little weight. She was on the thick to thicker side, yet I still was glad to see her. She still had a small scar on her face from where she was shot. If I hadn't been staring at it, it probably wouldn't have really been noticeable. *How you gon' be picky about somebody, Prince. Nigga you're locked up,* I thought, sitting down at the window for my first non-contact visit with Asia.

Before I could pick up the phone, Asia started smiling and waving. I tapped on the glass, so she eagerly snatched the receiver off the hook.

"Daddy! Heeeeeeeey, I've missed you," she replied, smiling with this distinctive smile.

"Hey, Butterfly! How are you?"

"I'm doing good, Daddy. You notice anything different about me?" She asked, grinning from ear to ear.

"Nope, I sure don't." I teasingly replied.

"Look closer," she instructed, as she put her face up against the glass, making me laugh.

"What am I looking for, Butterfly?"

"Daddy, my two front teeth fell out."

"They have? Man, Pooh, I didn't even notice that your teeth were gone. When did they come out?"

"Last Friday."

"Dang, let me see that hole in your mouth again?" I asked before bucking my eyes at her. "Wow! Asia, your mouth is a raggedy mess."

"Daddy, you're silly. Oh, guess what else happens soon?" She asked, without allowing me the chance to answer. "I'm about to start the first grade. Mama and I went school shopping last week."

"For real? What kind of back pack and lunch box did you get?"

"I got the Flyy Girls lunch box and back pack. It's pink, with yellow and purple flowers. I think that's what Mommy said. Is that right, Mommy?" Asia asked, looking at Zena for clarification.

"Um hum!" Zena replied, nodding her head.

"Asia, give the phone to your mom and let me speak to her for a second." As Asia handed Zena the phone, my eyes slightly watered. Over the past months, I'd really been missing my daughter. Actually, the hardest part was her being in my presence and me not to be able to touch her, which hurt my heart something terrible.

"Hey, Prince. Yoo..oo..u, you remind me of someone that I once knew," she greeted me singing.

"Oh, you on that new Mary J chick, too. I'm feeling that cut."

"Me, too. How have you been?"

"Good, Zena. Thanks for bringing Asia out to see me. I was dying to see her. Since Bean hasn't been out lately, I was wondering when I was going to get to see her again. You're really looking beautiful." I stated, lying through my teeth because I was grateful for the visit. "What have you been up to, and how is your mom?"

"I haven't been doing much. I recently opened up a home daycare. That way I'll be available after school for Asia. My mom is doing pretty well. She told me the other day that she doesn't think you killed Ray either. She said she wishes there was something we could do to assist with your release."

"That's nice to know, I wish you could, too." At that point I was at a loss for words. Zena knew I didn't kill her brother, but I knew she believed I had an idea of who did. The guilt from actually knowing bothered me, so I changed the subject. "Zena, you have done a hell of a job with our daughter. I could never give you enough props for the quality you've added to Asia's life. I hope you never stop showing her all the love you do. I believe that parental compassion is essential to a child's development."

"Prince, Asia is like you in a lot of ways. She has a mind of her own, and she's so easy to love. When I look at her, there's no way I could ever keep her away from you. All she ever talks about is her daddy this and her daddy that. I asked her the other day to give me a Prince Kiss like she gives you. She quickly told me that those kisses were for her daddy only. Man, she loves the way you adore her. As long as I am able to keep making provisions for her to see you, I will."

That afternoon, Zena touched my heart in a big way. After considering how I had initially lied about her being beautiful, I saw that she really was, and had to eat my words by the end of our visit. She wasn't as physically beautiful as she used to be, but her heart was. When they got ready to leave, I rubbed my face up against the glass with Asia. Though it wasn't the same feeling as when our skin touched, it carried the same meaning. I loved that little girl, and she knew it without a doubt.

That same week, Asia sent me a letter, which contained more compassion than I had experienced in some time. It didn't say a whole bunch, but it said all the right things. I put that letter right along with all the others in my footlocker for safekeeping.

**"Mail Call."**

August 21, 1991,

Daddy,

I had fun wit you. I didn't like you behind glas becuz I wonted a hug. Why did you have 2 visit wit cuffs on? I no they were hurten you becuz you had marks on your rist. I wonted to ask you if they were 2 tight but I didn't say nothin. I didn't wont you 2 be sad. Is that the way they make you visit at that prisen? If so I don't like the way they do you. Why don't you move? Them peple make me sick for bein mean 2 you. Hang in there. I know you can. You a Prince like me. If you need me rite.

Love,
Asia

# 14

## *Jackson State Prison*

My daughter's visit and her letter educated me. Because of the tenderness of our situation, I learned that whenever Asia was in my presence, she deserved to be hugged and loved like other little girls her age. Once I got my GED and lowered my security points, I was up for a move. Almost one year to the date of Asia's last motivational love letter and four months short of my twenty-second birthday, I rode out for Jackson State Penitentiary in Southern Michigan in August of 1992.

As soon as I saw the wall, I wasn't ready for Jackson. That placed housed about 5,500 inmates and was the largest wall prison in the world. Before getting rode in, I'd heard so many horror stories. To actually have it come up as a placement for me, literally made me ill. When I arrived at that facility, I had a chance to catch a complete glance of it for myself. All the prison stories in the world couldn't prepare me for what I saw. The wall that surrounded the prison had a very unwelcoming look. The brick seemed to have dark, cold eyes that gave off a chilling stare. The structure resembled a historical burial tomb with gloomy windows that had a mysterious glare and a sense of horrific pain. Based on all the other facilities I'd already served time in, it was extremely evident that Jackson was one of the oldest prisons in Michigan. Once I made it inside the walls of no return, I discovered that my conclusion of the facility was correct.

Jackson had galleries instead of small cellblocks. Each gallery housed five hundred plus inmates. Six by nine cages rose from the floor and stacked one on top of the other for four stories, resembling a large holding chamber for zoo animals. Prison bars could be seen for what seemed like miles, and the furniture inside each cell was the same as the other prisons, with the exception of being much more aged.

Every cell had open-faced bars, which allowed you to see straight into another man's house. I remember my first day on the gallery like it was yesterday. I was being escorted to my cell, and as we passed the small cell of one inmate serving life, we caught him jacking off on the toilet. *Privacy isn't an option here.* I thought, struggling to find any kind of humor I possibly could about my new living arrangements.

"Don't get caught slipping like that," Officer Reynolds stated.

"Trust me, I won't," I replied, scanning my new living quarters.

Jackson was the worst facility I had ever been in. But there were some positive attributes that came along with that gut wrenching facility, too. My being back in general population was one, and the ability to have contact visits with my daughter again was another. Daily trips to the yard and chow hall were a much-welcomed privilege that I looked forward to as well. Ionia Super Max had humbled me, the things I once took for granted, became a big deal. After that experience, I'd learned to appreciate some of the nonessential things some convicts and many civilians took for granted.

Huh, all prisons had their little cliques, inmate organizations or brotherhoods. The group in the joint I found most intimidating at Jackson was the Roaches. That place had some of the largest roaches I'd ever seen in my life. Whenever I considered defending myself, it was certain that they weren't going anywhere without a good fight. I remember one day I was lying on my bunk, reading a letter from Bean. Out the corner of my eye, I noticed movement on the wall next to my head. I slowly turned to zoom in on my visitor. Right in my face was this fat roach the length of my thumb, and the width of a fifty-cent piece. I rubbed my eyes for a second because I thought they were deceiving me. When that mug got a little closer to me, I leaned forward, grabbed my shoe, and fiercely slammed it against the wall. Bug guts splattered all over the wall and my pillow like a packet of oozing ketchup. "Shit!" I screamed out of frustration. I hated nasty bugs. *These almost reminded me of the roaches that lived in the projects at Chew's house,* I thought. The only difference was that they were bigger, and I couldn't get away from them. "Chew, man, I thought you were gonna look out for your boy up in this dungeon," I asked, looking up to the heavens with a smile on my face. "Oh well, I guess you're paying me back for always telling you to get your houseguest. Man, you're living up in the Penthouse where the streets are paved in gold while your dang bugs done aged and followed me to prison!"

One day after being on the gallery for a while, I was lying on my bed reading a magazine. My face was completely covered, which was my first mistake. I didn't realize someone was standing in my cell looking over me. Without any warning, I heard this deep voice say, "Li'l Punk, get off that damn bed, pull down your pants, and bend over right now." My heart was beating faster than it ever had before. I hadn't been charged up too much on that sissy drama, since I'd killed Big Man. I knew who ever was calling me out didn't know my history. I hesitantly lowered my magazine. I tried to proceed with caution as I moved to look my predator in his eyes. If a man thought he was about to rape me, he was gon' have to look me in my face and try to take my ass. I know I wasn't going out like a bitch, 'cause one of us was gon' die in the process. When I made eye contact with the face of the voice I heard, it was Raynard. He was standing over me, smiling for days.

"What's up, P? I had you scared, didn't I?" he asked, extending his arm to help me up off my cot.

"What's up, Man," I replied with sheer relief in my voice. "Don't play like that. You had a brotha nervous."

"When you get here?"

"I rode in a few days ago, and Man, this joint is raggedy."

"It ain't the best, but the last time I checked, we were doing time. P, every facility isn't gon' be plushed out like your ole girl's crib."

"Man, I know, but damn. These roaches are ridiculous. I hate to think of what the rats are looking like up in this joint."

"They big as hell, too."

"Damn, it's been about two years since we locked together? What you been up to?" I asked.

"Dang, it has been about that long, hasn't it? Man, I did a few years at Muskegon, but got rode out. They said I was influencing the younger inmates too much."

"Where did Louis end up riding out to?" I asked.

"Aw Dawg, don't even mention that trick to me. You should see Lou. He rode out of MR about six months after you. He's up in here on some different shit."

"Some different shit like what?"

"Man, them spirits done jumped on him."

"Spirits?" I curiously asked.

"Yeah, he got turned out shortly after he arrived. He's a straight trick. When I saw him, I swear I didn't even know what to say."

"Man, I know Louis ain't Butt Fishing?" I inquired.

"That boy so burnt up. When you see him again, it's gon' straight piss you off."

"What happened? I mean, how did they turn him out like that?"

"They caught him slipping. The rest of the story is history."

During our discussion, Raynard had given me some real "Jackson Jailhouse Knowledge." After he came in on me like he did that day, I never rested on my bunk to read nor did I ever completely cover my face for any reason again. I wasn't even trying to get caught slipping like Lou. That's why I made sure I always paid close attention to everything around me.

What I became in Jackson over the years was a beast that chumps stepped lightly to. I broke a many a broomsticks upside a niggas head for just looking at me like they wanted to do something. I didn't have any intentions on being turned out by anyone for any reason. I wasn't one to bother anybody, but if a sucka brought it to me, I handled him like a convict, not an inmate. For the record the difference between the two is that inmates try to peacefully do their time, convicts keep shit going, and don't care about nobody but they damn self, and sometimes that's even questionable.

In early January of 1993, I was fresh on twenty-two. A few days after the New Year, I was lying in my cell, feeling sorry for myself. Life was passing me by faster than I ever imagined it would. The thought that I'd lost my two very best friends on the same day still took me on an emotional roller coaster. None of us had the opportunity to go to the prom, graduate, get married or have a family of our own. We couldn't sing the latest rap songs together any more or argue over the new hottest babes in Hollywood. Since their death Hollywood had gotten a face-lift. When I thought about the arguments my boys and I would have had over babes like Mary J or Nia, I laughed, then I cried because all of us had each been robbed of our future.

Raynard popped his head in my cell, distracting my pity party.

"What's up, P?" he asked on his way outside.

"Man, just reflecting on my losses."

"Well, come on. They just called yard."

"I'm tight. I don't feel like going out."

"Man, you can't sit in here all day sulking or you'll stay depressed."

"Yeah, I know," I said, without moving.

"Get up, let's go, time's ticking on."

"I'm tight."

"You're not going?"

"Man, I didn't intend to go anywhere today. Plus, it's cold outside. My brother ain't sent the funds for me to get my new winter coat yet and the hawk ain't playin"

"Come on. Stop feeling sorry for yourself. If you stay on this pity party, you gon' make your time harder to do. Before you know it, it'll start doing you."

"Yeah, I know."

"What are you waiting for? Let's go."

"Coming," I hesitantly replied, pulling myself off my bunk. I threw on this thin winter coat, a skullcap and gloves, and I walked a few feet behind him. Once I exited out the door, I heard someone call my name. I hadn't made many jailhouse homies in Jackson, so I was uneasy. I looked, but I didn't see anyone I knew, so I kept walking. Again, my name was called, but this time it was a little louder. The person said something that caught my attention, which made me make sure I found the individual calling me.

"Prince, my cousin Carrington said, what's up?" After he said her name, locating the voice became a priority. I glanced over by the phones and there was Everett Storey, my homie from Atlanta.

"Storey-El, what's up? Mellow, I heard you were down with the nation now," I stated, giving him dap.

"Yeah, the brotherhood is serious. You should consider getting some of this knowledge we're offering. But, we can talk about that after I get out of my grandmother's pocket. I called you over here because I got someone that wants to say hello to you. Do you have a minute to talk?"

"Sure, who is it?" I asked.

"Carrington."

"Carrington! Aw naw, Man. I don't want to holla at her. Tell her I said, what's up. If I get a chance, I'll get at her later. I'm about to go to the benches to take care of some business right quick. Get at me when you get off the phone."

I walked away with mushy knees. My legs buckled the further I got away from the phone. I never thought I'd diss Carrington like that. But she was unaware of what I went through to recover from her not showing up that day. To add insult to injury, she didn't even think enough of me to attempt to reply to my letter. I wasn't giving her any more rope to hang me again.

After getting dissed by Carrington, I stepped up on my game. Most of the females I associated with out in the world were only for the sake of getting my needs met. I established a gang of pen pals, fat, skinny, cute, and ugly. It didn't matter. I needed someone to put money on my books, hook me up on a few three-way calls, occasionally visit when I wanted to be bothered, send letters, clothing, and provide me with some visiting room romance every now and then. My women were on it, too. So getting involved with Carrington would have been a set back that I couldn't afford to be caught up in ever again.

When Everett got off the phone, I asked him how he was related to Carrington.

"Our mothers are sisters. When I came from Atlanta, I lived with Carrington and her parents, until they put me out."

"Oh, that's who you were talking about back in the county?"

"Yeah. My girlfriend was Carrington's best friend."

"Mecca?" I asked.

"Yeah, you know her?"

"Hell, yeah. She and Carrington were a trip back in school. Whenever they got together, they got on most of my homeboys' nerves. Mecca had a look for yo ass that could kill you on the spot and Carrington was snooty. "

"They both have the kind of charm that steals a brotha's heart and they can own it forever, if they wanted to," he replied. "When I got caught up with Mecca's cousins, my family left me hanging. I guess they thought about it 'cause after I was sentenced, they told me they were at least willing to put a little money on my books and accept a collect call or two every now and then. That's how I got to speak with Carrington. She was visiting our grandmother and happened to be on the phone talking with me when I noticed you."

"Small world. I never would have put you with the Horton Family. They're way too uptight for you to be related to them. So how did I come up in your conversation with Carrington?"

"I said your name, then she wanted to know if I was referring to, DeMarques Prince. When I told her yes, she wanted to speak to you. After you didn't get on the phone, her feelings were hurt."

I laughed when he said her feelings were hurt. With the way she had dissed me, she should have felt honored that I didn't get on the phone and curse her out. I know that drove her crazy. Carrington was the type that likes to be the center of attention. When I didn't jump to her music, I know I broke her face.

### "Mail Call."

*January 13, 1993*

*Happy New Year my precious son, it's been some time since I've seen you. I miss you more than I can begin to express. I've paid all my fines, and completed my community service hours, so I guess we're back in business. I hope that all is well with you. You haven't written in a few months, which worried me. KeKe and I are coming to see you on Friday. We have truly missed you my dear, so don't keep us waiting. Everyone sends their love. I'll see you soon.*

*Bean*

*Hum, I know Bean ain't tripping out 'cause she hasn't heard from me. I've been dealing with my own stuff. Her letter is unusually short for this time of year. Maybe she's feeling the effects of us not seeing much of each other over the past few years.* I thought, moving on to my next letter, since I had gotten a few pieces of mail that day. I sat Bean's letter on my desk, figuring I would go back to assess it later. When I picked up my second letter, it wreaked the scent of a woman's perfume. Once opened, it was written on this cute stationary.

January 13, 1993

Prince,

Happy Birthday, Merry Christmas and Happy New Year. Like always, I hope when this letter finds you all is well. I'm so sorry about not coming out to see you the day I promised I would. My intentions were good, but the night before our visit was to take place, Derrick's mother died. With me being his girlfriend, I opted to stay with him to get things around her house organized before his family arrived. Once I got back to Atlanta, I had every intention on writing you to tell you what happened. Unfortunately, I got back a few days after classes had already started. Since I was in my senior year, I was playing catch up for the first few days. Due to my hectic schedule, every time I said I was going to sit down and write, something would always come up.

How is little Miss Asia? How old is she now, about 8 or 9? Wow, it seems just like yesterday that Zena was carrying that little monster around. The next time you see her give her a hug for me.

Okay, enough beating around the bush. Why didn't you get on the phone to talk with me that day? Are you that bitter with me? I know I can be forgiven for a simple mistake that was beyond my control. Prince, you need to stop holding a grudge, and get over it. I'm back in Detroit to stay for the time being. Derrick and I recently broke up, so I moved back home. You can write me back at the address on the envelope if you like, if not I understand.

Missing you so much
Your Friend,
C'

*Carrington has a lot of damn nerve*, I thought, putting her perfume scented letter in my desk drawer. *How is she gon' tell me that she was too busy to reply to my fucking letter for two years and expect me to fall for that bullshit? I'm a convicted felon, not a damn fool. She's trying to play me like I'm straight stupid. She better come again though 'cause I ain't the one.*

When I considered if I should reply or not, my heart was for it, but my brain said, "Hell No!" I decided to listen to my brain for a change. My heart already had me out there like a sucka when it came to her, so I wasn't allowing it to be the leader that time.

I needed a moment to consider my reply, and I didn't want her to think that she mattered so much to me that I'd just drop everything to respond. Not that I was really doing anything, but she wasn't about to play yo-yo with my emotions. I don't know why she thought she could pop in and out of my life at her leisure. She must have thought that was a cool thing to do to me. Well, it wasn't. Hell, being incarcerated didn't mean that I wasn't deserving of some form of consistency or respect. After considering the way she'd treated me, even if I wanted to write her back, I was so mad at that point, I left her letter in my desk for weeks. I didn't think twice about my decision not to contact her either.

That following Friday afternoon, I was called out for a visit about 2:45pm. When I made it to the visiting room, I was escorted to the booths for a non-contact visit with Bean and KeKe. Before I entered the room, the officer gave me tons of instructions. Finally, she motioned for my family to walk over to their seats positioned in front of the glass.

"Prince, you may hug your mother one time while I'm present, after that, there will be no physical contact between the two of you. You are to go directly in your booth afterwards. Any violation of these instructions will result in the termination of this visit. Do I make myself clear?" The officer asked, pushing her glasses up on her nose. *These damn female guards think they're the shit. If I wasn't in here, I'd break this little white bitches back. Who the hell does she think she's talking too?* I wondered. "Yeah, I got you," I disrespectfully answered, looking at Bean.

I was so anxious to get over to her, and when I did, I hugged my mother like there was no tomorrow. We hadn't touched each other in over three years. It felt wonderful to be held in her arms. I hadn't exhibited my childlike ways in over seven years, but I did that afternoon. When I got in my booth, I sat down, reaching for the phone. Bean and KeKe were all smiles. I looked at Ke for about ten minutes. She was blossoming into such a gorgeous woman. That girl had filled out and was looking like a young version of Jada P. Her eyes were a grayish green, like GG's, and she had a beautiful, smooth, golden-brown complexion.

"Damn Ke, you're just fine. How old are you now?"

"Seventeen."

"Are you dating?"

"Yep!"

"Yep?" I repeated. "Bean finally let you have a boyfriend?"

"Boy, yeah. I've had a boyfriend for a year now."

"Are you having sex?" I sarcastically asked, being silly.

"Yep!"

"What the hell did you say?"

"You heard me! I said, Yeah. "

"Damn, you could have lied. Bean, you know she's having sex?" I asked, hoping to hear her say that Ke was lying.

"Yeah!" She nonchalantly replied. "I got her on the pill as soon as I found out. These kids are too grown now days. Shoot, I ain't like some of these other mothers who are in denial. I'm not ready for her to make me a granny. Therefore, I did what I had to do."

I didn't want to think about my little sister having sex period.

"Where's everyone? Why did Ant let you drive out here by yourself?" I asked with a slight attitude. "He swore that you wouldn't be making anymore solo trips to the prison after we got busted. So what, he didn't want to come see me?" I asked, looking for some clarification.

Neither Bean nor Ke said a word. When I looked into their eyes, I knew something was wrong. Everyone knew how much I loved Ant, so their silence was related to their fear of how I would receive the news they'd come to share.

"What is it?" I asked in the calmest tone I could conjure up. Bean said nothing at all. She still wasn't any good at giving someone bad news. Finally, Ke said something.

"Ant's dead, Prince. He was shot up last week sitting in his car. He was out in front of his house, and someone did a drive-by on him. He got shot several times, but the doctor at the hospital said the fatal bullet went in his head. Ant was dead on arrival. Silk told Bean that he had so many bullet holes in him, he really didn't stand a chance. This morning we called everyone that needed to be contacted here at the prison. The family is trying to see about having you transported to the funeral. We haven't heard anything yet."

"When is the funeral?"

"Tomorrow."

"That shit's too expensive for the family right now. Besides, I don't want to see Ant in no casket. I want to remember him the way he was the last time we kicked it as a family. Do they know who killed him yet?" I asked, wiping my eyes to clear tears before they fell.

"Prince, Ant was talking on his cell phone when everything went down. The investigators believe that someone was trying to rob or car jack him, but no one really has all the details."

"Where was Melvin? Was he in the car with Ant?"

"No, Ant was with Renee's little brother."

"How could someone do that to him?"

"I don't know. Silk said half of Ant's face was blown off. But it was actually just a really big bullet hole. The funeral home said they'd do the best they could with him." Bean replied.

"Have they arrested anyone for his murder yet?" I angrily asked, trying to imagine my brother's pain. Then I tried to picture him with half of his face gone.

"Not yet, Prince. But I know they will. Once they do, will you please promise me that you won't do anything foolish if you ever lock with his killer?"

"Bean, I'm not one to bother anyone, I only defend myself when provoked. If Ant's killer comes to the joint, I can give you my word that I ain't gon' do him. One of my mellows might though."

As we continued to talk, I wanted to break down on our visit. However, after serving so much time, my spirit was growing too somber for that. Prison made me cold towards life. Seems like the more years I served, the less tears I shed. Besides, I just didn't want to shed any tears in front of everyone visiting if I could help it. I was grieving on the inside when I thought about not being able to console my mother as she laid her eldest child to rest. I felt like I needed to be strong for the moment. Although they didn't allow me to touch Bean again, I put my hands on the glass a few times to show her some compassion. I wanted her to know that I was with her. Even if I wouldn't physically be able to attend the funeral, my spirit would be in her midst. "Bean, my heart is with you," I whispered, fighting back my tears.

We could have visited until eight that evening. Unlike usual, a two and a half hour visit was all I could endure after the bad news. I stood up in the middle of Bean talking and blew her kisses.

"Okay, you and Ke need to go on and get on the road. There's too much going on in the world, and I don't want y'all traveling so late by yourself."

To be honest, terminating my visit wasn't so much about them, as it was about me, and the pain I could no longer conceal. The thought of not being able to see or ever talk to my brother again had taken a toll on me. It was getting hard to keep our conversation going, which made it evident that I needed some time to myself.

As they prepared to leave, I hugged myself and blew them three or four kisses. Bean and Ke waved bye and blew kisses back, which depressed me. My inability to hug or touch my mother for over three years had already intensified my desire to grow closer to her. Losing my brother just made the desire more intense. Actually, when thinking about my entire experience during my incarceration, I believe my separation from Bean caused me to love her more than I ever had before. I was pleased that over the past seven years we'd developed a real mother-son bond. Though I never knew a father's love like my daughter, I was blessed with the opportunity to get to know my mother and the benefits of a mother's love, which was most comforting to my soul.

When they left, we waved goodbye until we couldn't see one another any longer. Once they were out of my presence, I tapped on the glass to alert the officers that I was ready for my strip search. From the moment I entered the room to be checked, a dark mood came over me. I undressed and went through the procedure. "Okay, Mr. Prince, you're clear to go back to your cell," an officer in training informed me. I walked back to the block like a zombie, and then I flopped on my bunk without undressing. I was miserable, and watched the clock for hours in total silence. **"Lights out!"** A senior officer yelled, before the gallery went black.

# 15

## Protective Custody

I never recovered from my brother's death. After about five months, I regained my composure, and started trying to live in my environment once more. In early June 1993, I finally heard from Carrington again. However, this time she didn't write, instead, she came to see me. When I entered the visiting room, I walked over to where she was sitting, barely smiling at her. I was still very bitter about being stood up, but I did smile enough for her to know I appreciated her coming.

"Hey you," I whispered in her ear, embracing her. "What brings you to the "Belly of the Beast" on this beautiful spring afternoon?" I asked.

"You! Why didn't you reply to my letter?" She sassily inquired.

"For the exact same reason you didn't respond to mine," I cynically responded. "I was busy. Carrington, with my hectic schedule, I just couldn't find a free moment to write. Every time I wanted to sit down to reply to your letter, something came up. Plus, I've been so caught up with trying to deal with the death of my brother, I haven't had time for anything else, but me. I got to worry about my own well-being, you know 'cause nobody else is. Hell, some people don't even care if they leave you wondering for over three years why they never showed up for a visit."

"Don't be a smart ass. You're trying to be funny, but you're not. I told you what happened in my letter."

"Yeah, years later."

"There you go trying to be hard again."

"Carrington, I'm not being anything, but me. This place changes you. It makes you deal with reality while striving to survive from day to day. Your world is different from mine. You have no idea what my life is like or what a visit and letter means to me. Niggas go years without any correspondence. They try to act as if it's no big deal, but under these circumstances, it fucks with a person head more than you know. Some of these men in here are cold. They'll bust your ass for breakfast, and then try to turn you out over a period of time. I'm not about to be turned into nobody's bitch. That's why my demeanor is different. Babe, you have to conceal who you really are to make it in this place."

"Prince, but you're cold and bitter now. You're not the same person I grew to know and care about. You're not that same warm individual I came out to visit some years ago. What happened to you? Have you given up?"

"Did you hear what I said? You try spending seven plus years of your life falsely convicted for a crime you know you didn't commit. Then talk to me about change. Spend years of your life away from your family, your child, and people you love. Then try to endure the pain of your best friends being murdered somehow due to knowing you. Most importantly, try stomaching the pain of your brother's death. Then make that brother someone you love more than you love yourself. To add some additional pain to that situation, imagine not being able to attend his funeral because you don't want to degrade yourself or embarrass the family by being shackled and escorted by guards. Carrington, all I know is heartaches. After so many encounters with deep seeded emotional pain, I've become numb. Imagine being in love with someone since you can remember. Then imagine what kind of pain one feels when they love someone so much, but they never get anything in return. All you've ever provided for me is pain and stories about Derrick. Finally, imagine being incarcerated and that person you love promises to visit, then they don't ever show up or bother to explain why."

"I did explain why I didn't make it," she angrily replied.

"Almost three years later." I counted, holding up three fingers.

"Okay, I'm sorry. Tell me what I can do to help you get through this slump?" she asked.

"There's nothing you can do. I'm not in a slump. This is what life consists of for me now. When I think about things I need, there are so many things I require that are beyond you that I don't even know where to begin."

"Prince, I may be able to help, but if you don't open up and tell me what you need, then you're right, there's nothing I can do. Why don't you give me another chance? Try to give me an example of what you need, so I can see what I can do."

"In order to get my case back in court, I desperately need money for an attorney. I've got to shed these bogus charges I've been framed with. I need a good attorney to represent me. They don't come for free nor are they cheap. In the mean time, until I can hustle up on the money needed for my appeal, I need to be closer to my family and my daughter for a sense of peace."

Carrington sat quietly because she didn't know how to receive all of my needs. She sat back in her chair, looking around with her arms crossed. Suddenly, she smiled. From the way she was grinning, I thought she had devised a master plan, but that was not the case.

"What are you smiling about?" I asked.

"Look who just walked in the visiting room," she stated, pointing.

"Aw, Storey-El. That's my boy!"

"Oh, so you and Everett are real cool, huh?"

"Hell, yeah. That's my boy. He should've been out of here, but the parole board likes to flop inmates to keep generating revenue for the state. E is the kind of man that generally stays to himself. Lately, he's been embracing a lot of these young cats, trying to lace them up on some knowledge, but they're dummies with a lot to learn about prison like we had to."

"What's up, Baby?" Everett stated, walking past our seats.

"Hey," Carrington replied.

"What's cracking, my Man?" I asked.

Everett sat about five feet away from us visiting with Mecca. Carrington and I whispered over to them a few times during their visit just for the adventure. We chatted back and forth for about ten minutes. However, that didn't distract me from getting back to our discussion.

"You still haven't replied to my statement from earlier. I presented my needs, and I'm waiting for an answer," I abruptly reminded Carrington.

"I know. I've been thinking about what I can do to help. I'm going to let you know something soon. Don't lose faith in me this time."

*Yeah right,* I thought before we changed the subject all together.

"So honestly, why didn't you ever write me back?" I asked.

"Prince, after I graduated from college, I moved to Washington DC to be closer to Derrick. He's a Neurological Surgeon now. Can you believe that?" she asked, smiling.

"Yeah," I jealously replied with my face squinted.

"Anyway, I was trying to focus on our relationship. I severed all ties with all my male friends. I got a job working in DC as a Pharmaceutical Sales Rep, and while Derrick finished up in Med School, I worked. The first year things were great between us, so we got married."

"Married? What the hell did you do that for?"

"Let me finish!" She insisted, cutting me off. "We got married and again things were going well. At first I thought I could handle Derrick being away from home so much. After a while, I started feeling extremely lonely. We were supposed to be a family, but often we weren't. Most days, he was married to his books while preparing to take his boards. And that damn hospital occupied all of his other time. I became so jealous, that I accused him of being involved with another woman. I told him his residency wasn't supposed to take up his entire day, everyday. He assured me that all of his time was devoted to his profession."

"Yeah, sure it was," I responded, hating on him.

"On December 11, 1992, I gave birth to my beautiful daughter, India. While I was in the hospital, I met this gorgeous nurse named Dante. She was helping out on the maternity ward the week India was born. Because she, too, was pregnant, the two of us hit it off. I inquired as to when her baby was due, and she told me April. From there somehow my parents coming to visit from Detroit came up. That's when she informed me that her baby's father Derrick was also from Detroit. Turns out, we were both pregnant by my husband. I gave him a girl, and Dante gave him a boy. Which, by the way she named him, Derrick Jr."

My mouth fell open, "Hell Naw! That chump was cheating on you. I can't believe he got someone else pregnant," I replied in disbelief.

"He sure did! After my parents came to DC, I packed up everything and moved back home with them. I was still on maternity leave. Fortunately, after I settled in, my company had an opening in Detroit, so I transferred."

"What did Derrick have to say for himself?"

"Nothing really. He told me that he loved me, but he was confused after we got married. Dante was a girl that he dated in college, and they'd fallen in love. They dated for over two years without me knowing a thing. He confirmed that the distance between us made it easy for him to date us both at the same time. I rarely visited him during school, and if I did, it was only for a week here or there. He said when I told him I was moving to be closer to him, he broke up with her a few months before I arrived. They were still in love, but with me coming, he knew he couldn't have us both. They weren't having any kind of problems in their relationship, so Dante was puzzled when he instantly cut her off. And because she was sincerely in love with him, she tried to work things out after I arrived. Derrick always made excuses as to why it wouldn't work between them. He never bothered to tell her about me when they dated, so after I moved, she didn't even know that I ever existed. Sad part about it is after we got married, he still didn't bother to tell her that he was married or that he had a baby on the way."

*Damn! Ole Derrick had more game than I gave him credit for,* I thought before sarcastically stating just that.

"So I see you understand pain also," I deviously replied, feeling some pleasure in seeing her hurt.

"Yes, I do."

"What are your plans for Derrick and your family?"

"I don't know. My mother said, 'Go home and try to work it out.' My dad says, 'Fuck him.' He's real bitter about the way Derrick did me. He jokes about sending Derrick to prison for being a loser. Huh, Daddy always says, if Derrick still lived here, he'd lock him up for a simple speeding ticket."

"Yeah, I'm sure Judge Horton is hot. You're his baby girl, too. Everyone thought Mr. Derrick was an old Choirboy. He showed y'all, didn't he?" I asked, smiling. "Carrington, I can't explain it, but most men don't rest well when someone messes over their daughter."

"My father included."

"What do you think you're going to do? Everybody else can offer their opinion, but you're the one that has to live with whatever decision you make. Therefore, you ultimately have to decide what to do for yourself."

"I know. That's why I don't know what to do. I have a daughter to think about, but I'm not feeling Derrick at all. What do you think I should do?"

"Oh, you don't want to know what I think." I answered, grinning.

"Yes I do or I wouldn't have asked."

"I told you years ago to drop that nerd. Now I really don't know what you should do. Seriously, I guess you should do whatever makes you happy."

"To be honest, I don't know what'll make me happy."

"So, you need to take some time and think about it."

Our visit lasted for over four hours, and after hearing of her painful encounter with the other woman, I felt positive about the outcome of our friendship. Honestly, I thought we were on our way to becoming pretty good friends again. Once more, I decided I would try to trust Carrington. But if she wronged me, I made up in my mind that she and I were done forever.

Mecca and Carrington rode to the prison together that afternoon. Everett was ready to end his visit, so we wrapped up our visit, too, with a better understanding, some hugs, and a few innocent pecks on the lips. After returning to my cell, I thought about my visit with her. Had I known things were going to turn out so pleasant between the two of us, I would have considered contacting her earlier.

While I was meditating, some guys making loud noises out on the gallery disturbed me. My curiosity forced me to get up to see what they were doing because they were going nuts. When I looked out, I saw Louis cutting up.

*Louis!* I thought. "What the hell is that sissy out there doing?" I yelled to Freddy B.

"Showing out and acting like a damn fool," he replied.

Louis was on the lower level putting on a show. He was flirting with this bi-racial cat named, Roscoe. What I found totally disgusting was that some of the niggas looking on were really feeling the way he was shaking his ass like a straight ho. As they cheered him on, I heard a few of them whistling while referring to Lou as sexy. That was all she wrote for me. I leaned over the rail, looking him dead in his eyes, as if to say, "Cut that ho shit out. RIGHT NOW!!!!!" When he saw my expression, followed by the look in my eyes, he immediately stopped. I walked back into my cell without ever saying a word to finish reading a letter from my daughter.

"P, is that you?" I heard someone ask before turning to see who it was.

"Nigga, you know it's me. What the hell is that all about?" I asked, gesturing for him to look at himself.

"When did you get here?" He asked, walking over towards me for a hug."

"I ain't hugging no sissies, but I will give you some dap." I coldly affirmed before answering his question. "I've been here almost a year. I heard you were here. But forget that, again I'm gon' ask my question. What are you doing?"

"P, this is what life has come to for me. This is who I am now." He firmly stated, putting his hands on his hips.

"Why?" I asked clearly confused.

"What do you mean why?"

"Just what I said. Why would you go out like this, Lou? What's all this foolishness about?"

"I'm not carrying on, P, this is me. And for the record my name ain't Lou anymore, it's Lo-Lo."

"Lo-Lo! Man, you better get the hell out of here with that, I'm not about to refer to you as no damn Lo-Lo. You gon' always be Lou to me. Yo damn Adams Apple is bigger than mine, so how you gon' be a fucking Lo-Lo. I was hanging with you when we first came in the joint. I know you got playa genes in you, so what happened to them?"

"When I first got here, I was on that one hundred percent Mandingo kick. After working in the kitchen, my life changed."

"What, cooking made you want to act like a bitch?"

"Nooooooo, silly, I was raped."

"Raped by who?"

"I was cleaning the counters before shutting down for the evening. When I went into the storage room to put up some supplies, someone walked in behind me then locked us in. I was hit, gagged, then gang raped by Cal Lovelace, Joey North, and Dave Williams while some of their clique held me down."

"Hold on. Repeat that."

"Repeat what?"

"Did you say Joey North?" I asked, as my voice shook in anger.

"Yeah, why, do you know him?"

"He's one of the two that gave false testimony on me."

"You're lying. I forgot all about that. He sure is," Lou replied grabbing his mouth like a woman.

"Is he still here or have you seen him lately?" I anxiously asked, trying to ignore his feminine tendencies.

"I think he's still here. They moved him to another block, but I can find out."

"Do that," I suggested before encouraging him to go on with his story.

"Prince, I ain't been the same since they violated me. It's been so long, I don't even know what to do or if I can change now."

"Damn! What did they do to you to make you wanna stay like this?"

"They held me down and raped me. I tried to fight, but there were too many of them. Man, I couldn't defend myself. Prince, I've never told anyone about this story, but you've always looked out for me. A year ago I would have been embarrassed to even tell you, but it's me now, and I'm no longer ashamed."

"Okay, if you say this is you, then it is. But you can't be that turned out?"

"Man, I haven't had no pussy in years. After a few of them niggas forced me to give them blowjobs, while the others ran a train on me, I was mentally fucked in the head. After they finished rough riding me, I had to get fifteen stitches in my ass. My mind ain't been right since. What you just saw me doing a minute ago, well, I do that for attention, and sometimes to get on the guards nerves. I blame them for what happened to me. If they were doing their jobs, I would have been protected. It's a few officers around here on some bullshit, they doing major favors for various convicts, and I was one. So now every chance I get, I cause a disturbance to make for a long day."

"Lou, I ain't with that. When you're around me, I don't want to see that mess. If you see me, take that shit to the house. I can't stand to watch you go out like a sucka and I won't."

It hurt to see Lou go down like he had. I knew he appeared weak on our ride to the joint. For him to be as gone as he was, made me think he was borderline bitch from day one. From that moment forward, I avoided him as often as possible. I didn't want anyone to associate me with him. I wasn't like him, and I didn't want anyone to think I was. If anyone ever stepped to me with that drama, I was going to the hole for stabbing somebody.

♦♦♦♦♦♦♦

About four weeks after Carrington's visits, I got a letter from her older brother, Christopher Horton Jr. He was a criminal defense attorney, and was going to handle my appeal. He sent the letter, notifying me of a visit he planned to make to the prison for a meeting with me sometime that week. In his letter, he suggested that I have everything from my prior case together for his review. I was ecstatic about finally getting some good news for once in my life. After reading his letter, I went to the yard to call Bean. I had to immediately share my good news with her. We talked for about forty minutes, and when I was on my way back in, I ran into Joey North. When he walked past me, I'd swear he saw a ghost. He knew I had major beef with him because he lied on me. When I started over his way, he froze in his tracks, trying to scare me with a stare down. Looks weren't killing any damn body in the joint, but shanks were, which he was about to get. If I could step to him without being seen by an officer, I was gon' do him.

"What's up, Nigga?" I said, deliberately bumping into him on my way through the door.

"Look, Man, I don't want any problems. I ain't got no business with you."

"Oh Bitch, you got business with me. The day you sat in court and lied on me is when we established some business. Why you lie on me?" I asked.

"I ain't explaining my actions to you or anyone else," he coldly replied, as if he had no remorse for what he'd done to me.

"You gon' explain something or you gon' be on ice."

"I don't want any problems like I said earlier."

"When you lied on me in court years ago, you should have known once our paths crossed, it was gon' be some problems. I see you're not that bad when your boys aren't around. And now that the police don't have your back, what you got to say?"

"I don't want no problems, I'm just trying to do my time without static."

"Fool, you lied on me, destroyed the rest of my life, and now you're talking about you just want to do your time. I really ain't got nothing to lose at this point. I might as well catch a legit Murder One charge." I stated, lowering my shank out of my sleeve to move towards him.

Joey's eyes shifted, which made me stop to look behind me. A correctional officer walked up, insisting that we keep moving because we were blocking the entrance. Joey started walking away with the officer as he passed. I gave him this look that all convicts and inmates alike understand. "Nigga, you're dead." I whispered right when he passed me to exit the building. Had it not been for the fact that I was hopeful about a lawyer appealing my case I probably would've stabbed him that day. Once I returned to my cell, I thought about what he'd done to me, and I became angry. I wanted him dead so bad, I didn't care about my appeal.

That entire week, I walked around with a shank in my boot, hoping that Joey would cross my path. If only for five minutes, I didn't care if he was in front of an officer, I was gon' stab the hell out of him for what he'd done to Louis and me. Word on the block was that he went to Protective Custody the day after our run in. Joey obviously heard from someone that I was a man of my word because him going to PC proved he took my threat seriously.

The first week in August, my attorney filed my appeal. By the end of the month, we heard back from the Judge. He had ruled in my favor. I was on my way back to court, which I thought was a good thing. I knew I shouldn't get my hopes up too high because the prosecutor was sure to appeal the judge's decision. If he appealed and won, just like that, I was back to serving my life sentence. I rode out to the Wayne County Jail in Detroit to await my hearing. While I was at the county, I tried to make myself useful. Since I had already been to the penitentiary, I made it my business to talk to the younger guys waiting to be transported to Riverside. It was my intent to give them a more realistic view of what to expect than I had been given. However, they were hardheads just like I was. As I tried to warn them, I laughed at times 'cause many of them reminded me of myself as a boy.

As the days ticked by, I befriended one of the counselors at the county. Her name was Mary, and she was the Head Case Manager. She provided contract services for the state. While working at the county, she served a caseload of 55 felons. I happened to be one of them. One evening while I was on my way to a visit with Carrington, I met Mary in route to the visiting room. I spoke to her out of common courtesy, but her vibes weren't right. She was slightly flirting with me, which I'd never experienced, especially not from staff. *Damn, she spoke to me like she wanted some of this dick,* I thought, stroking my own ego.

Later that evening, I noticed her a second time in the visiting room. She was out there purchasing a drink, so I nodded at her. Once my visit was over, and I was back on my floor, I saw her again. She was talking with a seventeen-year-old that was due to ride out to Riverside for quarantine the following morning. She wasn't the most appealing woman, but she stood out to me. Hell, I hadn't been with a woman in years, and she was repeatedly making nonverbal passes at me. It had been a minute since I'd been flirted with, which is why I talked myself out of flirting back. Though, I was sure she was feeling me, I just chilled. All the signs were there, if she wanted me bad enough, she was gon' have to make the first move. Before she left the area, she walked over to me to let me know she would be calling me out the following morning. *What does she want to talk to me about?* I thought before replying, "Okay."

Wednesday morning arrived, and at ten o'clock, I was called to go see Ms. Austin. When I got to her office, I knocked on the door. She was talking on her phone, but motioned for me to come in. I walked in looking around, admiring many of her artifacts. Some of them were authentic pieces of fine African art that looked like very rare collector's pieces. After she hung up the phone, I commented on them while taking a seat on the opposite side of her desk. She spoke, and then smiled at me.

"I'm fine thank you. Are you doing okay today?" I asked, smiling in return because I was uncomfortable. This woman was a big chick, and she made me feel like a loaded turkey sandwich, which she was about to devour.

Mary was about six feet tall, weighing in at three hundred fifty pounds. She wore a blond Bob weave, which went into a bald fade in the back and lots of make up. While she talked to me I couldn't get past her glued on eyelashes, which had make-up caked up on them. *I know she's feelin' me, but damn, if she offers me the dugout, she's gon' be a little much for me.* I stood about five-foot, six-inches tall and Mary was way taller than me, so if she wanted to take advantage of me, she easily could have.

I figured if she was gon' force herself on me, then I needed to find something appealing about her. I looked her up and down from head to toe, but I got stuck at her feet. She had the ugliest, crustiest, hammer time feet I'd ever seen in my life. *Damn, I know women doing pedicures on a daily basis, do you know anything about that?* I thought. I gave her superficial smiles, here and there because this woman didn't know me from Adam. My stay at the county was temporary, and I was a convicted felon. In my eyes there was nothing we needed to discuss. She certainly wasn't the kind of woman I'd go after. With her being a professional woman, I couldn't imagine me being her type either. Sacrificing her career for five pumps and a nut certainly wasn't worth it to me.

Finally, Mary started asking me personal questions about my past. At first, I apprehensively answered them. However, the longer we talked that morning, the more I wanted to talk. Her dialogue sparked my interest and stimulated my intellect, and I can honestly say that I found her to be a very interesting woman.

An hour and a half had come and gone. Before I knew it she had shared just as much about herself, as I had shared about me. When I left her office, I knew she had clearly violated some of the ethical standards for a licensed clinician. I could sense a little weakness in her, but if getting to know her better could work in my favor, why not learn all I could. It was obvious from the manner in which she shared with me that she had some personal problems, including low self-esteem. I mean, why else would a professional woman on her level sacrifice her career and fall for an inmate she'd met in prison. That had me stumped.

"Come by anytime you need to talk," she informed me.

"Thanks, I'll see you tomorrow," I joked.

Turns out, I ended up staying in the county for over three months. Everyday, I'd visit with Ms. Austin, hoping to learn more about her each time we talked. The more I visited with her, the more comfortable I became. Finally, after months of chitchat, weeks of spending time together everyday, and hours tied up in conversation on my plans for the future, Ms. Austin confirmed that she was attracted to me. I didn't feed into her like I could have because I thought I was going home.

In mid-November the Prosecuting attorney appealed the Judge's decision to grant me a new trial and won. I was stunned. As I prepared my mind to go back to prison, I avoided all contact with everyone for days.

"Prince, your case manager wants to see you," an officer stated, approaching my cell. I crawled off my bed and walked down to Mary's office.

"You need to see me?" I asked.

"Why haven't I seen you in a few days? What's the problem?" she asked.

"I lost my appeal. I'll be going back to Jackson or somewhere soon."

"You lost it?" She asked in shock.

"Hell, Yeah! And I don't want to go back to Jackson either."

"Hey, I have a couple of friends in some high places. Let me see if I can pull some strings. Maybe I can help you get into Ryan, here in the city while you keep trying to get a new trial."

"Do you mind if I use the phone? I'd like to call my family to tell them the news."

"Not at all," she soothingly replied as I picked up the phone.

"Hello."

"Bean. I lost my appeal," I sadly stated without greeting her in return.

"You lost it?" she repeated before crying.

"Yeah, and my attorney said he couldn't represent me for free the next time either, so I need y'all to try and raise $5000.00," I desperately suggested.

"Prince, we don't have money like that," Bean replied.

"Ask Carrington for the money or at least a portion of it."

"I'm not going to do that. I'm not comfortable asking that girl for anything. Since she's your friend, you can call her if you like."

"Okay. Will you ask Silk for a donation, while I see what I can arrange with Carrington?" I suggested.

"I will."

I pitifully looked at Mary after hanging up. "Do you mind if I make one more call, please?"

"Sure, what's the number?"

As she dialed Carrington's number, I scribbled on a notepad that was sitting by the phone. When Carrington answered, I made small talk for a moment, before asking if Chris informed her of my defeat. Once she replied, I quickly took advantage of the moment.

"He said he can't represent me for free next time. If I want him to handle my next appeal, I'll have to pay."

"How much is he asking for?" she asked.

"$5000.00"

"I can give you $2000.00. I'll take it to your mother's house tomorrow. I don't want Chris to know that I'm giving you anything, so make sure that no one mentions that I did."

"$2000.00! Thanks, it's a start. " I stated with disappointment in my voice. I know that sounds ungrateful, but I was hoping for the entire $5000.00 from her. I wanted to call Bean back to let her know that Carrington was going to bring money by the house, but Mary was leaving for the day, so she said we'd call the following morning.

"By the way, write your mother's address on this paper." Mary suggested.

"My mother's address?"

"Yeah, I'm going to give you the difference for your attorney."

"You're going to give me $3000.00?" I asked.

"Un' hum."

She caught me off guard, but I needed the money. If she wanted to help me out, I wasn't going to dispute her offer. That same day, she stopped by the house to drop off $3000.00 in cash for my attorney fees.

When I went to her office to thank her the following morning, she was ready to collect three thousand dollars worth of me. Before I could get in the door good, she got up and closed us in.

"You said you came by to thank me. How do you plan to show your appreciation for $3000.00 dollars of my savings?" she asked, easing up on me.

"What do you have in mind?" I asked.

"I know it's been a long time since you've been with a woman. Why don't you let me remind you what it's like to climb aboard, ride, and dock in some good pussy."

"Good pussy!" I repeated, looking down, only to capture a glimpse of her toes. Even if I hadn't had any in over seven years, her feet made me want to give her a refund and run out the office. How was I supposed to put in any kind of work with those things up in my view?

I didn't want to seem ungrateful. She had just given me $3000.00 of her money. It was only right that I show my gratitude in some way. Hell, I knew I couldn't pay her back anytime soon. Therefore, I felt like I didn't have any choice, but to play her game. "How am I supposed to get some in this office? Someone might come by and then what?" I asked.

"Easy! Let me show you," she stated, pulling me towards her desk. She lit a scented candle, which she always burned. Next thing I recall was her easing up her skirt to expose this black thong that was completely lost between her butt cheeks. To add more pressure to the equation, she brushed my hands across her butt, forcing me to focus on meat, dents, and dimples. As she tried to ease up on her desk, thighs went flopping everywhere. *Now how li'l ole me gon' get up in all that woman there,* I thought, trying to sike myself up on an erection. Usually that just came naturally, but not then. All my efforts would go in vain. My dick didn't want to play with ole' girl, and refused to get hard.

Mary eased me inside her mouth, then worked them jaws like a trooper. I gasped for air like I was asthmatic because it had been a long times since I'd had a blowjob. Plus, the mouth work reminded me of the time Felicia got a hold of me in Ant's Benz. I remember the way I skeeted all over

Felecia's face, and guess what, I did the exact same thing to Mary. The only difference is that she at least tried to pull back. I think it was only because she was at work. Ole girl had real freak tendencies, too. Since I had an erection, she insisted that I at least attempt to penetrate up inside her big thick poodie lips that protruded like swollen, hairy camel toes in desperate need of a shave.

Since she had given me some satisfaction, I slid her to the edge of her desk. I thought about Carrington and every other Hollywood beauty I could possibly bring to mind to get a hard on. Once Mary eased back to spread her legs open, I tried to stand between them in order to get up in it there. She had far more extra meat on her inner thighs than I was used to working with. It kept getting in my way, so I asked her to climb down off of her desk and assume a standing position with her back to me. Once she turned around, I pushed her over on the desk, spread her legs, slid her thong to the side, and gave it to her Doggie Style. I don't think I put in any significant work, but to her I had. As long as she was cool with that, I was, too.

# 16

## Letter of a Lifetime

**"Mail Call."**

December 27, 1994

*DeMarques,*

*I have done a lot of soul searching since I met you in Jackson. I don't know where to begin, but I want to start off by apologizing about the situation I put you in. It is from my very own experiences of heartache and survival during my incarceration that I realized exactly what I've robbed you of. When I testified against you, I was young, stupid, and offered an opportunity of a lifetime. Really, a second chance to get my life back on track. Unfortunately, I didn't take advantage of it, which is why I'm currently in prison serving a life sentence myself.*

*I struggle to look at myself lately because of the guilt I feel from what I've done. After finding God, I am clearly aware of what is expected of me in order to have some peace.*

*Man in 1986, Delvon and I were 16 just like you. If convicted, we were looking at some serious time for some car jackings we had done. After an intense interrogation down at the 102$^{nd}$ precinct, Officer Thompson made us an offer we couldn't refuse. While waiting for your trial to begin, we were allowed to have conjugal visits, specials meals, and privileges other cats in Juvie Hall didn't get. The best offer of all was a plea bargain we couldn't refuse for a testimony against you.*

*The DA and the officers knew you had a solid alibi, so they had to have someone testify against you in order to get a conviction. That's where Delvon and I came in. They had us rehearse our story over and over, until we had it down. We'd repeated it so much that by the time we went to court, it was convincing. Man, both of us were immature. Other than freedom, we really didn't know what we were agreeing to. We didn't know you, so it wasn't like we felt any remorse about what we'd done. Had I not met you in Jackson, I may have never written this letter. To see you, and be able to relate to what I robbed you of, bothers me daily. I ain't no monster, though my behavior was something you'd expect from someone of that caliber. I've thought about our encounter over and over at Jackson, Man, I'm sure glad you didn't have a chance to kill me. 'Cause truthfully, I'm probably the only one that can help you regain your freedom.*

*Whatever I have to do to help you, I will. I'd be more than willing to write a statement and sign an affidavit on your behalf. If I'm subpoenaed to court, I know I'd be charged with perjury, but I believe what I'm doing is the right thing to do. I'm prepared to deal with any of the consequences I may face. Have your counsel contact me. I'll do whatever's necessary to help you win an appeal.*

*Joey North.*

Damn, after seven years, I get the letter of a lifetime. I couldn't believe what I was reading. Tears poured from my eyes like a major thunderstorm. That afternoon, I sat in my cell and cried until I couldn't cry any longer. Actually, as I reflected over some of the things that I'd been through since my ordeal, I cried for a number of reasons. Most of all, I cried because I missed my brother. Things finally seemed to be working in my favor. The sad part was that Ant wasn't going to be around to see me regain my freedom.

Mary was a blessing in my life in more ways than one. She turned out to be good friends with Judge Christopher Horton, Sr. Because Carrington and I were friends, the two of them asked the judge to make a few calls to see if he could use his pull around the city to get me moved to Ryan Correctional Facility in Detroit. After listening to their explanation, he considered the request, made a few calls, and within a matter of one person owing someone a favor, it was a done deal.

I sent my attorney a copy of Joey North's letter. Within no time he had secured a signed affidavit from not only Joey, but Delvon Stevenson as well. *We are finally on our way,* I thought. I tried not to worry too much with what the courts were going to rule in regards to my appeal because when I worried, I wouldn't eat. As a result of stressing there were also times when my hair started thinning in the top. Being closer to home was what I tried to put more of my energy into. It was a real blessing to be right in the city. That way Carrington, Bean, Zena, Asia, and Mary could frequently visit me. During one of my visits with Carrington, she admitted that she was developing feelings for me. At first I was hesitant to entertain her admission. She had already let me down several times, but it seemed like deep within my heart, I believed Carrington was my soul mate. Once I considered the feelings I had for her, I finally allowed her to wear me down.

Visitation was everyday except for Tuesdays and Thursdays. We were allowed eight visits a month so, Carrington used four, and the others were split between Bean, Zena and Mary. Suddenly, Carrington was all into me. She became faithful with visits, letters, and cards. She kept money on my books each month to assist with my personal needs, and inspired me to stay positive. The thought of her leaving me at the end of each visit became harder and harder.

I remember during one visit, we discussed the possibilities of us becoming a couple. Carrington vowed that she was ready to be with me. She said that though she had to maintain her responsibilities as a single mother, she would never miss a beat when it came to me, which she believed would prove her sincere interest in developing our relationship. Some days, we kicked around the thought of her bringing India out to meet me. I told her it was best not to expose her daughter to the prison environment or me until we knew what we wanted to do for sure. I thought before we got all off into that, it was best to make sure we were going to seriously be together. I never personally met her little girl during my stay at Ryan. I did occasionally talk on the phone with her once or twice. Carrington also sent me pictures of the two of them together on a monthly basis. The older India got, the more I loved her. With the way I felt about her mother, I always thought she should've been mine, and sometimes I wished she was.

Prior to falling in love with Carrington, I never knew what it felt like to really be in love. Chew and Julius always said I was weak behind her, but I never associated it with being in love with her because I wasn't. After years of being denied by her, I had to finally see things their way and agree. She had this kind of hold on me that I just couldn't shake or explain. Once she came back into my life, she introduced me to a sample of feminine tenderness that I craved like an addict. During my incarceration there had been several women I communicated with, but none of them turned me on like her. As a matter of fact, none of them meant anything to me at all.

After months of us dating, it was established that Mondays and Saturdays were Carrington's usual days to visit. Everyone knew that those two days belonged to her, so I didn't allow anyone else to come at that time.

One week she missed her Monday visit and showed up that Wednesday, which happened to belong to Mary. I was sitting on a visit with her, when I looked over at the entrance and noticed Carrington being searched. "What the hell!" I whispered, watching her walk into the visiting room. She stopped to briefly talk to one of the officers, then he pointed her over to the area where I was sitting. Mary had her back facing Carrington, so she didn't see her walking up, but as she approached, I could see she was pissed.

"Prince, what is she doing here?" She asked, talking with some slight bass in her voice.

"Carrington, what are you doing here today? I wasn't expecting you," I calmly asked.

"Who is this? I know you're not trying to be no jailhouse playa."

I was trying to think of a response, but nothing came to mind. I could only wonder how and why she was allowed to come back. Generally, if I was already on a visit, I couldn't have another one on the same day. Good thing for me Mary was thinking. She was quick, and her suave reply saved my ass.

"Hello." she stated, standing to shake Carrington's hand. "I'm DeMarques' Case Manager from the county. I was in the area, so I stopped by to make sure things were going okay with him. You must be the love of his life. He's always talking to me about Judge Horton's daughter, Carrington. Would that be you?"

"Yes."

"It's nice to finally meet you, Carrington." Mary stated with real class.

Afterwards, Carrington felt embarrassed. She repeatedly apologized for her jealous outburst while taking a seat. When she sat down to join us, Mary became somewhat uncomfortable with our situation. She stayed making small talk for an additional ten minutes before deciding to leave. Carrington's episode made me somewhat irritated. I tried to pretend like I wasn't bothered to prevent us from arguing. I hated that Ms. Austin was put in such a compromising position, too. We had become good friends over the months, and though she wanted me, she knew my heart would always belong to Carrington. What she and I did at the prison was nothing more than my way of providing her with a service to thank her for her financial help. Three thousand dollars and a blowjob was a lot for a woman in her position to sacrifice. My fifteen minutes of pumping, and the nut I got, could never compare to what she'd done for me. I knew that before I boned her. I just still wanted to express my gratitude for her help the best way I could.

On future visits, Mary never said much about the incident with Carrington. Since she didn't address it, neither did I. The day she actually met Carrington was like a reality check for her. After that, she never talked about us being together again period.

◆◆◆◆◆◆◆

In January 1995, everyone came out to see me for the New Year, Bean, Ke, GG, Daddy Ruenae, Asia, and Carrington. Everyone looked so good walking in together. I immediately noticed Carrington because she had on some tight jeans. I locked in on her ass 'cause it appeared to be getting fatter. The whole package was a turn on. Those bowlegs, and that sexy walk of hers, had me dying to get some. I smiled in lust as I watched Carrington approach me. Her hair was flowing, her dimples were inviting, and those lips were moist and beautiful. I puckered, and then stuck my tongue so far down her throat, she swore I was trying my best to taste her dinner from the night before. It was rare that I ever kissed her like that because I knew she hated it. She tried to push my tongue out, but I wasn't budging, so she bit down, making me quickly pull it out.

"Sorry, Baby, I was horny. Sometimes your kisses help me get off," I whispered, looking down. Li'l nosey Asia was standing right by us listening. She was impatiently waiting on me to give her some attention. She had her nose turned up like she was disgusted.

"Dang, Daddy. Y'all is so nasty." Asia said with attitude.

"Aw, you want some affection, too?" Carrington asked, pulling her in for group hugs.

"I want some affection, but only from my daddy."

"Oh, excuse me," Carrington responded, backing out of my arms to give Asia her space.

"Alright li'l Miss with your bad attitude. What I tell you about being so sassy?" I asked, embracing her.

"I know Daddy, but every time we come with Carrington, I always got to wait and get hugs after her. Then she hogs you for the whole dang visit. That's why I hate to come when she's coming. My mama told me the next time Carrington intrudes on my time let both of y'all know that I'm here, too."

"Butterfly, I'm sorry." I said, hugging her. "I know you're not jealous of my girlfriend, are you?"

"Sometimes. Only because you spend most of our visit all into her."

"I'm gon' do better……. Okay?"

"Okay, if you say so. We'll see next time."

My daughter had her mother's outspoken personality and had called me out. I felt real bad for a minute. She wanted me to know she felt neglected, and that's exactly what she did. After that day, I tried to make sure she never felt that way again. I had already picked my brother over her once, so I vowed that she would never take a back seat to anyone else, not even Carrington. I kissed Asia on her face as a peace offering. When she walked over to her seat, I laughed to myself because she'd wiped my sugar off.

"I saw you, don't be wiping off my kisses."

"You saw me?" she asked, laughing.

"I sure did."

GG, Bean, Ke, and I all kind of group hugged. They weren't too picky, and that was good enough for them. I still hadn't made it to my grandfather. Daddy Ruenae was patient, so he waited for me to finish with the women. I hadn't seen him in years. Actually, I almost didn't know who he was 'cause he'd lost so much weight.

"Hey, Daddy Ruenae," I stated, hugging him almost afraid to apply pressure out of fear that I might break his bones.

"Hey, Son, you're sure looking handsome in your old age. You almost look as good as your ole granddad."

"Yeah, I'm trying to hold up in this place. You know I got to try to hang on to my Prince-Appeal. When I get out of here, I still want to be good looking like you."

"I sure hope you do keep your good looks, Prince. But…. I'm afraid your Granddad isn't going to be around to see the day you walk up out of here."

"Come on, Man, you're only seventy-six. You're still young." I replied with a semi-smile because I could sense that something was wrong.

"Prince, I'm sick. My body is tired, and I'm tired of hurting. When Bean told me they were coming to see you today, I made sure I was in the car. I don't think I'm going to make it another month. However, I wanted to see you while I was feeling up to it. Most days I don't feel like doing anything. I've been praying to my Father, asking Him to spare my life until I could get here to see you one last time. God's given me the desires of my heart. If he took me on our way back home today that would be fine with me. I was holding on just to see you and now my mission is complete."

"What's wrong? What are the doctors saying?" I apprehensively asked.

"I originally had Prostate Cancer. But I'm afraid your granddad's old body is now infested with cancer. They've given me two weeks to live."

"Two Weeks?" I repeated.

I was in clear shock. My heart literally started aching from his news as tears fell from both of our eyes at the same time. I was choked up, but my granddad continued on because he had more to say. "Prince, your Daddy Ruenae wouldn't leave here without saying goodbye to his favorite grandson. Man, I love you so much, and I'm proud that our paths crossed. You are a noble young man. Son, God's going to save you from this place. Keep fighting for your freedom and trusting Him for deliverance. You have a fighter's spirit. God has created you with the heart of a warrior. Prince, you're fighting for a cause far greater than you realize. Remember that you have a spiritual enemy, named Satan. He's trying to devour you, but this storm that you're going through right now is temporary. There's something you're supposed to learn from this experience. Ask God what you're to gain from this encounter and then blossom from it. When He removes you from this bondage, know that He's preparing you today for your real mission in life. God's Word says, "Do not be afraid. Stand firm and you will see the deliverance the Lord will bring you." Prince, don't be afraid to boldly face His assignment. GG and I have taught you to have faith in God. Boy, there's a battle in front of you that must be won. Son, we didn't raise you with the spirit of fear. I expect great things from you as a Prince because one day in this family, you'll be our new King. I'll be smiling down from heaven when that happens, too. "

There was no reply on my behalf. My granddad's faith in God's power along with his tears moved me. There was obviously so much that he needed to say to me that he'd literally begged God to keep him alive until he could see me one last time. Granddad almost talked non-stop, which led me to believe that he obviously wanted to share that spiritual knowledge with me for a reason. As Daddy Ruenae continued on with his thoughts, I took a moment to get myself together. As we stood in the middle of the floor, my need to cry that day didn't concern me one bit. I wasn't worried about what the other inmates would say once we went back to our cells. I was saying goodbye to my Grandfather face-to-face for the very last time. I was hurting so badly that I wanted to crawl up in a tight space and lay in fetal position for the rest of my life. My heart ached so much that my soul cried out for a comfort that no one in the room could provide, not even Carrington.

"Prince, I'm gonna always love you. My soul won't rest until you're out of this hellhole. Trust God, Son. He's going to certainly work this out for you. I know He is 'cause I've been praying about your situation. He knows my heart, the pain I've endured from this issue, and the dreams I have for your future. You apologize to God for your wrongdoings, and then put this problem in His hands. Prince, you must remove self, I mean, step back, brace yourself and watch God work in your favor. Son, victory will be yours."

"I know, Granddad," I replied with some apprehension.

"Now one last thing. I've set aside the money for you to attend my funeral if you want to. There's enough money to pay for your transportation, your security, and an outfit for you to wear. I guess what I'm asking is do you want to come to my Home Going Service?"

"Granddad, no disrespect, but I want to remember you just the way you are today. When I think of you, I want to remember you teaching me how to spell, how to do math, how to ride my bike, and the way you used to get onto me about the phone ringing all hours of the morning. I will always cherish you teaching me about God. I will never forget you making me help G pick weeds out the garden. Most of all, I will forever remember the comment you made to me at my sixteenth birthday dinner. Do you remember what you said?" I asked.

"Nope." He replied, adjusting his glasses on his face.

"Remember you were in the front of the line waiting to fix your plate?

"Yeah. I do remember that," he laughed.

"I told you that GG cooked dinner for two kings."

"Yeah, I remember that, too," he said snickering even louder.

"Well, you told me, 'You must've been one of those Kings, 'cause I was the Prince.' Granddad you were right, you've always been a king in my eyes. You've done an excellent job at modeling for me what a man of quality lives like. Man, I thank you for loving me when my own father didn't. Most of all, I thank you for being there for me when my mother walked out on Ant and me. Granddad, may you bust heaven wide open exemplifying the same kind of love to your heavenly family that you've shown your earthly one. Man, I hope to one day mimic just a small portion of your character to my grandchild."

"Son, you will. You're already headed in the right direction," he replied, embracing me.

I sat next to my granddad for the duration of our time together holding his hand. Once we started to communicate with the rest of the family, I asked Bean why she didn't tell me Daddy Ruenae was sick. "I wanted to, but Daddy made everyone promise not to tell you because he planned to do it himself." I couldn't be mad at her for respecting his wishes. I knew Daddy Ruenae was the kind of man that said very little about most things, but when he spoke up, he meant what he said and said what he meant. He would have had a conniption fit had anyone else said something to me about him dying after he requested it be kept confidential.

We had a six-hour visit that day. When my family left, I hugged and then kissed my granddad on his forehead. I remember watching him slowly walk out of the room. Suddenly, he stopped in mid stride, lifted his fist in the air, and replied, "I know about your sacrifice. Fight with the Lord on your side and you'll win with the lord on your side. Your secret will go with me to my grave." From his comment, I concluded that he probably knew the truth, and from his expression, I acknowledge that we'd never see each other again. And we didn't.

On April 12, 1995, Daddy Ruenae died from complications related to cancer. As I thought about his life and what he meant to me, I felt honored, better yet very blessed that God allowed me to be a part of him. As I sat thinking about my Granddad, one thing I knew for certain about his death was that when he died, he loved the Lord.

Money wasn't going to be an issue for my GG afterwards either. She would never have to worry about how she would make ends meet because he had enough insurance policies put away to take care of her for the rest of her life and part of mine. Daddy Ruenae worked in the maintenance department at Ford for over thirty-five years. His retirement benefits were of high quality, and he always believed that insurance policies were for those living and left behind. When I was growing up, I remember him always telling me that a man should always ensure that his family is better off when he departs to meet his maker than they were when he was living. 'You may not get to enjoy one dime of your riches, but you won't have to worry about those you leave behind making it from day to day.'

In all the days of my life, I had only been exposed to three influential men in my time. No one could have ever told me years ago that at the age of twenty-six, two of them would already be dead. Out of the three, Silk was the only one left. After being convicted, I felt a little different about him. He hadn't made one trip to the prison to see me. With the way I loved and looked up to him that made me a little bitter. The few times we spoke on the phone, he claimed he didn't want to see the inside of no prison.

"Unless the joint is my new residence, I don't care if I ever get to see that place," he'd always say when I invited him to come out for a visit. I couldn't argue with that. I understood that he had far too much going on with his drug empire to take a risk on coming to see me. However, when you really love someone, I always thought you were supposed to make sacrifices. Due to the Feds being on him, he claimed he was laying low. That was just an excuse he used, which was fine. *One day I'm gon be free and Silk better look out. I ain't gon' have no kick it for him*, I frequently thought the week of my granddad's funeral.

My Grandmother always told us, "After being clean, you could only waddle in the dirt with dogs for so long. Eventually, your fresh scent wears off, and then you come up smelling like a dirty dog, too." Silk was so scantless to me that he was on the verge of not only being a dirty dog, but a dirty dog with fleas.

Carrington went to my Granddad's funeral to represent me. She read a resolution I had written for him once the minister opened the floor for remarks. Afterwards, she presented a copy to my Grandmother. When the family headed to the cemetery, Carrington came to the prison to sit with me. That day the warden allowed her to arrive an hour before visitation actually started to provide me with a little time to mourn in private. While Carrington stroked my neck, we sat in a conjoined chair holding hands for the first hour in total silence. As I rolled my head from one side to the other, I wondered how my family was doing. I repeatedly thought of GG and wished I could be with her for support. As tears fell, Carrington tried to console me. *How could my family be burying another one of the most significant people in my life and I not be a part of it,* I thought, wiping tears from my eyes.

"My situation has to change." I mumbled.

"What did you say, Baby?" Carrington asked, lifting her head off of mine.

"I've got to get out of this place. I can't see another person in my family die from this side."

"Be patient, you're gonna beat this. You'll see."

"It's got to happen soon because I can't take much more of this."

# 17

## A Cursed Man

I felt like my life was cursed. I was experiencing every kind of loss there was. My friends, my freedom, appeal one and two, my brother, my grandfather, appeal three and then four, and by the end of 1995 Carrington and I were also falling off.

Prior to her slacking on me, Carrington mentioned that she'd met a guy named Bobby in Greektown at one of the summer festivals. I couldn't get mad. I understood that she had physical needs. Hell, there was only so much pleasure she was going to get from talking nasty to me on visits and writing dirty letters. Shit, as big as her ass was getting, I knew somebody was putting in work 'cause that mug was getting phat, phat. I loved her so much that I tried very hard to keep her focused on me. I did all the little sentimental things I could do from prison, but my resources were limited. The more fascinated she became with the attention this Bobby guy provided for her, the less she stayed in contact with me. Until eventually there were no contacts at all.

I was losing the woman I'd spent a lifetime trying to win over. I was literally going nuts inside that prison every time I thought about Bobby possibly fucking my girl. I was very possessive over that coochie, even though I'd never had any. To me, I was supposed to be the next one to get that. Point blank, in my eyes the pussy was mine. It belonged to me and only me. The more I thought about her giving it away to somebody else, the crazier I became. I got so irate at times, I didn't even know myself. I'd make collect calls to Carrington to try to resolve some of my pain, but she would refuse the charges or hang up in my face. Due to the circumstance, my hands were tied. I was helplessly in love. My girl wasn't allowing me to express what I felt, my heart was crushed, and when Carrington treated me as if I didn't exist, I turned into a damn lunatic.

"Bitch, you ain't shit!" I'd screamed after the automated recording on my collect call instructed me to state my name. I felt like if she wasn't going to take my calls, she was going to at least hear what I had to say. When she deliberately refused my calls, I'd hang up and call right back.

"Fuck you, Slut." And I'd go on and on some days with obscenities for hours. There were times when I got a rush from cursing her out. After regaining some of my manhood, I returned to my cell to wallow in my sorrows. I wasn't eating, socializing, reading or calling my family. Most days, I couldn't think straight. The stress I was under affected my rest at night to the extent of causing me to suffer from sleep deprivation. All the pain I was going through made me reflect on the times I'd dogged Zena out. I remember she warned me that I'd one day reap what I had sown. Damn, had I known it would be as painful as it was, I would have done much better by her.

As awful as I felt about myself, it pleased me to know that someone thought enough of me to try and relieve me of some of my pain. With Mary being older than I was, I valued her opinion. I felt like I could count on her for some suggestions on ways to win my woman back. Sometimes, I'd call her to process what I was feeling. The few times she came out to see me, she allowed me to vent most of the visit. I know at least ninety percent of the time all I talked about was Carrington or how much I loved her. It was obvious that I was severely heartbroken and struggling to recover. Her words were often brutally honest, sharp like a razor, and slashed into my broken heart like a freshly sharpened blade. "Carrington doesn't want you anymore. Move on," was the summary she provided regarding my heartaches.

I tried to take heed to what Mary was saying. I attempted to find some new things to venture into, which is why I found a fresh ray of hope in "Religion." I needed some God in my life. As a child, I was exposed to Christianity, but since my incarceration, I became unclear as to which religion was right for me. Some of my Muslim friends called me a Babbling Baptist in need of the light that Islam provided; I didn't quite know if that was factual, but I set out to see if that was the case.

The Nation of Islam was massive in the joint. I considered the Moorish Science Temple of America because they received much respect from other inmates, as well as gave it. I believed I also possessed some very influential leadership skills, which could add value to that group. Everett had the privilege of becoming the Acting Grand Sherik or the spiritual advisor in Jackson and had actually inspired me to join the temple in Ryan.

Because of Everett's powerful leadership role in the prison community, he hit five different prisons in less than a year and a half. His fifth move brought him to Ryan with me. Over the years, he had become like a brother to me, so it was a real blessing for us to be locking on the same block again. I'd missed our friendship, which is why I was thrilled when he arrived. Everett always had my back. I could talk to him without feeling embarrassed about the manner in which I loved his cousin after she dogged me out, and he never made me feel stupid about the degree of love I had for Carrington. Though I was suspicious by nature about most of the characters in prison, I grew to trust Everett. He was the only person I shared most of my darkest secrets with. I guess that's because I knew we could always talk in confidence. Most of all, I knew he wasn't going to view me as weak or share my business with someone else.

One day while chilling in the dayroom, Everett and I were catching up on lost time. Out of the clear blue, he informed me that it was one of his partners that got Joey North and Delvon Stevenson to come forth with the truth. They applied some real pressure to those clowns, basically letting them know that they were either going to let the truth finally be told or deal with the consequences. Good thing for me those chumps made the right decision.

It was genuine loyalty like that, which made Everett highly respected by other inmates. He displayed a spirit of oneness towards the brotherhood and expected the same from all the members affiliated with the temple. After learning what he'd done for me, and the manner in which he helped me move on with life after Carrington, I realized that prison had taught me some valuable lessons about something other than survival. I learned that there were also some real values that came along with the bond of true friendship, which I'd developed with a man who was forced into a terrible situation like myself.

Everett was coming up on the end of his bid. In late March, he was granted Parole, and was due to discharge in May 1996. We kicked it hard for the last two months, and I knew when May arrived, I was going to miss him like I missed my brother.

"P, before I leave I want to tell you something that I heard right after you left the walls," which is what we called Jackson.

"I got to wait that long? You might as well tell me now," I insisted.

"Naw, you gon' have to wait like I said."

"Like you said! Chump, don't talk to me like that."

"Man, I'm not trying to hear that nonsense today. You always want to argue with me. What are you tripping about?"

"I got a lot on me. Sometimes I snap for no reason. I guess I'm under a lot of stress, and then you're about to get out on me, too," I paused to exhale. "Man, it occasionally gets kind of hard to see friends you bond so tough with come and go. You're like my brother, which makes your leaving even harder, especially when I consider that I may never get to go home myself."

"You need to rest that young mind, and get rid of those distractions that prevent you from giving your fifth appeal one-hundred percent of your attention. P' you got to let Carrington go, she's moved on. There's nothing you can do about that. That's just how romance and relationships go in prison. Here today, gone tomorrow. Carrington's out in the world enjoying life, you're in here stressing the hell out, and she ain't thinking about you."

"Man, I don't want to hear that. My tripping doesn't have anything to do with Carrington. I just want to know what you have to tell me that I can't know now." I replied, lying through my teeth.

"What I have to tell you is not about Carrington. It's about something that's far more meaningful to you than her. I'm going to tell you before I leave like I said. I will tell you that it's some deep shit, so get your mind ready because it's no joke." After E's last comment, I didn't worry myself with trying to figure out what he had to say. I knew he was a man of his word and before he got out, he would share his news as promised.

In late April, I started spending most of my free time in the law library. I was trying to work from the inside on my case as my new attorney Miles C. Lewis II, prepared a brief to rebut the prosecution's last appeal to the Courts. He was working closely with Gary Canadia, another highly respected attorney out of Detroit. Though Gary was up to his ears in clients, he took enough interest in my case to provide my attorney with some free consultation. As always, things were looking as though they might go in my favor, but we'd have to wait until after the brief was submitted for the Judge's reply.

I had come up with lots of cases similar to mine. I documented something on every one I ran across, then anxiously sent them to my attorney for further review. When I wasn't researching, I was reading; if I wasn't reading, I was working out with Everett in the weight pit. If I wasn't there, I was studying with my brotherhood, trying to learn more about my new religion. When I was idle, I read old and new mail to keep myself going. I did everything I could do to stay optimistic. However, there were times when I didn't know if I was going to make it or not because of the different obstacles that seemed to become new issues for me month after month.

Seems like no matter how hard I tried to move forward, something always occurred that mentally set me back. For the month of May, in 1996 it was Zena. I don't know what possessed her to send me a letter with such heartbreaking news, but all I remember is her letter shattered my world.

**"Mail Call"**

May 1, 1996

Prince,

I know with that survivor spirit of yours, all is well. I saw your mother the other day when I dropped Asia off and she looks a little ill. It seems as though she has lost a little weight. I was wondering if she was well, but I didn't bother to ask because I know how she gets sometimes. You probably should call home and check on her when you can.

I was sitting here watching the news the other day. Did you see where another inmate killed Charles Casey? I guess he finally ran out of favors with God and his last run in with death was his final meeting.

I know my letter comes as a surprise because it is rare that I write, but I wanted to take a few minutes of your time to say thank you for being a wonderful father to our daughter. She adores you. Prince, the only thing she would have different is you here on a full time basis. Asia made straight A's on her report card in March. I don't know if she mentioned that to you when she was there with your mother last month, but she did. I was real proud of her. I believe that much of her success comes from the love and support she gets from both of us.

I also heard that you and Carrington parted. Well for what ever it is worth, I'm sorry to hear that. I know how much you loved her. I'm sure it was a devastating experience for you. I hope that your heart is mending without reservation because to be honest, you were too good for Carrington anyway.

Prince, when I take your current heartaches into consideration, I hate to share my bit of bad news, but I know I must. My boyfriend Rodney moved to Chicago last week. He's invited Asia and me to come live with him. Rodney has been a part of her life for the past five years, so he's kind of been like a father to her. Asia is saddened by his move and sort of wants to go. But she loves you to death and has expressed to me that she doesn't want to move that far away, especially not without your approval.

Prince, I'm caught between a rock and a hard place. I'm looking forward to a positive change in my life. I need you to support me on this one. I've tried to be there from afar as much as I could for you, and now I'm finally looking for something in return. I'd like for you to talk with Asia. Tell her that I'm trying to make a better life for us, and that you'll be okay with her moving.

Please do this for me. Prince, she's fighting me tooth and nail about not wanting to go. Encourage her, and let her know that it's okay for her to leave. I think as long as she knows that you'll be at peace with her decision, she'll be fine with leaving. All she needs to know is that you'll love her the same, and that she can come see you in the summer when she's in Detroit visiting with your mom.

I guess I'll let you go. I'm sure that I've put quite a bit on your plate for one day. Please give my request some serious thought. Reply when you decide what you're going to do. Thank you in advance for your help on this one.

Zena

May 5, 1996

Zena,

Your letter comes as quite a surprise to me. I am crushed behind your news. Asia means the world to me, and it is very hard to see you move her to another city. Since I've been incarcerated I've tried to do everything in my will to be as much a part of her life as I possibly could. You may not realize this, but my Butterfly gives me what I need to go forth daily. There are days when I bear the weight of this dismal world all alone. It is thoughts of a visit from her that sometimes keeps me going.

I know you have a life of your own to live that doesn't consist of me, but it'll kill me for you to take my baby to Chicago. I won't call or write Asia to tell her that it's fine with me because it's not. This situation feels like one more slap in the face for me. Sometimes I swear I'm cursed. I don't know where this run of bad luck has come from for the past ten years, but it's taking a toll on my sanity. I don't know how much longer I can do this.

Sorry. Let me get off my pity party. My disappointments and heartaches have absolutely nothing to do with you. You've been good to me, even when you didn't have to be. Zena, I can't tell you not to go, but I will say that I don't want you to. If you decide to move, I'll be as supportive as I can. I won't tell Asia that it's a bad move for her. However, I won't tell her it's one that I support either. Kiss my li'l girl for me and tell her that her daddy loves her.

P.S.

As for Charles Casey, Yeah I heard he got a taste of his own medicine. "No Mercy." That fool was playing a game of cards out on the yard, and got caught slipping. A sissy named Louis stabbed him about fifteen times in the back and head. Charles was notorious for harassing people. Unfortunately, for his sake, Lou wasn't the one. His homeboys better watch their backs, too, 'cause niggas up in here are tired of their shit.

Take care,

Forever Asia's only father
A Prince in Chains

Zena killed me with her news. Her man of five years had relocated for a better job, and there was no doubt in my mind that she was going with him. She had invested years of quality time into building their relationship. I knew there wasn't anything I could say to keep her in Detroit. I tried to view things from her perspective in order to avoid being totally selfish. Yet, whenever I considered my daughter being that much further away from me, I couldn't clearly rationalize a damn thing.

Zena replied to my letter telling me that I wasn't right for my selfishness. She claimed I was being inconsiderate of her needs. Nonetheless, I didn't want to hear all that. I had enough on me, so I didn't get into a letter war with her. I expressed myself, she expressed herself, and that was that. As far as I was concerned, Zena was just gon' have to make her move and prepare to deal with the outcome. I knew Asia wasn't going without a fight. She was an eleven-year-old with much to say about everything. The more I thought about it, the more I was convinced that either way, I wasn't telling Asia anything regarding her move. If Zena decided against Asia's wishes, my baby was just gon' have to go. I knew she'd give Zena and Rodney hell all the way there, but as far as I was concerned, moving to Chicago was an issue that had to be resolved between them.

The day before Everett was released, we sat in the Law Library talking about his plans for the future.

"Man, I'm going home to get me a college degree. From seeing all these young brothas in the joint, I've been inspired to become a guidance counselor with some kind of juvenile facility."

"Boy, you've got to be kidding me. All these young hardheads in here ain't trying to get no kind of knowledge. So from seeing them all in here, you should know the ones out in the world ain't trying to be saved either. With the kind of skills you have, I see you benefiting more from becoming an entrepreneur. You're real business-oriented; working with these little knuckleheads is hopeless. Man, they'll kill your thunder."

"I don't think that will happen. Kids need guidance from people that have already gone through it. They respect us more 'cause we can relate to their struggle."

Ever since I'd known Everett, it was always in his nature to try to save the lost. His comment was so typical of him, which is why it didn't surprise me one bit.

We both had mixed feelings about our friendship after his discharge. Though I was excited about him moving on with his life, I got a little depressed when I considered that I was losing a great friend. Over the years another thing I learned was that constant change was part of the daily routine for inmates. Homies came and homies went. To see my partners go home always felt like a stab in the heart for a Natural Lifer like me. It was hard to see them cross over to the other side because I often wished it was me discharging instead.

"Okay, so what is it that I've waited all this time to hear?"

"P, I had you wait for a good reason." I looked Everett in his eyes like a man. I'd trusted him all that time with my most sacred secrets, so if he dropped some bogus news on me, I was gon' be heated. "Prince, I know who killed your brother," he confessed, with the most serious look in his eyes. I was speechless. I immediately started trying to figure out who it was, hoping he wasn't going to say someone we knew or had been jailing with. If he did, I was about to go off.

"What! Why didn't you tell me before now?"

"I didn't find out until I was getting ready to ride out of Standish. This young cat Byron Holmes was running his mouth about a dope man named, Silk. He said he was rolling for him and worked with Ant sometimes. I remember you always talking about your uncle Silk, so I knew there was a connection." *I figured Silk had Ant killed,* I thought, before allowing him to finish. "Byron said he was with Ant the day he was murdered. The guys that shot them told Ant right before they opened fire on his car that someone named Calvin Shaw sent them. Byron claimed Ant was big man on the totem pole, and quite a few of his spots had blown up. Ant was supposedly stacking some serious money during the time he was taken out, and his death freed up some territory and houses. Byron confirmed that Ant knew some of his closest friends weren't to be trusted, especially after he started coming up so fast. Ant believed that his new status put him in a different category, and it was only a matter of time before someone put a hit on him. Byron expressed that Silk was the only one that stayed on Ant about laying low. He believes your uncle is suspect 'cause he was the only one worrying about Ant getting too big, too fast. There were some other small pocket Ballas on the streets heated behind Ant's come up, but Ant refused to slow um up in spite of their threats."

"Calvin Shaw? Who the hell is that motherfucka?"

"I asked him the exact same question. He said he never met Calvin, but everyone talked about him. Byron said the odd thing about Calvin Shaw was that he was a big Balla and a big name on the streets that nobody really ever saw."

"Calvin Shaw. For some reason that name sounds so familiar. Seems like I know a Shaw, but I don't know why I feel that way," I said.

"Do you think Ant was living foul?"

"Hell naw! Ant was cool people. He had game, but my uncle taught him to conduct business with class. If my brother wasn't anything, he was loyal and legit. Ant was into some heavy shit the last time I saw him, but he never said what. He looked a little worried and real tired, yet I never asked him what was up 'cause we didn't talk about the family business inside the joint. I wish he had said something to me though. That way I might've been able to give him some advice or at least understand the magnitude of what he had gotten himself into."

"Man, what you've got to do is try to find out who Calvin Shaw is. Then you'll know why your brother died. It sounds like your brother was set up. I hate to say this, but Silk sounds guilty."

"Whatever! My uncle wouldn't kill my brother," I expressed, trying to give him the benefit of the doubt. I didn't want to think that a man I loved so much at once could turn on his peeps like that. "Whoever killed Ant did it for foolish reasons. Ant wasn't the one to get caught slipping. He would never be out there on the grind without a backup plan. He didn't let people get that close to him. Maybe this Byron guy killed him. I don't know, but I do know that someone Ant associated with set him up. For someone to walk up on him and blow his brains out, he had to have known them well enough to allow them in his space."

"I don't think Byron did it though. He was hurt behind Ant's death. He said the two of them were like brothers."

"Brothers my ass. The only people that were like brothers to Ant were T and Melvin. I know my brother and I'm telling you that he knew his killer. Byron's a fucking liar. He probably killed Ant, found out you knew me, and told you that lame ass story for you to do just what you're doing right now, be his advocate," I angrily suggested, slamming the book I was looking in closed.

"P, that's why I didn't tell you the first time, I knew you wouldn't listen to me. I didn't want to be drilled about this everyday until I discharged. That's why I held this information. You better listen to what I said. Let's find out who Calvin Shaw is, and we've probably found your brother's killer."

After I returned to my cell, the name Calvin Shaw kept running through my mind. I repeated that name over and over and over, trying to envision who he was, what he looked like, and why he wanted to kill Ant. With Everett mentioning that Byron said Calvin was a big time dealer as well, I concluded that Ant was killed over status in the dog eat dog industry on them Detroit streets. *Silk was getting 'em big time, too. His pockets were far bigger than Ant's, so if he wasn't Ant's killer, is he about to be hit next?* I wondered. Though we had grown apart, my new fear was if this Calvin person was gon' try to kill my uncle next. If that was the case, then all three of my male role models were going to be gone.

That entire night I tossed and turned. When the following morning arrived, I made my way to Everett's cell before he pulled out.

"E, thanks for everything. I thought about what you said, and I promise I'm gon' take your advice. I'm gon' find out about this Calvin Shaw, get some answers regarding my brother's death, and go from there." Everett extended his hand to give me some dap, followed by a hug.

"Stay up, Homie. You gon' beat this. Keep Allah first, and the rest is going to come," he insisted in a sincere tone. "P, I'm gon' be working this investigation from the outside to see what I can find out about Calvin. I'll be in touch real soon. And as soon as I get my stuff tight, I'm gon' come visit you."

"It's cool. Do your thang out there on them streets. When you get a chance, don't forget to hit a brotha up," I stated, turning to exit his cell. "E?"

"What's up?"

"Homie, you're about to walk the block one last time as a free man."

"I know," he smiled.

"Damn, how does that feel?" I asked, trying to visualize myself in his shoes one day.

# 18

## A Man's Choices Determine His Future

Zena moved to Chicago in August 1996. The day they left, she and Asia stopped by the prison to see me before getting on the highway. Rodney was with them, but waited in the lobby. They only stayed for an hour, but it was the most dreaded hour of my life. Asia held my hand our entire visit, crying. By the time they left, her eyes were starting to swell a little.

"Butterfly, I'm begging you to please calm down. To see you in this kind of pain is killing me," I stated, putting my arms around her. "Zena, do you mind giving us a few minutes alone?"

"No, not at all. I'll go to the restroom before we get on the highway."

"Butterfly," I said, looking into Asia's eyes. "There's no place in the world you could go that would stop me from loving you. You are my heart. Baby, I swear I love you more than I love myself. As soon as I can change my situation, I'm coming for you. One day we're going to be able to do something special together. Anything you want to do, you just name it, and it's done."

"That sounds great, Daddy, but, I know you're not ever getting out of this place. Mama told me years ago that you were going to die here. That's why I don't want to leave you. She said these men in here are ruthless killers, and you could be murdered at any time. I don't want you to die before I have a chance to make it back," she whispered, as tears flowed from her eyes. "Daddy, every night I pray to God like Daddy Ruenae and GG told me to. I ask Him to keep you safe. I ask Him to protect you, keep you secure from these evil men in here, and let you come home soon. But I know I've been praying for the past five years, and you're not home yet."

"Some things take a little longer than others. Asia, I don't know why your mom said I'll die in this place. Butterfly, I'm not, I promise. You give me so much to live for. Everyday of my life, I live with the intent of coming home to my three queens, You, GG, and Bean."

"Don't forget Carrington," she interjected with sarcasm.

"Don't be a smarty pants. You just worry about staying in touch with your old man. If you don't, I'm gon' be in Chi-Town looking for your li'l butt."

"Okay, Daddy. You know I'm gon' stay in touch. Man, if I go there and meet a boy....."

"Boy? Hold on……….. hold….on. You better not be trying to date no boys any time soon. I'll come to Chicago and do something I've never done before," I stated, cutting her off.

"What's that?"

"Spank that ass."

"You ain't spanking anybody. You'll be crying yourself before you ever swing the belt. Mama already said it's a shame how I got you wrapped around my finger."

"She's right, but I'll still tap that butt if you make me. Asia, bet-not no boys be trying to capture my Butterfly."

"Daddy, I'm getting too old to be called Butterfly."

"Asia, you're going to always be my Butterfly. You don't even know why I call you that, do you?"

"No!"

"I call you that because butterflies are one of the most beautiful creatures affiliated with God's divine plan on this earth. They are full of lively colors, they're graceful, they soar through the sky with pride, and no matter where they go, they are always going to capture someone's attention. Most of all, because of their presence, they bring smiles and joy to so many people's lives, just like you. You're a perfect replica of a butterfly. That's why the name is so fitting for you. Babe, you could be fifty and you'll still be my Butterfly."

Once Zena returned, it was a given that Asia and I had accomplished quite a bit in the ten minutes she was gone. I felt like cursing her out for telling my baby that I was going to die in prison. Out of respect for Asia and the occasion, I suggested that they leave, instead of going off on her. Considering the long ride they still had ahead of them, I stood to hug Zena, then bent down resting on one knee to say my final goodbyes to my daughter.

"Who loves you, Daddy?" Asia asked, with her lips puckered for a kiss.

"You do, Butterfly," I cheerfully replied, keeping my composure.

"Okay, now give me a Prince kiss," she insisted.

"You got it, Boo."

I watched Asia and Zena walk through the door and my heart throbbed. As bad as I wanted to cry, there were no tears to follow my daughter's departure. I was all cried out from years of pain. Now that Zena was moving on with her life, I hoped she would continue to do right by me in regards to our daughter. Only time would tell, so I had to wait and see.

After settling in, Asia sent me several letters. Sometimes they seemed real sad other times, they were just the opposite. The extra distance in our lives made a difference for me. I longed to see my daughter's face during the time she was away. Nonetheless, I'd have to wait until her summer vacations rolled around. Eventually, I adjusted to that arrangement, just like I had with so many others. Learning how to adjust was another lesson that came with being an inmate.

◆◆◆◆◆◆◆

In June 1997, my attorney contacted me to tell me we'd lost another appeal. Frustration built up inside of me from all my hard knocks, and my optimism was gone. I got to the point where I didn't think I could do time much longer. Eventually, I couldn't. I started to accept defeat and I was desperate. Prison had gotten the best of me. I started using drugs, hustling on the down low again, and assaulting officers. I was fighting with inmates, which I hadn't done in years. My conduct was horrible, and I was catching tickets every other day. Finally, I made my way back to solitary confinement, only to find myself going through mental torture once again. I was simply hopeless and had fallen into the cycle of becoming that "nothing to lose" kind of convict.

After serving so many years with every kind of personal loss imaginable, my spirit was broken. At that point in life, there was nothing else DOC could do to me. I was emotionally damaged, which aided in my time doing me.

One thing for sure, CO's had a way of dealing with hot heads. Frankly, I didn't give a damn about that either. My life was over as far as I was concerned. Staying out of trouble didn't matter to me anymore.

By October 1997, I rode out to Standish Maximum Correctional Facility, which was way out in Standish, Michigan. It was one of the newer, level five correctional facilities. I had been a level two for several years, so the structure was a whole new kind of living for me. I was back to a brand new kind of structure that I wasn't ready for. Most days I was pissed off with myself for being in that position. But eleven years of my life had come and gone right before my very eyes. Maintaining didn't feel like a realistic option to me anymore. I was about to turn twenty-seven and was still serving time. What else was I supposed to feel? How was I supposed to behave after trying to keep it together for so long, considering I was still being screwed by the system?

◆◆◆◆◆◆◆

One day, I stood looking at myself in the mirror for the longest. I was amazed with how much I'd aged. *Damn, I look older than I am. I guess that's what hard living does for you. P, you've got to get it together. Man, you know you want to go home to your family,* I thought, wetting a washcloth to wipe my face.

Since my incarceration, I hadn't had that many jobs. To make things a little easier on my mental status, I applied for a position in the kitchen. By March 1998, I had gotten a detail to work in the chow hall on the line. I was making seventeen cents an hour, and straight getting raped by the state. Day one, I walked into the kitchen all prepared to make a little honest change. Raynard was standing right before me, serving as head cook. Since I'd last seen him in Jackson, he'd picked up a little weight. That dapper physique my boy once bragged about was no more. As head cook, he was making thirty-two cents an hour. He'd been at Standish for a few years and had maxed out on DOC's pay scale. In other words, he was making a top dollar inmate salary for that particular job.

"What's up, Fat Man?" I screamed, walking up on him.

"P, what's up, Dawg?" he replied, grabbing me out of excitement. "Man, when you get here?" he asked.

"I've been here since October."

"October," he repeated.

"Yeah, but I had to do some down time. I caught major tickets in Ryan, so they had to reclassify me. After a few assaults on the law, they rode me out. To be honest, I've had some of the worst luck in the past few years, but, Man, you know your boy. I'm a survivor."

"Did you hear Charles Casey finally got iced out?"

"Yeah, I knew it was coming. That chump was too cocky for a nigga in a wheelchair. I'm surprised somebody didn't do him long before Louis did."

"When the last time you heard from E?" Raynard asked, stirring vegetables into a broth he was cooking.

"Everett paroled out of Ryan in May 1996. He said he was gon' be in touch with me when he got himself situated. I haven't heard from him in almost two years," I replied, observing Raynard because his attention was focused on someone else.

"B Holmes, what are you over there trying to do? Put those pots on that counter by the sink. Once I get the rest of these onions diced up, I'm going to sauté them in butter, and I'll need one of those skillets."

"B Holmes," I repeated. "I know a Holmes, what's his first name?" I asked as my heart raced.

"Byron, why?"

"Oh, I thought I knew him from the world. He looks familiar."

"P, Byron's from Detroit. He was out there getting 'em when he was in the world. He was down with Silk's empire. So I guess you can say he's part of the family as well."

"Is that right?" I asked, feeling numb from his reply.

"Looks like the Westside family's back together again," Raynard said, smiling with his arm around my neck. "Byron!" he eagerly yelled. "Come here. Let me introduce you to my boy, Prince."

As Byron walked over to the sink, I cased him from head to toe. *This simp knows something about my brother's death,* I thought, *and here Raynard is trying to make us boys.* After the intro, I just nodded my head without ever bothering to verbally speak.

"What's up, Man? Damn, you favor my boy Ant."

"Ant who?" I asked.

"Anthony Prince."

"Oh," I suspiciously responded, as my original thought of him seemed to be confirming itself.

He had to know that Ant was my brother considering that I'd just been introduced to him as Prince. To me, if he and Ant were like brothers then he should have known who I was. With the way my brother loved me, I know he talked about me to people he was cool with. For Byron not to know me or act like he didn't know who I was, I didn't think he was one of my brother's boys like he claimed to be.

Raynard didn't confirm that Ant was my brother after Byron made his comment. He knew me. If I didn't confirm I was related to Ant, there was obviously a problem of some sort between Byron and me. I went on about my business. I wasn't feeling Byron nor was I about to be chilling with the enemy. As a matter of fact, I beefed up my game over the months that passed to make sure I was always on top of what was happening around me. When I was working, I never allowed my back to stay facing anyone for long periods of time. I wasn't about to let anyone walk up on me and gut me without a fight.

One afternoon I was in the kitchen eating an orange. Raynard and I were laughing about a joke he'd made.

"P, with the way you're sucking that juice from those orange slices, it looks like you'd slurp the walls out of a coochie if you could."

"Ray, I never thought I'd say this, but one day I'm gon' get a chance to lick the hell out of some pussy. Man, I'm trying to get some practice in on something. I don't know anything about eating out, so I got to start somewhere. Remember, I came to prison at an age when that wasn't popular. Shit, Man, as a shorty, I learned how to tongue kiss by practicing on my arm."

"Boy, don't tell that story to nobody else," he laughed.

"Ray, all I knew in my younger days was thirty pumps and a nut. Back then, if a bitch would've told me to eat her out, I would have choked her ass to death, and then made her do me."

"P, you're a fool."

He thought I was playing, but I was horny and serious. There were so many things I thought about doing to a woman. At times, I didn't think I'd ever get a chance to experience any of them, but no one could ever take away my fantasies. Hell, even after I left the county, there were so many days I regretted not banging the hell out of Mary a few more times. There were so many moments I wanted to slap myself for not bringing a few more sessions of serious dick her way. As long as it had been since I touched a woman, I was tripping when I acted as though she wasn't good enough for me. Had I been in my right frame of mind, I probably would have hit that a few more times. I was so focused on going home to be with Carrington though. Huh, I guess the joke was on me. Had I known it might be another fifteen years before I'd see or feel the warmth of a woman again, I would've tapped that ass about three or four times the day she offered to let me dock in some bomb pussy. After pulling my dick out of her mouth, I would have found my way so far up inside of her that she'd still be looking for me today.

◆◆◆◆◆◆◆

After about a month, I was still leery of Byron. I believed he wasn't to be trusted. My reservation about him caused me to devise a plan for a hit on him. I don't know if God was on his side or if it simply wasn't his time, but the day he pulled me aside to say we needed to talk, actually saved his life.

"Holla at me about what?" I sharply asked.

"I can't talk here. Within the next few days get wit me. I'll let you know where later."

I couldn't imagine what he needed to talk with me about, but when he arranged a place to meet, I made sure I was strapped just in case I had to defend myself. I walked inside the library, picked up a law book, and sat at the table we agreed upon. If questioned by an officer while waiting for him to arrive, I'd pull out my notebook, which was full of cases to make it seem as though I'd been doing some research. I wasn't worried about the location because my back was facing a wall in the rear of the room. No one could sneak up behind me, which helped me relax. Therefore, I only had to pay attention to things going on in front of me.

"What's up, P?" Byron asked, approaching the table.

"Me! What's up with you?"

"Not much. The other day I had my mother send this letter I got some years ago from a good friend. When I was sentenced I told her to put it away for safekeeping. I knew I was going to need it in the future. For some reason, I've always felt like this letter would one day save my life. Today, I want you to read it, so you can tell me what you think."

I hesitantly took the letter from Byron carefully removing it from the beat up envelope it was in. I could tell it had been handled quite a bit because it was kind of worn. I delicately unfolded the piece of paper, and placed it inside one of my law books. Instantly, I focused on the writing. It appeared to be a script I knew really well. Actually, I knew it very well, and it gave me chills. It was a letter from Ant, which he entitled, "My request."

## My Request!

December 1, 1992

B, Smooth,

This note gon' be quick and to the point. I rarely put anything in writing, but if anything should ever go down with me, there are a few things I want you to handle. I have two hundred thousand dollars buried in my mother's backyard on the west side of her garage. If you walk about five feet from the side door, you'll be right in the area. It's stored in a black garbage bag and wrapped in rubber bands. Take that money, and open up five different bank accounts in my son's name. Deposit ten G's into each account. Make sure that no one touches that money before he's eighteen. Tell Li'l Anthony I want him to be the first male in the Prince family to go to college. With as much as I love the lifestyle I've lived, I don't want him to be like me or the other niggas in our family. One of us has to be on something more positive, and I hope it's him.

Give forty thousand cash to my mother. Tell her that ten grand is to go to my sister's college fund. Eighty thousand is to go to my younger brother, Prince, and twenty thousand is to be put into an account for his daughter, which she will be entitled to once she turns eighteen. It's hers to use as she pleases, but I would like for her to use it for college. The last ten is for you. I want you to have that for your loyalty to me.

I know you think I'm trippin', but there comes a time in a man's life when he realizes that one day his personal choices determine his future. When my day comes, I want to leave my family with something other than bills. That's something I learned from my wise grandfather.

Silk will take care of my funeral arrangements. Don't even bother to say anything to him about this money 'cause he'll want to use it. I have an additional bank account at Detroit Credit Union in Dearborn for my brother. If he ever gets out of prison for the crime I committed, I want to make sure that he gets that money. He knows our code and password. Tell him those numbers have been selected as the account number, too, with three zeros behind them.

If something should happen to him, you're the closest one to me. I'd like for you to have his portion of the money. I know that you'll handle this for me. Thanks for your loyalty, Li'l Bro.

Ant

Once again, I couldn't believe what I was reading. My brother was speaking to me from his grave. My soul was at rest, but as usual my heart was in severe pain. For Ant to write that note weeks before his death made me think he already knew he was about to die or Byron had him killed. Then again, if that were the case, why would he show me that letter? *He doesn't possibly think he can throw me off, does he?*

I didn't know what to think, but I still had a feeling Byron was kind of shady. Since I didn't know him, I still didn't trust him. Later that evening, I was edgy behind Ant's letter, so I called Bean to talk with her about Byron and my thoughts. I didn't want to go into too much detail on the phone 'cause calls were always monitored. But Bean confirmed that she got forty loaves of holiday bread from Renee's brother. Ten of which she gave to Ke for school. In simple terms, that meant she'd received forty thousand and gave Ke her ten.

"Do you know Byron?"

"Yes, I know him well. He's a good kid. Byron's always been very loyal to your brother, at times reminding me a lot of you. He looked up to Ant just like you did, which is exactly how he got caught up. When Ant's car was shot up, Byron was in the car, too. While trying to protect Ant, he'd been shot in the side. The only reason his life was spared is because when his gun ran out of bullets, he ducked to get Ant's extra gun from under the dashboard. The shooters opened fire on the car right as he bent down. Byron ended up killing one of the attackers with that gun. Though it was self- defense, the gun he used was also used to kill a police officer."

"All that for Ant?" I asked, feeling grateful for his sacrifice.

"Yeah, and I'm thankful that Byron didn't die because it would have been senseless for him and Ant to both die behind foolishness. Byron tried to resuscitate Ant after the other gunman ran off, but it was too late. Ant was already full of bullets and dead."

In all those years, I'd never gotten any real details on Ant's murder. I respected Byron for coming to my brother's rescue like he did, but troubled when I learned that he was like me in so many ways. Byron looked up to Ant so much that he, too, was willing to give up everything, including his life to show his loyalty. He was a natural lifer, just like me, and stupid for his sacrifice...just like me. Ant was dead and gone, but our loyalty caused us to serve his time. Maybe had I let him come to prison and do his own time, he'd still be alive. Huh, but who am I kidding? I would have still gotten into something and ended up incarcerated anyway. The only difference between Byron's charges and mine is that he was eighteen when he caught his case, yet he was still another young lifer, with nothing on his side but time.

In September 1998, my appeal finally made it to the Michigan Supreme Court. If they didn't rule in my favor I had one appeal left. If they ruled against me in the United States Supreme Court, I was going to be a permanent resident with the Michigan Department of Corrections. While Mr. Lewis continued to work on my case, I continued to try to find out who Calvin Shaw was. Byron was clueless. All he could tell me was that Ant talked about him from time to time, but Ant never introduced them. Byron did say the last time they all hung out, Melvin and Ant were beefing about a few of their spots that Calvin wanted them to do away with. He said Ant wasn't with closing down any of his spots that generated big money just because Calvin asked him to. Melvin argued that their houses were getting too hot because one of them was the location where the undercover cop had been killed. Ant had a mind of his own and wasn't in agreement with Melvin, so he refused to listen.

From my understanding, the cop-killing incident was a panic hit. Byron said a cop showed up trying to buy some heroin from one of Ant's spots. Melvin was across the street in another house with a silencer on his gun. When the officer left the porch, Melvin shot him in the head. After the officer fell in the street, Melvin walked away without being noticed.

I really didn't care about all those details. I focused more on the fact that Byron said Melvin and Calvin wanted Ant to shut down two of his houses. Though Byron didn't know Calvin, Melvin did, and to me that meant Melvin was suspect, too. *Did Melvin team up with Silk and set Ant up?* I wondered, trying to think of who I could put on Melvin for further investigation, but I hadn't seen him since '86, didn't know where to find him, and didn't have any legs on the outside to hunt him down, so I didn't stress about the Melvin issue for the time being.

# 19

## *Convicted But Innocent*

December 1998, Bean brought Asia to see me for the holiday. My little girl was blossoming into a fine young lady. She had sprouted breast, ass, and was working a shape that was gon' make me catch a case up in the joint. Inmates were checking her out, which I didn't like one bit. As she walked from vending machine to vending machine, I noticed a few of the guys gawking at her. That pissed me off. Before I realized it, I was up out of my seat, trying to inconspicuously mean mug convicts from my booth to get them to stop looking at her ass.

"Tell Butterfly to hurry up." I tapped on the glass, impatiently rattling to Bean.

"Asia, your dad said hurry up."

"Tell my dad to hold on, I'm trying to decide what I want."

Once Bean relayed her message, I got angry.

"Tell her to decide quicker or I'll decide for her." I hollered.

Bean finally told me to stop tripping. To avoid addressing her sassiness, Asia started telling me stories about Chicago, once she came back.

"Mom and Rodney have a pretty good relationship. But right now she's getting on everyone's nerves because she's pregnant again." While talking with her, I couldn't help but notice her sitting with her legs crossed. As I thought about her carrying on like she was grown, I smiled, thinking, *Asia has always been a real intellectual little lady.* For some reason she was a little more mature than usual. The more I looked at her, the more it hit home for me that my daughter was growing up. While wondering if she was sexually involved, my mind started going a million miles a minute. Before I knew it, I was asking that protective father question.

"Asia."

"Yes."

"Are you on the pill?"

"What kind of question is that, Daddy? Why did you ask me something like that out of the clear blue sky?" she asked, smacking her lips.

"Because, your butt's getting big. Actually, what I really want to know is, are you having sex?"

"Do I look like I'm having sex?" she asked with attitude.

"I didn't know that people having sex had a particular look. And you don't answer my question with a question. I asked are you having sex."

"No, not yet, but when I do, I'll write you or tell you about it in person."

"You said you gon' do what?" I asked as if she'd forgotten that I was her father.

"You heard me. I said I'll write you to tell you about it."

"Asia, those are a few details you might not want to share with me. Save that for your mother."

"Why not, we're supposed to be able to talk about anything, right?"

"Yeah."

"Why can't I tell you about my first sexual encounter then?"

"Because that's something that would kill me or break my heart. If you tell me anything like that, I'm gon' have a heart attack. No father wants to think about his baby girl getting pounded by no knucklehead. Asia, fathers enjoy having those conversations with our sons, not our daughters."

Asia laughed. I didn't see anything funny. Had I not cherished our little time together, I would have put my foot down. Thank God I took into consideration the tenderness of our relationship. Being that I didn't want to damper anything between us, I told her whatever she wanted to tell me, she could.

"But please remember I'm getting old. There's only so much I can take."

"Daddy, quit acting like an old man."

"Asia, I need to talk with Bean in private. Would you give me a minute alone with her, please?"

"Sure, Dad," she stated, hanging up her phone receiver. When she stood up to walk away, I started tapping on the glass.

"Where are you trying to go?" I asked, hoping she would sit there.

"Duhhhh, Dad. I'm going to use the restroom."

"I want you to sit there. These grown men keep checking you out. I don't like that."

"What do you want me to do then? I thought you needed to speak to Bean in private."

"I do."

"That means I'll have to move away for that to happen."

"Don't be up walking too long. Go and come right back."

"Okay." While Asia was getting up, I scooted closer to the glass to help Bean realize the significance of the discussion we were about to have.

"What do we need to talk about that's so confidential, Prince?"

"Bean, why didn't you ever tell me about the money Ant left?"

Complete shock filled her face before she finally replied with her head hanging in shame.

"Sweetie, I don't know. I just didn't."

"What the hell do you mean you don't know? I'm sitting up in this motherfucka rotting away for something I didn't do and that's the best you can say. I want to know why you said you didn't have any money when I called expressing my need for additional ends to hire an attorney." I angrily asked, speaking to her ruder than I should have.

"Because I didn't have any damn money!"

I looked at Bean as if to say, "Well, are you smoking?" But I couldn't bring myself to ask that question because I couldn't handle a reply of yes.

"Bean, I'm sorry for cursing. Just help me understand what you're telling me."

"Prince, when Byron brought the money to the house, he brought cash. I called myself hiding it until I could deposit it into my account. That Monday morning I got up to take it to the bank, only to discover that Renzo had stolen all but $6000.00 dollars. I called his cell phone to ask him about the missing money, but he never answered. He didn't come home that evening either. I called the cab company, only to learn from the dispatcher that he no longer worked for them."

"So you're telling me that sorry bastard took $24,000 dollars from you and bounced?"

"Yes," she replied, tearing. "There were so many things I wanted to do with that money. One of them was to get you an attorney," she said completely crying at that point.

"Why would he steal your money? And why didn't you tell me about this then?"

"Prince, I've made a lot of mistakes in my time. I haven't always been there for you, and I've exposed you to some things and men I shouldn't have. Renzo's an addict. He stole my money to support his habit, and I was embarrassed."

"His habit?" I asked, cutting her off.

"Yeah, Renzo has been a functioning Heroin addict for a few years. I really didn't know he'd relapsed until after he was gone. I suspected he had, but I found a few things around the house afterwards to confirm my suspicion."

"Plus most of your money was gone."

"Yeah," she answered in shame.

"But by then it was too late."

"I know. I never bothered to say anything to you about this because it goes back to my failures as a parent. You've been telling me about Renzo for years. I didn't want to hear those famous four words, "I told you so." I was already experiencing enough heartache."

I looked at my mother in disgust, as she sat weeping in her chair. There was no reason for me to further beat her down. I could see she felt horrible. As I sat quietly looking at her, I grew highly pissed about the entire situation. I was able to refrain from further disrespecting her. Yet, I couldn't help but think, *Dumb bitch, you suspected that your man was a fucking junkie, and you left thirty thousand dollars in the house with him? Bad move and we all lost behind that one.*

Although I thought Bean's actions were stupid, I struggled not to verbalize it.

"Bean we were supposed to be on some better shit when it came to our relationship. I can't believe you let a damn junkie steal my ticket to freedom. I'm disgusted with you. After that incident, I feel like even in prison you've let me down on this one. Was your self- esteem that low that you felt like you had to settle for a junkie?"

"Yes, sometimes."

There was nothing else for me to say. After sitting in silence for about two minutes, I tried to calm down again. I considered what I'd said to my mother, realizing that I really didn't mean most of what had come out. I was simply on a pity party. She didn't deserve half the stuff I said to her. Since my incarceration, she'd been my biggest cheerleader and my most inspiring supporter. I didn't want her to leave feeling bad, which is why I tried to be sympathetic and more positive before she left.

"Bean, no matter what kind of mother you were in the past, you've always been my mom. I love you in spite of our differences. We're going to make it through this, we're family. I know God will make a way. All of us have done things we're not necessarily proud about. What's most important is what we do to learn from our mistakes and better our situation and ourselves. No love lost, Beautiful. You keep being you and supporting me the way you have."

"I will, Prince," she sadly replied, exhaling.

Asia noticed Bean crying on her way back. I guess it was obvious that we'd had one of our intense conversations by my facial expression. She looked at me, then Bean, and decided to rescue her grandmother.

"Okay, Grandma, we need to go. You know Auntie Ke is taking me to the movies."

"Yeah, Ma, y'all better get on the road."

"Ma! Daddy, you never call Grandma, Ma."

"Yes I do."

"I haven't ever heard you call her that," she said looking at Bean for confirmation. "Grandma, has my daddy ever called you Ma."

"It's rare, but he has a few times in his life."

"Asia, be quiet, and give your daddy some Prince Kisses." I quickly interrupted before she asked another question.

"Daddy, I'm still your Butterfly, but I've gotten too old for Prince Kisses for real."

"Check you out. You'll always be my baby." I insisted laughing. "Asia, you've been a teenager for a few months. Now all of a sudden I don't rate kisses anymore?"

"Kisses are cool, but Daddy, I'm thirteen. I'm not about to be blowing kisses through glass. That's corny."

"So what! You said that like you're really old. *Damn, I'm starting to sound like Bean when she fussed me out about hanging out with Ant back in the day. I guess that comes with parenthood.* "Okay, you're thirteen, but you'll never be too old to show me love." I informed her, smirking.

"Bye, Daddy."

I just smiled, thinking, *She's so grown.*

### "Mail Call."

*February 6, 1999*

> P,
>
> *What's been up? Long time no hear from. Man, it has almost been three years since we had any contact. I know you're still maintaining. It's not in your nature to be doing anything else. I got a letter from Byron some months ago. He mentioned that he met you in Standish, which surprised me. I'm glad you took my advice and trusted my judgment on that one. See Prince, my judgment was right.*
>
> *The other day some guys came into my store. Stop smiling chump, it's not a big business, but it's paying the bills and it's legit. I became the entrepreneur you said you saw in me. I got a little clothing shop that I run out of my house. I sell designer bags, shoes, accessories, oils, and clothing for both sexes. After I got out of the joint, I hooked up with Thomas-Bey. He put me*

*down on this little clothing hustle. Man, you know me; well, I took it to the next level. Now I make a run every four weeks to New York to buy merchandise. When I bring it back to the city, I jack up the prices to make me a little profit, and that's how I'm surviving in the game.*

*I saw your girl, Carrington the other day. She's still looking as beautiful as ever, and also still just as stuck up as ever. P, she had another baby. This last one is by that cat Bobby she left you for. She said he's a little producer here in the city. Actually, Bobby has a few rap groups that just signed a major contract with Bling Inc. Records out of New York. They're supposed to be moving there within the month. Anyway let me stop talking about her. Go on pull the knife out of your heart.*

*As I was saying earlier, I was talking with this dude the other day that wanted to invest in my business. He claimed he could help me get a store on Seven Mile. He thought I had a nice little lay out at the crib. He swears his guy Calvin is a top dollar businessman. He's supposedly looking to invest his money in a few up-and-coming empires. He wanted to make me an offer for a piece of the action in Storey's Rags to Riches. I told him I'd meet this Calvin guy to discuss business in person, but I wasn't one to deal with the middleman. He is working on setting us up a meeting. See P, even in my freedom I'm still looking out. When I find out if this is our guy, I'll let you know something.*

*Don't reply until you hear from me again. If this guy is our man like I think he is, I don't want to take any chances on his boys shaking down my spot. You know how we do, just keep this to yourself. We can't trust anyone. If someone affiliated with Calvin finds out my connection to you or your brother, it could cost me my life. Stay up, and I'll be in touch soon.*

*One*
*E*

I hadn't heard from my boy for what seemed like forever. His letter came at a good time though. I always knew E was real, and his word was his bond, which is why I never worried about him not contacting me. He understood how important it was for me to find my brother's killer. That's why E couldn't help but look out for me.

♦♦♦♦♦♦♦

Byron and I brainstormed on ballas that might've set Ant up. To try to build our case, we discussed various things that happened days before his death. Though we kept coming up with dead ends, we kept going over as much information as we possibly could about the day Ant died. Neither of us knew much, but I wasn't giving up. Until I knew who Calvin Shaw was there was still hope. If E found out some low down news on him, and DOC didn't grant me my freedom, I was breaking out for the sole purpose of killing Calvin. Not only did I want to know who he was. I also wanted to know who this middleman was, too, and in what way he was linked to Ant, if any. As far as I was concerned, if there was anyone in or out of the joint that could give me any facts about Calvin, I wanted to speak with them.

I didn't tell Raynard, Byron or anybody else about E's possible business transaction with Calvin. I was on edge for weeks, then months, as I waited for some kind of information that might ease a little of the stress I was under. None ever came. I continued to question Byron on a regular basis to get him to remember any little detail he could about the time he spent with Ant. As he remembered things over the months, he'd mentioned them to me, I didn't want to forget anything he told me, so I logged everything in a journal. I was on a mission to keep up with all the facts he offered because I didn't know when Ant's killer would be brought to justice or if he'd be ordering a hit on me.

In June 1999, we finally got a decision back from the Michigan Supreme Court. They didn't rule in my favor. That was it for me. I was highly discouraged. I sat around for weeks wondering what I could do as an "Innocently Convicted" man to prove I wasn't guilty. My situation was making me hopeless. I had been fighting for my freedom at that point for over thirteen years, only to have one judge rule in my favor. To add disappointment to that one victory, the stupid judge allowed his initial ruling to be overturned in a matter of months. It seemed like my life didn't matter. *What the hell are these judges reading when they consider my case? Obviously not the facts,* I thought, reading the response from the courts over a million times. *These Suckas probably think I wanted to sue the damn state.* But had they offered me my freedom with one condition being no lawsuit, I would have taken their offer and ran.

I had all kinds of thoughts going on in my mind, one of which was the fact that I needed a Dream Team like OJ's. There was only one appeal left for me. I considered if I should stay with Miles Lewis or get the money Ant left to hire a new attorney for my battle in the United States Supreme Court. Finally, after hours of feeling sorry for myself, I got off my ass and went to work.

"Raynard!" I yelled, walking into the kitchen.

"What's up, P?"

"Man, they denied my appeal again in the State Supreme Courts."

"You're lying! What the hell are those judges looking at when they read over your material? If those bastards looked at the facts, they'd see that you've been falsely convicted. Shit, your affidavits alone should produce some damn concerns. Why the hell do they think you're spending all this money?"

"They're railroading me. They know if I win the state is going to owe me hella money. These assholes have robbed me of my youth, caused me to miss out on my daughter's childhood, prevented me from properly saying goodbye to my brother and grandfather, and forced me to live among hardened criminals, only to become one my damn self. I can't stay here much longer. Man, I've got to get me a bomb attorney to represent me."

"Who?" he asked.

"I don't know, but I don't have that much time to appeal, so I need to hire someone quickly." While sharing my plans with Raynard, Byron walked in.

"B, when you finish up, let me holla at you," I yelled.

"Cool, give me about ten minutes."

While waiting, I stood around listening to the fellas talk about a bunch of nonsense. That was one thing all brothas in the joint had in common. They all loved to shoot the shit about a whole bunch of nothing. Basic chattering made the day move a little faster, so everyone always had a story to tell. After Byron finished, he motioned for me to follow him out of the kitchen to a storage room.

"What's up?" he asked.

"They denied my appeal. I need to get to some of that money Ant had buried at the house for me."

"For real! How much are you talking about?"

"Ten grand."

"Man, I'll see what I can do. I'm gon' have to get wit the old girl to have her get the money."

"Get it from where?" I asked.

"I put the rest of it in a safe deposit box right before I came to prison. The box has been paid up for a few years now. There's also a small container Ant left for you in there. My mother just paid on it again just this year in order to maintain it."

"You said you put the rest of the money in a safe deposit box along with a container Ant left. What container and what do you mean the rest of it?"

"Ant had a grey box he kept in his room. He always told me if something happened to him put that container in a safe deposit box for you. He assured me that if you ever got out you'd know what to do with the box."

"Grey Box?"

"Yeah, it's the size of a cassette tape case."

"Oh, I remember what box you're talking about. But it's small. I'm sure it couldn't have anything of value in it."

"Man, he said put it up for you. That's what I did. Now as for the money, I had to pay for an attorney with something because I was looking at some serious ass time. I used what I needed from the money he left you, and put the rest up for a rainy day."

"Forget the fact that you spent some of it. How much is left?"

"About, twenty."

"Twenty thousand!" I replied in shock. "Damn, you spent sixty thousand dollars on what?"

"Some of it was spent on an attorney, different things I've needed in here, and maintaining that box year after year."

"How soon can your mom get to the bank to get Bean some of that money?" I asked.

"I'll call her later today. After I speak to her, I'll get back with you on that," he replied with little concern about my freedom or me. *I bet this nigga done spent all my fucking money,* I thought, getting up to walk away.

On my way to my cell, I was curious as to what might be in the grey box. I'd always seen it on Ant's dresser, but I never asked him what it contained. I do remember the box having a few marks on its side from being dropped so much. One thing for sure, I was convinced that whatever he stored in that box wasn't worth much.

I spent the next few weeks consulting with my attorney about his plans for my final appeal. After explaining his plans in detail, he insisted that I not lose faith in him. He said he, Gary Canadia, and his team were preparing a brief of a lifetime for the U.S. Supreme Court that was sure to bring me home. Mr. Canadia experienced a slight break in his tedious schedule and agreed to assist my attorney with the preparation of my final brief. Mr.

Lewis expressed that he had become so caught up on my conviction, that it was his personal mission to prove my innocence.

"Prince, I believe you're innocent. Proving that has become just as important to me as it is to you. To assure you that I believed in what I'm doing, we're going to do your last appeal for absolutely free."

"Free?" I repeated.

"Prince, save your money for the new trial we're about to win," he suggested.

For the first time during my incarceration, I felt a sense of peace. I knew that over the years my team of attorneys and I had put forth our very best effort. If my conviction wasn't overturned, it simply wasn't a part of the divine plan for my life. I didn't tell Byron that I wasn't going to need my money. It was mine. If he could get to it, I wanted it. Finally, weeks after our conversation, B came to me talking about only four thousand dollars of the money was left. I know he knew what happened to the majority of it, but I couldn't be mad. I wanted to raise hell, but when I considered his sacrifice, I felt like he was worthy of some of Ant's money as well. "B, that's cool; I'll take the four grand."

Days later we made arrangements for his mother and Bean to make the transaction. In September 1999, Bean deposited $700.00 on my books. I remember thinking how rich I was when I got my Inmate Financial Statement. I hadn't had that kind of money in so long that I laughed when thinking of a nice gift to send Asia. Here I was a few months short of my thirtieth birthday, and I hadn't been exposed to that kind of money in over thirteen years.

◆◆◆◆◆◆◆

December 5, 2000, I turned the big three/zero. I woke up feeling like it was just another day. I hadn't acknowledged a birthday in some time. As I sat around reading a magazine, an officer announced that I had a visit over the speaker. I didn't feel much like changing, so I got up off my bed then walked to the back hallway to be escorted.

"Prince, this is a non-contact visit. You have to go to the other side," a guard informed me. The only person I had non-contact visits with was Bean, so right from jump, I knew it was her. Considering it was my birthday, my feelings were a little hurt when I considered there would be no kind of physical affection between the two of us. As much as I'd been missing Bean, my heart was troubled behind the position I'd put us in.

It was straight to the cage for me that day. When I sat down, I touched the glass as always to show my mother as much love as I possibly could. She blew me kisses, while sitting down. I smiled at her acts of compassion like a five-year-old. When I picked up the phone, I was excited to hear her voice.

"Hey, Beautiful, you're sure looking good."

"So are you, Prince. Happy birthday, how are things going? Are you staying out of trouble?"

"Why do you always ask me that? You know I'm maintaining, like always." I paused, intently looking at my mother like I never had before. I could sense that she wasn't quite her usual self. To avoid nagging her, I started asking questions to get a feel for her look of concern. "How are you and the family doing?"

"Everyone is well. We miss you, Ant, and Daddy, but we try to stay afloat. Silk came by the other day. We hadn't seen him since we buried Daddy. He promised Ma he was going to slow down because he knows she can't take another loss. I believe he's seriously taking all these deaths into consideration and trying to do better."

"I can't take another one either," I replied as thoughts of my Granddad and brother came to mind. "Well, tell me something good," I suggested, forcing a smile to my face.

"Tell you something good. Hum….. Let me see." As Bean searched for a reply, I noticed she struggled to keep our conversation going. That was very unusual. She was generally a talk-a-holic, so I kept asking her if she was doing okay to see if she needed to talk about something. She repeatedly insisted that she was fine, so I immediately dropped the subject.

"How come you came alone?" I asked.

"I didn't, there's someone waiting in the lobby to see you for a contact visit."

"Who is it?"

"I'm not telling, but I am going to go ahead and leave, so they can come back before it gets too late."

"I know you didn't bring Carrington, did you?"

"Oh Hell No! With the way she hurt you, I sure didn't. I wouldn't take that bitch to a funeral if it were her own. I brought someone I thought you'd enjoy seeing."

"Quiet as it's kept, she'd be someone I'd like to see," I replied.

"Well it ain't her. Your other visitor is a surprise, so I'm not telling you anything," she responded, getting up from her seat.

"Love you, Bean."

"I love you, too, Baby, and again, happy birthday."

Bean blew me several kisses, before touching the glass to say goodbye. I lifted my hands to place them on hers, and then waved. As she walked away, I sensed she was in need of a hug from her only son. Man, I'd put us in a real bad situation. That was confirmed on every visit by the void and constant pain we experienced afterwards. I could tell that Bean was getting tired of the road trips. I knew they were starting to wear her down. I had some doubts about winning my final appeal, but for Bean's sake, I hoped my days of confinement were about over. I watched her completely exit before I moved. Within minutes of me sitting down, Everett walked through the doors. When he approached me, I smiled like a gigolo swamped by a harem of ho's. I was so hyped, about seeing my boy that once he made it over to me, I embraced him like an excited child.

"What up, Playa? I thought you were gon' write me about two months ago?" I asked.

"Yeah, I was, but I got real busy. How's DOC treating you?"

"Man, this place is taking a toll on me. I'm ready to blow this spot today. What has you out visiting the cons during your free time? I didn't think you'd ever come to prison again."

"Not to stay, but I would to see my Dawg. P, I got some good news I couldn't put in a letter with the way these nosey ass people read everything. I decided I needed to finally make my way out here, so I brought Bean along since it was your day."

"Good news? What kind of good news?" I asked, sitting back.

"The guy that handles all Calvin's business goes by the name Money. I've been trying to get his real name from so many people, but everyone on the block only knows him by that name."

"What does he look like?" I asked.

"He's a brown cat, short fade, and would be labeled in the joint as a pretty nigga. He's a slender build and is about 5ft'10in."

"Got me." I replied, shrugging my shoulders. "While you were describing him, I was trying to think if Ant did business with him back in my day. This guy doesn't sound familiar at all. Have you met Calvin yet?"

"Naw, we haven't met face to face, but I'm supposed to pick up some money from him next month. We're getting closer to hooking up. When we meet, I'll let you know."

"Cool, let me know how things go."

We both became heated the more we kicked it about Calvin and his errand boy Money. E changed the subject when I started talking loud. He was trying to calm me down, but his efforts were hopeless. Whenever I thought about my brother being murdered, nothing calmed me. I wanted to know the truth about Ant's death. Nothing, not even prison was going to stop me from getting answers.

When our visit ended, E made a few jokes about Carrington. I didn't find any humor in them because they were too personal. However, when I thought about him hating on me, I laughed. E actually kind of reminded me of Chew and Julius during our school days.

"Stay up, Homie," I suggested before E left.

"You too 'cause your day is coming soon."

# 20

## *Silk*

Asia was in Detroit for the Christmas holiday of 1999. Because she was in town, Bean brought her out to see me. That particular holiday season was much harder than all our previous holiday visits. I think I was stressing from the waiting that came along with hearing something from the courts. The thoughts of being in prison forever didn't help much either. I was back and forth on my pity parties. The fact that I was not able to hug my child or my mother took a toll on me as well. For the first time in the history of my imprisonment, I felt like killing myself. During my entire incarceration, I'd never felt as low as I did that day. After recapping the past fourteen years of my life, I felt worthless. All the hype about 2000 did not faze me one bit. *Shit, if the world was coming to an end grea;, I wouldn't have to suffer any longer*, I thought just about everyday until March passed.

During the first week of April 2000, my attorney came in to speak with me about the appeal he'd submitted for a new trial. I wasn't as nervous as I had been for some of the other appeals. I felt like what ever happened, happened. At that point, there was nothing else I could do. I had fought a great fight. Now it was up to God and the U.S. Supreme Court Judges.

"All we can do is wait now, Prince," my attorney stated once he was about to leave. "Get some rest. You look tired. As soon as I hear something, I'll be in touch."

To me his comment was easier said than done. It wasn't the rest of his life that was on the chopping block. If them tight collar, coffee drinking, Supreme Court Judges didn't rule in my favor, it wasn't a real issue to him. He was going to proceed with his life, get him a few new clients to represent, buy a new Benz to replace the one that had accumulated to many miles from coming to see me, and move on. I'd be stuck in prison with a constant reminder of the ultimate sacrifice I made trying to be my brother's keeper.

**"Mail Call"**

March 25, 2000

Prince,

What's up, Dawg? You're never going to believe this. I know who your boy is. There was a big Y2K party downtown on New Year's Eve at Danzel's. Your boy Calvin fell up in the spot clean as hell. He caught my attention because he was rockin' this phat, full-length fur, with a bad mink hat to match. I heard a few sista's talking about his platinum pinky ring that had a rock in it the size of an eyeball. The suit and gator's he was rockin' made him stand out like a sore thumb.

At first, I didn't know it was Calvin. Money never worked out our business transaction, so I didn't get to meet him. The day we were supposed to hookup, Calvin decided it wasn't in his best interest to invest in my clothing business. Anyway, there were about four other big balla's up in the house that addressed him by name. Plus, Money was right on his heals acting like a bitch.

Man, I was so close to him a few times, I could have done him just like that. He wouldn't have known what hit him. But, I ain't no fool. I do value my life and my freedom, so I stayed away, peeping him from afar.

I was just sending you a shout out. I'm gon' lay low for a little while. I promise when it's his time, he's getting served a blanket of carnations with some baby's breath.

P.S. I got my store on Seven Mile. Business is jumping off the hook, too. Man, if you ever get out, you know I'm gon' look out. Holla back,
E'

Damn, I couldn't believe E got that close to Calvin. I wanted that nigga dead so bad, my ass hurt thinking about it. For the weeks that followed his letter, I had restless days and restless nights. I was losing my grip on reality and on the verge of breaking. I needed any kind of good news because I was in bad shape. I moped around from sun up to sun down. I hadn't prayed in a minute, but the entire month of April, I stayed on my knees asking Allah to deliver me from the living hell I was going through. Some days while kneeling to pray, I thought about my grandfather and the God he raised me to serve and even prayed to Him in the manner in which my granddad had taught me. I'd ask God everyday in the name of Jesus to bring me out of the funk I was in. I needed Him to send me anything that would lift my spirits. But to me, my prayers went unanswered because as usual pain and heartache followed my month of prayer.

In July 2000, Ke and Silk came out to see me. As soon as I saw Silk, I knew something was wrong. It was either Bean or GG. Silk hugged me like a father would a son before telling me how much he'd missed me. His words meant nothing, which is why my reply to him was cold, and direct. "Yeah, Nigga right, that's why you've been in touch with me so much over the past fourteen years, right?"

Silk seemed shocked from my reply, but I was numb to his presence and unmoved by his fake expression of happiness. Had it not been for them bringing me bad news, and me not wanting my sister to have to try to tell me alone, I would have put his sorry ass out. After I got myself together, the best I could give Silk was my presence. "Excuse me, Silk," I stated, moving around him to embrace my sister.

"Damn, P! What's up with that?" He asked, stunned by my flat reaction towards him.

"Ke, how's GG and Bean?" I asked, ignoring his question.

"Not too good." Once I looked into my little sister's cheerless eyes, there was no need for additional words. I understood by her expression that one of them had taken severely ill or was no longer with us.

"Which one?" I asked.

"Mama."

"Mama?" I repeated, struggling to breathe.

"Prince, Mama died yesterday at work. She walked to the water fountain complaining of chest pains and fell dead, inches from her desk." I grabbed my head out of shock.

"Hell Naw!" I screamed out in pain.

I looked at Ke and then Silk, but I couldn't bring myself to words. To comfort myself, I leaned forward resting my head on my lap. As the news of my mother's death registered, I thought, *God no! I can't take another loss and especially not my mother*. As I softly moaned, tears uncontrollably fell from my eyes. When I thought about the relationship Bean and I had established, I became scared to go on without her. I had become so dependent on her. Her visits meant more to me than I can ever describe in words. I was empty. The thought of never seeing her again made me want to slit my wrist in the visiting room.

The more I cried, the more I kept trying to tell myself that I was only dreaming. Ke eventually started tearing as well, and tried to hug me. I pulled away 'cause I didn't want to be comforted. I had almost fourteen years of pain bottled up inside of me that needed to be released. I had been suppressing a real hard cry for so long that I needed to get that one off. All I'd been doing for years is dropping tears, but the death of my mother was more than I could bear. "Bean, how you gon' just die on me before I win this fight for us? I ain't held you in almost eight fucking years. Please don't leave me like this," I cried out, feeling alone.

My sister and I were fairly close, but since Ant's death, my mother had become my closest relative. I felt absolutely nothing in regards to Silk. Since we hadn't kicked it in so long, I actually didn't know him anymore. Seeing him that day helped me realize the degree of bitterness I harbored towards him, and the thought that he had something to do with Ant's death didn't help.

"Thanks for coming out to tell me in person," I replied, wiping my eyes. I stood, kissed Ke's forehead, and then turned to walk away. "Ke, I'll call you tomorrow. I wish I could be there with you. I love you, and be strong." I took about thirty additional steps before stopping again in mid-stride. "Silk, put Bean away like a Royal Queen who gave birth to a Prince. Though she didn't always act like a queen, over the past few years, she really blossomed into one to me."

Without saying another word to Silk, I tapped on the glass to alert the officer that I was ready to return to my cell. He motioned for me to enter the room for my strip search. As he attempted to make small talk, it was clear in my expression that I was uninterested in his conversation. As degrading as that process had always been, even strip searches had become as routine to me as brushing my teeth.

The week Bean's funeral arrangements were being made, I called home everyday. Silk told me he was paying DOC the $1100.00 dollars required for me to be transported to her services. I knew that was only out of guilt. I didn't want any favors from him or anyone else, but if DOC allowed me to attend my mother's funeral, I was going. I had already missed Ant's and Daddy Ruenae's funerals, which I regretted. It was a little different with Bean though; I felt obligated to pay my last respects to her. She was my mother, and no matter what it required for me to attend, I wanted to be there.

The morning of Bean's funeral, I woke up feeling sorry for myself. Officer Deznick came to my cell informing me that I needed to suit up for transportation. Before being escorted to the shipping unit, I put on some black slacks, a blue shirt, and tie. Officer Flemon and Wallace were my acting escorts and transported me to the McTemple Brothers Funeral Home.

When we arrived, Officer Flemon helped me off the van. Once I was situated the three of us walked in together. I remember walking into the building with my head down because I felt ashamed. Though we arrived early and there was still an hour until the service started, I cringed at the thought of my family and friends seeing me shackled. When I entered the sanctuary, I locked in on Bean's mauve casket at the front of the room. I could see the silhouette of her body, but no particular features because of the distance. As I walked, I could hear my leg shackles rattling. For a moment, I focused on them because the sound helped me pace myself. The closer I got to my mother, the more defined her image in the casket became and the shackles no longer mattered. I could feel my heart racing and my adrenalin flowing. My legs felt like mush, so I tried to pace myself to keep from falling. My shackles seemed to rattle louder as I took one step after the other, then suddenly I was standing beside Bean's casket.

I stood there for a moment in silence as tears fell from my eyes. When I thought about our last visit, my heart ached. After I considered that I wasn't able to hug her before she left, I cried even harder. That day, had I known I would never see or talk to my mother again, I would have shared with her how much I loved her and the difference she'd made in my life over the past fourteen years. When I thought about us never being able to visit or talk again, I lifted my shackled hands and laid them on top of hers. "They can't stop us from touching today." I whispered, leaning over to kiss her forehead.

When I felt her cold, stiff face, I kneeled down and cried out loud. I think the officers felt a little compassion for me, which is why together they agreed to take off my handcuffs. I eased a little closer to Bean and whispered to her. "Bean, why didn't you wait a little longer? You've left me here to fight this fight all by myself, and I need you. I've grown so use to spending time with you and talking with you that I don't know how I'm going to make it the rest of the way alone. I wish you'd shared with me that you hadn't been feeling well. I knew something was wrong during our last visit, but I ignored my instinct. I hope you know that I loved you so much. No matter what anyone thinks, you died a Queen in my eyes. But Ma, most importantly, you shed the name Mia (MIA), if that means anything to you now. I'll never forget the support you've given me. When I get out of this mess, I promise, I'm going to make you proud of me. Bean, I'm going to be the son that makes something of himself like you've always wanted."

I looked at her wishing she could reply. After staring in her sleeping face for about twenty minutes, I sat on the front pew thinking as I waited for my family and the service to begin. Finally, after about thirty minutes, people started arriving. I stood when my family walked in, trying to be as much a part of them as I could. Once Ke made it to the front, she sat right next to me. I held her hand for the majority of the service, and we often found ourselves repeatedly wiping each other's tears. GG sat between Ka'Nita and Silk, while Brian sat right behind her.

Ke's boyfriend Sam put together a Power Point slideshow of Bean's life to *A Song for Mama* by Boy's II Men. It was a beautiful presentation. It was very fitting for the occasion and a tribute to Bean that even brought Aunt Ka'Nita to her knees. Right as the video was ending, Ke went nuts. She ran out the sanctuary screaming. What hurt me most is that I couldn't run behind her to provide any kind of comfort. I looked over at the two officers who sympathized with my pain, but they gave me a look like, you better not move. When I looked up at the screen there was a freeze frame group picture of the Prince family. Three of the members were no longer with us. To be reminded of what we once were only made me question where we were headed as a family. One day the other six people on that photo were going to die as well: GG, Silk, Brian, Ka'Nita, Ke, and me.

By the time the funeral directors opened the casket for the final viewing, Sam had walked Ke back to her seat and sat with us. As people came to pay their last respects, they hugged and kissed me the most out of everyone. I tried to be strong for Ke, but when E, Carrington, and little India walked up, my pain was intense.

"P, be easy, Man. If you need me for anything, just let me know," E insisted, wiping his tears.

"Thanks," I said, embracing him and looking on at Carrington.

"Prince, I'm so sorry about your mother," she stated, hugging me.

"Thanks for coming," I replied, without giving her any additional conversation because I noticed my daughter viewing Bean's body.

"Daddy, I'm so sorry about Grandma dying on you. I know this is going to be hard, but you've still got me and Auntie Ke," Asia replied, crying extremely hard.

"Thanks, Butterfly. I love you. Write me when you can."

Asia tried to sit with me, but because she had not been sitting there since the beginning of the service, the officers shook their heads to let me know she couldn't stay. When the family on the first row stood for our final viewing, I had to stay seated, so Ke sat back down with me. Everyone except for the two of us said their goodbyes and exited. Ke and I approached Bean's casket hand in hand. As we provided support for each other, we stood there crying over Bean for a long time. I looked at my mother, and finally she appeared to be at rest. "Bean, no more suffering," I whispered, bending over to kiss her forehead one last time. "I can't believe you're leaving me like this. Who's gon' love me and support me now?" I loudly cried out, like a small child, lowering myself into her casket. "Who's gon' love me now?" I whispered again, comforting myself. Once I got up out of the casket, I regained my composure, and hugged my sister.

"Prince, I'm glad you didn't make me do this service by myself. I love you so much and thanks for coming. You're all I've got now. No matter what, we have to do better about staying in touch."

"I know, Beautiful. You better go on and get up there with everyone else. Sam's waiting on you, and they're ready to take Bean's body."

"Okay, I'll be out to see you later this week." Ke stated, walking away.

Sam waited in the sanctuary door until Ke made it to him, and the two of them exited together. I wished like hell I was leaving with them. After the room was empty, Officer Wallace re-cuffed me, and I was escorted to the van. All the way back to Standish, I didn't say a word, but once we pulled through the gates, I thanked them for removing my cuffs and standing off to the side to spare me some embarrassment.

Once I made it back to my cell, I changed my clothes. I grabbed Bean's obituary before relaxing on the bed to read through it. I didn't make any calls home that evening nor did I go to work. I didn't socialize with Raynard or anyone else. I sat around the remainder of the day reflecting on that Power Point slideshow of Bean's life, my childhood, my brother, my family, my life, and my freedom, until I finally fell asleep.

◆◆◆◆◆◆◆

Ke visited me that same weekend just as she had promised. Every other weekend that followed for the next seven months, she made that long trip over and over again. Our first few visits, she seemed to talk very scattery. She was scaring me for a while, talking about things that didn't make any kind of sense. She told me she saw Ant at Bean's funeral when she ran out of the Chapel. I knew she was gone after that. I was worried about her psychological well-being or the possibility of her having a nervous breakdown. I wondered if she might need some kind of counseling. I spoke with her about seeing a shrink, considering that we had experienced three major deaths in our family. She wasn't in favor of that. Ke assured me that she wasn't crazy, and I respected her views.

Some weekends when Ke came out, we'd talk about things pertaining to our life or what Bean would want for her. Some days we didn't say much at all. There were a number of weekends she'd come, sit in the visiting room with me, and not say one word for hours. Though she never said, I think she needed to be around me due to the connection we shared as siblings.

Once we finally found ourselves healing, we were in a new year. Ke and I talked a little more about my mother's death and the role I could play in her life from prison. She was only ten when I left, so our bond wasn't what it could have been, though we were working on establishing something special.

"Prince, when Bean first died, I often felt alone. More so like an only child because I had no siblings to comfort me after her funeral. I didn't have anyone to visit in the city on the days I felt most lonely, which is why I started making the long trips to see you. Somehow us just being in one another's company made me feel better. You were all I had, and though GG was there for me, she didn't provide the same kind of comfort as you did."

Ke coming to visit like she did provided me with a sense of family security that I knew I was going to lose after Bean died. I never told her that her company was good for me as well, but it was. As painful as my mother's death had been for me, if we had to mourn the loss of her all over again, I'd want things to be the exact same way they were between us. I wouldn't want to do anything differently, considering that my sister and I had become best friends.

◆◆◆◆◆◆◆

In February 2001, I was informed that I was being transferred to Thumb Correctional Facility in Lapeer, Michigan. That facility got its name because of where it was located. It was in the thumb portion of the mitt that gave shape to the state. I was clueless as to why I was being moved or if someone had put the transfer into motion. When I arrived, I was placed on level two. I literally thought I'd died and gone to heaven. Thumb was one of the nicest facilities I'd locked in and most certainly my favorite. It was closer to Detroit, so Ke only had to drive forty-five minutes for a visit. Being closer also relieved some of my worrying when I knew she was traveling home afterwards. One thing for certain about Thumb, if it weren't for the correctional officers, and the razor wire, I could have almost appreciated doing my time.

As I settled in, I remained anxious about my last appeal. It had almost been a year since we'd heard anything, so I started getting antsy. When I felt discouraged, I called my attorney to ask questions about the appeal status or if he'd heard anything.

"When I hear something, you'll be the second to know." That wasn't particularly the response I was looking for, so at times, I didn't think he was doing enough on my behalf. That's why I'd have Ke following my case via the Internet. She could go on line and let me know anything she came up with. The more she checked on my status, the more frustrated she became with my case as well. After a while, I stopped asking her to check and impatiently waited on notification from the courts.

Some days she'd tell me, "If these stupid judges don't decide something soon, I'm gon' start personally emailing them myself."

"Right, and find yourself facing some harassment charges."

"Harassment charges for what?"

"First of all, they gon' doctor up your E-mail. You know these bastards in the judicial system all working together. They don't give a damn about a black man's future. All them in decision-making roles are scandalous as hell, and about one thing, getting a paycheck. Ke, "Fair Justice" went out the door, long before I went on trial."

One positive thing that came from seeing my sister's frustration was the confirmation that she sincerely wanted me home, which made me feel good.

**"Mail Call."**

April 5, 2001

Daddy,

I hope when this letter finds you all is well. I'm sure you've been wondering where I've been since I haven't written in a while. Man, I've been going through some things. I still haven't recovered from Grandma's death. I miss her so much. There are days I dial her number expecting her to answer. I think I'm going through a slight bout of depression. My grades are suffering, my skin was breaking out real bad, and I've lost about thirty pounds. Mom took me to the dermatologist two weeks ago. My skin looks way better, but now I'm having family problems.

Mom and her man are a trip. Lately, we haven't been getting along very well. They're pressuring me about being a role model for my little sister. I told them that's their job, not mine. They're her parents, not me. Why should I always have to walk on eggshells like I've given birth to some dang kids? I'm in the prime of my life. I'm supposed to be able to thoroughly enjoy myself, not worry about setting examples for someone else's kids. If I were worried about being the perfect role model, I'd have my own children. Anyway, my attitude keeps the three of us going at it every day. Mom says since I've turned sixteen, I think I know everything. Daddy, that's not the case. I've always had an opinion, now all of a sudden she hates the fact that I speak my mind. I think Mom wants me to allow Rodney to talk to me any way he pleases. I'm not having that. He's not my daddy. His child's name is Dynasty, and that's who he needs to be focused on, not me.

I'll be in Detroit in mid June to stay with GG and Auntie Ke. I'm sure we'll be out to see you.

Love and miss you,

Asia

I hadn't seen or heard from my daughter since the funeral. I didn't know why she hadn't written and couldn't worry about it either. I was going through my own thing; however, I was glad she at least let me know she was doing okay.

**"Mail Call."**

May 1, 2001

P,

What's upper? Man, my businesses are doing great. I got two real nice stores that are bringing in serious money. How's the appeal coming along? Hopefully you'll hear something soon. It's already been a year. I know they got to rule in a minute. From time to time I check on Ke and your grandmother to make sure they don't need anything. Ke's boyfriend is a nice young man. I cut real hard for him. He shows your sister lots of support. She found herself a good man when she got with him.

Hey, one of my little young homeboys found out Money's real name. Do you know a guy name Melvin Daniels? Well hopefully you do because that's Calvin's homies real name. If your brother knew him, I'm sure he's probably going to be our delivery boy.

Get at me when you can. Oh and by the way, I sent two hundred in for them to put on your books.

Holla,
E'

When E said Money's name was Melvin Daniels, I almost died. Melvin had been Ant's life long best friend since forever. I was hoping he wouldn't take part in setting my brother up, but anything was possible. What really hurt me most was that I knew Ant trusted Melvin more than he trusted some of our family. To think that he had something to do with Ant's death enraged me. *Shit, he was the only nigga that could get close enough to Ant to kill him without him suspecting anything,* I thought as I kicked clothes all over my cell. "Damn, Melvin! How you gon' sell out my brother like that?" I screamed, continuing to kick shit all over my cell. "Fuck you Calvin Shaw, you're a dead nigga," I mumbled, making an even bigger mess.

I was broke down after I learned about Melvin. At one point in my life, I loved him like a brother. I never told Ke what I found out because I didn't want her involved in anything. Plus, she would have told Silk and who knows what would've transpired from there. We already had enough deaths. Our family couldn't afford another one. *In time, some people gon' die for killing my brother. I don't care if I have to pay for that nigga to be got, he's goin' down,* I thought, cleaning up my mess.

# 21

## GG Basement

On May 21, 2001, I was called out to my Case Manager's office. *What now?* I thought, walking with some pep in my step. As I reached the door, I stopped, took a few breaths, and then knocked.

"Come in, Mr. Prince," he suggested. I entered the office thinking he was about to be the bearer of more bad news, when my attorney walked in.

"We did it, Prince!" he yelled, smiling like crazy.

"Miles, you got to be kidding me." I responded, as my heart dropped.

"Nope, I'm serious. You're going home. Not only did they think you deserved a new trial, but they saw that you'd been railroaded, which is why they demanded you be released."

"When?" I frantically asked.

"Immediately."

"Immediately! Aw, hell naw. You got to be kidding!" I replied.

"Nope, I'm serious, Man. You're going home today."

"Damn," I stated, resting my head on the desk in front of me to cry. Here I was fifteen years later a free man. I was innocent all that time and had practically lost everything I loved.

"Mr. Prince, you need to go get packed. You're leaving today." Mr. Woodard my Case Manager suggested.

I didn't know what to think, this was a day I'd only dreamed about, but I promise I never thought it would become a reality. Institutions had been my home for over the past umpteen years. My fear of the unknown scared me to death. I didn't know what life was like outside the prison walls anymore. I certainly didn't know how I was supposed to live my life without my mother and brother. I no longer had a connection to Silk, so I couldn't help but wonder what was expected of me since my life was starting over.

I went to my cell, crying as I packed my things. I couldn't believe that I was finally going home. I put all my cards and letters in a box with some of my pictures. Then stuck the rest of my belongings into a bag. One of the officers stood near my cell waiting for me to get my stuff. Once I was ready,

I stepped outside of the entrance with my old D.O.C laundry bag draped over my shoulder. I looked back in my cell on last time, reflecting over the past fifteen years. I saw myself entering the system as a small boy, then my ride to Riverside, which had me so frightened. I envisioned myself going through quarantine, followed by my experiences of growing up in one prison after another. Finally, I took my last walk on the prison block as a free man. Again, I found myself afraid of the unknown. I was uncertain of my future without some of the people I loved most being there for me. I immediately wondered if I had become institutionalized or if I'd go back to prison like so many of my friends from the past.

"Prince, what does it feel like to walk the block one last time as a free man?" Officer Henry asked.

"I don't know. There are so many thoughts going through my head right now. I feel joy, pain, fear, and resentment. Damn! Man, I feel some of everything. I wish I could tell you, but it's too much to give words to when you're convicted and truly innocent. Ask a real guilty man, and his feelings are sure to be different. But mine are indescribable because the system designed to protect me, didn't. The Michigan Judicial System has fucked me. Had it not been for someone helping me out, I'd be getting fucked until I die."

As soon as I made it to the other side of that Prison wall, I realized that I was truly a free man. Once we made it into Detroit city limits, I had my attorney stop by a trash dumpster in a shopping mall parking lot. I got out of the car, ran over, and tossed all my clothes into the trash. I didn't want anything in my possession that reminded me of prison or the hell I'd been through. My pictures and letters is all I kept, and that's because each of them were sentimental in some way.

"Would you like to call someone to let them know you're on your way home?" my attorney asked.

"Naaa, I'm going to surprise them."

"Where do you want me to take you?"

"Damn, I almost forgot about that. I didn't even consider that I was going to need a place to live. Could you take me by my mother's house? My sister lives there now. If she's not home, we can go by my grandmother's."

When we pulled up in front of Bean's house, it was just as I remembered. I sat in the car for a moment gazing at the house with tears filling my eyes. At first, I was terrified, and then my attorney told me to get out. I opened my door, placing one foot on the ground, and finally the other followed. I pulled myself out of the car and I was just like a kid. When I stood in the driveway staring a second time at Bean's house, it was as if I were seeing it for the very first time in my life.

"Bean, I mean, Ma, I'm home," I whispered, walking up on the porch to ring the doorbell. It's something how my first thought, once I made it on the top step, was of my mother opening the door, screaming out in delight when she looked into my thankful eyes. I was rushed back to reality when my attorney bumped me, informing me that someone had already asked twice, who is it?

"It's me." I quickly responded.

"Who is me?" Ke yelled from the other side of the door.

"It's me, Prince, open up."

The door slowly opened, and Ke peeked out.

"Prince! Oh my God! Oh my God! Oh...my...God! What are you doing here?" She screamed in excitement.

"Looking for a place to stay."

She grabbed me around my neck hugging me so tight that I couldn't breathe. "Prince, I can't believe it's you," she said, hugging me even tighter.

"I know. I almost can't believe it myself."

"Get your stuff and come in," she anxiously suggested, fanning her hands for me to enter.

I grabbed the few things I'd kept and made my way into the door. Everything about the house was pretty much the same except for Bean. Right away, I noticed that Ke had Bean's bedroom door closed. She said she hadn't changed anything in there since she died. Everything was pretty much still the same way Bean left it that morning she went to work.

"You mean to tell me that you haven't done anything to her room at all?" I asked.

"Nope. I don't want to ever bother Ma's stuff. I've simply left it like that because every now and then I'll go lie on her bed, hug a shirt she once wore, which still holds the scent of her perfume and cry. When I do that, it feels like Bean's still alive. I kind of feel a sense of closeness to her that I can't explain, but it's weird."

"Okay, if you say so," I replied, trying to be somewhat compassionate, but really thinking, *There she goes tripping on one of them nutty, coo-coo sprees again. First Ke said Ant came to Bean's funeral. Now she feels like if she left Bean's room the way it was before she died, it would seem like she was still alive.*

After my attorney left, I walked around the house. Ke called everyone to tell them I was home. My Grandmother thought she was lying, but once convinced, she hung up, and made her way to the house. My aunts, uncles, and cousins tried to pretend like they were so excited. Shit, they never bothered to come visit, write or anything, so their excitement meant nothing to me. I was hot with them all about forgettin' a nigga. After that, I didn't give a damn what they thought or if they came by the house or not.

"Ke, if our family gave a damn about me they would have visited at least once while I was in prison."

"Prince, seeing you there was hard. They didn't want to see you like that."

I didn't verbalize it, but that was some BS.

Before Ke finished making all her calls, GG was at the house. I had actually been holding up pretty well, until I saw her. When she got to the porch and hugged me, she cried like she was in mourning. She hugged me for a moment before she literally fell down to weep on the porch. I leaned down to pick her up. Huh, G was thick and she was also dead weight. It was a real task to try to lift her off the top step. I grunted, trying to pull her up, but she didn't move.

"Prince, let me sit here for a minute. When I get myself together, I'll get up on my own."

"GG, please let me take you into the house. This concrete is hard."

"Baby, thank God you have finally made it home. I wish your mother and granddad were still alive to enjoy this day. Daddy Ruenae told me on his deathbed that you were coming home. I was doubtful, but he made me promise that when you got here I'd give you this package he left for you."

"Yeah, I tried to never lose faith, G. I believed I was coming home one day, I just always hoped it wasn't in a body bag."

"Prince, I never stopped trusting God for a miracle in regards to you and your situation. I am so thankful to Him for making this day possible. Baby, you make sure that you take advantage of this second chance at life because everyone doesn't get this opportunity. God was in your corner. He blessed you with favor. That's what the power of prayer does. It creates miracles and testimonies."

I couldn't agree with GG more. There were so many people I was locked up with that were just like me, falsely convicted, unable to afford an attorney for an appeal, and not gonna get a second shot at living their lives. I saw it happening with so many inmates, but I am extremely grateful that I wasn't one of them.

"You gon' be proud of me G; I didn't lose all that time for nothing. I'm not making any dumb decisions nor am I ever going back to prison. I got a daughter I'm trying to get to know and a sister that needs me."

As GG got up, she lowered this big ole purse off her shoulder and unzipped it. I looked on as she dug into her bag searching for something. Whatever she needed or wanted couldn't wait until we made it into the house.

"Prince, your granddaddy gave me this money the night before he died. He put it in my hands, making me promise to give it to you the day you came home. He said, 'Gloria, the day my grandson is released, give him this money. Tell him that neither a Royal King nor a Heavenly one would ever leave the Prince without some words of wisdom and helpful treasures to rebuild the kingdom. Tell Prince I expect him to take our family to the next level or else.' Baby, in spite of your situation, your grandfather was most proud of you. He knew early on that you went to prison for Anthony. He told me the day he died that you were his hero because you were the only Prince that ever made such a senseless, but noble sacrifice for someone in this family."

Tears fell from my eyes as I watched my grandmother reached down into her purse and gave me a folded manila envelope that contained fifteen thousand dollars in cash, and a note that my Granddad had written four days before he died.

## April 8, 1995

Prince,

The two Kings in your life left this gift for you. May you truly understand the meaning of the ultimate sacrifice you made to save your brother's life. You are my hero. I hope you learn from your past, and build yourself one heck of a future. Buy a few things you need with this money, and make sure you stay out of trouble. I'm counting on you to take our family to the next level. **Prince, Read, Reflect, and Realize that your life has a Real Purpose**. I can't tell you what it is, but trust in God, and He will direct your path.

Love,

Daddy Ruenae.

His letter made me numb for weeks. I read it over so many times trying to comprehend my grandfather's hidden message. *What am I supposed to do now that I'm a free man?* I wondered. The more I thought about my life, the more I realized that I was no longer in a position to be told what to do. Part of becoming a free man was going to require that I plan and make decisions for myself.

◆◆◆◆◆◆◆

Asia made it to Detroit a few weeks after I got out. I never called her to share my good news. I wanted to surprise her. I wanted to show her that our prayers had finally been answered, and as promised, I didn't die in the joint. The day she arrived, I remember hiding in the kitchen, listening as she talked with GG.

"Hey, Granny," Asia stated, entering the house.

"Hey, Baby. I thought your mom was going to call once you made it to Detroit. You're lucky you caught me here. I was on my way to the grocery store."

"Oh, I'm glad we caught you, too 'cause Mom forgot to call."

"Where's your stuff?"

"Outside."

"Child, why you come to the door empty handed? And where are your clothes? You kids are so fast these days. You're walking around here half naked or half dressed. Whichever, neither one is cute to me."

"Yes! But Granny, this is the style. This is how we dress now."

"I don't care, it's disgusting. In all my seventy-nine years, I ain't never dressed like that, and I was sexy."

"Okay, Granny. I was trying to make sure someone was here before I pulled my stuff out. I got two large pieces of luggage in the car. I'll run and get them now."

"Just hold on a minute. I don't want you messing up your female organs trying to carry in no heavy bags. I done told you about that already; you aren't a boy. Those clothes you're wearing with all that cleavage showing confirms that. Let me get my neighbor's son to help you. Go in the kitchen, and tell Marques your Granny needs him to do something, please."

Asia came bouncing into the kitchen all prepared to deliver GG's message.

"Daddy!" She yelled. "Is that you? Oh my God! When did you get out?" She screamed, without moving.

"I've been out since the end of May. Stop looking so hard, and give your old dude a hug."

Asia hugged me just as tight as Ke and GG had. She grabbed my hand, and instantly drug me out to see her mother. Zena got out of the car all excited and hugged me like we were still an item.

"Prince, I'm so happy you're home. What happened?"

"I finally won my appeal."

"Great, Asia's going to love being here with you this summer."

"DeMarques, I'm Rodney. Congratulations, I'm excited for you."

I thought his words were nice. Then I considered how he had been a part of my daughter's life all those years.

"Nice to finally meet you. Thanks for being there for Asia when she needed a father or father figure and I was unavailable. I appreciate you stepping in and doing that for me."

"No problem, your daughter is a beautiful young lady. I love her like my own."

Afterwards, I grabbed Asia's things out of the car and the two of us walked into the house.

"Girl, what's this little ass outfit you got on? I'm not in the joint anymore. You gon' make me catch a real case out here."

"Catch a case? Be serious, Daddy."

"Asia, if you dress like that for the rest of the summer, I'll be in jail. I need you to cover up all that flesh you got showing before I have to bust somebody's ass for being disrespectful."

"Here we go. Daddy, don't even start trippin' 'cause I ain't havin' it."

"You ain't havin' it. Who's the parent here? The last time I checked, I was. Chump, you better remember that," I said, smiling.

"Daddy, you're talking way too much noise for an old guy. I got a few brotha's here in Detroit I'm feelin'. I'm not a baby anymore. I'm sixteen years old. Man, I've been dating for the past year and having sex for the past seven months. You can't come home and treat me like no kid, so don't even try because those days are over."

"Sex!"

"Yes, I've had sex."

"Butterfly, you're about to kill me, and you better check your tone. Though I haven't been home, I have been in your life. You're not about to be disrespectful to me like I just popped up on the scene."

"Sorry, Daddy, I don't want to argue with you. I'd prefer that you not fuss about my clothes. Rodney and Mom do that all year long. We have a different kind of relationship. You and I talk like friends, but now you're sounding like them."

"I don't mean to fuss, but I don't want you dressing so provocative either. Men don't think very highly of women who show all their goods. Asia, you've got to leave something to the imagination. With all you've got showing right now, a young man doesn't have to imagine much, 'cause you're revealing it all like a hoochie."

"Daddy, I'm not a hoochie."

"Don't dress like one then."

"Brotha's know I'm classy. Besides, this is the style."

"Style or not, I don't like what you have on. Half your ass and your entire thong is showing. Why would you even put on some jeans that rest that low on your waist? All I'm gon' say is don't put me in a bad position. If you're dressing that way and someone gets out of line, you won't leave me much of a choice. I will bust a nigga's head wide open for being disrespectful. Now that's all I'm gonna say about your attire. You decide the rest."

I ended our conversation on that note because I didn't want her to feel like I came home trying to treat her like a baby. We'd always been close; therefore, I needed for her to continue to feel comfortable openly sharing things with me. I'd never held my tongue when dealing with Asia and I wasn't about to start. She killed me with her news of being sexually active, so that entire summer, I kept her close. Neither of us had been anywhere together, so we went on a cruise to the Bahamas with some of the money my grandfather left. I didn't care about the trip being costly nor did I worry about where more money would come from for my future survival. I'd promised Asia years earlier that when I came home we were going to do something nice and that's what she wanted to do. We needed that time together, and the two of us had a ball bonding. We toured islands, went snorkeling, and got to know each other better. That trip gave us a chance to talk about a number of things, including her expectations of me. I knew that I'd been limited in the past as a father, so we talked about what she thought I could do to be a better dad.

After Asia's summer ended, I slightly started adjusting to being home. I was tired of staying around the house, which is why I let E give me one of his quick pep talks, which inspired me to get out a little. "Prince, when I first came home, I was scared to death. I really didn't have anyone to motivate me to get out there and test the free world. Man, I'm gon' tell you, once you get accustomed to being in control of your life again, everything you do will seem natural."

Most days, I hung out at Everett's busiest store on Seven Mile. Though he had opened a second store, he still ran his first one. I was up there so much trying to keep myself occupied that he eventually gave me a job. He spent months teaching me about the retail business. He taught me about good customer service skills, and then started taking me to New York to teach me the fundamentals of being a buyer.

By mid October, I was making clothing runs to New York alone. I had better taste than E, and the items I purchased were leaving the shelves faster than we could stock them. I remember one week, I had just returned from a turn-around trip. Late the following afternoon, I was unloading the truck. After staying in the store for a ten-minute break, E and I started talking about some of the new merchandise I'd picked up. I was standing at the register with my back to the door, when Everett started talking under his breath.

"Money, just entered the store."

"You're lying." I stated, never turning around.

"Money, what brings you into the store today?" Everett asked.

"I'm looking for a hot li'l birthday gift for one of my women. She's not one of my top notches, so you know the routine, something nice, but inexpensive," he replied.

I knew that voice, but I was hesitant to turn around. I didn't know if that nigga was gon' recognize me, and I didn't want to take any chances. Finally, he walked in the view of a security camera hidden on a garment rack. As I looked at the monitors on the back wall, I noticed Melvin's face. The diamonds on his platinum watch were blinging like crazy. I couldn't believe it. That boy appeared to be on top of his game and was sharp as hell.

"What the fuck?" I whispered, as I made my way to the office. *This scantless bitch set up my brother so that he could blow up alone. Prince, ain't nothing else for you to do but kill his ass,* I kept thinking, as I paced the floor like a caged dog.

While listening to him, I considered that I had just gotten out of prison. From the way things were looking, I was on my way back after I'd promised my grandmother that I would take advantage of my second chance. I had been off to a good start, but the more I thought about the fact that someone my brother trusted with everything, deceived and probably killed him, the angrier I became. I found myself resorting back to my survival skills in prison. At that point, I felt and was thinking like a vicious killer.

When Everett came into the office, we talked about how close Melvin and Ant were. That pissed him off because he was able to associate it with the bond we had. E believed in loyalty, so he knew from day one, Money or Melvin, whichever, was on some shady shit.

"P, we got to do something about that sorry Bitch. Whatever it is, we can't be involved. He's in here pretty often, so we'll set him up. We just have to be smart about the manner in which we put things into action. Neither one of us want to go back to prison. Getting him may take a little longer than you'd like, but we got to think this hit through wisely or it could cost us big time."

"I know. We can't rush. We need to devise one hell of a backup plan on this one. I'm putting a contract out on that chump. I just got to get my hands on a large sum of money."

"We're gonna do this together," E stated.

"We! Man, I'm not about to involve you in this. I done seen too many innocent people go down for someone else. I'm not with you going down for me."

Suddenly, I got quiet because I remembered the letter Ant left Byron. "I got to get in touch with Byron." I replied, walking out to finish unpacking the truck.

A week before Thanksgiving Byron's mother got in touch with me. While I was going to pick up the key, I took some time to see my nephew. That boy was twelve years old and looked just like Ant when he was a shorty. I hadn't seen li'l Ant since he was a newborn, so for us to hang out or spend any kind of significant time together was important to me. Before I left Mrs. Holmes' house, I made plans to hook up with him again at a later time. I wanted to hang with him and do some big Prince, li'l Prince bonding and she was cool with that.

As I was leaving, Ms. Holmes gave me the key to the safe deposit box.

"Now, Prince, I'm telling you in advance that there's no money left."

"It's cool, Ms. Holmes. The money isn't an issue. Whatever you used is fine with me. Your family deserved it as much as I did." Though I was thinking, seventy-six thousand dollars would have come in handy. Shoot, after splurging most of my money on Asia during her visit, my funds were a little tight.

I headed straight to the bank after leaving their house. The teller verified my information, before taking me to get the box, and then led me to a private room. After putting the box on the counter, she informed me that she was about to go to lunch, but someone would assist me once I was done."

"Okay, thank you," I anxiously replied, trying to see what it contained.

I took the key, which was on a gold key ring and inserted it into the lock. As I turned it, butterflies accumulated in my stomach. At that moment, I felt the same kind of uneasiness and uncertainty I felt the day I was sentenced. Once it was open, there was nothing in it but a sealed envelope with lots of papers and the small grey box. The papers consisted of the account information Bryon was instructed to open for the kids. There was an additional bank statement for the Detroit Credit Union in Dearborn and the account number had been blacked out. I noticed that Ant opened the account a few months before he died. I'd almost totally forgotten about it, until I thought about needing some quick money.

I picked up the little box, and found myself staring. It was as though I thought it contained my brother's ashes or his spirit. I daydreamed for a second, looking almost in a state of hypnosis at the numbers on the box. "Ant never told me the combination, so how the hell am I supposed to get it open?" I mumbled. I tried over fifteen numbers for about five plus minutes before I decided to try our code. "4357, Help," I whispered, talking to the container.

Wal-la, it popped open just like that. I hoped I was about to come across a check for some big money, but the only thing it contained was a letter.

October 5, 1986

P,

You've only been gone for a month, but there are times when it feels like years. I have so many sleepless nights from the guilt I have for allowing you to go to prison for a crime we both know I'm guilty of. All your life, I've tried to take care of you. I wanted to be the father figure for you that we both longed for. But I failed. Though neither of us ever knew our fathers, I'm glad we both had the chance to embrace an unconditional brotherly love to a far greater magnitude than so many other brothers will ever know. Prince, all your life you have been my boy. I'm very proud to call you my brother. I don't give a damn what anyone ever says about the Prince family nor our bond. I'll go to my grave knowing that my li'l brother sacrificed his own life so that I might have the chance to keep living my own.

There are days when I can't even face Bean. I look at her, and I can see the pain in her eyes from her loss. I can also see the disgust she has for Silk and me because she blames us for your situation. Sometimes I want to hug her for comfort, not hers, but my own. However, somehow the distance in our relationship quickly reminds me that you were always her favorite. Knowing what I've allowed you to do prevents me from trying to talk to her. There were only four people in the Prince family I felt any kind of affection for. It's real fucked up how the one I loved the most is away from our family on an indefinite basis. Maybe for the rest of his life or mine, whichever I think about, both make me feel terrible. Prince, no matter how you look at it, we both lost in the end.

I may not be here when you get out. But I'm writing you this letter today because I want you to know how bad I'm grieving. The way niggas been getting hit lately, I know somebody gon' try to do me soon.

If you ever get out and get this letter, know that I love you and I always will. I could never repay you for your sacrifice, but I do want to try. I've put away some money for you as a token of my appreciation. I hope it's enough to get you started.

When you get a chance, I need you to look in Bean's room for this key. You'll more than likely have to do it while she's away or at work. You know if she catches you in her shit, she's going to blow her cap, but by the time you come home, she'll probably be real soft on you. Nonetheless, in her room on the bottom of her underwear drawer, I have taped a key to a safe in GG's basement. It's hidden in the floor under the gold couch with the plastic covering. Daddy Ruenae allowed me to have it installed last week after I told him everything about our situation. Anyway, lift the carpet and you'll see the safe. The key will open the first door, which will get you to the combination lock. Once it's been unlocked the combination is the same as all the others.

Peace
Ant.

My brother was never emotional, but I guess my situation had gotten the best of him. I could tell he was crying when he wrote the letter because the ink on it was smudged in spots. I sat on the floor in a daze. I considered how we both endured some real mental anguish. It was sad Ant had to carry all that guilt for such a long time. He was so afraid of my mother finding out the truth that he had literally gone to such drastic measures to keep our secret. He was so ashamed of what he'd done that he kept his letter in the locked container.

My heart felt empty when I considered that here I was fifteen years later getting instructions from my brother on how to sneak around without being caught by Bean and she was already dead. Ant never thought she'd be deceased when he was writing that note back in 1986, neither did I.

I hadn't experienced any real financial struggles after getting out, but I was on the verge of having some serious money. I didn't suspect that I would be a millionaire, but I knew I could live quite well on whatever Ant had put away for me. Asia was graduating from high school that year and though Ant put money up for her, with the funds he'd left, I was going to be in a better position to make a contribution to her education, which made me feel good.

After I finished reading, I was more confused about my situation. I didn't want my brother's killers to go unpunished, but most of all, I didn't want to carry out a killing. I wanted Melvin dead, but not to the extent of having to go back to prison. I sat on the floor, wondering, *Do I want to take a chance on sacrificing my future once again for my brother?* I knew that carrying out the hit myself would cause me to run the risk of possibly getting busted. After spending time with Asia, I truly needed to focus on our future. I didn't want my daughter to be fatherless again, so I convinced myself not to act off of my impulses. I tried to be rational, which made me weigh out my options and think about my plan of action before striking.

# 22

## Big Fellas

When I made it home, I went straight to Bean's room to find that key. If Ke knew I'd been in that room, she was gon' have a fit. As I entered the room, I tried not to disturb much. I only bothered her underwear drawer, but it turned out to include more than panties and Ant's key. Carefully secured with tape on the back of her drawer was a small brown file. It was the length of an envelope, and had been labeled as important documents. Though I didn't know what it contained, I was curious. Actually, since Ke hadn't gone through most of Bean's things, I thought there might be an insurance policy or something in it that Ke missed. Since she said she didn't bother anything in Bean's room.

When I looked through the file, I didn't run across any policies. I did find our Birth Certificates, along with a copy of Ant's Death Certificate. First, I read the Death Certificate, since I couldn't attend his funeral, hoping to feel a little closure. Reading it didn't resolve anything for me. I put it back, then pulled out all of our Birth Certificates to read each one. I read Bean's, then mine, Ke's, and finally Ant's, because his was on the bottom of the stack.

"What the hell?" I uttered, as I read Ant's Certificate "He's a fucking what?"

"*Twin!*" My mind replied.

*Why have I gone my entire life unaware of the fact that Ant had an identical twin?* I thought. Then I couldn't help but wonder if he was ever aware of that news himself. *Naa, he couldn't have known because he would have told me.*

One thing I noticed that I never knew before was Ant's father's name, which was Robert Shaw. There was an old, discolored newspaper clipping attached to the birth certificate about this Robert guy being gunned down in front of a party store, so I knew he wasn't the killer. However, after reading Ant's certificate, I had questions.

I wanted to know why Bean never told us that we had another brother. I also wondered where he was all those years while we were growing up.

*Better yet, where was he now?* Nobody in the family ever talked about Ant's twin. I wondered if anyone knew he existed or if Bean had pulled another one of her stunts. My brain was going five hundred miles a minute. Suddenly, I heard the front door shut. I put everything back in the envelope, carefully returning it to the space it occupied. I got the key from underneath the drawer, and quickly pushed it closed.

"Prince, I'm home," I heard Ke scream.

"I'm in here." I yelled, waiting for her to come into Bean's room with one of her mysterious looks.

"What are you doing in here?" She asked, kind of territorial.

"I was trying your thing. I came home missing Bean so much today. I was trying to find a way to feel closer to her. I pulled out this robe of hers to hug. I thought it would make me feel better, but it didn't."

"Yeah, I hug that same robe all the time. To me it's the one thing in her closet that still smells a little like her."

I allowed Ke to think whatever she wanted to think as long as she didn't figure out I was in Bean's room snooping. We stretched across the bed talking for a while. After talking about my brother, we both found ourselves locked in on this family picture we had taken back when I was ten. I smiled when I thought about how much I wanted to be like Ant at that age. That was my boy. Bean always knew I loved him far more than I loved her. I think that's one of the reasons she despised him so much.

The phone suddenly rang, cutting our reminiscing short. Sam was on the line, letting Ke know he was on his way. They were headed to Tulsa, Oklahoma, for the holiday, and she needed to finish packing.

"Ke, I'm going out for a while. If I don't see you before you leave, have a safe trip."

I drove Daddy Ruenae's old hooptie to GG's house to go check out the safe. When I arrived, it was my intent to head straight for the basement, but I was detoured by an hour and a half of small talk with G. She was like most senior citizens living alone. Glad to have company when you stopped by, and certain to talk you to dang death about whatever. Since she was in a talking mood, I wanted to ask her about Ant's twin, but I didn't. I knew how Bean was, so I feared GG didn't know about him. At that point, it wasn't worth me exposing Bean's secret at the cost of defacing her. If G didn't know, she wouldn't know from me. I'd rather keep Bean's secret locked away, than make her look like shit for no reason.

"G, I'll be downstairs if you need me." I finally told her.

"Okay."

I walked down the steps straight to the gold couch. I carefully moved the sofa, lifted the carpet, and there built into the floor was the safe Ant described in his letter. I opened the first lock with the key, and then entered the combination. Once it was open there were all kinds of items Ant left in there for me, including a file like the one I found in Bean's drawer. I pulled it out, and was overwhelmed. Ant had pictures of him and his twin together that had been taken at My Fair Ladies back in 1984. As I looked through the additional pictures there was one other picture of Ant, T, his twin and Melvin, so someone did know about Ant's twin, I just didn't. I kept looking and reading, and looking and reading, and finally, I ran across his name............. *Calvin Shaw.*

*That motherfucka and Melvin set my brother up. They were the only two nigga's he would have allowed in his circle and they took him out,* I thought. As I remembered the discussion I had with Byron in the joint about the argument Ant and Melvin had, I knew Ant was probably on to Melvin shortly before he died, which is probably why his death was so brutal. While I kept looking through his things, I remembered Byron also saying that the guys that shot Ant said Calvin Shaw ordered the hit. "Ant was clearly set up," I whispered, flipping through the photos. The sad part about everything is that he didn't see it coming.

The more I thought about the way Ant died, the more I was convinced that he'd gotten caught slipping on his own motto, "Never trust anyone." *So that nigga went to Bean's funeral, too, which is why Ke kept saying she thought she saw Ant there,* I speculated while pulling all my facts together. "That nigga got some real nuts," I grumbled, pissed off about his boldness.

When I finally made it to the bottom of the safe, I came across another brown envelope. Once it was opened, I discovered a letter and one hundred and fifty thousand dollars cash.

## January 10, 1993

Prince,

I don't know if you'll ever get this money or this letter, but things are looking kind of grim and I'm on spook. Sometimes you feel good about the things you do in life and sometimes you don't. One of the best things that happened for me was you and my son. I hurt sometimes when I think about all the wrong I've done because I know that a time will come when I'll have to pay for it via DOC or my very own life.

I have put money in this safe every two weeks for you, hoping that a day will come when you can enjoy it. I don't know how much there is in here because I never count it. I don't want to feel tempted to take out a loan, (Smile) but I know it's enough to buy a house and car.

If you've looked through the other files in this safe, you've discovered some real dark family secrets. Yeah, it's fucked up how I had an identical twin and I didn't know about him until we ran into each other at the club one night. I had the cameraman take a picture of us, so that I could show Bean his picture. What a secret huh? Every now and then, after him and I became cool, I'd let him go by the house and play me. It's something how Bean gave life to both of us, but because she never gave us much of anything else; she could never tell us apart. Anytime he was playing me, Bean never sensed that it wasn't me. That's sad, considering she's our mother.

When I asked her why she kept one of us and gave the other away, she claimed that she didn't think her finances would allow for her to raise two kids, not to mention that she wasn't really ready to be a mother to one. I couldn't believe it, but Bean also said in the same breath that, she never wanted me either. I don't think Bean ever expected her secret to come out. I told her when you know people, like I do, and you get out on a regular basis, like I do, you'll discover just how small the world really is. Bean was on some shit when she left my brother, Calvin at the hospital nursery for our father to pick him up.

I was in disbelief when she said the morning she was to discharge, she called my father and told him she was only taking home one baby, and if he didn't get the other, no telling where he'd end up. My father arrived at the hospital right when she was getting into the car with Silk and me. I told her that the baby she left behind could've easily been me, instead of Calvin. She replied that it was almost Calvin and me that got left, so I needed to consider myself lucky that she had a change of heart.

Silk and Ka'Nita were the only ones that knew about him, which is why Ka'Nita always called Bean a MIA. I think it also explains why Bean always tried to change the discussion when Ka' Nita got on the subject. I had to know, so I asked Bean why she picked me over him. She told me that I looked more like the Prince side of the family and cried less.

Huh, that's your mother. By the way, *GG* and Daddy Ruenae were never informed about Bean having twins. They don't know anything about her giving up Calvin, so don't tell. News like that would kill them or divide the family.

To be honest, this is why I think Bean drank so much. I believe she felt guilty about giving away one of her children then half raising the others. P, she couldn't live with herself.

When you went to prison, I thought she'd die that first month. Man, she would drink for breakfast, lunch, and dinner most days. At times, she would miss every meal of the day, and refused to eat anything. I told her with the way she drank, if she kept it up, she'd eventually die from Cirrhosis of the liver or a fucking heart attack. But you know she's not going to take my advice with the way she feels about me.

Hey, I gotta go. I know you have lots of questions. Do me a favor, if I'm not around when you get this letter find my twin, Calvin. He'll have plenty of answers for your questions. When you meet him, you'll think you saw a ghost, but trust me, there are a few things different about us.

Ant

Prison made me very aware of dates and time. I always looked at dates to put me in mind of where I was when something was happening. Ant had written that letter a few days before he died. Maybe at that time, he still trusted Calvin. I didn't trust him, and I knew I wasn't about to go see that nigga to let him kill me. Yeah, I had questions, but he was gon' answer them looking down the barrel of my gun. There was no way I was gon' be fraternizing with that sucka and slip up like Ant had.

When I first went to jail, Ant had Daddy Ruenae open an account in my name. He was initially under the impression that the account was going to be used as my prison aid account. Ant told him transactions were going to actually be made by Bean, but Ant was going to maintain it. Ant knew the only way my granddad would open the account is if he lied because he wasn't with supporting no dirty money deals. From reviewing some of the bank statements, I noticed that they were initially sent to Ant's house. When he discovered that he was being watched by the DEA, he changed everything over to prevent the account from being taken by the feds.

A few days after meditating on all the news I'd learned from the letters, I went to the Detroit Credit Union in Dearborn to check the balance on the account. "One hundred and fifty thousand dollars," the teller stated. I was speechless. "Repeat that please?" I asked. When she did, my mouth fell open. *Damn, my HELP account is phat.*

After I made a substantial withdrawal, I stopped by the shop to tell E about my come up. After seeing how Ant was set up, I was back on my guard. I didn't get to talk very long with E about all of my discoveries because the store was jumping. It was a few days before Thanksgiving and everybody was trying to get suited up for the evening. There was a Gator party going on at Big Fellas in downtown Detroit, and everybody that thought they were somebody, trying to be somebody or knew somebody that was somebody was gon' be there. E and I were gon' be there partying like Big Fellas as well. When you compared us to some of the ballas that were gon' be up in the club that night, we were "Nobodies." E and I were simply two ex-cons trying to stay just that. Since I had a little money and Detroit was known as the city that loved to shine, E and I were gon' be "Gatored Up." But we weren't about to bust out in just any old gators; we were gonna be sporting **Top of the Line** shit. I wasn't settling for anything less. This was our first big event, and I was determined to find us some farm raised gator that was hitting for over a grand per shoe.

I think the discovery of all my money made me a little cocky. Three hundred thousand dollars was quite a bit of money. I wasn't going to totally waste all my finances, but I could afford to splurge a little and still have a nice savings.

"E, let the hired help run the store while we go for a ride."

"A ride where?" He asked, not wanting to miss out on his money.

"P, I can't afford to go today. Man, when the big man's away my employee's gone play. All their friends' gon' get a hook-up on me." Though his spot was jumping, E knew his employees were sometimes known to work the register for a five-finger discount and run a little store hustle here and there. I didn't even care about that.

"Man, don't trip, it's the holiday. The little two hundred they steal might bless them. I got a surprise for you anyway. Plus, I want to go somewhere to find us some gear that everybody else ain't gon' be rockin' tomorrow night."

After E agreed to go, our first stop took us to Alston White's Cadillac's, which was a Dealership in downtown Detroit. I was on a mission. I mean, I couldn't jump out of Daddy Ruenae's old busted hooptie. How was I gon' be styling a gator hook-up in that bucket? I just about paid off a Cadi Escalade for myself and made a substantial down payment on one for E. I picked a cream one off the showroom floor. It had the gold package, and was sitting on some twenty-twos with chrome rims. The screens in the headrest caught my attention. The fact that the brains were blown out made me have to have that particular one right then. E got a Black one and kept his modest. With all the good he'd done in my life, especially getting those letters from Joey and Delvon, I felt like a fifteen thousand dollar down payment was the least I could do to say thanks.

After leaving the dealership, we went to Gator's Isle and got our gear for the festivities that Thursday night. I was gon' rock an ocean blue hookup with one of Ant's furs. E was on this tangerine kick that I wasn't feeling. He called it burnt orange, but the salesman was in agreement with me and called it tangerine as well.

Once we finished shopping, we headed back to the store. When we pulled up, there was thirty minutes left 'til close. Right when I took a seat behind the counter, Carrington walked her fine self up in the store. E bumped me mumbling, "Keep your composure, your baby just walked through the door." I hadn't seen Carrington since Bean's funeral, but she still looked hella sexy.

"Man, I ain't thinking about that girl."

"Right you're not."

She immediately made eye contact with me. When she smiled, I nodded. As she approached, as usual, I locked in on that gap between her legs. *Ummmmm,* I lusted, watching like a nasty freak. I wasn't about to just stand in her face salivating like one of Pavlo's dogs, so I moved around.

"Yo, E, if you need me, I'll be in the office counting money."

"Okay."

I walked to the office, lusting all the way there. I watched Carrington on the camera, figuring I would be okay. Finally, I observed her through the one-way glass, which allowed me to admire her from afar and maintain my dignity. She still had big titties and beautiful lips. I noticed that her ass had gotten a little wider with age, but I'd chalked that up to the game. I figured that her man was putting in work and definitely hitting it right because her jeans clung to that cat like sticky paper, and her legs were still just as bow as ever.

Carrington knew exactly what she wanted, which should have cut her stay in the store to a minimum. She bought a classy pair of gator boots that four other chicks had also purchased that same day and a short fitted dress that matched.

"What's the occasion, Cuz?" E, asked.

"Oh, Mecca and I are supposed to go out tomorrow. I'm getting this outfit for the party at Big Fellas."

"You know me and my boy gon' be up in the spot tomorrow night, too?"

"For real, what are you wearing?"

"Oh, P and I went to Gator's Isle and bought some farm raised gear."

"Farm raised? Umm, that must have cost you a pretty penny. Everything up in there start at a grand. That was nice of you to set Prince out like that."

"I didn't set P out, he hooked me up."

"Yeah right, he ain't even been home a year yet. How he gon' set you out?" *Ain't that a bitch,* I thought, listening to her dog me out like I was a bum.

"P, got money."

"Okay, if you say so," she said in that stuck up tone of hers.

"Oooo, that Bitch makes me mad," I mumbled, grabbing my keys after I overheard her comment.

"E, I got to run by Triplet's Cleaners before they close. I'll be right back."

"Okay."

I walked outside and jumped in my truck, which was parked right in front of the store. Carrington watched me walk out. As I pulled off, I noticed she was all out the window. *Now who you calling broke, Skank Bitch?* I thought, cranking up my beats.

When I returned, she was still in the store. I walked back to the office like she didn't exist.

"He's still kind of bitter with me, huh?" I heard her ask.

"A little, I'm sure. You did dog him out pretty bad."

"Why don't you see if he'll let me come back and talk with him?"

"Carrington, I don't think that's a good idea. Why do you want to keep playing with his emotions? You need to stop acting like a big tease."

"Just hush, and see if I can. I don't need a lecture from you. I know what I need to do, we have some unfinished business. I want to resolve it."

"Where's, Bobby?"

"He's still in New York. He'll be here next week. You know I moved back to Detroit some months ago, so he's commuting."

"No, I didn't. Neither Aunt Jean nor Grandma mentioned that to me. Why you move back? Did you catch him cheating like Derrick?"

"Ouch, you act like you got a little attitude with me about something. With the way you're talking, I'd think you're still a little bitter with Mecca and taking it out on me."

"That's not the case at all. I just hate to see women take advantage of good brothas when they know they love 'em."

"Well, stop tripping, and go see what's up with your boy."

"Yo, P."

"Yeah."

"Carrington wants to know if she can come back," E yelled.

"Is she giving up some of that ass I've waited over seventeen years to get?" I disrespectfully blurted out.

"Maybe," she interrupted, quickly shutting E out of the conversation. "Can I come back?"

"Yeah."

As Carrington walked back, I could see E on the other side of the glass and in the monitors making fun of me. I know he thought I was wimping out. I guess in some ways I did. Carrington walked in the office smiling. She behaved as though she still had my head gone and had really come up. She sat her bag on the floor, closed the door behind her, and then approached me.

"Hi," she whispered, biting her lips.

"Hi! How you gon' say some shit to me like that after all these years and the way you did me?"

"I have no explanations. All I can say is that I've missed you."

"Missed me? Missed me my ass. I went......" Carrington covered my mouth.

"Shhhh," she said. "Let me make it up to you," she said, unfastening my pants.

"Oh you need to know with all the years I've waited on you, I'm not fucking in no office."

"Follow me home then or I can follow you." Before I could reply, E knocked on the door. "Come in," she said.

"P, I'm out. Lock up when you leave."

"No, we're out, too. Let's go, Carrington."

She picked up her bag and walked out of the store to her car. E set the alarm, while I held the door. As I locked it, he stood there making small talk.

"Carrington asked about two hundred questions after you left the store in that Cadi. Man, she's on your nuts. I hate to say that about my cousin, but she ain't shit. She and Mecca are two peas in a pod. They are some of the biggest gold diggers I know."

"Man, I'm about to go to her house. You got a few condoms?"

"Yeah, here you go. I grabbed them before I knocked on the office door. I was about to give them to you then. I knew with the hundred questions she was popping off that she was about to offer you some ass."

"Man, she's always been a tease."

"Naw, Homie, she gon' produce tonight."

"Think so?"

"Man, do we own new Rollouts?"

"Fa'sho," I replied, giving E dap.

"That's why I know. You gon' hit tonight."

"If I do, I'll give you the details tomorrow."

"Naw, I'm gon' pass on those facts. She ain't about shit, but she is my cousin. I don't want to know nothing about y'all bedroom secrets. And that's exactly what they gon' be 'cause you know she ain't about to tell nobody, especially not Mecca that you hit."

"I feel you."

E went his way, and I followed Carrington to her place in Southfield. She pulled up in the driveway. I parked on the street.

"Come on, Prince," she eagerly insisted.

"Okay, chill. I'm coming. I got to get my gun from under the seat."

After I entered the side door, I walked to her bedroom. She wanted to give me a tour of her house, but I wasn't there for all of that. I hadn't had any in a few weeks, so I was focused. My primary reason for being there was for nothing more than to tap that ass. Carrington went into the bathroom and ran bathwater in this huge bathtub. That mug was so big, I know they had to have had it specially installed. It was big enough for at least three people, which meant we were going to have enough room to get buck wild up in that j'ont. Carrington twisted off a top and filled the water with bubbles. She set candles around the bathroom, grabbed two wine glasses, and a bottle of wine. I remember seeing two speakers in the ceiling, and before ever asking why they were there, she turned on her stereo. This old skool CD bumped Luther and Cheryl, Rick and Tina, and a host of other great romance hits.

"Prince, here," she stated, handing me a glass full of wine.

"I haven't had a drink in so long. This wine is gon' have me messed up."

"That's good. I don't want you to be in control that way I can do whatever I want to you."

"Whatever!" I repeated.

"Umm hum. Whatever," she smiled.

Carrington pulled her hair back into a ponytail. She took off all her clothes, slid into a robe, and then slowly undressed me. *The old Carrington was way shyer. The new Carrington was very aggressive, which I liked.* Once she had all my clothes off, she pulled me into the bathroom. "There, get in," she insisted, smacking me on my ass. "What's wrong, Prince? Are you nervous?"

"Naw, I'm shocked."

"Shocked?" she repeated. "Shocked about what?"

"You."

"Well, enough of this small talk," she said, inserting my toes into her mouth to lick and suck each and every one of them. Carrington had me crawling and squirming all over the tub with some of the stuff she did to me. I think her blowing in my ass under water was the straw that broke the camel's back.

"Ut'un Carrington, I ain't with nobody doing nothing to my asshole. That's off limits," I said getting out of the tub.

"Where are you going?"

"To get in your bed. Get out and come on in here with me."

Carrington came into the bedroom with bubbles still on the back of her neck. I started there and worked my way down as far as her navel. As bad as I wanted to eat her out, I couldn't go there on her. I don't know if it was the image of all those stretch marks that turned me off or the thought of two babies and umpteen niggas being in the dugout that made me change my mind. Nonetheless, I flipped her over to avoid seeing her face or that stomach, slid on my condom, and beat the pussy up. I didn't want to look at her because her face even in the heat of passion reminded me of all the pain she'd put me through. After watching Carrington suck my toes, followed by her blowing on my ass cheeks, I no longer felt that same attraction I once had for her. I never thought she would feel like nothing more than a piece of ass to me, but that's all she turned out to be that night.

Now she did give me one of the best blow jobs I'd ever had in my life. That mouth and tongue of hers took me on a far greater voyage than Ant's ole girl, Felicia did. And even though she'd put in major work, it still wasn't enough to change my feelings for her or make me respect her again. That's why I skeeted all over that pretty face of hers, too, and made my record three for three.

I probably hit about three times before finally running out of energy. Carrington was good, but to think I'd waited all those years for what I got, was a disappointment. I had gotten better ass from Zena in high school. Hell, part of Carrington's problem is that she was trying too hard to fuck pretty. *Ain't nobody got time for this bucket head,* I thought, rolling over to get me a few hours of sleep.

"Goodnight, Sexy," I stated, hugging my pillow.

"Goodnight," she replied, snuggling up under me.

Seven the following morning, I was awaken by my cell phone. Ke and Sam were on the other end all jolly.

"Happy Thanks.......giv.....ing," Ke sung.

"Happy Thanksgiving to y'all, too. Are you having fun?"

"Umm hum, Sam's family is so nice and his mother is my girl."

"Sam, you better get my sister back home safely or I'm gon' break your little bird neck."

"Man, don't worry, this is my baby. I ain't about to let nothing happen to her."

"Good, y'all have a great holiday and call me when you get back on the road."

I laid back down for another ten minutes, then Carrington was all over me. "You think I could get a little of this dick for breakfast?" she asked.

"Oh, you done got hot with age."

"Nope, it's you. I've been hot for you since high school."

"Yeah, yeah, yeah, save it," I said cutting her off. "I'm gon' have to pass on the breakfast nookie. I told my GG I'd help her cook," I replied, lying. "This is our first holiday together in fifteen years and since she's alone, I need to get over to her house."

"Oh, well you better get in the shower. You surely don't want to go to her house smelling like hot sex on a platter," she suggested, getting out of the bed. As I caught a glimpse of her stomach, I cringed. *Not my beautiful, precious Carrington,* I thought, concluding that her stomach was the ugliest thing on her body. With me being as old as I was, I'd never seen a woman's stomach after she'd had a baby, and if they all looked like Carrington's, I didn't want to see many more.

"Naw, I'll take one at the house. I have to get dressed anyway," I mentioned, pulling up my jeans.

Carrington walked me to the door. "Thanks for coming over," she said, kissing me like she did when we visited at the prison. The only difference was that she didn't turn me on like she had in the past. "Prince, see you at Big Fellas tonight."

"Okay."

"Make sure you save me a dance. You know I'm gon' be the hottest thing in the house tonight.

Since E and I were gon' be in the club, I figured Carrington and Mecca would try to make a grand entrance. They loved attention, but by no means would they be the hottest sistas in the house. Carrington was in for a rude awakening. I knew I was gon' fall up in the party with one of the finest women in the city, but it wasn't gon' be her. The honey I planned on taking was so fine, she had me bout ready to pop the question on sight. I even met her in my granddad's hooptie, so I knew she was diggin' me, and not the fact that I might have loot. She was so on point that even Ms. Berry with her fine, sophisticated ass would have to give my girl Veronica Teretta Kilpatrick some major props.

I'd met Teretta three months earlier in Westland Mall. She was a natural sexy, which is why she immediately caught my attention. She was built like

Halle, bow legged like Nia, hair like Jada's, and attitude like Vivica's. Though Carrington was fine, my baby was the one honey that would take her damn breath away. When I called her to wish her a happy holiday, she answered the phone in that sensual tone I'd grown to love.

"Hey, Beautiful. Are you still meeting me at Big Fellas tonight?"

"I wouldn't miss it for the world, our date's still a go. I'll be there looking my best, so you better come correct. Don't forget a few of my girls are coming with me."

"Yeah, I'll set E up with one, and his boy Scoot's gon' entertain the other."

"Okay, see you tonight, and Happy Thanksgiving."

"Same to you, Baby."

Thanksgiving went by real slow for me. Although I had come into all that money, it still didn't compensate for the mental anguish I felt from missing my family. I hadn't spent a holiday at home for years. My sister was out of town with her boyfriend, my immediate family was dead, and loneliness overwhelmed me. GG and I were invited to go to my Aunt Ka'Nita's for the holiday, but I still felt some resentment towards her. My loyalty was strictly to Bean. Besides, I knew Bean would have been cursing my black ass out from her grave as she struggled to come through the dirt and pimp slap me for eating with the adversary. I passed on the invitation to go to Kay-Kay's, which is why GG decided she wasn't going either. At about two o'clock, we ate. G talked about how our family had significantly changed since we had the dinner for my sixteenth birthday. As she talked about my grandfather and his role on Thanksgiving, I thought about Bean and the meals she usually prepared. One thing missing was those funky chitterlings, which I know would have made the menu had Bean or Daddy Ruenae been alive.

I called E at seven o'clock to see what time he was rolling out. He said his boy Scooter was cool with the owner and had called to have our names put on his VIP list. I was with that 'cause the club was gon' be off the chain, full of women, and a much needed outing for me. I was hype 'cause Teretta was meeting us there with some of her girls, too. After getting off the phone with E, I hit Teretta up one last time to tell her that I'd be at the club about midnight. After we hung up, I showered, had me a drink, and pulled out my gear. At about ten, E called me to see how far along I was.

"I'm walking out the door now."

"Good, meet me and Scoot at the Club in thirty minutes."

When I pulled up, Scoot was parked in front of the club chilling in his Metallic Blue Escalade. It was sitting on some Spreewells, and the Chrome on those babies was shining so serious that I saw a reflection of my Cadi that made it look like it was moon walking. His beats were humping so fiercely that you could hear him coming from a mile away. He had that mobbed out tint on his windows that made onetime nervous. And wherever he went, hella gold digga's always jocked him. Scoot had a li'l style about him that I was feeling. In a lot of ways, he reminded me of my brother. What really tripped me out is when that nigga stepped out of his ride Gatored up in baby blue, with the mink coat and hat to match. *Oh, that's Ant fa'sho.*

The line to get into Big Fellas was so long that it draped around the corner for at least three blocks. As I passed all the half-dressed honeys in their fly Motor City outfits, I was lusting and flirting for a moment. We bumped into Carrington, but didn't stop. I spoke, but kept moving 'cause I noticed our guest about seven people ahead of Carrington, Mecca and their crew. When I walked up on Teretta and her girls, I noticed from looking at the line there was at least a fifteen to thirty minute wait before they got in.

Teretta was looking so hot that I had to flaunt her. I pulled my boo by her hand, and told her and her two girls to come with me. She stepped out of line looking like a true dime in her thigh high gator boots. I was too out done when I realized that they matched this short mini dress she was rocking, which was nothing more than a few scraps of fabric.

Everything about her was off the chain that night. From her fur to her hair, she was making a statement. As we made it past everyone to enter the club, I sported her on my arm with real pride. Once we got to the door, Scoot didn't have to say a word.

All the security was like, "What's up, Serious Money."

"These are my peeps," he replied, hitting the checker off with two fresh Benjamins to take care of our coats.

"If they're with you, they straight. Your table is on reserve in BBO," the head bouncer Ty stated, pointing us in the direction of the elevator.

Big Fellas had this section in the club called BBO, "Big Ballas Only" This section was for nigga's I called, "P Diddy Wanna Be's." It was a highly secure area where the elite niggas with big chedda chilled with their guest, and sipped Cristal all night long.

*Our table's up in the Big Balla's Chambers,* I thought as Scoot flashed his Platinum BBO Card. *Damn we got it like that tonight,* my conscience rattled. "Now that's what I'm talking about," E stated as we were allowed to enter the secured elevator. As the glass elevator started to move, I found myself fascinated with the view of the club's two dance floors. When we made it to BBO, the doors slowly opened and the room was unbelievable.

Right away I saw big money represented all over the place. There were brothas gatored up everywhere. As I made my way to my seat, I observed fine ass females all over the place. Many of them were over in the Balla's Corner, posing for high quality photos taken by Derrick Brown. That brotha could capture the moment, and the constant business he got all that night confirmed just how lethal he was with a pose, the right lens, and some film.

Once I sat down, I noticed the platinum nameplates on each of the reserved tables. The glowing gold letters immediately caught my attention. *Damn the owner of this club got loot,* I thought, looking around. After I ordered a drink, I noticed Calvin Shaw's name on the table directly next to ours. At that point, I said nothing. I didn't know what kind of relationship Scooter had with Calvin, but I knew he wouldn't be that close if they weren't tight. For all I knew, they could have been setting me up. Finally, I asked a few questions to make it seem as though I was interested in the club. My inquiry got me some valuable information. Calvin Shaw was the owner of Big Fellas. With the dough floating around that spot on a weekly basis, it was a given to me that Calvin was stacking major dollars, and not to be fucked with.

I started putting two and two together and figured with Scooter's table being so close, he too was one of Calvin's loyal homies. I felt for my gun, and remembered I'd left it in my truck under my seat. I thought they'd be searching for heaters at the door, which is why I left it. I didn't want it to be found on me then I'd have to go back to my truck. With Scooter getting the kind of love he did at the door, I was sure he was packing. Had I known he was down with the club affiliates like he turned out to be, I would have been strapped, too. I started tripping a little, but didn't want to bring unnecessary attention to myself. I immediately started devising a backup plan. While considering my next move, I noticed Melvin walking around in BBO. Suddenly he turned to approach our table and I panicked.

"E, there's your boy. Did you bring your heat?" I whispered.

"You know I did."

I was relieved after E said he was strapped. When Melvin got to our table, he chatted with Scoot. I didn't want him to recognize me, so I held my head down.

"What's up?" he asked, giving Scoot dap. I moved my head close to Teretta's face to conceal my identity. I pretended to be whispering in her ear.

"Yo, Playa. The club is off the hook tonight." Scoot stated.

"Yeah, we're expecting about six hundred. Good thing you're up here 'cause downstairs gon' be packed."

"Hey, let me introduce you to my guys. This is E, and......"

"I know E. I frequent his stores from time to time," he interrupted.

While he was explaining how he knew Everett, my girl and I got up from the table to go dance. By the time we made it back, Scooter had introduced Melvin to the other ladies at the table and he'd gone on his way.

Though I had a watch, I remember this neon clock in VIP keeping me up on the time. I didn't want to bring any unwanted attention to myself by constantly checking my watch, so the clock was a relief. At about two thirty, Calvin came up to BBO. He was wearing a plush, baby blue tailored made suit, and some gators almost the same color as mine. When he got close enough for me to look him in his face, we both looked at each other in shock. He looked exactly like Ant and his style of dress was quite similar as well. I mean that nigga looked so much like my brother that I got the creeps from just looking at him. They were the same height, same build, same expression, same smile, same hairline, same style, same everything. With us not growing up together, it made it impossible for me to tell them apart. He made his way over to our table to speak to Scooter. I didn't even attempt to hide my face or leave. Though I was out of my comfort zone, I wanted to look my brother and my brother's killer in his eyes. He had no real emotion at all, and repeatedly kept popping this fat cigar he was smoking on in and out of his mouth.

"What's up, Cuz?" He asked, taking a puff of his cigar.

"You." Scooter replied, while I continued to stare him down.

"Are these your guests for the night?" He inquired.

"Yeah, this is my boy E, his date Jacaria, my boy P, his date Teretta, and my date Meko."

"How's everyone tonight?" he asked the group, appearing to be full of himself.

"Fine," everyone replied except for me.

"Hey, Young Buck, are you enjoying yourself?" he asked looking at me.

"I'm straight," I grimly replied.

"Good. I sure hope you're enjoying yourselves, welcome to Big Fella's. If you need something, don't hesitate to ask one of the attendants. I'm sure my cousin Scooter is going to see to it that you all have a good time at BF's tonight. It was nice to meet you. All drinks are on me 'til close. So drink up." He stated, lifting his cigar to his mouth again.

After Calvin moved away from our table, I noticed him looking over in my direction a few times. He really wasn't fazed by my presence, and didn't have to be. There were about fifty Warren Sapp look-alikes ready to beat down anybody that got out of line.

*I know Calvin remembers me*, I thought. I didn't know what might go down nor did I want to be caught slipping or spoil Teretta's evening. In order to keep our date pleasant, I suggested that we go down on the lower level to dance. Actually, I was trying to make sure I could escape quickly if it came to that without giving her any signs of my paranoia.

Once we made it to the dance floor, DJ Dangerous Dawn started bumping Snoop, and the stage got packed. Miss Lady had on one of those hottie dresses with all kinds of holes and slits all over everywhere. The opening on the front of her dress went all the way down to her navel. Each side was attached to her breast some kind of way, and I was enjoying the attention it got from everybody. I think she told me part of the dress was taped to her breast, but it obviously wasn't working because every now and then, she'd turn just right and I'd get an eyeful of her pretty ass titties. The more we partied throughout the night, the more I was feeling the li'l hookup she had on. I think it was my favorite because she was coming home with me, and I knew I'd have her out of those scraps of fabric in two seconds flat.

That was the first time I had kicked it like that since my release. I actually enjoyed myself, and everyone in our group partied. As a matter of fact, we were clowning so much that I eventually noticed Carrington and her girls looking over at us. A few times while we were all hugged up on the dance floor, I caught Carrington and Mecca checking me out with their noses turned up like back in our school days. The two of them stood off by the bar talking and pointing over in my direction. I assumed they were talking about my date for the evening because they kept looking at us all night long. Plus, I knew with as proud as Carrington was, she wasn't about to tell Mecca she gave me some a few hours earlier, and then I barely acknowledged her.

The two of them didn't keep my attention very long. Teretta was dancing slightly provocative, and her moves demanded my attention. She was working with an authentic beauty that was a definite showstopper as well. That had to burn Carrington up because that meant she had to share the spotlight.

Scooter, E, and the girls stood on the balcony cheering us on. When I glanced up to shoot them two deuces, Calvin and Melvin was looking down at me. I wasn't about to trip on those niggas. I had my buzz going, and a fine ass, half naked woman grinding all on my dick. If them chumps had beef with me they would have to see me later.

The last forty-five minutes the DJ played old skool hits and the club went nuts when *Fire and Desire* by Rick James and Tina Marie came on. I pulled my girl closer to me and started singing in her ear in the same key as Rick.

Well, I wasn't quite as crisp, but I was in the ballpark. Renee and Angela's song, *My First Love* came on next. As I held Teretta, I immediately thought about Carrington because that was her favorite song back in the day. She looked over at me as if she thought I was going to send my princess away to dance with her, but I knew that wasn't about to happen. I palmed a hand full of Teretta's firm ass, which stood at attention like a polished soldier on graduation day and loved all over her. I looked at Carrington, shot her the peace sign, and winked to be spiteful. She understood my message, "Your loss Bitch." For her to see me having such a good time with another woman drove her crazy. To defend Carrington, Mecca flipped me off. But I wasn't bothered by her actions because she was half of Carrington's problem. Since E had fired her bossy ass, she was a lonely, miserable, troublemaker, too.

When E's store was in his house, Mecca dogged him out about being a real business owner. He wasn't good enough for her anymore, so she started going out with some cat that worked for one of the auto plants. Looks like she and her girl lost in the end. I know if they could have gone back in time and knew then what they later learned about E and me, they would have hung in there for the financial come up.

# 23

## A Family Connection

We left the club about four, maybe even closer to five o'clock that morning. I took Teretta to breakfast, and then she ended up coming home with me. All that clowning I'd frequently endured from Raynard in the joint about sucking on oranges finally paid off. My vision of genuine beauty was hot and ready to make love to me. After I took off her clothes, and showered, she was ready for me to venture there. I licked all over her body, making my way down to some of the juiciest pussy I'd ever eaten. Oral sex was nothing like I imagined it would be. Her stuff was so fresh, I know I could have stayed down there until I was a registered senior citizen. From her size, I could tell that she hadn't had any kids because her stomach was gorgeous, the coochie was still tight, and it farted like crazy every time I pushed up in it just right. Hell, that girl's stuff was so good, I was damn near ready to give her a fourth of my inheritance and buy her a house.

Considering I was out of practice, I knew when we finished, I'd put in some work. After we were done making love, she left my bed soiled and had destroyed my clean sheets with what seemed like gallons of her juices. I hadn't had a chance to get down like that since I'd been out of prison. With the way she was backing that thang up and riding me, there was no doubt that I had to bring fifteen years worth of pumping and grinding out of somewhere to get off the nut of a lifetime.

Once I came, I wanted to come again, and again, and again, but after nut number two, she informed me that her lips down below were swollen, sore, and too beat up for me to get off one more. I couldn't complain. My girl had worked it like she was in training for a heavy weight fight. Once she wiped herself off, I scooped her up. While we were embraced in each other's arms, she rubbed the top of my head in a circular motion, which was so soothing. Before I knew it, I'd lowered my head on her naked titties and slept like a newborn baby.

Late that afternoon, my cell started ringing off the hook.

"Hello," I rudely answered after about the seventh call.

"What's up, Chump?" E asked.

"I was sleep, but not anymore. When I woke up, it was my intentions to be getting me some, but you done messed that up."

"What are you talking about?"

"Teretta got out of the bed about two calls ago. Now she's in the shower thanks to you."

"Why you didn't answer the phone then?"

"Nigga, like I said, I was sleep. What you want anyway?" I asked.

"Nigga, who you calling a nigga. You better be glad I'm calling you on legit business or I'd hang up on yo ass. You know I don't play that nigga shit. Wash your stankin, sweaty-ass balls and meet me at the store in an hour."

First of all, I knew I was tripping when I didn't answer the phone. E wasn't the type to keep calling if he didn't have something important on his mind. I quickly got up, threw a jean hook up on the bed that I'd picked up from the cleaners the day before Thanksgiving, and jumped in the shower with my Boo.

"Thank you for a wonderful evening," she stated.

"No problem. Thanks for spending your holiday with me. I would have been real lonely yesterday without someone special to spend my time with."

We embraced for a few seconds, but I was on a mission, so the only thing I could do was look, feel, and quickly caress her body.

"Come stay with me tonight," I suggested, slapping her on her butt. She gave me this look like I wasn't gon' get none if she did, so I jokingly replied, "But stay your fine self at home if the beaver don't want to spin around on no wood tonight."

♦♦♦♦♦♦♦

I got to the store about ten minutes early. I sat in the back office talking with one of the store managers while I waited on E.

"P, let me holla at you in the truck," he insisted with the most serious look on his face. I followed him out the door in order to talk in private.

"What's up?" I asked.

"After you left the club last night, Melvin started asking me about you. I know he remembers you, but I think he was trying to see if you remembered him."

"Inquiring about me like how?"

"He wanted to know who you were, where I knew you from, what side of town you grew up on, and if you were balling."

"Why that Bitch wanna know about me? Did you tell him anything?"

"P, who am I? Man, you know I always got your back. I done told you that once. I told him we did time in the joint together and you dated a female I knew."

"What he say after that?"

"Nothing, but it's time for us to get that nigga's toe tagged. He made me nervous with his twenty-one questions. He's coming over to the store today to pick up a bag for one of his girls. We got to clear out the store. I'm gon' send everyone home now 'cause around five this evening some contractors gon' pay our boy a li'l visit. He's supposed to be here before six, so lay low 'til then."

"Good, it's pretty dark about that time. Go on and send everyone home right now with pay for the day, and I'll work the rest of the shift. When he comes into the store tonight, we're closing down. I'm taking him into the office before we have his ass killed. He gon' tell me why he turned on Ant after years of friendship."

"That's cool, Man, but make sure you don't put your hands on him period without gloves. We don't want shit to be traced back to us, that's why I didn't do any talking in the store. You never know who is listening," E replied.

I sat watching the clock for the hours that passed. Finally, at about six o'clock, Melvin pulled up to pick up his girl's purse as planned. I walked out the back door, through the alley, around to the other side of the store, and through the front door again. Barry and Recardo, two of the three hit men working for us walked in behind me. To make sure no one else entered, I locked the door. Once I closed the store blinds, they immediately rushed Melvin like he had robbed their great grandmothers.

"What the fuck is up with y'all li'l young nigga's? Do you know who I am?" Melvin asked with clear fear in his eyes. As he was being punched, I pulled his legs and drug him to the back office.

"Yeah, nigga, I know who you are. You that ho that betrayed my brother and set him up. I noticed that you ain't smiling as hard as you did last night when you were getting yo shine on. It's a different feeling to be the one looking down the barrel, ain't it?" I asked.

"Prince, chill."

"Oh, so you know me today. But I find it real funny that you didn't acknowledge me last night while you were with my brother's twin."

"P, you know I always cut hard for Ant."

"That's what you say, but word on these streets and the joint say differently. I heard you a snake-ass nigga that ain't to be trusted. Everybody told me about how Ant was blowing up and you started beefing with him

276

about slowing down 'cause this Calvin Shaw motherfucka put you on the payroll."

"Man, you don't know what that hell you're talking about. If you kill me, it's gon' be a big mistake."

"Are you threatening me? Are you trying to insinuate that if I kill you it's gon' start a blood war?"

"I'm saying it's not gon' be nothing nice."

"Fool, I'm not hearing you. The shit I went through for the last fifteen years wasn't anything nice. Those big-ass roaches I shared my house with in prison wasn't nothing nice. But you and your boy Calvin Shaw, on the other hand, are small change compared to what I've spent the past few years of my life surviving."

"Man, don't do this to me. I didn't kill Ant. I loved that nigga and that's on everything."

"Where's your boy, Calvin?"

"I don't know."

"Bitch, you know," I replied, slapping him with the butt of my gun.

"P' chill man, don't do this," he begged.

"Melvin, you got two minutes to figure out where your boy is, call him, and get him here or I'm gon' bust a cap in yo ass. The only difference between your death and Ant's is that you gon' die slow."

"Prince, he can die, but not here. This is my source of survival. Do what you gotta do, but take that shit somewhere else," E quickly informed me.

"Melvin, you call Calvin or your begging's in vain. One or the other, but yo time is running out."

"I'm going in my pocket to get my phone." Melvin stated.

"Ut'un, I'll get it. Try anything shady if you want to, and it's lights out for you," I stated, extending my arm to hand him his cell. Melvin hesitantly took the phone. Realizing that he was about to die, he dialed Calvin's number.

"Cal! It's me, Melvin. Do me a favor and roll down to Storye's Rags to Riches on Seven Mile. I've got someone with serious money you need to meet." Calvin said something, and then Melvin replied, "Okay. I'll see you in about twenty minutes."

I started that pacing back and forth, which was a bad ass habit I'd developed while serving time, and when twenty minutes came and went, I walked into the back room, raising hell.

"Where is your boy? His twenty minutes are up, and yours is, too. Get this chump out of here." I ordered, walking out of the room. I heard Melvin scream as he was put in handcuffs, and God must have wanted to show my man some favor that day 'cause right when he was on his way out the door, Calvin arrived alone with an envelope. I opened the door, and looked into his eyes with a most vicious stare, drawing my piece on him.

"What's up?" I asked like Calvin already knew what I meant.

"Where's Melvin?" He inquired, looking around like he was worried he'd been set up.

"He's in the back dead, where you about to be for killing Ant." Silence took over, and then after thirty seconds, he started talking.

"Prince, Man, damn! I know you didn't kill Melvin."

"Yeah, Nigga, I did. He violated the rules of the hood, and you violated the rules of the family when y'all killed my brother. Ant looked out for Melvin. They were like brothers. Why he turned on him for you got me wondering." He remained quiet. "Calvin, all I want to know is why you would want to kill your own fucking blood? I know with you being Ant's twin, he would have cut hard for you like he did for me. That's the kind of guy he was. So what you pay Melvin to set Ant up?" Calvin looked at me but refused to answer any of my questions again. "Since, he ain't got nothing to say, cuff him and take him for a ride with his boy. I'll call you from a payphone later to make sure that it's been handled. Give me that envelope he's holding, too."

When Calvin saw that I was serious about killing him, he agreed to tell me what happened between him and Ant, but we had to speak one-on-one. I knew the pussy was trying to buy some extra time, but I didn't care; I wanted to know what happened to my brother and why they set him up.

"Give me ten minutes, and then I'll be ready. E, take this envelope and see what's in it," I stated as everyone left the office.

"Prince, sometimes we do things that we aren't always proud of. I regret my decision behind killing my twin everyday of my life. Seems like I wish I could have done some things differently after the fact, but when you're caught up in the game, you start to feel powerful and then invincible. Sometimes we're dealt a bold hand and we can't go back and start over. You can't relate to some of the dark pain I've been carrying, but I'll share a story with you. In 1959 our mother had a set of twins, and though I don't have all of the specifics, I can say this for certain. She only brought one of us home, while the other was left to be raised by a father that never loved him and a grandmother who tried. The father was abusive, mentally, physically, and verbally, and the grandmother rarely intervened. The twin always wondered who was gon' be on his side, who was gon' love him and educate him on the gentleness of a mother's love. Nobody ever stepped in."

"And your point."

"The other twin, he got to go home with his mother, but she didn't really want him either, so his grandparents ended up raising him as well. The only difference was that he had to endure the pain of his mother later bringing home two additional children that she loved far more than she loved her first born. He was faced with the same struggle as his twin. He wondered, *Who was going to love him and educate him on the gentleness of a mother's love?* Nobody ever came to his aid either. Bonita Prince dogged me and my twin brother. We suffered from a case of unbearable neglect at the hands of our parents. After me and my twin met, we ended up hating each other. We stayed in constant competition, instead of embracing one another, and that's where we dropped the ball."

"So you and Ant hated each other?"

"I hated the family life he was exposed to. All this glamorous shit means nothing to me. It has and will always be about family. When Bean died, as angry as I was, I went to her funeral and stayed at the back of the damn church because I didn't want the family to see me. I knew I wasn't even going to be able to participate in the final viewing the day of the service, which is why I had to go to the funeral home at night before they closed to say my goodbyes." He paused, apprehensively looking at me, but kept my undivided attention. I was clueless as to what I should say because he shared some of the same pain that Ant expressed in his letters. I could also relate because before I was incarcerated, I once felt the exact same way. I clearly understood the pain he was talking about, and wanted to tell him that, but as I was about to speak up, he started talking again.

"Huh! Ain't that a bitch? Even in my mother's death, I was still kept a secret. I was mourning the loss of our mother right along with the rest of the family. Prince, nobody ever bothered to embrace me to help comfort my pain. Not one person, not even the only two relatives that knew I existed. Silk nor Ka'Nita acknowledged me. They knew I was aware of Bean's death and didn't call to say two words to me. What hurts me more than anything is the fact that Ka'Nita is married to my father's half brother. She and Bean didn't hate each other to the magnitude they did just over money. KaNita hated Bean for selecting one of her children over the other. Then after her and Silk kept Bean's secret, she was still neglectful to the twin she decided to keep." I looked because I was stunned by his remark. "Oh yeah, KaNita and Silk knew about me."

"Why did Bean give you away?" I asked

"No one has ever answered that question for me to this day, and I guess like my twin, I'll go to my grave not knowing."

"If you're so family-oriented, why the hell did you kill Ant."

"You remember the day T was found murdered right? Melvin said one of the guys rattled something about Silk and then T started screaming, well turns out that T was set up. Remember the day you got picked up and y'all did that drive-by on Zena's house. There was a police officer that pulled you over. If you think back you might remember what he said when he let y'all go?"

*How this nigga gon' quiz somebody at a time like this,* I thought, trying to refresh my memory.

"That was almost twenty years ago, I don't remember. What did he say?"

"He called Ant or who you thought was Ant, Mr. Shaw."

"Yeah, he sure did and what's your point?"

"My point is this, you thought it was my Alias, but it wasn't. It was Calvin Shaw pretending to be me. Prince, I'm not Calvin. I'm Ant but I've stolen his identity because the feds were looking for me." I looked and wondered if he were telling the truth. He looked like Ant, he sounded like Ant, and his style was like Ant's, but I didn't know if he really was Ant.

"Man, Hell naw! You're trying to straight fuck me up in the head with this nonsense. I almost fell for it, too. You ain't Ant because I would know. Why you didn't you just say that you were Ant from jump, instead of giving me all this nonsense about one twin and the other twin?"

"Prince, my twin Calvin set T up and used Silk as a decoy. He was pissed with Silk because he wouldn't put him on and Silk knew he was having tough times. He sent his boys up in one of our spots to rob the place, but T wasn't giving up any hiding spots for our dope until they started torturing him. I got to the point where I didn't trust anybody, so I was making runs in and out of town in a rental. I wasn't telling anybody when I was leaving, sometimes I didn't even tell Melvin. The night all that stuff jumped off with Zena, Calvin called Melvin pretending to be me. He told him that he'd lost his key. Melvin had my spare keys and took them to Calvin, thinking he was me. I left my beeper in the Benz that weekend, which is how he ended up picking you up from Julius' house. When he did that drive-by and y'all got pulled over by the police, that's when Melvin realized that it wasn't me and got my li'l homie DC to roll my Benz into the lake. I met them on the outskirts of Detroit and cursed Melvin out for slipping up like he had. What most people didn't know is that the drive by wasn't about Zena, it was about killing Calvin's boys who could and were going to rat him out once our guys got a hold to them about T's death. When you got caught up, I would have known you took my extra gun because I frequently switched it out. Calvin wouldn't have known because he didn't know it was there."

"Um hum!" I replied.

"Calvin wanted to fix things between us. But I was hesitant to trust him after that. I wanted to know that I could depend on him, which is why I allowed him to grind out of one of my booming spots with Byron. That is my son's uncle. He also became my right hand guy at the time along with my l'il homie Alex, who picked Calvin over me. Byron thought Calvin was me, but I was setting Calvin up to steal his identity. I had some of my guys run up on them the day I let him be me. Byron wasn't supposed to die, which is why he's alive. I told them when they shot Calvin to tell him that the hit was ordered by Calvin Shaw, so that he'd know I set him up. Prince, I'd gotten in so far over my head as Anthony Prince. It didn't mean shit to me for Ant to die that day and take on Calvin's identity. The Feds were sweating me something serious. I was looking at pulling a life sentence for being caught with 456 grams of Coke earlier that year. By killing Calvin and leaving the family alone, I gave up some things, but once again, I got to maintain my freedom. The only difference is that now I'm someone else."

"So all life is about to you is making someone else do the punishment for your crime?"

"Naw, not at all."

"Why didn't you tell me what was going on then? Man, if you were about to change your identity, why didn't you at least tell me about your twin or say goodbye for that matter?"

"It was so much going on. I didn't want to involve you or have you stressing out about me. You were trying to win your appeal. That's all I wanted you to focus on. Prince, I've always wanted the best for you. Man, I wanted you to go to school, make something of your life, and raise your daughter. Prison was never an option for you in my mind. That's why I kept telling you to stay out them damn streets."

"Well, why did you let me go to prison in your shoes then? And if you can't answer that, why the hell did you let me rot in that bitch for so long? I can't believe you were stacking all that loot and didn't bother to get me an attorney on Cochran's level or any damn body that could help free me."

"Man, I know I didn't do right by you. That's another issue I live with. I'm sorry. But you're free now. When Melvin called me this evening, I figured you were here, which is why I came. I brought you some money as a way to apologize for letting you do my time. In that envelope is fifty grand. You can have that, plus I want us to run Big Fellas together and move on from here."

"Fuck running Big Fellas. I don't believe you! You're not my brother." I firmly replied.

"Man, what you mean I'm not your brother. P, look at me! I don't look like your brother?"

"Yeah, you look like my brother, but you're not the brother I grew up with."

"Boy, your ass is trippin' for real now. Tell me what I got to do to make you believe that this is me?" he asked.

"Write me a letter like the ones you left for me. Mention that you're leaving me the Club if anything should happen to you. Date it for early September and sign it." I stepped out into the hall and yelled for someone to bring Melvin into the room.

"You said Melvin was dead," he replied.

"Remember you told me never trust anyone, right?"

"Yeah, and I see you have done well."

"Why would I kill Melvin? Someone has to witness you signing your club over to me just in case you're fatally wounded, right?"

"Yeah, I guess so!"

"Nigga, I'm glad you agree 'cause if you ain't who you say you are that's what's gon' happen," I rattled off, waving my piece in his face.

After twenty minutes his letter was finished and Melvin signed as the witness. I didn't even bother to read his note at that time. I slid it back on the desk and sat real close to him. After his cuffs were put back on, I looked in his face trying to remember any specific feature on Ant's face that I could. Calvin looked so much like Ant that I couldn't tell them apart.

"If you're really Ant, I got two questions for you. First what was the name of the chick from Palmer Park that gave me my first blow job."

"Come on, Man, I know you got one harder than that," he replied smacking his lips. "Everybody knows Felicia slobbed on yo knob."

"Good answer. Now you get two for two and I might believe you. All my life you've always told me never trust anyone, not even the people in our family. We established a code when I was ten. What is it?"

"4357! He quickly rattled off, smiling. "See P, I told you it was me. Man, now get me out of these cuffs before I bust yo li'l ass. You trying to be a Big Man up in here, avenge my death, and about to accidentally kill Mel and me on some BS."

"Yeah, you were almost a dead brotha, and you still might be if you don't finish the question."

"I answered it," he replied clearly aggravated.

"Nope! You didn't, you answered part of it. Actually, you didn't answer the most important part."

"What's that!"

"What does 4357 mean?" I asked with a cold, dark stare of limited trust and no expression at all on my face.

I knew Ant was one to occasionally share a story or two, but Melvin was there when I got the blowjob, and Ant might have said the code because I called him with it a lot when I was young. But because it was our brother in distress call, I knew he never said what it meant unless it was just the two of us. Ant guarded that password like it was a rare diamond. He wasn't gon' ever let the meaning get out to anyone.

"You said what does it mean? Man, I don't remember. Prince, it's been almost twenty years."

"If you don't remember, you're not Ant. Kill them both," I stated, walking out the room.

"Ant, remember the damn password," Melvin yelled out of fear as he was being gagged.

"I don't remember. I've been so caught up on being Calvin Shaw, that there are times when I remember very little about living as Anthony Prince."

"You better give us something or you're drowning tonight. Keep this shit up and DC's lake is gon' store more than stolen cars." E suggested.

"P, you gon' let them weight me down and throw me in the bottom of one of these lakes?" Calvin screamed. I ignored him because he already had my mind all fucked up. I didn't know if I was killing the right man or what to believe about his story. "Prince, I'm Ant. I swear I'm the brother you grew up with," he replied out of desperation. "You're going to regret this if you allow them to kill me."

"Shut up!" I finally yelled. "Shut the fuck up. I don't know who you are. You can't give me the password that you came up with and you want me to believe what you're saying? You fucking died on me and left me rotting in that prison and I'm supposed to trust you."

"Prince, as much as you loved me as a shorty, I can't believe you don't know this is me."

"Gag him." I screamed, walking into the front of the store because the more he talked the more confused I became.

"Wait!" He screamed before his mouth could be covered. "Prince. Let me holla at you one more time. Please, don't do this to me."

I never went back into the office to listen to him share his side of the story again, and his begging became too much for me. After they had taken him and Melvin away, I was sitting in the office questioning my decision to kill him. "Was he Ant or wasn't he?" I repeatedly asked myself. No matter which twin he was, he was my brother and I shouldn't have killed him.

*Have I made a mistake?* I wondered for weeks. For the next few months all the news channels ran stories almost everyday on Calvin and Melvin's disappearance like they were celebrities. I smirked to myself a few times as I listened to the news anchor report on them. The way they were worshipped, pissed me off because I remember Ke saying that Ant's death barely made the six o'clock news. The two of them obviously held more weight in the city than I realized. From the way folks were tripping, it was a given that we'd taken out two of Detroit's "Biggest Fellas" in the game. Too bad for them they got caught slipping, and backed away from the round table with a half-ass backup plan. Had they killed Ant and never said anything about Calvin Shaw, I would have never found out who murdered my brother. But obviously they weren't hip to the little slogan Silk and Daddy Ruenae taught me as a child, which was "Loose Lips, Sank Ships."

◆◆◆◆◆◆◆

In April 2002, E and I established a partnership. We maintained the clothing stores, but they were on an entirely different level. We were no longer moving knock-off bags and clothing. We had the stores gutted out, refurbished, and changed our merchandise to top of the line suits and dresses with matching gator footwear and accessories. We offered clothing by some of the most popular designers on the market that Detroiter's loved to rock. The Store was no longer called Storey's Rags to Riches, but *Top of the Line Fashions.*

Right up the street from Big Fellas, I opened up a trendy sports bar and grill called **Asia's,** and on the same block about a half a mile down, I opened up a soul food joint called **BEAN'S Spot.** I knew that didn't really sound like a name for a restaurant, but as a child I always called home, "Bean's spot!" So I figured she should always have a place that others acknowledged as her spot as well. Ant always told me that he wanted me to make something of myself. Well, I did.

In all that time, I never bothered to read the letter Calvin had written the night he was killed. E didn't want anyone to find it either, so he put it in the store safe and just so happen to run across it one day while he was locking up some money.

"Prince, do you want this letter or should I shred it?"

"What letter?"

"The letter that made you full owner of Big Fellas." He sarcastically replied, laughing,

"What, you still got that letter? I thought your scary ass trashed that long ago?"

"Nope, I still got it. I figured one day you might want to read it."

"Why you figure that? Did you read it?"

"Yep, and that's why I kept it for you."

"Where is it?" I asked.

"Right here," he stated, handing me the letter.

When I grabbed the paper, a cold sensation came over me. I sat at the desk in our newly plushed out office and read my brother's last words for the first time.

*September 5, 2001*

> *Prince,*
>
> *Everyman gets too big for his own good sometimes, and when he does, the consequences can be costly. I never understood the family concept, because I never lived it. Today you have shown me what it means to love your brother to no end. You've also shown me what the consequences are for any outsiders that violate the family bond. I hated Anthony because he had what I always wanted, "A Family Connection."*
>
> *Though I was your brother, and I violated the rules of the family, the only thing I lacked was the bond. Therefore, you had no remorse for wanting to kill me. But tell me this, if we had a bond like you and Ant, would you still kill me if the circumstances were the same?*
>
> *Prince, I was your family. We were brothers, too. So did you violate the rules of the family as well by killing me, and if so, who's gonna avenge my death?*
>
> *Calvin*

I paused because he presented some deep points, which I couldn't answer. As I moved on to the second sheet of paper, I noticed that there was plenty of space for him to finish his note, but he started it on a fresh sheet.

*September 5, 2001*

> *Should something ever happen to me I want to leave everything I own, including my club Big Fellas, to the only relative that gave me an*

*opportunity to share what family meant to me, my brother De Marques Prince.*

*Calvin Shaw*

*Melvin Daniels Witness*

With Calvin writing his beneficiary note on a separate sheet of paper, I concluded that he seriously wanted me to have his club. He knew I couldn't claim it had he written it on the letter that revealed my having him killed, so he started an entirely different sheet of paper to prevent that from happening. I don't know, maybe he didn't think I would follow through at first, and with my head being as fucked up as it was that night, had I read his letter after it was written, I probably wouldn't have. He was right when he said, "He was my brother, too." But because we lived in separate homes, we lacked the bond, but we didn't lack the bloodline, so yes, I violated the rules of family as well.

When I thought about cashing in on his club, I considered how much I wanted it and the consequences that might come along with producing that letter. I wasn't about to hang myself because one thing I'd learned early on was that all money wasn't good money. Therefore, I decided not to claim what rightfully belonged to me. I didn't want anyone to become suspicious, especially since nobody even knew he had a little brother. Besides all my businesses were doing well, so I really didn't need his money.

In June 2002, Ke, E, GG, Teretta, and I drove to Chicago to see Asia graduate. It was a real emotional time for me. I was so proud to see my baby accomplish something in life that I could only dream about for myself. I had earned my GED while I was out on DOC's all expense paid vacation. The only thing glamorous about getting my GED was the little certificate they sent to my cell. In my mind there was nothing like graduating from high school. *My baby has done it,* I thought as a few hard to restrain tears fell from my eyes. She didn't graduate valedictorian, but she was the Senior Class President. To me that was just as good as being one of the top graduates in the class.

When she gave the occasion for the gathering, her classmates cheered her on. She approached the podium, grabbed the mic, and began to speak. I carefully listened to everything she said, but when she spoke of her daddy, she had my undivided attention.

"Finally, I want to thank my dad. Daddy, throughout my life there were so many times when we were apart that I wished I could reach inside my dreams or my heart to pull you out for a tender hug or a Prince kiss. Your love for me has been like a trophy stored in a locked vault, which was my heart. I always knew that we would one day be together on the other side of the walls. You are my hero, and a fine example of what having faith in yourself can restore to one's life. I love you more than words will ever express, and may we never be apart again. After being able to access you when I want, I could never go back to just pulling you out of my dreams. I thank you for loving me and being the best father you could possibly be, when the circumstances were tight and prevented you from being the super dad you desired to be. Thanks for enlightening me on your definition of a butterfly. I have carried that with me since the day you shared it. I want you to know that you, too, are my Butterfly, but you're more like a moth because they're a little more rugged and manly."

The entire family cried, but not me. For once, I'd held it together, well, until Ke hugged me, talking about she was so happy. I was doing fine 'til then, though I was already feeling sentimental. Her comment sent me over the edge, and tears flowed from my eyes like crazy.

Weeks after returning home from Asia's graduation, GG died. Her death was hard for me because once again, I had to deal with a loss. Saturday, June 29, 2002, three family cars and a host of friends, family, and associates drove one behind the other in a procession to Woodlawn Cemetery on Woodward to lay Granny Gloria Arnell Prince to rest in the same family plot for five that Daddy Ruenae, Ant and Bean were already resting in. The fifth plot was for Silk whenever he died, which didn't seem like it was far away.

Since I'd been home, I'd never gone out to the cemetery to view any of their graves. When I saw them, I cried as if it were their funeral that day. Each of their headstones bared pictures of them. Though I know it was selfish of me, I couldn't help but ask before leaving their grave "Damn, why have all y'all gone on to glory and left me and Ke here fighting the daily test of this world alone." In my mind, I heard all four of them reply at different times, "To tell the story of the Prince family and carry our legacy to a new horizon."

In July 2002, KeKe married Sam. Though Renzo was her father and had shown back up on the scene after he'd stolen Bean's money then disappeared, I paid for her wedding. I also gave her away 'cause that sorry sucka was still broke as hell. Her wedding was another proud moment for me. I stood at the front of the church listening to her recite her vows. I felt honored that I was there to share that moment with her, though I wanted to get stupid on Renzo for what he did to Bean. When the minister pronounced them man and wife, I winked at her, as tears flowed from both our eyes. I'm sure there were a number of things going on in that mind of hers, but it was her day, and I told her to make the very best of it.

Ke and her husband honeymooned in Hawaii. After they returned to the city, we packed up the house. She was moving to Houston. Sam was an established engineer and had accepted a job with NASA.

I finally decided that it was time for me to move on with my life as well, so when Ke moved, I moved out of Detroit to the suburbs in West Bloomfield. The day the movers packed up the remaining things in the house, I stood in the living room reliving my childhood, the arguments Bean and I used to have, and the last family Christmas gathering we all shared together. I'll never forget the whole family waiting for me to come home from the hospital before anyone opened their Christmas gifts when that car hit me. That was something that only a family that really loved you would do.

For a second, I became trapped in that recollection because so many other painful memories came with that day. "Hum, if Chew and Julius could see me now, they would trip." I laughed. "And yeah chumps, I ended up with the finest woman out of everybody," I replied, looking to the heavens. Finally, I had to laugh at myself when I thought about calling my brother hood rich many years ago. Hell, after thinking about my come up, I discovered that I was just as hood rich as him. Shoot, I was parking my Cadi at Bean's Spot, and I know my truck cost just as much as her house did.

"Mr. Prince, that's it. Everything you wanted is loaded up. We will see you at the other house." The movers stated, interrupting me.

"Okay, someone should be there to let you in."

"Goodbye, Bean," I said to my mother one last time, shutting the door behind me. Then I walked down the steps to the grass and pounded a *For Rent* sign in the lawn. When I backed up to the sidewalk to look at the house, someone honking disturbed my thoughts. When I looked up, it was Carrington in her company car, a Taurus I believe it was. I smiled before greeting her because even with as bad as she had treated me when I was at Ryan, I had forgiven her and my life was better because of it.

"Hey, Prince. I see you're moving," she stated

"Yeah, Ke's gone, and the house has so many memories that it would kill me to live here any longer. I just bought a place in West Bloomfield. I'm gonna try to start a new life for me and my family out there."

"Family! Are all y'all moving to West Bloomfield?"

"No not all of us, just me and my girlfriend."

"Girlfriend?"

"Yeah, Veronica and I are expecting a baby."

"Veronica?"

"You know, the young lady that was with me at Big Fellas on Thanksgiving night."

"Oh, yeah. I remember her, but E said her name was Teretta."

"Her middle name is Teretta."

"Oh, well why are you moving way out there instead of Southfield?"

"I don't want my son to get caught up on that ghetto madness, like I did. I don't want the dope man or crack heads to be his role models. I want him to see how affluent black lawyers, doctors, professors, CEO,s and common hard working people with dreams, some faith, and a little dedication to make things happen are living. My son's going to see that you can come from nothing and have anything you want with hard work. He's gon' be different from me. Hell, he's even gon' learn to play the piano. I already bought him a little black Baby Grand, so when he's ready, he can jump on it and get busy. I don't care what it sounds like at first; in the end, he's gon' master that skill."

"That sounds great. But moving out of Detroit isn't necessarily the answer. Crime's everywhere. I grew up in Detroit and look at me, I was fine," she replied kind of snooty.

"You're a female and the pressures for a man in Detroit by far out weigh those of a woman. Shit, the pressures of the Ghetto in any city period for a male, by far out weigh those of a woman. I want to raise my child in a nice neighborhood. That way he'll get a better education, and be able to do what I should have done when I was a shorty, focus on school, not slangin'."

"Prince, I'm really proud of you for whatever that's worth."

"It means a lot. Thanks, Carrington."

"You know, I should have stuck it out."

"Yeah, you should have cause I loved you so much."

"But it got hard."

"That's fine, I've moved on with my life, and so have you. I've learned some things throughout my vicious journey. At times, you were my best teacher. But that's not a bad thing. You taught me patience and that just because something looks good, it doesn't always mean that it's good for you. You weren't for me and vise versa. Baby, there are no hard feelings, and I sincerely wish you nothing but the best."

"Yeah, me, too," she sadly replied. "Okay! Have a good one, I better get busy," she abruptly suggested. "I've got to get back to work before I get behind. Again, it was so good to see you, and if you see me out sometimes say Hi."

"I will. Come by one of the restaurants sometimes with your family and the tabs on me," I replied, waving goodbye.

That was the first time I had a conversation with Carrington in all the years that I'd been knowing her in which I was able to stay in control of our conversation. She'd always made me a little weak, but not that time. It was clearly evident in the manner in which she looked at me that she finally realized what she could've had and what she lost. We had our memories, our one night of romance, and our story of how we hurt each other. Oh, yeah, Carrington was crushed to learn that she turned out to be nothing more than a one night stand or a booty call. I never called her again after we fucked. She buzzed me up a few times, but I didn't have time for her anymore. I was on to a new fantasy, and she was having my baby.

As a boy, I'd learned a valuable lesson from Zena about Carrington. I most certainly wasn't about to go through the same experiences as a grown-ass man with Teretta. I didn't give the conversation I had with Carrington a second thought. I picked up the scrap wood off the grass, and left the house thinking about my woman and my new family to be.

## *24*

_____    _____

# *Finally a Prince*

GG left her and Daddy Ruenae's house, along with a hundred thousand dollar life insurance policy to Ke and me. Seems like she felt obligated to us after we lost everyone. She left Silk, Brian, and Ka'Nita the money that was left from Daddy Ruenae's policy, which came to about ten thousand a piece.

I couldn't believe that Uncle Silk was one of the greatest ballas in his time, but had fallen down on his game. I wasn't going to live in GG's house, and he needed a place to stay, so I let him live there under the agreement that he maintained the annual taxes on the property. Seeing a man like Silk, who was once one of the greatest ballas in the history of Detroit get down on his luck, helped me appreciate that I had taken a different route for myself after getting out of prison. His decline in the game also taught me the importance of investing and respecting the inconsistency of the all mighty dollar. Several of the Old School Ballas could relate to the saying, "here today, gone tomorrow." Dope money was shifty, even a crack head could tell you that. One thing for certain, I took all that dirty money Ant left me and made it work in my life.

In August 2002, Teretta gave birth to my son, DeMarques Anthony Prince. I gave him a fraction of Ant's name and a fraction of mine. I felt like by doing that, through him, both of us would get a second chance at doing something great. The only thing I decided I wanted for my son's existence was for him to be something far greater in his life than my brother or I had been. Sure his dad had become a successful businessman after years of hard knocks. I'd also done well for myself, considering my past, but I hoped that the new Ant in my life would take full advantage of his opportunities. Not to mention that I wanted him to make his family much prouder than I had.

Calvin's body was also found in 2002, which I was completely unaware of. As popular as his story had been in the city of Detroit at one time, I don't see how I missed the news the day of his discovery. The state had been looking for his next of kin to claim his body for several weeks and after it sat in the morgue for a few months they gave him a city burial. They put him in the pine box that looked like an old school Dracula coffin, and buried him in the cheapest cemetery in the city. He didn't even have no head stone, just an old round white cement circle, which served as a grave marker. As for Melvin, he never surfaced. I guess he's still in the bottom of the lake making his keep as fish food.

As for E and I, well, he's my son's Godfather. We're still the best of friends, and we continue to experience good fortune. For example, in November of 2003, two years almost to the date of Calvin's death, I received a letter from the courts. Ke and I had been named the beneficiary of his estate after they concluded that he didn't have any living parents or children. I was shocked the state found us, considering we were never a part of each other's lives. A nice portion of his inheritance was used looking for us; nonetheless, since we were his next of kin, we got everything he owned, including Big Fellas, which was no longer the happening spot.

Once I got the key to the building, E and I went in to see what kind of potential the club had for future business. Upon checking things out, we found a secret safe in the wall that was hidden behind this ugly painting of something we couldn't make out. I suspect that's why the safe wasn't ever found. The picture was so horrid that it wasn't worth taking off the wall. We just so happened across it because E snatched the painting off the wall, insulting Calvin's taste in fine art as he flung it across the room.

Everett played around with the combination lock for a while, but none of the numbers he tried worked and just on a whim, I told him to put in 4357.

"If those numbers work, maybe I actually had the real Ant killed, and he honestly forgot the password due to the pressure he was under," I sarcastically replied, never thinking the numbers would work.

"4...3...5...7. Bingo! P, were in," E replied.

"You're lying." I responded in clear fear, because I thought I might have killed the wrong guy. "Well, what's in there?"

"Some kind of a log and some pictures."

"Let me see. Pass 'em to me," I eagerly suggested, hoping for some confirmation on which twin I'd killed.

There was a receipt from a painter for the work done on Bean's house in 1990, and some pictures that had been taken at a few different functions, one of which was my Birthday-Christmas dinner. There were a few pictures of Bean, Ke and GG. And there was an 8 x 10 of the twins taken at My Fair Ladies. Once I opened the log, I discovered that it was a journal. *Who ever heard of a gangsta keeping a journal?* I thought, sitting on the floor by the safe to read it in its entirety. Ant told me in his letter to find Calvin Shaw and I'd get answers. After I finished reading their journal, I discovered that he was absolutely right, and it goes like this.

Initially, the journal belonged to Ant. I know that because it had several personal confidential entries written by him. Somehow, Melvin got a hold to it and learned that Ant was suspicious of him. Melvin stole the damn thing from Ant and gave it to Calvin with the intent of removing evidence from Ant's place. After a while, Calvin ended up sporadically making additional entries. Nonetheless, the story was out. In 1983 when T was killed, Calvin set him up, but Melvin helped carry it out, which is why he was on the phone with T before he got killed. The story about the guys mentioning Silk before killing T was used as a decoy. Melvin called T to tell him that a few of his runners were coming by to pick up some money, which is how Raymond and his boys were able to get into the house so easily. T was actually killed for nothing more than the fact that he knew Melvin was dirty.

Melvin and Calvin had been friends for about as long as Ant and Melvin. But one summer after they met at the Boys Club, Calvin made Melvin promise not to ever tell Ant about him. Melvin spent the summers with his father's mother, and Calvin's grandmother lived on the same street. The day Ant met Calvin in the club for the first time was not by coincidence either. Melvin knew him and Ant were going to be at My Fair Ladies and told Calvin he thought it was time he met his twin.

Turns out that Melvin and Calvin used that meeting to their advantage. After the twins met, whenever Ant was out of town on a drug run, Melvin was generally the only one that knew because they were trying to break off from Silk and build their own empire. Since no one knew when Ant was gone, Melvin would often give Ant's keys to Calvin and allow him to pretend to be Ant. Melvin had the only set of spare keys to Ant's car and house. This was one way Calvin was able to spend time around the family, which is how he came up with some of those pictures in his safe. This also explains why Bean used to always tell Ant he was changing. Sometimes we were dealing with Calvin and other times we were dealing with Ant. Calvin's temperament was different from Ant's, which made it seem like Ant was on a constant mood swing. Bean should have been able to tell the twins apart, since she gave birth to them. However, being that she rarely gave Ant any attention, and never saw Calvin, she was unable to tell her own son's apart.

Most often, we thought it was Ant at the various family functions, but it wasn't, sometimes it was Calvin. After Ant and Calvin became a little closer, he didn't mind Calvin being him because he knew Calvin wanted to be around the family, and it also kept Silk in the dark. When things started going wrong, Ant put a halt to the game, especially after his Benz had to go for a swim.

Raymond was killed because him and some of his crew killed T. The Casey boys actually really didn't have anything to do with T's murder, but they knew Melvin was involved, which is why the day Ant got out to confront them at the school, Melvin stayed in the car. He knew after that encounter, it was too risky to let them live. Melvin ordered an additional hit on the Casey's after it took Silk's boys longer than he expected to carry out their murder for hire contact for Chew and Julius' death.

When I thought about the day Ant bonded me out of jail, I considered how he didn't remember catching me in his car. However, after I suspiciously looked at him, he played it off because he knew it was Calvin who caught me instead. The night Zena was shot, Calvin and Melvin picked me up before we did that drive-by. That's why the police officer referred to the driver, whom I thought was Ant as Mr. Shaw. I simply thought Ant was on top of his game with an alias, but that was not the case either. Once everything happened, Melvin called Ant in Chicago to let him know what went down. After Ant threw a fit, he cut his business trip short, had them strip the car, and then they met him half way to dump it in the lake. Because he was rushing when they met up, he didn't think about getting his spare gun until he got to Bean's house. All this information also explained how Calvin knew our secret code, but not the password. When I beeped him the night the Casey's ran up on me at the theater, he was too casual about my call. Had that been Ant, he would have been frantic from jump when he saw my beeper number and the code. I never said anything about needing HELP when Calvin and I spoke, which is why he didn't know the password he needed to live that night.

A lot of scandalous stuff went down with Melvin once him and Ant started building their own territory. Ant got real suspicious of him, which is why he started scooping young Byron under his wing. He was teaching him the game of the underworld just in case something happened to him. The saddest thing about the gun Byron got caught up with is that it wasn't Ant's original spare. Melvin switched it out, hoping to pin a murder on Ant when his body was discovered. Melvin was the only one that knew that gun had been used in a 187, so he took advantage of the opportunity to pin his cop-killing on someone else. Melvin also knew Ant kept a spare under the dash and would possibly trust him enough to briefly go in and out of his car. That's how he was able to make a switch right before the shooting occurred. The two of them had been having some differences about finances for a while, so he was ready for Ant to get picked off. Ant confronted Melvin about two hundred thousand dollars that came up missing hours before he was killed. After the confrontation, Melvin realized Ant was onto him, so he had to take him out because the money he stole from my brother was used to establish Big Fellas.

Melvin, not being man enough to kill Ant himself, geeked Calvin up and encouraged him to order a hit on Ant because he said he was getting too big for himself. He also told Calvin that Ant was about to cut him off due to their carelessness. Finally, Melvin made Calvin believe that Ant was considering having the both of them killed, which was a lie. Calvin, not really liking Ant to begin with and feeling as though it was either him or Ant, struck first out of paranoia and made a bad decision.

It wasn't until a few weeks before Calvin himself died that he realized Melvin had set him up, too. He was actually in the process of planning a hit on Melvin, but I just so happened to beat him to it. All that I had read was a lot for me to comprehend. The shit I was reading sounded like a real gangsta movie, but huh, it was a part of my life.

Once I finally read the letter Calvin wrote at the store that night, I felt troubled for months. I comprehended the fact that though we had absolutely no relationship, he was still my brother. I figured since I was going to benefit from his wealth, I had to put him away better than he had been. I had Calvin's body exhumed from Michigan Pastures Cemetery, purchased him a nice oak casket, with his name engraved on the side, "Calvin Latrell Shaw-Prince," and buried him out in Woodlawn Cemetery in Silk's plot next to our grandparents, our mother, and our brother. "Now you'll forever be a part of the family you should have never been without. Finally, you're a Prince, too," I whispered, sitting a blanket of flowers on his grave. I stood there tearing when I thought about what I'd done to my brother. Due to our mother's ignorance, and because we grew up in separate households, when I thought about what we'd lost out on as siblings, my head started to pound. I was supposed to be my brother's keeper. Well, I had dropped the ball big time on one of them.

I briefly snickered when I thought to myself, *There you go crying again, Prince. You're supposed to be hard. Uncle Silk and Ant always told you 'Real nigga's don't cry, they deal with the pressure and then move on.'* I know half the world probably believes that real men don't cry or aren't supposed to. And the golden rule is that Balla's and Playa's most definitely don't. But, that's bullshit. I've shed more tears in a twenty-year period of my life than some eighty-year-old men have in their entire lifetime. I've endured so many heartaches and so much pain throughout the years that my tears have taught me some valuable lessons about life and being *a real man*.

One of which is this, a man's tears don't symbolize his weakness, but the fact that he is human, and if he allows himself to be that, (human), he, too, will gain some knowledge on the emotions that move him from one phase in his journey to the next. These feelings consist of, but are not limited to compassion, heartaches, disappointments, failures, struggles, perseverance, and most of all what he needs to focus on after he's weathered the storm in order to move forward. After weathering the storm, a man needs to determine the crucial steps he must take in order to advance to his maximum potential, and then proceed in that direction. I believe the singer Kemistry described this process best when he sung *A Matter of Time.*

After having my brother Calvin buried with the rest of our family, I decided that in order for me to be that role model I needed to be for my son and daughter, I should pursue a degree and participate in some kind of graduation for myself. In January 2004, I enrolled in a Junior College and got involved in one of the retention programs designed to help non-traditional college students experience academic success. After my first year of college, I married Teretta. We had a beautiful wedding, and now we share a beautiful life together. I know she was one of the many blessings God gave me for my sacrifices. Another one of my blessings came when I upgraded my Escalade in 2005 to a Benz G 500. The day I saw R Kelly rocking that SUV on one of his videos, I vowed I was gon' get me one. At the time, my boys thought I was dreaming too big, considering I was a convict, but I proved dreams can and do come true.

On a more serious note, I would have to say that the ultimate accomplishment for me was securing my Associates Degree in Business Management within three years. I figured if I was going to be this big time entrepreneur, I needed to know the specifics about running a lucrative business.

My nephew Anthony Lavell Prince II is twenty-one years old now. My brother would be so proud of his son today. He's about to graduate from college with his degree in Agriculture, Ag-Business to be exact. I know Ant would trip the hell out to know that his son selected such an unusual profession considering that he came from the Motor City. But Li'l Ant had the ambition required to make the impossible, possible, and will be graduating from an HBCU in Langston, Oklahoma, with honors this spring.

Asia, well, she's still a brat and a daddy's girl for life. Years ago I had to hear her fuss about Carrington, now she fusses about Teretta. You'd think with the way she behaves that she was my woman. When I bought my wife her first fur coat, Asia had such a fit that I had to buy her one, too. When I bought my son, his first little battery operated Benz, you would have thought I made a real purchase. Yes, that's right; I had to buy Asia a Benz as well. A few years ago, I called her at work right before Christmas and invited her to lunch. When she came out to the parking lot, I had this big red bow on the hood of her cute little platinum C-Class. I told her that's it for her for a while, but I know my daughter, whatever my next purchase is, she'll be comparing it to what she has. Out of guilt, she might catch me slipping and have her way. She's currently a Social Worker, and though it's not a high paying job, she enjoys what she does, and it's a rewarding career for her. Therefore, if she's happy, I'm happy for her.

KeKe and Sam have two children and are doing very well in Houston.

Louis received an additional sentence of life for murdering Charles Casey. I heard another punk in the joint recently killed Lou for the same thing he picked Casey off for. Raynard and Byron are still pulling their Natural Life sentences. Every now and then, E and I drive out to pay them a visit. I submitted a copy of the information in Ant's journal to my Attorney to see what could be done in regards to freeing Byron. He is in the process of writing an appeal for him now.

No one would have ever believed that "The Prince in Chains" would be the one to break the shackles of financial struggles and fast living, which basically kept our family in bondage, only to legally become one of the most legitimate "Big Fellas" in Detroit.

My Grandfather said in his final note to me that he hoped I truly understood the meaning of the ultimate sacrifice I'd made to save my brother's life. Ultimately, I believe I've figured it all out. See, my life has been a test. It is because of my trials that I've learned about faith and trust, which in turn has helped me develop hopes and dreams. My hopes and dreams gave me the determination required to become someone destined for greatness. Because of my sacrifice, I am "The Prince" that was stripped, reformed, polished, and then forced back into the world to learn how to soar far beyond my expected potential. I was created to establish a new family legacy, which I have done. Had I never gone to prison, I know I would have been in one of the family plots today. Actually, at the rate I was going, I probably would have beat Ant, my granddad, and Bean to the dirt. And when I think about Chew and Julius, I know that's a realistic fact.

"DeMarques, before we end, I want to thank you for sharing with *Big Successors Magazine*. I have personally followed your story since you were released. This interview chronicling your life is certain to send sales off the charts for next month's issue. You are a highly respected businessman in the city. So many Detroiters are quite impressed with your achievements. It's very rare that anyone spends over fifteen years in prison, discharges, and becomes a millionaire in what seems like over night. There were so many nominations from people in the community, recommending you for next month's cover story."

"Ken, that means a lot. But, if you don't mind, I want my family to grace the cover with me."

"That's fine, is there any certain reason for that?"

"Yeah, Man, my wife's my rock, she loves me, and if it wasn't for her, there are some days I wouldn't make it. She's a great mother to my son and an awesome companion for me. She's my confidante when I need her to be and a shoulder when I'm falling short on support. Most of all, she has shown me what real love is all about. My children have to be on there simply because they are the main reason I strive to make something better of myself."

"That's real cool."

"Oh, by the way, here's your recorder. You can turn it back on now."

"That's funny. Prince, I go on the record stating that per your contract with our company most of this interview cannot be printed due to the possibility of legal ramifications. I'd like to thank you for your time and close by saying, you have one hell of a story. As one of your former classmates, I want to also acknowledge how proud I am of you for your accomplishments, especially after hearing the details of your story for myself."

"Thanks, I appreciate *Big Successor's* interest in my struggle. Years ago had anyone told me in 2009 I'd be a millionaire, I would have laughed in their faces. It's hard to believe that at one time in my life, I was just trying to survive in the hood. Now when you look at me today, you'll discover that I'm straight *"Hood Rich"* and loving it. Not material wise either. And unlike what Ant said years ago about hood rich only being a state of mind, I disagree; it is by far way more than that. Growing up in the hood taught me morals, gave me quality, life-long friends, made me respect the value of my family, as well as myself, and forced me to develop honest alternatives for survival, in order to avoid ever having to go without my freedom again. Now with priceless stock in my life like that, tell me the hood didn't make me prosperous."

"Yeah, when you put it in terms like that, you're very "Hood Rich.""

"Ken, sorry, about making you turn off your recorder, but I've got too much to lose. No hard feelings, right?"

"Man, I'm honored. Don't worry about it. Your story was so good I actually forgot to take notes. That's why I record."

"Huh, not this time."

"Before we close, is there anything else you'd like to add?"

"Yeah, there is. I'd like to dedicate all my struggles, losses and life long lessons to my seven-year-old son. Throughout his life, he, too, will learn about sacrifices, and the real definition of being his brother's keeper. I want him to know that he'll be the one to carry on the Prince name and our newly defined legacy. In spite of trials, he needs to remember that I want him to soar on without ever looking back because that will cause him to second guess himself or have doubts. Like me, the two Kings in his life will also leave him some personal treasures. They will be called dreams, trials, faith, and triumph. I hope he understands that determination, faith and self-confidence are the key ingredients necessary to conquer each of them. DeMarques, Duce, always remember that I am "The Prince" that contributed to your ability to dream, but you are the Prince that will make your dreams a reality."

"Wow, that's powerful food for thought."

"Naw, this is powerful food for thought. Long before my young brothas and sistahs secure themselves three hots and a cot or a life sentence they can't overturn with D.O.C, it is my hopes that all who are lost like I was or exposed to negative things like I was, will Read, Reflect and Realize that their life has a Real Purpose. Young people, strive to be purpose-driven, not material-focused. Two years in lock up is way too long, especially when one takes a moment to consider all they missed out on or all the positive things they could have accomplished during the lost time."

**"*Hood Rich*** is far more than driving around in a fancy car or sporting some iced-out jewelry. It's more than a certain state of mind or even having the finer things in life. In spite of all the negativity thrown my way, real Big Tymers allow hard times and bold environments to transcend us into prosperous achievers based on the knowledge we gain from the hood......*Like Me*"

Just because we fall, there are no rules to life that state we have to stay down.

*Learn From Your Hard Knocks*
*And Grow*

*Read, Reflect, and Realize that all Urban Lit, ain't Bullshit*

# *About the Author*

Crystal Perkins-Stell was born April 5 in Newark, New Jersey, and raised in Detroit, Michigan. She is a three-time Who's Who inductee, who vowed to her mom at a very young age that one day she would do big things in life.

Crystal is a double major, who completed her undergraduate degree at Langston University with scholastic honors. She obtained her Master's degree in Human Relations, with an emphasis in professional counseling from the University of Oklahoma, where she graduated Summa Cum Laude. She is a proud member of Delta Sigma Theta Sorority Inc., and a 2004, honorary inductee of Tau Beta Sigma.

Crystal has written several short stories and poems, which led to her involvement in a HIV and AIDS Awareness project sponsored by NFL players Kenny Blair and Ron Fellows. Crystal, along with two other local lyricists, wrote and performed a song entitled, "The Magic Touch," which they dedicated to Magic Johnson. She also composed a campaign jingle for the Oklahoma State Senate Election for the Honorable Vickie Miles-Lagrange, who is the first black female, United States Federal Judge appointed in the 90's by President Bill Clinton.

In 2001, Crystal started working on her first self-published novel, *Soiled Pillowcases, A Married Woman's Story*. In 2002, she organized, Crystell Publications, Marketing and Distributions, Inc., a sole proprietorship. She is now on a mission to become a bestselling author while raising money to give scholarships to first-generation and low-income college students.

# *Quick Order Form*

**Fax orders:** (405) 216-0224. Send this form to

**Telephone orders:** Call (405) 414-3991. Have Your Credit Cards Ready

**E-mail orders:** www.crystalstell.com click on Order link. All Credit Card purchases are handled through Paypal

**Postal orders:** Crystell Publication, Attn: Crystal Stell, PO Box 8044 Edmond, Oklahoma 73083-8044

**Please send the following book(s):**
___*Soiled Pillowcases: A Married Woman's Story*

___ *Hood Rich, Sex, Status, and a Baller's Confession*
**The sequel** Big Tymers, **is under construction**

___*Never Knew a Father's Love*

Name:_____

Address:_____

City:_____State:_____Zip:_____

Telephone:_____

Email Address:_____

**Sales tax: Please add 8.75% sales tax to all purchases.**

**Shipping by air**
**U.S.:** $4.00 for the first book and $2.00 for each additional book.
**International:** $9.00 for the first book and $5.00 for each additional book.

**Payment:** _____ Check ___Visa ____Mastercard ___Discover

**Card Number:** _____

Name on card:_____Exp. date:_____

# I Almost Kept This To Myself

✓ Hood Rich was written in 45 days

✓ Too many words to tell you

✓ Cover changed three times

✓ Original Title ... A Prince in Chains

## The Characters

*Model:* **Teretta** resides in Dallas, Texas. She is new to the modeling industry, yet she's already been featured on J'Lo's Website. See more of **Teretta** on Derrick Browns website or www.Teretta.net

*Photographer:* **Derrick Brown** is an Award Winning photographer out of Austin, Texas. He's been in the business for over ten years. If you're ever in search of a photographer of high quality, look him up at **www.dbrownphotos.com**

*Model 2:* **Jermaine Chiles** is my peeps. He's an individual of quality and a li'l cutie who resides in OKC.

*Silk:* **Chris** is my peeps, and currently resides in Dallas, Texas.

*Ant:* **Mook** is the owner and operator of Shuntes Kollege Korrner Greek Paraphernalia store. If you want to check him out, go get your shop on at 810 E. Clarendon, Ste. A, Oak Cliff, TX 75224.

# CRYSTELL PUBLICATIONS

### Presents
### The M. Alexis Stell

## COURSE BOOK SCHOLARSHIP FUND

Eligibility Requirements: This scholarship is designed to assist first-generation and low-income, minority college students with the purchase of course books. The applicant must meet the following requirements in order to qualify for this scholarship.

### The applicant must:

1.) Must be a first generation or low-income continuing student.
2.) Be a U.S. Citizen
3.) Have a grade point average of 2.9 or higher (on a 4.0 grading

scale at an accredited 2 or 4 year College or University.)
4.) All applicants must provide a current official transcript with a

College or University seal and 2 letters of recommendation from a faculty or staff on institution letterhead.
5.) Include a 500 word type-written, double-spaced essay best describing the applicant concluding with his/her long term career goals. Essay should include full name, current address and contact number
6.) Include a photo and submit all material no later than May 30, for consideration of fall awards.

**Scholarships will be awarded the 2nd week of the semester. Submit applications to:**
CRYSTELL PUBLICATIONS,
Attn: Karolyn Lewis, Scholarship Coordinator
PO BOX 8044
EDMOND, OK 73083-8044
**Any questions, please e-mail comments to**
cleva@crystalstell.com